Static

Charge

By

T.E. Smith

ISBN:
Copyright © 2021
First Edition,
Published in the United States of America
Or Canada, UK, Australia, etc.

DEDICATION

To my mother, Loretta, who was always willing to listen to one of my stories. She heard me tell her about this book. However, she left us before I was able to write it.

To my wife, Sharon. All my love and thanks for your patience, understanding and your help in bringing my wish of writing a book to reality. Without your help, this would not have been possible.

To Kacie Jones, a fine young man who is battling ALS.

To Mary Dougherty, my publisher who helped me with all the ins and outs of getting my book out to the public.

Introduction

My publisher asked "Why did you write the book?" To be honest, in the beginning I had no set purpose for writing this book other than to see if I could.

As the book took hold, I realized I could use it for a lot of good. That's when I decided that ALL proceeds will go to the following charities:

The American Cancer Association because cancer has hurt my family and taken friends.

Multiple Sclerosis because I have had it for over thirty years and it affects thousands of people each year.

ALS (AKA Lou Gehrig's Disease) because a young man I know is fighting this disease and it robs people of a normal life.

Feeding The Hungry because the need to help feed people will never go away but we all need to do what we can to help.

ALL proceeds for this book will go to these charities.

We can all help. Please donate to a charity of your choice and make a difference in someone's life.

I hope you enjoy reading this book as much as I enjoyed writing it.

T.E. Smith

Epigraph

From the beginning of time, men would invent things to enhance and prosper mankind. But there is always someone who subverts its use to something evil.

Orville Wright and his brother Wilbur invented the airplane. Orville experienced its destructive use during the years of WWII. When Orville was asked about how he felt seeing their invention used this way, he answered as best he could:

"We dared to hope we had invented something that would bring lasting peace to the earth. But we were wrong! No, I don't have any regrets about my part in the invention of the airplane, though no one could deplore more than I do the destruction it has caused. I feel about the airplane much the same as I do regarding fire. That is, I regret all the terrible damage caused by fire, but I think it is good for the human race that someone discovered how to start fires and that we have learned how to put fire to thousands of important uses."

I feel just the same about my father's invention as did Orville Wright about his.   Professor John Northrop

(This quotation came out of the book by David McCullough "The Wright Brothers")

Chapter 1

It was just before noon on a Monday morning when Professor Sharon Northrup let her biology class out. She headed outside herself to enjoy the day for a little while. She had two hours before her next class, and she was determined to enjoy every minute of it.

It was a fine spring day. She paused, took a deep breath, and looked at just how blue the sky was. The air was clear for a change. No smog today. That's unusual for Pasadena. She was a little hungry, so she headed for the campus cafeteria to grab a little lunch. The next stop was the little park inside the school campus.

Finding a bench in the sun, she had a little time to herself and she meant to make the best of it.

Her thoughts drifted back to Brittany, a young lady in her class. She's trying hard, but even after tutoring, she's having a hard time keeping up. I really think she's in over her head. I hope I'm wrong. She's a good kid.

As she sat there on the bench enjoying the sunshine and the lunch that she bought, she couldn't help that nagging feeling that just wouldn't leave her alone.

It's been six weeks since her last period, and she's never been this late. With all the precautions her husband Paul and she have taken, it's not possible for her to be pregnant. What she's thinking just couldn't happen, or could it? No. Just stop thinking about it. If nothing happens by next week, I'll need to call my doctor.

Before she knew it, her two hours were up and she was headed back to her last class. This was her longest class of the day. Two hours in the classroom and another two hours in the biology lab. She wasn't really complaining. This was her best class of students and they were doing very well. She very much enjoyed working with them.

She has been teaching here for three years following her own graduation at the very same school. To her great surprise, she had been offered a position right after she completed her PHD in physics and biology. She was a little overwhelmed by the offer, but after teaching the first year she decided this is what she was meant to do.

It's a bit of a walk from the classroom where she taught to her apartment on the campus. The walk always gave her a chance to think and unwind at the end of the day.

That nagging thought came back. Having a child was never in the plans that she and Paul had made.

I know Paul won't be home for hours. His last class is over at four, but he always stays after to help his students. Then he heads over to the lab to work on who knows what or for how long.

Paul is just one of the mechanical engineers teaching at Cal Tech. He's been there for almost ten years. He holds a master's degree in engineering from MIT, a master's degree in both physics and technical science from RIT in New York, in addition to a master's degree in mathematics. He is a brilliant man.

He has an unending thirst for knowledge. He believed that through knowledge a person could change the world around them and help people everywhere.

His wanting to help people is what attracted me to him in the first place. Professor Paul, as everyone called him, was filling in teaching a physics class for a professor who was out with a back problem. It was during that time that I became interested in this man.

I realized he was several years older than me, but I hadn't really given that much thought.

One day after class, I asked him for his help on the last assignment. He is always willing to help one of his students when asked. I found out later he would start out helping you by asking a question.

"Why do you need my help? Were you not paying attention in class or haven't you done your reading and your research?"

It was a question I had not anticipated nor was I ready to answer. After a long moment I said yes and yes. "The reason I asked you for help is that I believe you didn't fully explain the purpose of the next research paper."

"Why do you need a purpose? The assignment I gave may not have a purpose. It may just be an exercise."

"If this were an undergraduate class, I could see the need for an exercise paper. This is a master's degree program. I don't feel we need to spend time on an exercise report when we could be working on something that matters."

"I hear what you're saying and you make a valid point. Miss?"

"Michaels, Sharon Michaels."

"Miss Michaels. I don't give assignments with no purpose. I have a well-defined reason for giving them. I believe if you do the work and the research you will discover my reason. Is there anything else I can do for you?"

"No. I guess not."

"Miss Michaels. I appreciate your comments and applaud you for speaking up. Most of my students never say anything."

"Thank you, Professor. I have never been one not to speak my mind."

"That may serve you well in the future or get you into unwanted trouble."

"Maybe, but it's who I am, and I don't think I will change anytime soon. Good day professor. I will see you next week."

"Good day to you as well Miss Michaels."

Two weeks later after class Professor Paul asked to speak with me.

"I would like to go over your last paper with you."

"Why, what's wrong with it?"

"Oh nothing. In fact, I want to compliment you on your work. It's very well done."

"Thank you. I don't often get feedback from my professors."

"Yes, we tend to be a little self-involved. Funny, I promised myself I wouldn't be that way if I ever became a teacher. I guess I broke that promise. If you have time, I would really like to go over your report."

"I have time right now. My next class is this evening."

"Very well then. It's almost lunchtime so why don't we go down to the cafeteria and we can talk there."

"That works for me, I haven't eaten anything today. I got a late start and I missed out on breakfast."

At lunch we talked over my report for a little while. The conversation soon turned to many other subjects. Like where are you from? Why Cal Tech? What are your plans after graduation? Before we knew it an hour and a half had passed.

He had to run to get to his next class. I had very mixed feelings about this guy. At first, I wanted to get to know him, but after asking for his help, he really got in my face about the assignment. I lost some of that interest. Now after getting to know him a little better, I was even more interested in him.

Truth be told, he was right. I did see the purpose once I was done. Time passed and I finished his class. We started seeing each other more and more. Before I knew what was happening, I realized I was falling in love with this man. I hoped he felt the same way. Apparently, he did because four months later, to the day, he asked me to marry him.

We had a small wedding right there on the campus with only family and a few friends. The next three years were a blur. Paul and I were both teaching full time. We had little time to ourselves. When we did have time for each other we made the best of it. Paul was always into something new. Always telling me about his latest great idea. I never got tired of listening.

On the other hand, I became interested in what was happening to our environment. Our ecosystem. Visiting San Francisco on a very smoggy day will get you thinking that way. What are we doing to ourselves?

One time during a Save the Planet rally, I made Paul go along with me. He went kicking and screaming the whole way. However, after seeing what's been happening and realizing for himself that climate change was taking place, he became interested.

From that point on it was all he talked about. What could we do to help save our environment? His thinking led him to exploring clean energy. What we as a country were doing was not good enough. He became obsessed with finding a clean energy source. There were times I wished I had never taken him to that rally.

Our lives were going pretty much as planned. However, this nagging feeling I had needed to end. I made an appointment to see my doctor next week. No reason to wait. I wanted to know what was going on. Even if it was what I feared.

The weekend was over before I knew it. Monday morning, I was walking into the doctor's office. Dr. Lisa Anderson is one of the most caring people I know. I really liked her. She seemed awfully young to be a doctor but look who's talking. I was young to be teaching as a professor.

She had a very pleasant smile on her face as she came into the room. Her mannerisms always put you at ease.

"Good morning, Sharon. What can I do for you today?"

"Good morning, Doctor Anderson. Well, I haven't had my period in a little over seven weeks, and I don't know why."

"Are you and Paul trying to have a baby?"

"Oh no! We certainly aren't trying to have a baby. It's not in our plans at all. We are careful about that."

"Okay then, let's see what's going on. First, I want a urine sample and then a blood test. How have you been feeling as of late?"

"Good. Just a little anxious about this."

"I understand. Let's get that sample and we'll go from there." I turned in the sample and went back into the room. When Doctor Anderson came back into the room, I could see from the look on her face she was struggling to find the words to say something. So, I asked her, "Do you want a blood sample?"

"No, that won't be necessary. I know what it is. You're pregnant."

"Lisa. Are you sure? Can't there be a mistake?"

"No mistake. I checked it myself."

"I don't understand. We're so careful."

"Sharon, it happens. Sometimes, no matter how careful you are, one of those little guys gets through. Next thing you know, you're having a baby."

"So, what now?"

"That's completely up to you. We do have options these days. You're only about nine weeks along and we can easily abort this pregnancy."

"No, that's not an option! Paul and I were both raised as Christians. We don't get to church like we should, but we believe that only God gives life, and only God can take it away."

"I'm glad to hear you say that. Too many people don't believe that life begins at conception. As a doctor, I can tell you it certainly does. You can always put the baby up for adoption. There are many good couples that would love to adopt your baby."

"Yes, that may be our best option. Neither one of us wanted children. I just don't understand how this happened."

"Well, Professor Sharon, when a man and woman have intercourse..."

"I know how it happened! I just don't know how one of those little suckers got through."

"Oh, they find a way. They're pretty determined little guys." "Well, now that you are pregnant, I want to set up regular appointments for you. If you're going to have this baby, I want to keep both of you healthy."

"Yes, that would be a good idea I suppose."

"I will see you in four weeks."

"Thank you, Doctor. I'll see you then."

The drive back to campus was short even with all the traffic. I called in and canceled all my classes for the day. I needed time to get this settled in my own head before I told Paul. I'm more than a little nervous about how he will react. I hadn't prayed in a long time, but I prayed a lot that day.

Of all days, today would be one of the days Paul came home early. I tried to act as normal as possible under the circumstances, but it didn't take long before he realized something was bothering me.

"What's wrong?"

"Nothing, I'm fine."

"Sharon, I know you well enough to know when something's bothering you."

When I turned to face him, I lost it. I started to cry for the first time in years.

"Honey, what's wrong? Whatever it is, we can fix it."
A typical response from an engineer. They think they can fix anything.

"You can't fix this, I'm pregnant."

"What?"

"What do you mean 'what'? I'm pregnant."

"Are you sure? Have you seen a doctor?"

"Yes, just today."

"How pregnant are you?"

"Paul, there's only one way to be pregnant, either you are or you're not."

"I mean how far along?"

"Nine weeks."

At that point neither one of us could think of anything else to say. After a couple of minutes or so he asked me, "Are you planning on keeping the baby?"

"If you mean having this baby, yes! I intend to have the baby. If you mean keeping the baby after it's born, I'm not sure what I'm thinking right now."

"I thought we decided not to have children."

"I didn't plan on this, but it just happened."

"How is that possible? We are always so careful."

"That's just what I told the doctor, but she said it doesn't matter. Sometimes it still happens."

"This is my fault, you told me a long time ago to get a vasectomy, I should have listened to you."

"It's nobody's fault. It just happened."

"How do you feel about having a baby?"

"I don't know how I feel right now. I guess I'll find out in the next few months."

"Well, you know I will help anyway I can."

"Yes, I know."

Well, that offer didn't last long. The first time I threw up in the bathroom he just yelled from the bedroom "Are you okay, honey?" Yeah, a lot of help he was!

Three months down the road and it's obvious that I'm pregnant. That's when all the questions started. Are you pregnant, when is the baby due, is it a boy or a girl? I thought you said you didn't want children.

I quickly tired of hearing all the questions. I wish people would just mind their own business. Then one evening about five months into my pregnancy, I was sitting at my desk grading papers.

I got my first kick, and what a kick it was! I almost jumped out of my chair. It wasn't just a kick in the side, it was a Kick in The Head and a Kick in my Heart.

I am pregnant. There's a new life inside me. A baby that someday not too long from now will be my son or daughter. I was overwhelmed by this feeling and started to cry. I couldn't stop crying. For the next half hour, I must have looked silly. Crying and laughing all at the same time.

I sat there and thought about what I had said to the doctor. Only God gives life. He must want me to have this child, or I wouldn't have gotten pregnant in the first place. I said a little thank you prayer and then told God I would take good care of this child whether it's a boy or girl, no matter what. This time I couldn't wait to tell Paul how I felt.

He didn't come home until long after I went to bed. Next morning, I was up ahead of him. I put the coffee on and waited to tell him all about last night and how I felt. Once he came out, I gave him a big hug and a long kiss.

Paul said "Well, you're certainly in a good mood this morning!"

"I'm in a great mood!"

"Well, I have some news that will make your mood even better!

"Let me go first. I want to tell you something."

"Okay, you go first.

"Well, last night the baby kicked me for the first time. It made me feel like I could be a real mother for this child. For the first time since I've gotten pregnant, I really feel excited. We're going to have a baby."

"Yes, honey, I know. I'm glad you're excited. Let me tell you what happened to me, or I should say for us yesterday. They have agreed to support my research and finance the whole project. Isn't that great news?"

He hadn't heard anything I said. All he had on his mind was his research.

"Honey, not only that, but the US defense department also wants to support my work on a new battery. All that in one day."

"So, why is that so good for us?"

"Honey, with that kind of funding I will have my own lab, right here on campus with my own team of scientists and engineers. I'll be able to complete my work in a couple of years, not ten years from now."

"So, I'll see you less now than I already do!"

"Sharon, you know how hard I've worked for this. It's my dream. Very few people get a chance like this."

"Yes, I understand, but did you hear me? We're going to have a baby?"

"I know, but once we've adopted it out, you'll be free to join me in my research."

"Did you hear me? I want to be a mother."

"I thought we decided we would have it adopted out?"

"Stop calling the baby it. This child is yours and mine."

"We haven't decided. We only talked about it."

"I've decided, I want to be a mother."

"But I thought,"

"There are no buts. I'm going to be a mother and you're going to be a father." He looked at me, turned around and walked over to the counter to grab a cup of coffee.

"Sharon, you know that was never in the plans. We talked about this from day one."

"I know that, but now that it's happened, I've changed my mind."

"You have. I haven't."

From that day on things changed. I still love him, and I know he loves me but what we had was gone. Everything changed. He buried himself in his work and we spent little time together.

Chapter 2

"Gentleman, before we get started, let's introduce ourselves to each other. My name is Ted Benson, the Dean of Engineering at Cal Tech."

"Good morning, everyone, I am General James Wellington of the United States Army. These four gentlemen with me are two of my best mechanical engineers and two gentlemen from our science department. You don't need to know their names at this point. All information will pass through me until I advise otherwise."

"Good morning, I am Professor Paul Northrup. I will be overseeing all of the research here at Cal Tech and out in the field."

Dean Benson said "Very well. Gentlemen, let's get started. Who has the first question?"

Paul said "General, before we get started on that, I just want to thank you and the defense department on behalf of Cal Tech for coming this morning, for your support on this project and joining with us to make this happen."

"Thank you, Paul. We're glad to be here. Now Paul, the army has purchased hundreds if not thousands of the batteries you designed here at Cal Tech. They work better than anything we've ever had before. That's what brought us back here. Now Dean Benson told me about the improved battery but failed to tell us it's not ready for field use."

"That's true General, we have yet to solve the overheating problem."

"Dean Benson, you told me they would be available soon. That was two months ago. Just what is your definition of soon?"

Dean Benson looked a little embarrassed and then said "General, at the time I felt they would have resolved this overheating problem. We're finding it to be more difficult than we first thought."

"Okay then Paul, what's your estimate of when they'll be ready?"

"Honestly General, roughly six or seven months at best."

"I find that unacceptable. If it's going to take that long, we will buy our batteries somewhere else! I'm sure we can find batteries that are just as good."

"Excuse me General, but you won't. We are years ahead of anyone else. Other companies come to us for help. They are nowhere near where we are."

"You're certainly sure of yourself Paul."

"General, they are still trying to get their batteries to the level of the batteries you've been using for the last four years."

"You better be right about that Paul."

"Don't worry General. I am."

"We've already been waiting months as it is. Six or seven more is unacceptable."

"General, we'll do the best we can. The last thing you need is to have a battery catch fire when they're inside something strapped to one of your men."

"You're right about that. It would be a disaster. Okay, we're done with that. So, tell us about this new project of yours. This electrical experiment you're talking about."

"Yes sir, I will be happy to. Gentlemen, you all know that everything we do today is powered by some sort of energy. That energy comes from either atomic plants, coal, oil, gas or hydroelectric power and a little wind power. But the power produced by the wind is less than 1% of what we need. Wind is unreliable and cannot produce nearly what we need. Importing oil puts us at risk of other countries cutting off our supply. Coal is plentiful, but is also the biggest polluter of our environment causing untold damage to our atmosphere. I am sure some of you have children and would like to leave them a cleaner planet than we have today. My plan is to use clean energy that is abundant and free."

"Excuse me Paul, just where do you think you're going to find that? You never mentioned that clean energy source in your request for more funding."

"You're right General, I did not. I wanted to explain this to you face-to-face. I plan to use a natural source, lightning! I can see by the look on your faces you think I'm a little nuts. So did most of my colleagues before I explained my plan. Your reaction to using lightning is the same reaction I got when I set out to design a better battery. I believe the new batteries are working well. A new and even better battery is now in the works. I firmly believe the problems with using lightning can be resolved just like we did with the batteries. We have some of the best people in the world right here at Cal Tech to solve those problems."

"Now wait just a minute Paul, even if, and I say if you can harness lightning, how in the world could you collect it?"

"General, we already know where lightning strikes the earth most in the United States."

"Even so, you don't know when or where or how frequently it will happen."

"True, but we do know that lightning strikes the earth a hundred times a second with the average being one billion volts per strike. All the energy goes right into the ground and is of no use to anyone. Why not use it?"

"Why hasn't someone already done this?"

"General, I believe that we've been fat and happy with just what we have right now. We have all the oil we need, large coal reserves, our atomic plants seem to be working well for now, and we've been told wind power will be a great resource in the future. Although, I can't see that wind power will ever happen. The other big reason is, up until now, we haven't had the technology to do this. Just stop and think about the damage we do by burning these fossil fuels. To say nothing about the radioactive rods that come out of our atomic plants. They will still be radioactive a thousand years from now. We can't continue this way. Eventually we'll just kill ourselves with all this pollution."

"Paul, I don't believe anyone sitting here would disagree with you, but could we get back to how you plan on doing this?"

"Yes, General. Sorry, I do tend to get off track when it comes to the environment. It's one of the main reasons I want to do this."

"Well, whatever your reason, what makes you think you can?"

"Because I already have. Let me explain."

"Please do."

"Gentleman, lightning is only a large charge of static electricity. Inside a cloud, tiny ice crystals collide with each other. This colliding causes the cloud to become charged either negatively or positively. When the charge builds up high enough, you get a lightning strike. Simply put, it's just static at a very high level. Have you ever walked across a rug and then touched someone or something and received a shock? I'm sure you have. In my lab I was able to create such a charge, direct it to a receiver and record the voltage."

"Maybe you can do that in your lab on a small scale but doing it out in the open on a scale you're proposing is a whole different matter altogether."

"Yes, sir it is, but every great advancement in science and technology started out with a little idea. Thomas Edison and Nikolai Tesla had what you may call a small idea back in 1878 and look at where we are today. They laughed at them back then. Who's laughing now?"

"Okay you made your point. Suppose you can find a way to do this? Where are you going to put it and who gets to use it?"

"It doesn't matter where we put it. Everyone will be able to use this energy. This is how we will collect the energy. We will build our collecting rods in a circle. The voltage collector will be in the center surrounded by six towers each being about one thousand feet high. These towers will pick up any lighting strike within miles of the site funneling the energy to the collector. Once the energy has been converted to usable power, it can then be sent to the grid or anywhere we like. General, once we've collected and stored this energy, we just tap into the infrastructure we already have."

"That's fine for the general public, but what's in it for the Army?"

"Glad you asked. With the new tech knowledge, we will learn from designing the new collectors, we feel we will then be able to supercharge our new battery. This new battery will be much smaller and will be able to run anything you put it in, and we won't be polluting the environment in the process. General, what are some of the problems you have with your tanks?"

"What do you mean? Our tanks are the best in the world!"

"That may be so, but they are powered by a diesel engine. They're noisy and at night their engines give off a very distinctive heat signature. Anyone with an infrared device can find them, true?"

"Yes, that's true."

"Just imagine if that tank had an electric engine. Now it's quiet and no more heat signature from the engine. Wouldn't that make it even better than it is right now?"

"You mean to tell me this new battery will drive a tank?"

"Yes sir, I do. If my research is right, we can put a battery the size of a shoe box in an eighteen-wheeler and drive it for a month, or in a car for up to six months."

"Pardon me for being skeptical, but it sounds a little unrealistic. Dean Benson, what do you think about all this?"

"Well General, Paul has done some groundbreaking work here that has surprised us all. I wouldn't be supporting him if I didn't believe his ideas would work."

"Very well. At this point I would like to speak with my team. Could we have the room for a few minutes?"

"Certainly, General. We'll be right outside. Call us when you're ready for us."

"Paul, that was very well done."

"Thank you, Ted. I hope it was good enough. Do you think they will go ahead with the funding?"

"I really don't know. The General can be a hard sell on something he can't see or understand. Let's just wait and see what they say."

The general stuck his head out the door and said, "Gentleman, would you please rejoin us. We've talked it over and we're not completely convinced. This is what I want to happen. I have two other professors at MIT that I trust very much in these matters. I want Paul to go there and tell them just how you're going to do this. If they agree, then you'll get your funding."

Paul said "General, I'm not going to give my designs to anyone. It's my work and it stays here."

Ted said, "Hang on Paul, the General is not asking you to give anything away."

"That's right I'm not. I just want you to tell them what you told me. If they agree with your concept, then I'll be satisfied."

"Okay fine with me. When can they meet with me?"

"I will set it up and let you know in a couple of days."

"The sooner the better."

"I understand. I know you want to get started as soon as possible. By the way Paul, just how long will this take?"

"General, I can't give you a date, but short side maybe three years, long side five."

"Try to make it on the short side."

"Yes sir."

"Ted, can I see you in your office for a minute?"

"Yes, General, follow me."

Paul left the meeting feeling that it had gone very well. He hurried home to tell Sharon how it went.

"Paul, you're back, I didn't expect you so soon. How did the meeting go?"

"I'm not sure. I need to meet with two professors at MIT in New York. If they approve, then we'll get the funding."

"When is that going to happen?"

"Sharon, I don't know right now. They're going to call me in a couple of days and set it up."

"Well, I hope it's soon for your sake."

Chapter 3

"Dean Benson, it's been three weeks. How can it possibly take three weeks to set up a meeting?"

"Be patient Paul, you know the government doesn't do anything very efficiently and time doesn't seem to matter to them, unless they want something. How are your classes going?"

"They're fine, but I'm getting a little tired of teaching. I want to get into my lab, get it set up and get started. I need to get my research started before I lose the people that I'm counting on to help me."

"Relax, Paul. I don't think any of them are going to leave. They're just as excited about this as you are."

"Maybe, but they are all at the top of their field. They could be pulled away by a better offer from a private company. They certainly would make more money."

"They're not in it for the money, Paul. It's the intrigue of inventing something new that keeps them here."

"I hope you're right. I can't afford to lose any of them. That could set me back months.

"Hello, Paul. It's Ted calling."

"Hi Ted. I hope you have some good news for me this time."

"Well, yes and no."

"What do you mean yes and no?"

"They called to set up your meeting today. The good news is they can meet with you. The bad news is it won't be for six months."

"Six months! Are you sure?"

"Yes, I'm sure. They're both out of the country and won't be back before then."

"Isn't there someone else I can meet with?"

"I'm afraid not. The General insisted it has to be them."

"I don't believe this will ever get off the ground."

"Paul, I want you to come and see me tomorrow at my office at ten o'clock. Can you make it?"

"Yes, I'll be there."

"Good. I'll see you in the morning and we can talk more then."

"Okay, I'll see you then."

"Good morning, Paul. Come right in and have a seat. Look, I know you're upset by the timeline of this meeting. So am I. I want you to take the time to prepare."

"I'm already prepared."

"Maybe so, but you have six months to get ready to convince those men who don't know you or what you've done. You have to convince them your idea will work."

"I'll convince them. Don't worry about that."

"You better. There's a lot riding on this. If you don't, neither one of us will get any funding."

"What do you mean, neither one of us?"

"Your ten-million-dollar project is only part of the story. Your project receives ten million and the school gets an additional five million."

"What! Why isn't it all going to the project?"

"Paul, look around you. Do you have any idea what it takes to run this place? There are over 2,200 students attending this year. We have over three hundred faculty members, one hundred and fifty staff support people, and the maintenance crew alone is fifty-five. We have sixty-five people in the cafeteria. Do you know how many toilets we have on this campus? How often they stopped working. Last year alone we spent over $14,000 just fixing the plumbing around here. Look, a certain amount of all the funding we receive here goes into helping keep this place running. Do you really believe this place runs on tuition alone?"

"I guess I never thought about it."

"I know, that's why I brought you in this morning. Now you understand why I want you to be prepared for this meeting. It's important for both of us. Like I said before, there's a lot riding on this, so make sure you're ready."

"I'll be ready, you can count on it."

Chapter 4

For the next six months, Paul was consumed with his classes and preparing for the meeting that was upcoming. I barely saw him, and he didn't even realize how close I was to having this baby. The meeting came and went with no clear decision on the funding. Three weeks after Paul came back from that meeting at MIT, we brought little Johnny into this world. Paul was so distracted with his research he hardly spent any time with me or his son. Almost one year to the day after Johnny was born, word finally came about the funding. It was finally approved but was to be spread out over the next four years. Not what Paul wanted, but it would do.

After Paul set up his lab, I saw even less of him. He became a ghost who came and went without ever being seen. Over the next four years, there were many ups and downs. They made progress but it was slow. Paul's work on the new battery was complete and sent to the army. However, the work on using lightning as a power source was still far off.

Paul was granted funding for an additional four years if he first finishes his work on a new field radio for the army. Work on the radio was complete and given to the army. The additional work done on collecting and storing the energy for lightning was still out of reach. After eight years with no positive results, the Army refused any further funding.

Paul continued for the next three years using the money he'd received on his design of the latest battery and the new field radio. Most of Paul's staff left. They lost faith in his idea and moved on. I can't say I blame them. There were times I wanted to leave him myself. He continued with the help of two new assistants that did their best to keep up with him.

After eleven years, the college pulled the plug. No further work was to be done on collecting energy from lightning. Paul's notes on the project reflected that even if it had worked, it would never fill the need for the electrical power this country needs.

One particularly good discovery that had come out of all that work was a power receiver that did work. That was a huge milestone for the team. This receiver, as Paul called it, could receive mega units of voltage then convert the voltage to watts and store it like a giant battery in the blink of an eye.

After the lab was closed, they mothballed all of Paul's work. His only option was to go back to teaching.

That only lasted about three years. Paul never gave up on finding a way to produce clean energy. He came up with a new plan and it consumed him once again. Our son Johnny, as I like to call him, was seventeen at this point. Paul had missed almost everything he had accomplished. The only time he spent with him was when I insisted that he take John with him. When he did take him, all he talked about was his latest great idea. I had managed to keep teaching all those years and keep our little home running on a shoestring. Any money Paul made went into his new inventions.

Chapter 5

My mother is a brilliant woman. I really don't understand how she ever got involved with my dad or put up with being left alone so much. She raised me almost completely by herself. Yes, I had a father, but you wouldn't know it. In the early years of my life, he was just this man that came and went. I think he made it to my ninth birthday, but I'm not even sure of that.

I believe I was fourteen and about to graduate from college with a degree in mechanical engineering when he finally took an interest in me. Yes! At fourteen, I was just a little ahead of my years. My mother tried hard to raise me like any other boy my age. It didn't work!

By the time I was four, I could read anything you handed me. I could do advanced math in my head by the time I was eight. So, you can see, I was not like other kids. What would you expect from two people like my parents who have remarkably high IQs. Of course, a child with a high IQ of his own. She gave up trying to treat me like a normal kid. In fact by the time I was six, she would take me to her classes. I pretty much understood what she was teaching. I read every book she put in my hand and could memorize large volumes of material. There were many schools pursuing me, but Mom put her foot down. She would homeschool me and that was that.

I finished high school by the time I turned eleven. I could attend Cal Tech at twelve because both my parents taught there. I knew from an early age I was different from other kids. I had no interest in what they were doing. It seemed childish to me. It wasn't them. It was me. I finally started to realize it when I went to college. I was only twelve, but everyone else was eighteen or over. I didn't fit in at all. Some of my classmates really resented me being there, but others treated me very well.

In fact, a couple of the girls treated me like a little brother. That was nice of them, and I paid them back by helping them with their schoolwork. Too bad the guys didn't catch on. I guess they weren't smart enough. I graduated in three years with a bachelor's degree in mechanical engineering and applied science. Then I stayed on at Cal Tech for my master's which I received in two years. I was seventeen at this point and that was just about the same time my dad got his new idea... building a static charge machine. My mother warned me not to get involved in another one of my dad's ideas, but I didn't listen. She was right. Surprise, surprise. Three years later I told Dad I'm done working on this. We're getting nowhere.

I applied to Cal Tech for a teaching position and got accepted. I began teaching and very much enjoyed it. My second year of teaching pretty much changed my life for the better. About two months in, I was walking down the hall and just stepped around the corner when out of nowhere I got blindsided by some clown running down the hall.

This was my first encounter with BJ, Brad Johnson. Little did I know at the time but he would become my best friend. Before I could get my bearings, he picked me up off the floor and began to apologize for running into me. I hadn't seen this guy before, but he left quite an impression on me. He had to be at least six two and weigh 220. It felt like I had been run over by a truck. He kept saying how sorry he was. I told him not to worry about it. "I'm okay, I think." He offered to make it up to me by buying me a beer.

Brad said, "How about meeting me at Berries Beer and Burger Joint?"

"Thanks, but no thanks. I have a lot of work to do tonight."

"All right man, I'm sorry, but if you change your mind, I'll be down there around 8:30."

"Okay, thanks, but I don't think so."

Later that night as I was going over my students' latest reports, I sat back and looked at the clock and it was almost 8:30. I thought, why sit here by myself. I'll give it a try and see if I can find this guy at Berries.

Berries was certainly a college hangout, full of students having a good time. I stood there looking around and thought this was a mistake. I don't fit in here anymore than I did in high school when I was eight years old. Even though I was the same age as a lot of these students, I still didn't feel like I fit in. I turned around and headed out the door. Just then, this big hand grabs my shoulder and all but yanks me off my feet. It was Brad.

"Hey, you made it. Glad you decided to come down."

"Yeah, but I don't think"

BJ interrupted me. "Follow me. I've got some friends I want you to meet."

Next thing I knew, I was at the bar with a beer in one hand and a shot of whiskey in the other.

"Here's to you, sorry. I don't remember your name."

"That's because you never asked. It's John."

"In that case, nice to meet you, John. I'm Brad Johnson. Just call me BJ everyone else does, and sorry for knocking you down."

BJ swallowed the shot and took a big gulp of beer. I guess it was my turn. That whiskey burned all the way down. I had to drink the beer just to cool my throat. I had tears in my eyes, and I started to sweat.

Brad laughed! "Is that whiskey a little too much for you?"

"No, not at all! It just went down the wrong way."

"Well, in that case, let's have another."

"Not right now, let me drink this beer first."

"Ok then, John, this is Lisa and Sally."

"BJ, we already know Professor Northrup. We are in one of his classes."

"Say what? You're shitting me!"

34

"No! BJ, I'm afraid not. They are both in my class."

"How can you possibly be a professor? You can't be over twenty years old."

"Actually, twenty-one, but who's counting."

"I don't get it."

"I started young."

"I guess so. How long have you been teaching?"

"This is my second year."

"I didn't know I ran over a professor. Now I'm really sorry." The girls started laughing. Sally said, "You ran over the professor?"

"Yeah, but I didn't mean to. I was in a hurry. I was late for class."

"No, not BJ. You, late for class?" Lisa mocked him. The girls laughed.

"He only knocked me down the hall about ten feet."

"Okay professor, so what are you teaching?"

"Mechanical engineering, applied science and physics when they need me. Also, a little biology. That's the class I know Lisa and Sally from. They are both doing well in my class."

"Professor Northrup makes it very interesting."

"Please, tonight it's just John, and thank you. I do try."

A couple of beers and two more shots. I was well on my way to a place I had never been. BJ handed me one more beer. I took a sip and almost lost my lunch. BJ must have seen what was coming. He grabbed me and pulled me into the men's room just in time. Ten minutes later, he had me outside in the fresh air. He called me a cab and sent me home.

Next day, my first class wasn't until one in the afternoon. Good thing, I barely made it as it was. I didn't eat anything all day, but I drank a ton of water.

Later that evening, BJ called and asked me how I was doing. "We're all down at Berries if you want to try again" he said laughing.

"Are you kidding! I don't ever want to do that again."

"The girls are here, and they would like to see you."

"No thanks. I made a fool out of myself and I have no intention of doing that again. Besides, I haven't gotten over last night yet."

"Okay, maybe next week."

"I don't know, we'll see."

Chapter 6

Two days later, on Saturday, I met up with my dad for lunch. We had a little small talk over lunch. Afterward, he asked me to come to the lab. He had something to show me.

"Okay, but just for a few minutes."

"John, look at this."

"What's that?"

"It's a new type of generator."

"What's new about it?"

"It produces a static charge that I can direct. See that titanium tube on the end there."

"Yes, I see it."

"I have wound copper wire around the inside in a very tight pattern. It makes the electric charge run straight out the end just like a lightning bolt."

"So, what does that do for you?"

"This one, as you can see, is small. It only produces a charge equal to about 10,000 volts, not much. However, it's a start."

"Okay, so how much electricity do you use to reproduce that small amount of electricity?"

"Only about 13,000 volts."

"So, you still are not close to getting more out than it takes to put in."

"Not so fast there, John. It takes 13,000 volts to get the generator running. After that It only takes about 8,500 volts for the second charge. I still get 10,000 out."

"Really?"

"Yes, really!"

"How long can you do this?"

"Only three times, then the generator needs to recharge."

"So really, you're still only a little on the plus side."

"That's true, but I am on the plus side, and no one has ever done that! John this is only a prototype and a small one at that. Can you imagine this on a large scale? Think about how much more it could produce."

"Where are you going to get the money for this larger generator? Certainly not from the college."

"No, my plan is to ask General Wellington for it."

"I don't think that's going to happen. He was very unhappy about your last failure."

"I know but this is different. I'm sure the General will see the value in this. This is a great opportunity for everyone. I'm awfully close this time. I really need the General to come through for me."

"Why is that?"

"The college has given me notice. They want me out of the lab."

"What do you mean, they want you out of the lab?"

"I'm afraid I've been using the lab, and I spent a little of their money without authorization."

"You've been using the lab and spending their money without them knowing it?"

"I'm afraid so."

"Does Mom know about this?"

"Not yet. I haven't had the nerve to tell her."

"That's great, that's just freaking great. Wait till she finds out."

"John, I was hoping you would help me tell your mother."

"Oh no, you're on your own for this one. All the sacrifices she's made for you and now this. You should be ashamed of yourself."

"I am, but you must know I didn't mean for this to happen. John, you of all people, you should understand why I needed to keep my research going."

"No! I don't need to understand. You've spent all these years trying to do something that can't be done. How many people told you you're wasting your time? But you think you're smarter than everybody else, and now what have you got. Nothing. I hope for your sake they don't want Mom to leave as well."

"Her position at the college is fine. They just asked me to leave."

"Well, thank God for that. I can't believe you did this. I'm leaving."

I headed back to my apartment and got madder by the minute. By the time I got there I was so pissed I couldn't sit down. I just kept walking. For a man that was so smart, it was the stupidest thing I've ever heard of. How could he do that to himself and my mother? He never even thought about how this would affect her. All he ever thought about was his stupid experiment. Nothing else ever mattered, including my mother and me.

I just kept walking and before I knew it, I was downtown. It was getting late in the afternoon and I was getting hungry. I found myself a block away from Berries. I never did get a burger in that place. I was there, so why not give it a try. As I walked in there was no one in there that I knew and that was good. I doubted anyone would recognize me, but you never know.

I sat down at a table in the corner and ordered a burger and a glass of water from the waitress. I finished my food and just sat there staring at the table. I thought about how my mother was going to react to the news. This would break her heart. Before I knew it, the place was filling up and getting loud, so it was time to get out of there. I was just about out the door when who did I run into? BJ.

"Hey John, good to see you. What are you doing here? I thought you were never coming back here."

"Hi BJ. I've been having a bad day and just ended up here. I was walking it off and before I knew it, I found myself downtown. I'm on my way home right now. Good to see you. Catch you later."

"Not so fast man. Is there anything I can do to help?"

"No, not really. I've just got to work this out for myself. I'll be fine."

"No better way to work things out than with a cold beer and a friend to listen to your problems."

"Thanks, but no thanks."

"Why not? You're here so you might as well have a beer and talk it out. What do you say, just one and it's on me."

"Yeah right, just one. That's what you said last time and look what happened."

"Honestly, man, just one and after that you can go home."

"Okay just one and I'm going to hold you to it."

"Great, let's grab a beer and find a table."

"So, what's the problem man?"

"You wouldn't understand."

"Try me. I'm a little smarter than you might think."

"Okay, it's my father. We're not too close but he can still make me crazy."

"Why, what did he do?"

"He's been spending his whole life trying to come up with a way to make clean energy."

"That doesn't sound like a bad thing. What's wrong with that?"

"What he's been trying to do won't work, and everyone knows it except him. You have no idea how much time and money he's wasted. It's so ridiculous. It's taking a huge toll on my mother. I can't believe she's still with him. Wait till she hears the latest news."

"Why, what happened?"

"He's been working in the lab at the college and spending money without their consent. He got caught, and now he's been asked to leave."

"Leave the lab?"

"Not just the lab, but the college as well. They removed him from his teaching position."

"Oh man, that does sound bad. So, what do you think your mom's going to do?

"I'm not sure, she'll probably keep teaching, but I'm not sure she's going to stay with my dad."

"Wait a minute, you're telling me your mother is a professor too?"

"Yes, she teaches biochemistry at the college."

"So, your mom, your dad and you are all professors at the college?"

"We all were, but my dad is out for good I'm afraid."

"That's too bad. I'm sorry about that. I've never heard of a whole family all being professors and teaching at the same college. That's just crazy."

"My mom and dad are intelligent people. They've been teaching here for years before I was born. I guess that's where I get my good genes from."

"I guess so, they must have passed on some really good stuff to you."

"My mom and dad are a little above normal."

"A little above normal? I'd say they're a lot above normal and that goes for you as well. I mean that as a compliment. To do what you're doing at your age, that's just nuts, man."

"Well, I wouldn't say you're normal either. Look at all you've accomplished since you've been here. All the things you've done with your sports, and I understand you're going to join the army as an officer once you graduate. How many people can say that?"

"Well maybe so, but that's nothing compared to what you've done."

"Don't sell yourself short, BJ. I think you're going to do good things in the future."

"We'll see about that! How about another beer?"

"Okay, one more then I've got to go."

Chapter 7

Around noon Sunday, I got a call from my mother. At first, I thought she had been crying but she was just angry. I couldn't blame her. She had every right to be. My father had just told her what happened. She was so upset with him that she kicked him out.

"I said good for you Mom, that's just what he deserved."

"Johnny, I don't know what I'm going to do with him. He lost his teaching position, and all his work is for nothing."

"Yes, I know. He told me the other day."

"I must have told him a thousand times not to go back to that lab and keep working, but do you think he would listen to his wife? Not me, he thinks I don't know anything."

"I'm sure that's not true, mom. It's just he's so driven he can't see anything else. He doesn't care about the cost, not to himself or anyone else."

"You're right son. I understand that better than anyone."

"So, what are you going to do now?"

"I'll keep teaching, but I don't know if they will let us keep living on campus now that only one of us is teaching. I guess if they ask me, I may have to move."

"I hope it doesn't come down to that. I can talk to Dean Benson for you. We get along pretty well."

"No, I can speak with him myself if I need to."

"Okay let me know what happens."

"I will."

I don't know for sure what happened between them, but a few days later my dad was back home, and they could stay on campus. Things were quiet on the home front after that, at least for the next couple of months.

I kept busy teaching classes and checking on my mother. Every so often, I would meet BJ down at Berries Burger Joint to grab something to eat and have a few beers. We got to be good friends. He invited me to go with him on one of his work outs. I thought he was trying to kill me. Every muscle in my body hurt. I hurt in places I didn't know I had. First and last time I did that.

BJ was always trying to fix me up. Every time I would meet him down at Berries, he would try to introduce me to some girl. I never found any of them interesting, not that I didn't try. They just had different interests than I did. Some of them had been in a class I taught which was strange.

Having BJ as a friend is both a blessing and a curse! There is no one else I would call if I needed help in any way. He is a true friend in every sense of the word. He's loyal, honest to a fault and can be trusted to keep any secret. I hope he feels the same way about me. However, on the other hand, he can be a royal pain in the ass!

Shortly after we became friends, he felt I was open game for him to play all his practical jokes on every chance he got! There was the time when he put clear contact cement on the floor at the podium where I was teaching. When I stepped up to the podium, I couldn't move my feet anymore. I had to step out of my shoes to get free. Then there was the time he oiled every door knob in my apartment and greased my toilet seat with Vaseline.

One night at Berries, he paid a hooker to come on to me. She introduced herself to me at the bar and asked me to buy her a drink. We talked for a little while and soon she started to come on to me in a big way. She started kissing my neck right there in the bar. Next thing I knew, she was running her hand up the inside of my leg right to my crotch. I couldn't help but get excited and she grabbed me right through my pants. She kept at it and kept telling me to take her back to my place and have sex with her.

This was so out of the realm of my world I could hardly move. Little did I know that BJ and a few others were standing in the back of the bar watching the whole thing. I left the bar with this hooker hanging on my arm promising to meet her at her place. She headed for her place and I headed back to my apartment to take a cold shower. My virginity was still intact. Two days later, BJ confessed to setting me up.

Well, I decided that one good turn deserves another. So, with the help of two of his football buddies I got my revenge. We paid a gay young man to come on to BJ. We also had the help of the ladies that used to hang out with BJ at the bar. That night at the bar, the girls wave BJ over and introduce them to our gay young man. They told this young man all about BJ and his passion for football, so they hit it off right away. Before long, our young man was hanging all over BJ. We just sat back and watched. The more our young man hung on BJ, the more you could see him getting uncomfortable. When our young man put his arm around BJ's waist and tried to kiss him, I thought BJ was going to jump out of his skin!

I was laughing so hard I could barely breathe! Fortunately, BJ's buddies stepped in to save our young man. I'm not sure what BJ might have done. Within minutes everyone in the bar knew what had just happened. BJ would never live that down for the rest of his time at Cal Tech.

When BJ found out it was me that had set him up, all he could say was "Good One!". It was shortly after that when I felt that we had become friends for life.

Chapter 8

One night near the end of the school year, BJ called me. He said "Meet me at Berries tonight. I've got someone I want you to meet."

"Thanks, but I'm kind of busy tonight."

"I don't give a s*** how busy you are. Get your ass down here. I want you to meet this girl."

"Okay, when you put it that way, I guess I better show up."

"What have you got to lose? See you around nine."

"Okay fine. I'll be there."

I wasn't really interested in going down there. The school year was almost over, and I had plans for the summer. I got there just about nine and found BJ at the bar.

"Good, you made it. I really want you to meet this girl."

"Is she different from any other girl you've introduced me to?"

"Just wait and see. She'll be here in a few minutes."

A short time later as I was enjoying my beer, I turned around and looked towards the door. As I looked, I saw this young lady walking in our direction. She was about five six and might have weighed all of 110 pounds. She had on a light blue top with a dark colored dressy jacket. She was wearing a pair of faded blue jeans that really showed off her figure. She had sandals on her feet and a dark blue choker around her neck. From across the room, I could see this pretty soft face with bright blue eyes surrounded by long brown hair that fell well below her shoulders. She had the brightest smile I've ever seen. She really caught my attention, as well as half the guys in the bar. I was sure this girl was here to see BJ. He always had the best-looking woman hanging all over him. I felt sure he would keep this one for himself. She walked right by me and up to BJ. She gave him a hug and a little kiss on the cheek. I was so jealous of him right at that moment. I guess you need to be a football star to catch a girl like that!

BJ looked at me and said, "John, I'd like you to meet Mary."

I almost hit the floor. For all the great brain power I have, all I could think of to say was "Hi."

Mary smiled that beautiful smile of hers and said "Hi John. Nice to meet you. BJ told me a lot about you."

"I hope it was all good."

"Well, most of it. Only kidding. It was all good. I heard you're a professor at Cal Tech."

"Yes, I am, but I've only been there two years."

"I've been going there for a year now, but I've never seen you on campus."

"Cal Tech is a big school. That's probably why you've never seen me."

"Cal Tech might seem big to you, but it's nowhere near the size of the school I first went to."

"Why, where did you go before you came here?"

"Oklahoma State. There are over 25,000 students on that campus."

"I guess Cal Tech is small compared to that school. What was your course of study there?"

"I received my bachelor's degree in education, sign language, and I studied a little Latin."

"So, what are you studying here?"

"French and Spanish."

"That's probably why we haven't crossed paths. I teach mechanical engineering and applied science on the other side of the campus."

"I'm sure that's why. Why don't we grab a table? I've been on my feet all day."

"That sounds good to me. Lead the way. I'll follow you." I would have followed her anywhere.

Mary turned to BJ. "Are you coming, BJ?"

"No, I'm waiting for someone else. Thanks."

That was the right answer as far as I was concerned, whether he was really waiting for someone or not. When we got to the table, I offered to buy her a drink, and to my surprise she asked for a soda. She said she had enough last night when she was out with her girlfriends.

"So, why the language classes?"

"I want to teach but I'm just not sure where. It will most likely be in the states, but I may want to teach in France or Spain. I just don't know at this point."

In my mind I was praying she would teach here in California. We sat there talking for the next three hours and got to know each other well. She was the most interesting woman I've ever met, besides my mother. It was getting late. She said she was worn out from the night before and needed to head home. As we stepped outside to leave, I asked her if we could meet again.

"Are you sure you want to? I talked your ear off."

"I loved listening to you. You're one of the most interesting girls I've ever met, not that I have met that many."

"You really think so? Most guys can't be bothered."

"I think you'll find I'm not like most guys."

"I guess not. You're the only guy I ever met who is a professor at your age."

"Is that a problem?"

"Not at all. I just feel a little intimidated."

"Don't feel intimidated. It's just who I am. I'm really no different than anybody else."

"Maybe, but you're smarter than anybody else I've ever met."

"Well, I can try to dumb it down for you if you'd like."

"Oh no. Don't do that. I find you interesting and refreshing for a change."

"Good. That makes me feel better. How about lunch on Wednesday?"

"That would work well for me. I have class until 11:30. How about meeting at the little park on campus?"

"Great, that works for me. We can grab a little lunch and talk then."

"Good, I'll see you then."

She gave me a hug and walked away. I just stood there watching her until she got out of sight. I could feel my heart racing and I was breathing a little faster than normal. I wasn't sure what was going on, but I think I liked it. I have never been interested in girls before, but she was a different matter altogether.

I was just turning to leave when I felt this big hand on my shoulder. It had to be BJ. As I turned around, he said "So, what do you think?"

"Where did you come from? Have you been standing there watching us?"

"Not really, but I was headed out and I overheard you and Mary making plans. So, what do you think?"

"She's something else."

"So, are you going to see her again?"

"I'm going to see her a lot if I have anything to do with it."

"Seriously, who would go out with you more than once!"

"Ha, Ha! Very funny, wise ass."

"Well, maybe, if you asked in a really nice way, she might go out with you again."

"I will beg if I have to. I think she's fascinating and I can't wait to see her again."

"Funny thing. Other guys that have gone out with her and tell me she talks your ear off."

"Well, I find that to be a very charming part of her."

"Okay, glad you do, because she's a real talker. I've got to run and get my beauty rest. I have a game tomorrow, the last one of the season. Are you going to make it to the game?"

"You need a lot of beauty rest for that face."

"OH, you're so funny."

"I think so, I don't have anything else to do. I'll try to make it."

I did make it to the game, and I was glad I did. BJ threw for over 300 yards and scored four touchdowns. It was the best game of his season. BJ had a half dozen pro scouts looking at him. He could have played for just about any NFL team he wanted to. I couldn't understand why he would pass that up to join the Army, but I really respected him for it.

Chapter 9

Wednesday finally came and I found myself standing in the campus park by 10:30, a full hour before Mary was coming. 11:30 finally got there but no Mary. I waited almost half an hour and decided she wasn't coming. I couldn't believe how disappointed I was. I just started walking away when I heard a voice calling.

"John!"

I turned around and there was Mary running in my direction. I could feel my heart rate increasing the minute I saw her. When she finally caught up to me, she was all out of breath.

"I'm so sorry I'm late. I was helping one of my classmates with his French. The time just got away from me before I realized it. I'm glad you waited. I was afraid you had left already."

"I was just about to leave. I thought you weren't coming."

"What you will find out about me is that if I tell someone I'm going to do something, you can be sure I'll do it."

"I was afraid you stood me up."

"I would never stand you up, that's not the way I do things. If I didn't want to see you again, I would tell you to your face."

"That's good to know, I like people who are direct. I want you to know I will always wait for you."

"So, who is your French teacher?"

"Her name is Professor Kelly. She's really an awesome teacher."

"I know Professor Kelly. She's a friend of my mother's. My mother taught her class for three weeks when she was out with the flu."

"You mean Professor Sharon Northrup?"

"Yes, they've been friends for years."

"Is Sharon Northrup your mother?"

"Yes, she is."

"I don't believe it. I never would have thought you are her son even though you have the same last name. How weird is that?"

"Well, it's not that weird, we do have the same last name."

"Yes, but who ever heard of a woman having her son teach at the same college she teaches at."

"Well, there's a first time for everything."

"Now, I suppose you're going to tell me your father teaches here too."

"Well as a matter of fact he did, up until a few weeks ago."

"You're kidding! And what was his name?"

"Professor Paul Northrop."

"I never met him, but I did hear the name. Didn't he have some big project here on campus?"

"Yes, he did."

"I remember reading about him. Did his experiment work out?"

"No, and that's kind of why he's not teaching here anymore."

"What happened?"

"It's a long story. I'll tell you some other time."

"So, what have you been doing for the last three days?"

"Not much."

Not much, turned into an hour and a half. I don't think she took a breath the whole time. I never met anyone so full of life! BJ was right. She could talk your ear off. I finally held my hand up and told her I had a class I had to get to.

"Mary, I'm sorry we didn't get a chance for lunch."

"Oh, that's fine. I never eat lunch. I believe in a good breakfast and dinner. That's all a person needs. We eat way too much food in this country. There are way too many obese people walking around."

"Well, if you don't eat lunch, how about dinner tonight?"

"That would be great!"

"Give me your number and I'll call you later."

I met her at Wontons Chinese around seven. We had a nice dinner and we talked, or I should say she talked until they closed the place. It wasn't that far from the campus, so we walked back. When we got back to her dorm, I said good night and turned to walk away. She grabbed me around the waist, gave me a hug and a big kiss on the lips.

"I hope you didn't mind that. I'm really starting to like you."

"Do that again and I'll let you know." She laughed and gave me another kiss. "No, I guess not." What a stupid response. She stepped back and started to laugh just a little. I guessed from the look on her face she could tell how stunned I was.

"I take it you're not used to having girls kiss you first?"

"I think I could get used to it, if it's you. You can kiss me anytime you want." She said thanks for a great night and disappeared into her dorm.

By the time I walked back to my place my heart rate had slowed down and my breathing was back to normal. What a great night. I couldn't believe how lucky I was to have met Mary. I guess I owe BJ for that one.

When I got home there was a message on the phone from my mother. "Give me a call. I need to talk to you about your father." My heart rate may have gone down, but my blood pressure just went up. What now?

I couldn't get back to her until later the next day. "Hi Mom. What's up?"

"Your father's at it again."

"What did he do this time?"

"He wrote a letter to General Wellington. Can you believe he is coming out to see your father and Dean Benson?"

"What! After that last fiasco?"

"You heard me. They're meeting next Tuesday at ten in the morning."

"Why would Dean Benson be at this meeting? Dad doesn't even work for the college anymore."

"I know, but the general wants him there and he agreed to be there."

"I don't believe this after all that's happened."

"John, what has your father been working on?"

"Same old thing, just another way. He hasn't told me much about it and I didn't ask. It gets me a little too wound up."

"John, I want you to go to this meeting and find out just what's going on. Your father's not telling me anything and I don't want this to start all over again."

"Don't worry. I understand your concern. I'll make sure I'm invited."

Mary and I spent the weekend doing things together. Saturday, we drove to Pasadena and spent the day shopping for clothes for me. She said I was a little out of date and behind the times. Maybe just a little. Sunday, we drove to the beach. When we got out onto the beach, she laid out a blanket in the sand and a basket full of goodies, along with a bottle of wine. It was the first time I saw her drink wine. I guess I shouldn't have been surprised. She was two years older than me. I'm sure it wasn't the first glass of wine she'd ever had.

"I'm a little surprised you brought wine. You usually have a beer."

"I have been drinking wine from the time I was about fourteen. After all, I grew up in wine country."

"Here in California?"

She laughed. "Not even close. I grew up in a little town called Tannersville in New York. It's in the finger lakes area of the state."

"Never heard of it."

"That's a surprise," she scoffed. "It has a population of five hundred and thirty-five, and you've never heard of it?"

"I guess I must have missed it in one of my geography classes."

"Even so, isn't fourteen a little young to be drinking wine?"

"Not if your parents own a winery."

"Your parents own a winery?"

"Yes, and an incredibly good one at that. They have an incredibly good wine selection of their own and they also bring in some of the finest wines from France. So, you see it's not unusual for me to have started drinking wine at fourteen."

"I guess not. Tell me more about your parents, but not right now. I want to go for a swim."

She was wearing a long dark cover up and I couldn't wait to see what she was wearing under it. When she finally took it off, I found myself staring at her. It wasn't long before she caught me. She smiled and said, "I guess you like what you see."

I must have looked like I'd been sitting in the sun for a week. I could feel the embarrassment on my face. I'm sure I was turning bright red.

"Sorry, I didn't mean to stare."

"Don't be sorry, I'm glad you're staring. I'd be disappointed if you didn't."

She leaned over and gave me a kiss and then ran into the water. We had a great day at the beach. Before I knew it, the weekend was over. We only had one more week before the semester was over.

Chapter 10

Tuesday morning, I found myself in Dean Benson's office by nine o'clock. I wanted some time with him before the meeting.

"Dean Benson."

"John, just call me Ted. We've known each other for a long time."

"Okay then. Ted, what the hell is going on with this meeting?

"I'm not all that sure John. The General called me about two weeks back. He said your dad had written him a letter. He had talked over the letter with a couple of his staff people and apparently it sounded interesting to them. So much so, they wanted this meeting and asked me to run it."

"Do you really think my dad has come up with something new?"

"John, after the last go-around I have my doubts. However, the General wants to talk and when he talks, a lot of people listen. I'm one of them. The General has given millions of dollars to this college. When he asks me a question, I try my best to answer him."

"I understand that, but he got nothing out of the last program."

"I wouldn't say that. The new batteries that he's using are working well and no one else in the world has them."

"I understand that, but I still don't see how that counts for much."

"Let's just wait and see."

We were all there by ten, right on time. The General, his staff, Dean Benson, my father, and me. After a little small talk, they turned the meeting over to my father. Three hours later and after a lot of questions, we were done. The General took the report, thanked Dean Benson and my father and left.

After saying hello to me before the meeting, the General never even looked at me. It was like I wasn't even in the room.

My father and I talked for another hour. I must admit after hearing my dad's report I was impressed. He might just be onto something. He sure made you want to believe. I walked out of that meeting thinking, here we go again.

Over the next three weeks my father was his old self. Things seemed to be going good with my mom and dad for a change and I was glad to see my mother happy. Even if I knew it wouldn't last. Shortly after that meeting, I taught my last class for the year. Mary had her last class on Friday. That night, we all got together at Berries. It had become a routine for us almost every Friday and Saturday night. However, this night would be the last one for many of us. I had made a lot of friends because of BJ and Mary. I was grateful for that. Later in the evening I pulled BJ aside to let him know what his friendship meant to me.

"BJ, until I met you, I had no real friends and I really didn't know how to get along with people, to say nothing about how to drink whiskey and beer."

"Well, it's a good thing I ran you over!"

"I guess so. I really want to thank you for introducing me to Mary. I think I love that girl."

"How would you know that? Have you ever been in love before?"

"No, but I think I am."

"Better be careful man. It's like the song says, 'sometimes love can hurt', or something like that."

"I guess I'll just have to take that risk."

"Well, I hope for your sake she feels the same way."

"I think she does!"

"Why don't you just ask her and find out for sure?"

"I will as soon as I work up the nerve to ask. BJ, I know you have to report on Monday. When do you think you'll be back?"

"No idea man, the Army is not one to tell you much. My basic training is over, and I report as an officer. I go for advanced training, then it's off to Ranger school. That's for a full year. Most of it is here in the states, but three months of it is out of the country, and I have no idea where they're going to send me."

"That sounds rough!"

"Maybe for some people, but I can't wait."

"I know you're a cut above the rest of us. You're so much different than me."

"I don't think that much. We are both alike in some ways. We both like women and beer" he laughed.

"Well, I guess we have that much in common, I'm really going to miss you. You've been a great friend."

"Yeah, I'm going to miss you too."

"Make sure you write and let me know how you're doing."

"I'll try, but I'm not much of a writer."

"You take care of yourself and try to stay out of trouble."

"What fun is there in that!"

That was the last time I saw him for almost two years. In all that time I only got three letters and every time he was hurt and in the hospital. Just like BJ. He couldn't stay out of trouble. The last time he wrote was when he broke his leg jumping out of an airplane. Part of his training, I think.

Mary and I spent most of the night saying goodbye to our friends. Most of them we will never see again. I guess that's just life. Friends move on to new places and make new friends. It's kind of sad but true. We left Berries around two in the morning. I believe it was one of the few times I ever left there completely sober. That night wasn't about drinking. It was much more than that. It was about saying goodbye to good friends one last time. Most of the friends I had made I would never see again. As bad as that was, the thought of saying goodbye to Mary was killing me. I knew saying goodbye to Mary would be terrible. I wasn't sure I'd even be able to do it. She had told me weeks before she was headed to New York, some little town in Rochester. She had a teaching job waiting for her there and she would be close to her family. I wanted her to stay for the summer, but she wanted to get to New York. She wanted to get ready to teach in the fall. She needed to find a place and get settled in.

We got back to her dorm and as always, I gave her a long kiss and hugged her so tight. I just didn't want to let go. I finally let her go and as I turned to leave without saying anything, she reached out, grabbed my hand, and turned me around. "You're not going home tonight. You're staying with me."

I could feel my heart starting to race. She led me into the building and up to her room. We had never been intimate with each other up to this point. I had no idea what I was doing or what to say. We walked into her place and she locked the door. She took my coat and tossed it on the chair. She gave me a long hard kiss and I kissed her back just as hard. She pushed hard up against me and held me tight up against her. For the first time I reached down and caressed that beautiful firm butt of hers. I was shaking with anticipation of what I hoped was coming. I think she felt my excitement because she whispered in my ear, "Just keep that guy ready for a few minutes. I'll be right back."

Before I could catch my breath, she was back wearing a long pink nightgown that buttoned all the way down the front. She found me right where she left me. I really couldn't move. My mind and my feet weren't connecting anymore.

Mary came over, took my hand, and slowly lifted it to her breasts and left it there. My heart was pounding so fast I was sure she could hear it. I didn't believe it could beat any faster. I was wrong. She reached down and found the pounding erection in my pants. I thought my legs were just going to give out. She undid my belt, unzipped my fly then gently pulled my pants to the floor. As I stepped out of them, I could feel her hot breath on my erection.

She stood up slowly pressing her body against mine. She lifted my shirt over my head and tossed it aside. Then she took hold of my boxers, knelt down and pulled them to the floor. I heard her say "Oh, that looks nice." She stayed right there for a long time and I could feel her face pressed against me. I had never been naked in front of a girl before, but the excitement was incredible. Mary stepped back just a little and said, "Now it's your turn. Unbutton my nightgown."

I was shaking so bad she had to help me. Together, we got the job done. She pulled her nightgown back and slowly let it fall to the floor. She had the most perfect body I had ever seen. I just stared at her. Her tan lines accented each one of her full soft breasts. I gently caressed each one. After a few moments she reached down and grabbed my throbbing penis and pulled me close to her. I have no idea where the lotion on her hand came from, but it felt incredible. I had no idea how good a simple touch could feel. She began to slowly stroke me up and down. I thought for sure my legs would give out. She put me between her legs, never letting me go. Then she slowly started rubbing her body against mine up and down in a slow rhythm that just made it feel all the better. It wasn't long before I felt myself losing control. I wanted to tell her to stop but it just felt so damn good. She pushed her mouth against mine and I could feel her tongue pushing into my mouth. She started pushing harder against me moving up and down at a quicker pace that drove me crazy. Before I could say anything, I had lost control and was erupting in her hand. She just kept going. I grabbed that beautiful ass of hers and joined in the rhythm. Soon, I could hear the soft sound of her coming. She picked up the pace even faster and we were both rubbing hard against one another. Her breathing was coming hard and fast. I heard her soft moan and felt her body relax. She never let go of my manhood the whole time.

I had no idea if I had done what she wanted or not, all I know is that she made me come more than once. I was kind of amazed because after all that I hadn't relaxed even a little. My erection was just as hard as ever. She pushed me down on the couch and laid on top of me. She grabbed my erection and gently guided me inside her. What an incredible feeling! I could never have imagined how good this could feel. She slowly began to move up and down on me. My body just shook from the feeling. She began to increase her rhythm and within just a few minutes it was happening all over again. When it was over, she laid down on top of me and put her head against my chest. We laid there for a long time and just enjoyed each other. She got up after a few minutes and disappeared into the bathroom. I didn't know what to do so I just laid there. Two minutes later she reappeared with a warm wet washcloth. She came over and gently started to clean me off. A minute later she pulled back and said "Oh my. You look like you are ready for me all over again. What would you like this time?"

I had no idea how to answer that question. I didn't have to. Mary answered the question for me. Soon we were locked together, and she was having her way with me. This woman was incredible. I had no idea sex could be this good.

"I want you to know John. I've never been this way with anyone. I didn't know I could be this way."

We spent the night sleeping and occasionally waking to enjoy each other once again.

When I woke up in the morning, she wasn't in bed with me. I could hear her in the kitchen, and I could smell the coffee and hear the bacon cooking. She came back to the bedroom and crawled under the sheets with me. Just to tease me she reached down and took hold of my manhood. I came to attention almost immediately. She started laughing and said, "I guess breakfast will have to wait. You're really enjoying this, aren't you?"

"Mary, you have no idea how much I'm enjoying this."

We made love once again. We enjoyed each other a little slower this time. She had the most incredible body and I just didn't want to ever let go of her.

By the time we got to the kitchen, the bacon was pretty burnt. We really didn't care. After breakfast we took a shower together. That was the most fun I've ever had in a shower. I eventually got dressed and helped her pack some of the last things in her apartment.

I only had her for one more day and then she would be gone. The thought of her leaving was making me very depressed. I wish I had met her long before I did. How could I ever let this woman leave after last night? We talked a little bit that morning before I had to leave and meet my mother. I promised I'd be back later.

"You better be."

"Don't worry. I'll be back."

I would have gone back even if my house were burning down. I had to see her one more time.

Chapter 11

When I walked into my mother's place, I could tell from the look on her face something was wrong.

"What's wrong, Mom?"

"Your father got the grant from the army."

"Isn't that a good thing?"

"No, not really. Dean Benson will not allow him to work in the lab here at the college."

"Why not?"

"Because your father abused that privilege and now, they won't let him back in."

"That's a little harsh, don't you think?"

"Yes, I think so."

"Would you like me to talk to Dean Benson?"

"No. I already did that, and he won't budge."

"So, what's Dad going to do now?"

"He's planning on setting up his own lab."

"Where is he going to do that?"

"You remember that little house he bought years ago at Lake Havasu."

"Yes, I remember, but that's not a house, it's more like a shack. It needs a ton of work!"

"It's not that bad. He promised to fix it up before we moved in there."

"Moved in there? You're not planning on going with him, are you?"

"Yes, I am. Your father will need my help."

"Yes, until he kills himself working on this stupid idea of his. I can't believe you're going along with this."

"John, he's my husband and I can't abandon him now."

"What about your teaching here at the college?"

"I'll find something out there."

"There's nothing out there but desert."

"There's a nice little town not too far from the house. I'm sure they could use someone like me."

"Maybe so, but they sure aren't going to pay you what you're worth."

"No, but your father will have more than enough money to support both of us."

"Mother, you know that all the money he gets from the government will go towards his experiment."

"Not all of it. The grant is in both our names."

"How did you pull that one off?"

"I had a long talk with that General. We came to an understanding. I wasn't born yesterday, John. I know how your father thinks. I need to try to control him as best I can."

"Well, good for you! When is this all going to happen?"

"Fairly soon, I think. The army is anxious for him to get started."

"So, who's going to build this lab anyway? Certainly not dad."

"Believe it or not the army's going to build it."

"They really must think this is going to work or they wouldn't be doing it."

"Well, they've made quite a commitment to your father and me, so they must think so."

"I heard his spiel to the army, and he certainly makes you want to believe it'll work, but there are so many problems he needs to work out. It could take years."

"Well, that's what your father does. He works out problems. He's been doing it his whole life."

"I hope we can find someone to help him, he's certainly going to need it. I still can't believe you're going with him on this."

"Don't worry about me. I'll be fine."

"Well, I've got something to tell you. I have a girlfriend and I want you to meet her."

"You have a girlfriend? I was beginning to give up on you. I didn't think that would ever happen. So, when am I going to meet this girlfriend of yours?"

"I'll bring her after lunch. I can't wait for you to meet her. She's something special."

"I guess she must be. You're pretty excited about her."

"I am. She's perfect in so many ways."

"Let me be the judge of that. I don't want you falling for just anyone."

"Don't worry. She's not just anyone. I've got to go. I'll see you in a little while."

I left my mother's place and headed right over to Mary's. She was pretty much done with her packing. I helped her load some boxes into her car. Once that was done, I took her over to meet my mother.

My mother met us at the door. "You were right, Johnny. She is a beauty."

We sat and talked for two hours. My mother and her got along like old friends. I could barely get a word in. We had a little snack and hoped my father would show up. He never did. After a couple hours, it was time to go and my mother made her promise to write. She said she would. We got back to her place and she jumped out of the car. I really had to bite my tongue to keep from asking her to stay. I knew she wouldn't'. She really wanted to get to New York and take on that teaching job. We had one more night together and we made the best of it.

The next morning, we had a little breakfast. I could tell she was anxious to get on the road. We loaded the last of her belongings into the car. It was time to say goodbye. I tried hard to be a man about this, but I could feel myself starting to lose it. I had tears in my eyes. I could barely talk. I hadn't realized until that moment how much in love I was with this girl. The thought of saying goodbye to her was terrible. She handled it far better than I did. She promised me she'd stay in touch and try to talk to me every day. As she drove away, I just stood there and watched her go. There was so much I wanted to say before she left but I didn't say any of it.

I tried teaching that summer, thinking that would keep my mind off Mary, but it didn't work. We talked often, but it just wasn't enough. Every so often I would go down to Berries and have a beer. It just wasn't the same. Everyone was gone for the summer and it just seemed empty to me. The days I had spent with Mary were the best days of my life. Talking with her only made me miss her that much more. I couldn't deal with this anymore. I had to do something.

My mother knew just what I was going through. Somehow, mothers just know. My mother, bless her heart, told me I should move to New York to be with Mary. I said I would love to, but I need a job. She made a phone call for me to a friend of my dad's at RIT in Rochester, right near where Mary was teaching. Next day, I received a call from the head of the engineering department. They had an opening if I was interested. I couldn't say yes fast enough. This was too good to be true. I would be back together with Mary and teaching at one of the finest colleges in the country.

I couldn't wait to call Mary and tell her! Then I thought no, I'll just go there and surprise her. I liked that idea even better. As soon as summer classes were over, I packed what I needed and headed for New York. I hated to leave my mother, but she knew I had to go. I tried to call my dad. He was already in Lake Havasu watching over the building of his new lab. I couldn't reach him. No surprise there. I decided to stop there on my way to New York, even though it was out of my way.

I hadn't been to the house (if you could call it that) in at least five years. It was the last time my parents made me go. I had a hard time finding the place. It was located on a dirt road a mile off the main road and nothing but desert. As I drove up, I was amazed at all the activity. There were army trucks and cranes everywhere. There must have been a hundred men working in the lab. The building was much larger than I had imagined. It had to be a hundred feet by two hundred feet. The walls were halfway up and some of the equipment was already in place. It took me a few minutes to find my dad. He was busy giving orders to everyone. I finally got a chance to pull him aside. I told him I was leaving for New York.

"Why would you go there? I could use your help right here."

"Dad, I'm going there to be with Mary."

"Who's Mary?"

"If you had come to the house when Mom called you, you would have met her there. She's my girlfriend."

"You have a girlfriend?"

"Yes, I have a girlfriend, and she's wonderful. I wish you had met her. I'm in love with this girl."

"I guess you must be if you're moving all the way to New York. What about your teaching position here?"

"I already have a new teaching position at RIT."

"How did you get that position? You know, I went to school there back when I was your age. I even taught there for a year."

"I know, that's kind of how I got my teaching position. Mom called and talked to a friend of yours in the administration department. They offered me a position teaching in the engineering department."

"Well, I guess I'm glad for you, even though I could use your help here. If it doesn't work out, you can always come back here and work with me. I could surely use your help."

"That's not going to happen. I want to be where Mary is."

"John, don't you realize what I'm doing here? This will help millions of people all over the world."

"You keep saying that, but after 20 years you still have nothing to show for it."

"John, I'm very close this time."

"I've heard it all before, and I'm not listening anymore. I've got my own life to live and it's not here. Sorry, Dad, I've got to go. Make sure you look after Mom. She's a better woman than you deserve."

"You're right about that. I'll make sure I look after her. Please call us and let us know how you're making out in New York."

"I will."

CHAPTER 12

I spent the next three days on the road. What a magnificent country we live in. I had never driven cross country before, but I promised myself I would do it again as often as I could. I hope next time it will be with Mary. The morning of my fourth day I pulled into the parking lot where Mary's apartment was. It was a nice place in a little town called Brighton. I was so excited to see her I started to shake. I had picked up some flowers on the way and planned on holding them in front of my face when she answered the door to surprise her.

I found her apartment number and started knocking on her door, but no answer. So, I knocked again a little harder this time, but still no answer. I just stood there for a few minutes not knowing what else to do. I was so disappointed, but it was obvious she wasn't home.

I sat on a bench outside her apartment for a little while and then decided to go sit in my car. I was tired from my drive out and before I knew it, I was sound asleep.

I don't know how long I was asleep, but when I woke up someone was pounding on the window of my car and shouting my name. It was Mary and I almost fell out of the car. She grabbed me around the neck so hard I started to choke. I gave her the longest kiss I could ever remember. She started asking me questions.

"When did you get here? How did you get here? Why are you here? Did something happen to your mom?"

"Slow down a minute and I'll tell you. I have a lot to tell you. Everyone is fine back home."

"Did you lose your teaching position?"

"No, I didn't lose it, I gave it up."

"Why would you do that?"

"Because I have a new one."

"Why would you take on a new position? You love teaching at Cal Tech."

"Because my new teaching position is right here at RIT in Rochester."

"Are you serious? Do you really have a job here? When did all this happen?"

"Hang on, one question at a time."

"John, you better not be lying to me or playing a joke. Are you seriously moving here to New York?"

"Yes, I'm serious. Do you think I drove all the way out here just to say hi?"

Mary threw her arms around me again and started to cry. Then she told me how much she had missed me and was thinking about moving back to Pasadena.

"I've missed you so much. Sometimes I would cry just thinking about the months it would be before I would see you again. I cried all the way out here to New York. I can't believe you're here. I just can't tell you how happy I am! Where were you planning on staying?"

"I was hoping to stay with you."

"You better say that. My apartment is a little small, but we'll make it work. Let me help you move your stuff inside."

"I don't have much. I left most of my things with my mom. I told her I would have them shipped out once I get settled. All I have are my clothes and some books."

"Good. Let's get all your things inside."

We moved everything inside and started to put things away, but that didn't last very long. The unpacking could wait. We hadn't seen each other in quite a while, and we had a lot of lost time to make up for. We spent the next two hours making up for lost time.

Once we came up for air, we started catching up on all that had happened since we had last seen each other. Mary talked nonstop about her new teaching job. She had been to the school, met the staff and saw her classroom.

She was so excited she couldn't sit still. I told her I would be teaching at RIT in the fall and was excited about that as well.

A couple days later we got settled into a good routine. We would have a little breakfast each morning and then go for a jog at a nearby park. Then off to run errands and get ready to teach in the fall.

School started early September for both of us and before we knew it, it was early December. Mary's classes we're going along very well, but mine not so much. I had several students who liked nothing more than to challenge me and my assignments. I was sure it was because of my young age. They couldn't get used to a professor that was their age.

Things between me and Mary just kept getting better. We loved spending time together. I occasionally made calls home to see how things were going. My mother had given up her teaching job at Cal Tech and moved with my father next to the lab. She said she was happy, but I had my doubts. I hoped that she really was.

Everything was going well until I got a call from my mother in mid-December. Little did I know that this was one of many calls I would get in the future from my mother.

"John, I need you to come out as soon as possible. I'm afraid your father is in a lot of trouble."

"Why, what happened?"

"I'm not sure, but during one of his experiments he shut down the power grid for miles around. Will you be able to come out? I will pay for your trip out here."

I knew my mother needed me out there, or she never would have called. I squared away things at the college and the next day I was on a plane to Lake Havasu. When I got there most of the power grid was back online. The army had sent out a small team of engineers to help figure out what went wrong.

This was my first meeting with the local sheriff, Paddy O'Flynn. Not the way I wanted to meet him! As I pulled up in front of the house, the sheriff started making his way over to me. The sheriff looked to me like someone out of an old western. He had on a cowboy hat and cowboy boots, but was dressed in a well-kept uniform. Not what I was expecting. I introduced myself.

"Hello, I'm John Northrup, Paul's son."

"Good to meet you, John. Can you tell me just what the hell happened here?"

My mother came over just as we started to talk, gave me a hug and told me how glad she was that I was able to come out.

"Sheriff, I'm really not sure what I can tell you. I just got here. Give me a chance to talk with my dad and maybe I can tell you something after that. Just how much trouble is my dad in anyway?"

"I really can't say right now since I'm not sure what happened. Without some more information, I really don't know what to do right now. That army lieutenant won't tell me a thing."

"All I know right now, sheriff, is that my dad is under contract to the Army. He's involved in an experiment that, if it works, could benefit millions of people. That's all I can tell you at this point. Let me see what else I can find out and I'll try to fill you in."

"Thank you. I would really appreciate that. Your mother has my number. You can call me at my office."

After the sheriff left, I spent a few minutes with my mother asking her if she knew what happened.

"John, all I can say is that your father shut down the grid for three days and that's not helping anyone."

"Did anyone get hurt?"

"Not that I know of, but there sure are a lot of upset people in town."

"I can't blame them for being upset. I would be too."

I headed to the lab and caught up with a lieutenant who was in charge. "Can you tell me what happened here?"

"During one of your father's experiments, he overloaded the grid and shut it down. We found three blown out transformers, and a couple thousand feet of line that had to be replaced. I really can't tell you why, but it sure made a mess. It shut down the power for twenty miles in every direction."

"How much power did he draw?"

"No way to tell. Everything was so fried, there was nothing left. It was a complete meltdown."

I thanked him for his help and made my way into the lab. I found my dad in the back working on a panel with one of the army engineers.

"Hello Dad. What's going on out here?"

"Oh Johnny, it's good to see you. I didn't realize you were coming out."

"Mom called and asked me to come out. She told me you were in trouble."

"Not really so much. Yes, there was a problem and I understand that we shut the grid down for a couple days."

"You don't consider that a problem, shutting off everybody's electricity for three days?"

"Yes, I understand it was an inconvenience for a few people but, what I'm doing here is important. In a few years, they'll all thank me for what I'm doing here."

"Well, maybe so, but you better not let it happen again. The sheriff is upset with you and if it happens again, he's going to shut you down."

"The sheriff can't shut me down. He has no authority here. I'm under contract to the army."

"That may be so, but he can still make life miserable for you."

"Don't worry, we're taking steps to keep it from happening again."

"So, what's going on out here anyway?"

"Come with me and I'll show you. Do you see this?"

"Yes, what is it?"

"Do you remember that little prototype I showed you back at Cal Tech?"

"Yes, I remember."

"Well, this is it's big brother."

"Big brother! I guess so, it doesn't look anything like the prototype."

"That's because it's not. I had to completely redesign it from the top to the bottom. No one has ever seen a generator like this."

"How did you come up with this?"

"John, I don't have time to tell you right now. If you want to know more about it read my notes. I keep them in the filing cabinet right next to my desk."

"Maybe later. Tell me how you shut down the power grid."

"That was just a minor inconvenience and it shouldn't happen again. I've taken steps to keep that from happening."

"I hope they work for your sake."

"I can't worry about that right now. I've got bigger things to worry about. John, there's something I want you to see as long as you are here."

"I didn't really come out here to help you work on this."

"I know, I know, but you're the only one that could possibly understand my notes and you might just come up with the answer I need."

"What makes you think I can help you?"

"You're the best engineer I've ever worked with. The three years you worked with me at Cal Tech showed me just how good you were."

"Maybe so, but we got nowhere."

"You won't say that after you read my notes. They will prove just how close we really were."

"Why what changed?

"Read my notes and see for yourself, I know you'll understand."

Now that he had my curiosity peaked, I would have to read his notes just to see for myself if he was really close. I spent the next two days reading his notes and going over his new designs. To say the very least, I was impressed. He had come a long way from the last time I looked at his work.

The new collector he had designed was three times more powerful than the last design and could store far more voltage than the last one. That was a huge breakthrough. As for the generators, that was still the biggest problem. I couldn't believe myself, but I did have an idea. It would take me two or three days to come up with a good concept, and I wanted to get home to Mary. I told my dad about my idea.

He said "John, take my notes with you. I have copies. When you have something you want to show me, just send it my way. I won't be ready for another test for weeks."

"You shouldn't do another test without my design. You could ruin a lot of your equipment without it."

"Fine, I'll wait, but try to get them back to me soon."

I jumped on a plane the next morning and headed home. As I boarded the plane, I was kicking myself. I hadn't learned anything from the past. I had only come out here for my mother, just for a day or two. Now I was headed home with a new project that I had never intended to get involved with. My dad just had a way of sucking me back in.

I spent the whole flight reading a copy of his notes and working on my design. I could only scratch things down on paper, but it was a start. By the time I landed in New York I had the concept half done, and it looked like it might just do the trick. We landed just before eleven in the evening. Mary was waiting for me at the gate, I picked up my luggage and headed home. She had a

75

lot of questions for me but the first thing she wanted to know was how my mother was doing.

I told her mom was fine and she seemed happy with her teaching job at the little school in town. She was teaching 6th, 7th and 8th grade and had made a lot of friends in town. It wasn't anything like living and working at Cal Tech, but she said it was new and exciting and she was happy. From the conversations we had, I believed she really was happy.

Once we got back to the apartment, we had a little snack and then headed for bed. I had been gone for almost a week and Mary was very anxious to welcome me home. I was more than happy to let her.

After my welcome home, Mary fell asleep in just a few minutes. I laid there and started thinking about my new design and the upgrade to the generators. Before I knew it, I was at the kitchen table working on the new designs. It struck me as I was sitting there. Was I becoming my father? Lord, help me. I hope not. Mary woke up around 5:30 and noticed I wasn't in bed. She found me at the kitchen table and asked, "What the hell are you doing up at this time in the morning?"

"I couldn't sleep, this idea I have just won't let me go. I'm close to having it worked out."

"You know you have a class at eight this morning."

"Yes, I know. In fact, I might just throw this problem at my class and see what they can do with it."

"You can't do that!"

"Why not? I've been teaching them to think outside the box, and this is way outside the box, trust me."

"Wouldn't the college be upset with you if they find out?"

"Even if they did find out, they would have no way of knowing that it wasn't a teaching problem. No one, and I mean no one, has ever seen a concept like this."

"I still think you're taking a chance."

At eight o'clock, I walked into my class and the first thing I realized was the class was a week behind. They were right where I left them. Apparently, my fill in did nothing while I was gone. So much for throwing my designs at them.

After my last class I headed right to the lab to use one of the advanced computers there. I was making incredibly good progress when I realized I was the only one left in the lab. It was way past the time I should be home. I printed out my designs and headed home. Mary was not too happy to see me. She had eaten dinner without me two hours ago.

"I see you're becoming your father's son. You just can't let go of something once you've started."

"Sorry, I'm so late. I just got caught up in what I was doing."

"Just what are you doing? You really didn't tell me much about what happened out there."

"There's not really that much to tell. My dad's latest experiment shut down the power grid because it overloaded the system. They have it all fixed now, and it shouldn't happen again. That's about it."

"So, what are you working on that's so urgent?"

"It's a problem with the generators. They overheat so fast they will never hold up long enough to produce the power they are capable of. If my new design works, it will allow them to run constantly."

"So that's what you're working on. I thought you didn't want anything to do with this."

"I know, I keep saying that, and I really don't, but this time even I can't deny he's onto something. If I can help with this problem, it might make a big difference."

"How long will this take?"

"A week, maybe two. It all depends on how much time I get on the computers at school."

"Can't you work from home?"

"No, our computer has nowhere near the power I need."

"So, you really are becoming your father."

"Please don't say that, it's the last thing I want. Two weeks later and a lot of time away from Mary I was done. I put my designs in the mail and I was out of it. At least that's what I thought.

Chapter 13

Things went along very well for the next three months. We had our first Christmas together, and I got used to shoveling snow and cleaning off my car every time I wanted to go somewhere. Just our luck! New York was having a record snowfall that year. No one told me about that! We made many new friends and enjoyed all that this little town of Rochester had to offer. I spoke with my mother many times, checking on her and asking her how dad was doing. It seemed like all was going well, then in early April I got another one of those calls!

"John, your father needs your help."

"What now?"

"He said he tried your designs, and they didn't work. He wants you to come out and fix them."

As it turned out the following week was spring break for RIT. Mary's school was letting their kids off the same week. We had been planning to get away that week and had not really made any plans to go anywhere specific.

Problem solved. We were headed to Lake Havasu. I told my mom to send me two tickets and we'd see her next week. We got to the house in the afternoon. We hadn't even got out of the car before my father came charging out of the house. He met me as I was opening the car door.

"John, come with me. I've got something to show you."

"Dad, could you at least say hi to Mary?"

"Oh yes, good to see you, Mary. You can come and see as well if you'd like."

"No, no, that's fine, you boys go play with your toys. I'll see it all another time. I'm going in to see Sharon."

"John, come with me. You gotta see this."

I had never seen my dad so excited. He almost ran to the lab.

"I've been waiting to show you."

Once in the lab he went right to the control panel. As the power came up on the generators, they started to turn slowly at first and then faster and faster. They got to the point where you could feel the floor vibrating under your feet. It seems to me they were running way too fast.

"John. Here put this over your ears and put on these glasses."

As I was doing that, he threw another switch and a third machine started to turn. It was not a generator, but a large fan of some sort blowing air at 90 degrees to the generators, aimed right at the large receiver across the lab. I could feel the vacuum from the fan and if I had been any closer, I think it would have sucked me in.

"Okay, John, watch this."

He threw one more switch and the biggest bolt of lightning I had ever seen came out of both generators. The two lightning bolts met in the middle just as they were hit by a tremendous airflow that directed them to the receiver across the room. The combined lightning bolts were turning the face of the receiver red and within seconds it began to glow so bright I could barely watch it. Just about ten seconds later there was a tremendous boom like a clap of thunder, and everything shut down.

It scared the s*** out of me. I must have jumped back 10 feet.

"What the hell was that?"

"Sorry, John. I should have warned you."

"YOU THINK! It would have been nice to know that was coming!"

"Yes, yes, sorry. So, what do you think?"

"I think I need to go check myself. I'm sure I filled my pants."

"John, seriously. What do you think?"

"Tell me what I just saw and then maybe I can tell you what I think."

"What you just saw was two generators putting out a large static charge. It equals many, many mega volts of electricity directed at that receiver. That little, short sample could power New York City for a week. I can only run this system for ten seconds at that level before it overheats and shuts down. That big boom you heard at the end; that was everything shutting down."

"Oh, I heard it all right!"

"John, the design you sent me got me this far. Before that I couldn't even get the generators up to speed before they overheated. We need to find a way to keep them running for a long time. The other problem is I'm losing way too much voltage when the air hits the charge, but I need the air to push the charge to the receiver."

"It looks to me like you're going to melt the receiver if you run it any longer."

"Not a problem. The face of that receiver is covered with the same panels that cover the space shuttle for re-entry."

"Where did you get those?"

"Never mind about that, I need your help on this overheating. It's just like the batteries. We had to control the heat before we could use them, but now they're fine."

"Yes, but you're talking heat on a huge scale. I can feel the heat coming off the generators from where I'm standing."

"So, you understand the problem."

"I would have to be an idiot not to! How often can you run them?"

"Once every three days, but I don't really want to. I'm afraid I will damage them. That would set me back at least a year. I can't just go to the hardware store and buy more."

"Yeah, I guess not. I am only here for a week. I 'll see what I can do."

Sheriff O'Flynn came out twice that week to talk with me. We kind of became friends. It turned out he was a good guy. He offered to help if needed. I asked him to stop by occasionally just to check things out and he said he would be happy to.

The week came and went before I knew it. I did come up with a new design and I had a lot of confidence it would work but had no time to prove it. I had spent little time with Mary that week, and she reminded me on the way home. It was supposed to be our first vacation together. It was not much of a vacation for either one of us. I promised to make it up to her.

Chapter 14

Our first year teaching in New York ended in late June for Mary and I was done in early May. We made plans to go camping in the Adirondacks. We had been told it was the place all New Yorkers go camping in the summer. They were right. We spent two weeks there and enjoyed every minute of it, except for the black flies and mosquitoes. We went hiking, fishing (even though I didn't catch anything) and canoeing. We climbed a couple mountains and enjoyed a campfire every night. What a great place to spend two weeks. It was everything people told us it was. When we got home, I got this feeling that someone had been in our apartment. Nothing was broken or missing, but a few things just seemed out of place. I told Mary what I was thinking, and she said, "What makes you think so?"

"I'm not sure, it just feels like something's not right."

"Well, I don't see anything missing or broken."

"I know, I guess it's just a silly feeling I have."

After a couple of days, the feeling left me and I forgot about it. We spent the rest of the summer traveling around New York State and the Finger Lakes region. We spent many days at her parent's winery in the Finger Lakes. I had no idea how much went into making a good wine. We visited there for five or six weekends over the summer. We had just come back from visiting their winery and as we walked into the apartment, we found a message on the phone. BJ was coming to town and he wanted to take us out to dinner. He had found a nice restaurant and he wanted to try it out. We both laughed a little bit since we could never remember going out to dinner with BJ. It had always been a bar, mostly a sports bar.

We were both looking forward to seeing him. It has almost been two years since the last time we had seen him. We were sure he had many fascinating stories to tell us. The following Saturday we pulled into the parking lot of a very upscale restaurant. We were pleasantly surprised at the place BJ had found. As we walked into the restaurant, we saw BJ waving at us from the table where he was sitting. As we headed to the table, he stood up. He was dressed in a black button-down long-sleeve shirt and a pair of black slacks. He was as fit and trim as I've ever seen him. He looked to be two inches taller and 20 pounds heavier than the last time I had seen him. BJ was certainly someone you didn't want to mess with. Standing there with a short haircut and a very stern look on his face, I wondered, was this the same BJ I had always known?

When we got to the table, he broke that look with a big smile and a very warm greeting for me and Mary. Still, something about BJ was different. We had drinks and ordered dinner. We did a lot of catching up over dinner and dessert. After dinner, we headed to the bar for more drinks and more catching up. Mary and I both ordered a glass of wine, but BJ ordered a glass of water. Okay, BJ had certainly changed. I never saw him pass up a free drink, especially if I was buying.

"What's up BJ? You're not the BJ I used to know. You never pass up a free drink."

"I suppose you're right John. I'm not the same guy you used to know back in college. You can't see the things I've seen and not change a little."

"What sort of things?"

"I really can't tell you much. It's all top secret you know. My squad was asked to take on special assignments about a year ago. We are now one of the highest trained assault units in the army. Right now, they have us doing recon work. They send us to gather information on countries and the people that run them. We are only allowed to observe. We can't take any action. We're not allowed to engage in any action at all. We can't do anything to help the people that we see being tortured or killed. It's awfully hard to watch that going on and not help them. Helping people is exactly why I joined the army in the first place. All we do is gather information and walk away."

"Why aren't you allowed to do anything?"

"Because we aren't supposed to be there in the first place. As far as the army is concerned our squad doesn't exist anymore. We don't carry any identification that would connect us to the US. In fact, if you went looking for someone called Brad Johnson you wouldn't find a single thing about him. The army completely erased my existence."

"Why would they do that?"

"Simple. If we ever get caught, they can deny that we exist. They can claim they don't know anything about us, and no one can prove otherwise."

"You mean if you get caught, they wouldn't step up to try to help you?"

"That's right. They would completely deny that we even exist. We are on our own out there."

"That's terrible!"

"I know, but it's the way it has to be."

"Where have you been lately?"

"Sorry John. Can't tell you anything about that."

We talked for another hour about the days at Cal Tech. We enjoyed a good evening with BJ, but we left with a lot of questions. He said goodbye and told us that he would be out of the country within a few days. I asked him to stay in touch as often as he could, and he said he would try. On the way home we talked about how BJ had changed. Mary said, "It's so unfair what they asked him to do and then they won't stand behind him when he's in trouble."

"I agree with you, but that's what BJ signed up for. He knew what he was getting into."

"Maybe so, but I still think it stinks. He's putting his life on the line for his country, and they won't stand up for him."

"The government can't take the chance. It could start a war if they tried to protect them. Every country has people like BJ, doing just what he's doing. You just don't hear about them."

Chapter 15

I was back teaching by the middle of August. Mary started right after Labor Day. Summer was over and we were back in our old routines once again. Everything was going along as it should until the end of October.

Once again, a call from my mother had me on a plane to help my father. His latest experiment had caused problems for the local town. The lights kept going on and off. That wasn't really a big deal, but I know it annoyed everyone involved. We got that taken care of in a couple of days. The only big change that I saw was that the Army was putting up a twelve-foot-high fence all the way around the property. When I asked them about it, they said that the fence was needed to keep the locals out. I thought that was a lot of bull shit! I called the sheriff to find out what was really going on. He told me there hadn't been any problems with anyone going out there, only a few complaints about the lights. I was concerned about the fence going up, not really understanding why, but since it didn't bother my mother, I kind of forgot about it. Mary had not come along with me on this trip. She was too busy with her kids and her artwork, a new hobby that she had just gotten into. I had only been home a couple of hours when the phone rang. It was General Wellington.

"Hello John. How are you?"
"Good General, thanks for asking."
"How's that lovely wife of yours doing?"
"She's doing fine, thank you."
"Glad to hear you're both doing well."

.I wondered to myself where this was going. The General never calls just to see how you were doing. There's always a reason for him to call.

"John, I need to know how your dad's doing."

"Why don't you just call him or go out and see for yourself?"

"I have called, and all he says is that everything is good and he's very close."

"Yeah, I know that line, he's been close for years. By the way, what's with the fence?"

"I believe it's to keep the locals out."

"General, you and I both know there's no problem with anyone in this town. What's the real reason?"

"John, you need to keep this to yourself."

"Why, what's going on?"

"We are a little concerned that someone might be trying to steal your father's work."

"What! Why would you think that?"

"We're not sure. It's only a suspicion at this point but being the Army, we take precautions. The other big reason is we want to protect our investment."

"That makes more sense than anything else I've been told. I can understand that. General, if you come up with any more concerns, please give me a call."

"You'll be the first one I call John. Don't worry about that.

Time went by with no more calls from the General, and that was fine with me. Winter came early that year and with it the snow. I wasn't looking forward to dealing with that again. Every time I went out to use my car, I had to scrape ice off it. I never had to do that in California. My car was always clean except for maybe a little dust. Mary might have been okay with the snow, but I was having second thoughts about living in New York State. I was very content with how things were going until Mary started dropping hints about getting married and starting a family. We had been together for almost two years. It wasn't that I didn't love Mary or

88

hadn't thought about marriage. I just thought it would come down the road aways, not quite so soon. Thinking about having children gave me chills. I might be ready to get married but having kids was another thing altogether.

Chapter 16

I'm not one who believes in fate. I do believe in God, but I confess I don't really understand Him very well. My quandary is this. I have been taught that God made this world, that He put me and everyone else here, and that He is in control. If that's true, why doesn't He fix this mess? I've also been taught that He knows all things, past, present, and future. If that's true, then He must have seen this coming. Why wouldn't He stop it? If I were God, I would have.

As I sit here in this cavernous C-130 Army transport plane, the noise is almost deafening. Those four prop driven engines that pull this monster through the air with ease, rattle and shake this thing so much you can barely hear yourself think. This thing they call a seat, which is no more than a bunch of straps put together to look like a seat, is the most uncomfortable thing I've ever sat in. The only way you can hear yourself think is to plug your ears, not that I want to think about anything anyway. I would much prefer to not think about anything that's happened in the last three weeks ever again, but that's next to impossible. I wish there were a way to shut off my brain. Sitting across from me are two of the best electrical mechanical engineers I have ever met. The army sent them over to help stop what was going on. They are as wide-eyed and pale as I must be, and they don't know half the story.

Just down from them, sits six of the best Army Rangers the US has to offer, and each one of them has been wounded in some way. They seem to be able to take all this in stride, but it's what they do. It's their job. Their concern right now is not for themselves, but for two of their own. One of them is William T Wright who gave his all for his country. His fellow brothers are looking at a box covered with an American flag. How will they tell his wife and kids that he gave his life to save theirs? Hanging from a makeshift sling is the other soldier, their lieutenant and my best friend, BJ. The doctors that came over from the states are doing the best they can for him. BJ needs far more than they can do on this plane. They know the bullet that went through his protective vest is lodged somewhere near his heart and they're doing all they can just to keep him alive. They want him back in the states at Walter Reed Hospital. There is a surgeon there they hope can take the bullet out and save his life.

I haven't stopped praying for him since the moment they carried him on board. He looked more dead than alive. How could someone lose so much blood and still survive? If anyone could, it would be BJ. I have known from the first time I met him, he was not your average human being. He is a cut above the rest of us. It will take all he has and then some to get through this one. I wonder about the ones left behind. I worry if they will make it out alright. Is it over? Not for me. It won't be over until my friend survives. If he doesn't make it, it may never be over for me.

As my gaze drifts back to the two engineers, my heart goes out to them. One of them can't hold it back any longer. He buries his face in his hands and starts to cry uncontrollably. His friend tries to console him and then he starts to lose it. I can feel the tears running down my own face, but I refused to give into the fear and contemplation of what could have happened. If this had not been stopped or taken under control by the General and the men left behind, well, God bless them. God help all of us if they have failed.

We have three more hours riding in this monster they call a plane and then what? All I know is that I'm glad that I told Mary to stay home and not to come over to visit. I can't wait to see her, but I have no idea what I'm going to tell her. The truth? Probably not. Why put her through something that should have never happened. For now, I guess I will just tell her what I would tell anyone on the street. I was called to help the army and I can't talk about it. After all, isn't that the line they always use when they don't want to tell people what they know or what they're up to? I wish these two men would stop sobbing. I think it's starting to get to the rangers. Some of them look to be getting a little uptight. Those guys are trained to deal with what they've seen, but not us. I don't think any of us had any idea of what we were getting into. It's a nightmare that I will relive for years to come. How did I ever get pulled into this?

A little over three weeks ago I was a happy professor teaching my class at RIT in New York. The phone rang and then everything about my life changed. It would never be the same. It started out like any other Friday night except that this was the last Friday in the semester and I had a full weekend of work to look over. It would take my whole weekend to grade all the papers my students turned in. As I left the campus, I was stopped by one of my students. He hadn't made it to class at all that week, and had not turned his paper in. He came up with all kinds of excuses as to why he wasn't there. I stopped him and said, "Look I've heard it all before".

He did have his final paper done and asked me, more like begged me, to take it. After a good tongue lashing and a little browbeating, I did take it. The short ride back to our apartment was uneventful, other than the miserable traffic. I always seem to be going home during rush hour. I stopped at our local deli to pick up our favorite sub, something me and Mary started during the winter. We just stayed in on Friday nights. I was planning on getting a head start reading and grading papers. It's a short walk from the parking lot to our apartment. I headed up the stairs to our place. Mary had been home for hours and was waiting for that sub. We sat and talked about how our day was as we always did. After our little dinner, I grabbed a cold beer out of the fridge and sat down to a full night's work grading papers.

The phone rang about 7:30, and of all people to call me, it had to be BJ.

"Hey, John, it's BJ. I'm in town this week and I have the night open. What do you say, you, Mary and I go out and have a beer or two?"

Now that sounded like the old BJ. I was thinking, I just don't have time for this tonight. I asked Mary if she wanted to go out.

"No thanks, I have friends coming over."

"Sorry BJ, Mary's tied up and I have a ton of work to do. I'll have to take a rain check, maybe next time."

"Hey John, that's what you said the last time I called you. Come on man, you owe me a night out. You're not getting out of it this time. I'll come over and drag your ass out of there if I have to."

"Okay, okay, but just a beer or two."

"Great, I found a really nice sports bar that you're going to love. I will pick you up in about an hour."

This was the old BJ, I wondered what had changed? BJ was right on time. I answered the door and in steps BJ, bigger than life. He gave me a hug that squeezed the air right out of me. Mary came over and gave him a kiss.

"Mary, why don't you come out with us?"

"I would love to, but my friends will be here any minute."

"Well, bring them along, the more the merrier!"

"I don't think so, BJ. I don't think they could handle you. They're too conservative."

"Okay then, it looks like it's just you and me Johnny. I think you're going to like this place."

I swear BJ gets bigger every time I see him. He was no small guy in college. As an athlete he was outstanding. He was a two-time national wrestling champ and an All-American quarterback for the football team. He only got bigger after college. The Army must have done that for him.

While I was studying physics and biology, BJ was all about getting into the army. His goal was to become a ranger and run his own platoon. It's a wonder we became friends at all, but without a doubt, he is my best friend, and I would do anything for him. Including going out drinking with him, even when I didn't want to. As we pulled up in front of this place, I could see it was an old brick building and they certainly hadn't done much to clean up the outside of it. I'm sure this was an old factory a long time ago. I hoped the inside was better than the outside. As I stepped inside, I was not disappointed. Much to my surprise, the place was nice as far as sports bars go. It had to be one of the better ones I've been in. No matter where you looked, you could see a large tv screen whether you were sitting or standing. Every sport you can think of was on a screen - golf, tennis, Nascar, soccer, college football, basketball. You name it, it was on. The inside was clean, and it didn't smell like stale beer like most bars do.

The place was well-lit, the floors were clean, the booths and chairs looked almost new, and I liked the music I was hearing, A good place to have a beer. As we got further inside and up to the bar for our first drink, I couldn't help but be impressed by the effort someone had to put into this building. I liked the old-fashioned wooden bar yet with a very modern look. BJ was right. I did like this place. I could see myself bringing Mary back here once or twice to catch a game or two. We both love football, and it's a lot of fun watching at a bar.

The bartender asked, "What will you have?"

Before I could open my mouth, BJ said "Two Coronas and two shots of Jack Daniels."

"Coming right up."

I said, "I thought you said a couple of beers?"

BJ laughed "Hey man, you didn't really think you were getting off that easy. You brushed me off the last three times I was in town. We've got a lot of catching up to do. Let's get our drinks and grab a table. I've got something to tell you."

We grabbed a table over in the corner. BJ said, "I'm a little anxious right now."

"You anxious? I don't think I've ever seen you anxious or nervous about anything."

"My team is being called up and they're not telling us anything. They usually tell us something so I can get my men prepared to go. This time all they said was get ready to go at any given time and bring everything you've got. We've been working as a recon team for months now, so we don't normally carry anything more than a pistol. Being told to bring everything you have leaves me with a lot of questions. They didn't give me much to tell my guys. I can usually figure out what's going on by what I see in the news or when I hear the CO's talking a little too loud. The other thing that's unusual is, we just got back last week. I've never seen a team turn around this fast. They're keeping everything on a need-to-know basis."

"Is that unusual?"

"Yes, I always get a heads up. Something else I can't figure out is there are no real hot spots happening right now. Everything I know about is pretty quiet right now."

"You're right about that, things seem to be kind of mundane on the news lately. So, what do you think it is?"

"I have no idea. Remember, I told you we have been strictly a recon team for some time now."

"Yeah, you told me."

"Well, this time we're going in fully armed."

"Why the change?"

"I don't know, but I do know, it's time for another beer."

The rest of the night was just about the same as many others we shared in the past. Talking about past nights out, chasing any good-looking female that walked by. Except for me now, skirt-chasing was out. Ever since I met Mary that all changed, not that I was any kind of a girl chaser anyway. BJ had introduced me to some fine females in the past, but I never got anywhere with any of them. Not that I wasn't interested. I just had things to get done. I never took the time for girls until Mary. A couple beers and a shot or two later, it was time for me to head home. Mary would be getting concerned. I gave BJ a hug and headed for the door. He was still going strong. He had a good-looking brunette hanging all over him.

"I'll call you tomorrow and catch up then."

He turned to me, slapped me on the back and said, "Told you you'd like this place."

As I walked out the door into a cool dark night with a light rain falling, I could see the street lights reflecting off the wet road. I made my way down the sidewalk to a cab that was waiting to pick up people leaving the bar. I jumped into the back seat and the cab reeked of cigar smoke. The seats were so bad I could feel the springs poking through.

The cabbie asked me "Where to?"

I told him "Home."

"Okay smartass, where's home?"

I told the cabbie what my address was, put my head back and closed my eyes and wondered what BJ was getting into this time. What seemed like only a few minutes later, we pulled up in front of my place. As I made my way up the sidewalk, I could feel the rain on my face and it felt good. Fumbling with my keys, I made my way inside the apartment. I was thinking, man I'm going to pay for this in the morning. I was not used to going out anymore. I headed for the bedroom and glanced down at the table loaded with all the papers I had to grade. This was going to be a long weekend.

Mary was sound asleep, and I tried my best not to wake her. My head hit the pillow and I was sound asleep in minutes. Around three o'clock that night, less than two hours later, the phone was ringing. You know it's never good when you get a phone call in the middle of the night. This one would change my life forever.

Whenever my dad would do something to get himself in trouble, Mom would call me and she would insist that I come out and help. I would have to make a three-day trip. I would help as best I could, although half the time dad would have the problem solved by the time I got there. I told myself not this time. I'm not going. I don't care what he did this time or what his problem is. I have way too much work to get done to leave. I let the phone ring three more times before I picked it up. Mary was awake now.

"Hello Mom. What did he do this time?"

There was a long pause, then I heard a voice I knew well.

"Hi John, it's not your mom. It's Sheriff Patrick O'Flynn. John, I'm not sure how to tell you this, but there's been an accident."

"Hi Pat, what did Dad do this time? Shut down the power grid again? Turn all the lights off in town? Or blow another transformer?"

"No John, this accident is a little different. Your mom called me and said that she heard a loud noise and went out to your dad's lab to check on him. When she got out there the whole place was dark, and she couldn't open the door. You know your dad never locked that door. I got there as fast as I could, John. I couldn't open the door either, so I went around to the side where the windows are and broke one of the windows. As I did, all the glass went inside with a loud rush of air. I thought that was strange, but I didn't have time to think about it right then. I tried getting to the window, but it was too high off the ground, so I went back to the front door. This time the door opened easily. Your mother and I tried to go inside to find your dad, but after only a minute or two inside we both became very winded. I grabbed your mom and headed back outside. I tried one more time before I gave up. There was also a strange smell, so I called the HazMat team.

They got there quickly. They gave me a breathing mask and I followed them inside. Once we got inside, we tried the lights, but nothing worked. We started looking for your dad and ended up almost all the way in the back where your mom thought he would be. We got back there, and we found your dad. I'm afraid we were a little too late, John. He was just sitting there at his desk with his head down on his notes. He still had a pen in one hand. I don't know what to tell you John. He looked fine. He just wasn't breathing. They tried to resuscitate him, but nothing worked. John, are you still there? John?"

"Yeah. I'm still here. Just trying to understand what you're telling me. Pat, how's Mom doing?"

"She's okay for now. You know how your mom is. It takes a lot to rattle her. She's taking the news like a real trooper."

"I know that's the way mom is. We always had a feeling this could happen. I guess I never thought it would."

"John, one more thing. I called the coroner to come and get your dad. Once we got the lights back on so we could see and had time to look around, we noticed something very strange. Everything in the building was burnt. Not so much burnt but charred. The edges of all your dad's notes were burnt just a little. Everything we looked at was the same way. Your dad's hair had a burnt smell to it, but it wasn't burned off. The coroner noticed the same thing. Any idea what would make that happen?"

"No, Pat. No idea at all. Was there a fire inside the building?"

"No fire. Not that we could tell, just everything singed. When are you coming out John?"

"I'll get there in a couple of days. Do me a favor, Pat. Lock the place up until I get there, I want to see it for myself."

"I'll try to do that John, but you know we need to do an investigation to see what happened here."

"I understand that, but try not to move too many things around. I'd like to see it just as it was."

"Okay John. I'll try."

"Thanks, Pat. Is Mom there?"

"Yes, I'll put her on the line."

"Hi Mom. How are you doing?"

"John, I'm so sorry you had to hear this over the phone, and it wasn't me who told you."

"Don't worry about that, Mom. Nobody wants to give that kind of news to anybody. I've always worried that something like this would happen. He was always taking chances on things that he couldn't control. He knew better, but he did it anyway."

"You're right, John. That's what made your dad who he was."

"I know, Mom, but this time it cost him his life. I can't see how it could have been worth the risk."

"I guess we'll never know. Johnny, when are you coming out?"

"I'll get there as soon as I can. I need to find someone to fill in for me. It's the end of the semester and I have a lot of papers to grade.

"Okay, I understand, dear. Come out as soon as you can. I want you to help me with the funeral arrangements."

"I'll do my best to find someone who can come over and stay with you."

"No. I'll be fine. Just come out as soon as you can."

"I will, Mom. I love you."

"I know, dear."

"Mom, is Pat still there?"

"Yes, he's right here. I'll get him for you."

"Hi John, this is Pat."

"Could you please check on Mom from time to time? She may act like a trooper, but I know how much she loved my dad. She must have loved him with all the crap she put up with all these years. I don't know how she'll be when she's there by herself."

"Don't worry, John. I'll check on her twice a day."

"Thanks, Pat. See you soon."

I put the phone back. I just sat there sitting on the edge of the bed. I could hear Mary softly crying behind me. I turned and pulled her close to me. My head was spinning from the news. I was still a little groggy from the beer and lack of sleep. It was hard to comprehend that I just lost my dad. Was that real? Could I have heard them wrong? I knew it was real all right. I just couldn't get my head around it. Mary asked me what happened. "I really don't know right now. There was an accident in the lab, and before they could get to dad, he was gone."

"Why couldn't they get to him?"

"I'm not sure, the sheriff said he couldn't open the door. It makes no sense at all. I need to get out there as soon as I can."

"Yes. you do. Your mom needs you."

"I have to find someone to dump my workload on, I need to pack some clothes, and I need to get a plane ticket. Who should I call first?"

"You can't call anyone right now. It's three o'clock in the morning."

"Should I call BJ? What about the funeral arrangements?"

"John, you're not thinking straight right now. You can't do anything tonight. Try to get some sleep and we will get this all done in the morning."

Thank goodness I had Mary to lean on. I'd be lost without her. I laid back down, then it hit me. I just lost my dad. I laid there and just started crying. Mary pulled close to me and just held on to me. I felt like I was the only person in the world right then. I couldn't believe it, but I did fall back to sleep out of sheer exhaustion.

I woke up the next morning at 6:30. Mary was already up and packing my clothes. As I thought about my dad, my eyes started tearing up. How would my mom handle this? What would she do now? I felt like I needed more sleep, but I knew that wasn't going to happen. I had to get moving. One phone call to an associate of mine and my workload was taken care of. Mary was on the phone with the airline. For some reason, she couldn't get me on a plane until the next day. I decided to drive. I would need a car out there and the drive would help me think. I had breakfast with Mary, kissed her goodbye and hit the road.

After three days of hard driving, I was pulling up in front of the sheriff's office. I wanted to stop there first to see if he had figured out what had happened. The first face I see is Sheriff Pat. As I headed across the room where Pat was standing, we looked at each other. There were just no words to say. After we hugged each other for a minute or two, I started asking Pat a lot of questions. Pat repeated everything he had told me just a couple days ago.

I had a thousand questions but the only one that came out was "How's my mother doing?"

"She seems to be fine. Every time I talk to her, she tells me not to worry about her. Your mom is a tough lady. I believe she's over at the funeral home talking with Fred right now. If you hurry, you might catch her over there."

"Thanks, Pat. Catch you later. When this is over, I want to meet with you at the lab sometime after the funeral service."

"Sure, John. I'll be glad to meet with you anytime you want. Just call me."

I headed right over to the funeral home. This small town is located on the edge of the Colorado River ten miles west of Lake Havasu on the California/Arizona border. Main Street is only eight blocks long with many empty storefronts. Just one bank, one gas station, one church, a small school, where I assumed my mother was teaching, a post office and the funeral home. Not too hard to find. As I pulled up, there was Mom's car, an old Ford wagon. If it had been back east, it would have rusted away a long time ago. I wasn't sure how my mom would react seeing me, but I should have known.

"Johnny, come over here and sit. Fred was just telling me what we can do for your father."

101

That's my mother, all business. A half hour later, we were walking out with funeral plans finalized. It will take place this coming Saturday at 11 a.m. in the only church in town. I followed her back home and as we pulled in the driveway, I had the strangest feeling. I knew this place well, even though I never lived here. I've been here a hundred times. That little brown house they lived in didn't look any different from the last time I had been there. It certainly was showing its age and needed some work. The roof was in bad need of repair. It needs new windows and a new door. Apparently, my dad had not done the work he promised. No surprise there!

The yard hadn't changed. It was still that sandy brown gravely desert substance that they called dirt. How they grow anything out here is beyond me. The old broken-down fence around the house with no gate was still there. It hadn't been that long since my last visit, not more than five months, but somehow it felt different.

One thing that was different was that twelve-foot-high fence the army had put up. I was looking around when it hit me. I would never see my dad there again. That was such an empty feeling. About two hundred feet behind the house was the laboratory that my father had built. It was built with strict and specific instructions from my father. This lab was built with money from the US government, specifically from the defense department. The government was his sole supporter currently. Back when he was at Cal Tech, he had all the financial support he needed from the college and three energy companies, hoping to cash in on what he was developing. After years of waiting with no results, they walked away and took their money with them. That's when the government came calling.

I followed Mom into the house. As I looked at her, she seemed to be much older somehow. It hadn't been that long since I'd seen her. She looked very worn down and her hair seemed a little grayer, but still well kept. She had a somber look on her face, her wrinkles looked a little deeper and those blue eyes that always sparkled when she saw me had no sparkle on this day. Even her voice seemed different. I have never seen my mother look so down. She might say she's doing alright, but my father's death had taken the life right out of her. She had put up with him all these years, gave up her own professorship and followed him no matter what. She never lived in the house she deserved or lived the lifestyle she should have had. Every dollar they had went into his research and now he was dead, and for what. A dream he had that never happened. What did he leave her with? No money, a house that was falling apart, no future. Suddenly, I was not filled with so much sorrow. I was getting angry with my father for dying and leaving my mother nothing.

I never realized how selfish my father had been until that very moment.

Mom and I talked until well after the sun had gone down and the stars had come out, filling what otherwise would have been a very cold and dark night. We finally headed for bed. I said good night, she gave me a hug and whispered, "I love you" and went to her room.

The tears in her eyes were the first tears I'd seen since my graduation from college. My mother was in a lot of pain. By the time I got up the next morning, Mom already had breakfast on the table and hot coffee waiting for me, just like she always did every time I came to visit. This was the first normal thing I felt since arriving there. The one big difference - Dad wouldn't be joining us. Today would be hard, meeting with the reverend at church, calling friends and deciding on lunch after the funeral. I'm not sure how much help I will be with all that. I will be there for all the support she needs and anything else I can do for her. After breakfast, we headed into town to make all the final arrangements for the church service, ordered flowers and food for the luncheon. Afterward I dropped Mom off at home, told her I'd be back in a little while and headed into town to meet up with the sheriff.

As I pulled up in front of the office, I had the feeling this might not be the time to ask Pat a thousand questions that were bouncing around in my head. I'm here so I might just as well go talk with him. No surprise, Pat's not there. He was called about an accident some thirty miles outside of town and he wouldn't be back anytime soon. So, I headed back to the house and decided I would start looking around without him. Once back home, I realized I can't get in the lab. They had locked the place up and boarded over the broken window. Okay, now what? I had calls to make that I've been putting off. I guess it's time to start making them. I owe it to the people I care about. The first call is to Mary. I knew she would be anxious to hear from me. She has always been concerned about my mother being so far out of town. After three rings Mary picked up, "Hello Hun, it's me."

"Hi Hun, how are things going? How's your mom? I was starting to worry about you. It's been a couple days since you last called."

"I was still on the road when I called you last. I'm with my mom now and she seems to be holding up well."

"I wouldn't expect anything less from her."

"I have been busy helping with all the arrangements."

"Tell your mom I'm praying for her and wish I could be there."

"She knows you would be here if you could."

"What did you find out about your dad?"

"We aren't sure. It was an accident and by the time they got into the lab he was gone."

"John, I don't know what to say. I know you and your dad haven't been really close the last few years, but I know how much you loved him. You're sure your mom is doing ok?"

"She is putting up a good front for everyone, but I can see how much she's hurting. My dad was her whole life. She gave up everything for him. I still don't understand it. I guess I never will."

"Your mom is a wonderful lady. When she said until death do us part, she really meant it, no matter what. She must have really loved your dad."

"I guess so, but now he's left her with nothing. I don't know what she's going to do out here all by herself."

"John, your mother will be fine from what I know about her. She will get through this and move on. Your mother is not one to sit around feeling sorry for herself."

"You're right about that, but this is a hard one."

"When is the funeral service?"

"Saturday at 11 o'clock."

"Saturday that seems awfully fast. Why so soon?"

"That's what Mom wanted. I think she wants to get that part behind her."

"I can understand that, but what about all the people that may want to come."

"I asked her that and she said it's not about them. He's my husband and that's what I want."

"That doesn't sound like your mom."

"I know, she always puts others first. I think she is so hurt she just wants to get it over with."

"I can't blame her for that. It's such a hard thing to deal with, losing someone you loved so much. Is there anything I can do to help?"

"Not right now, but if I think of something, I'll let you know."

"What about calling the people at Cal Tech and all the friends he made while he was working there?"

"I already did. They know about it. I don't know if anyone will come, but they know."

"They should after all he did for that school."

"I understand what you're saying but there's two sides to that story."

"I don't care. They should still come."

"Well, we'll see. I'll let you know when it's over."

"How long will you be out there?"

"I'm not sure at this point, but at least a couple of weeks. I want to stay long enough to help my mother get through this. I really want to figure out what happened to my dad. I haven't been given any good explanation at this point."

"What do you mean? Don't they know?"

"Not really. All they know is he was dead when they got to him."

"Do they think it was a heart attack?"

"We don't know. I haven't seen the coroner's report, so I might not know anything until next week."

"Please let me know if there's anything I can do for you."

"I will."

"I love you, John. I wish I could be there for you."

"I know. I love you too. I will call you in a couple of days and let you know what's going on."

"Please do. I'll be waiting for your call. Bye for now."

It's too bad that Mary can't make it out right now. I could really use her help with my mom. The two of them always get along well. She might understand better what my mother is going through. Probably a lot better than I do. My mother would talk to her more than she talked to me. The girl-talk might help.

My next call was to BJ. This one should be easier than the last one. At least that's what I thought. The phone was ringing but no answer. Just as I was getting ready to hang up, he picked up the phone.

"I'm here, so talk."

It's just like BJ to answer the phone that way. "BJ, it's John."

"Hey John. Did you call to thank me for taking you out the other night? Told you that you'd like the place. Was I right?"

"Yeah, you were right. It's a good place."

106

"Did you see that brunette I was with? We really hit it off. She wants to see me again. I think I may have a future with this one. I really like her."

If I only had a dollar for every girl, he said that about.

"So did Mary give you a hard time for being out so late?"

"Not at all. She knows how good friends we are. I did have a good time, but that's not why I called. I called to tell you", then it hit me like a wave crashing on shore. My voice was gone. I just couldn't get the words out. I could feel the tears beginning to run down my face. My heart was pounding, and I tried to take a deep breath, but it didn't help.

For some reason telling BJ became much more difficult than when I told Mary. BJ knew my dad from several years back when I was teaching at college. He would sit and listen to my dad talk about how he could do so much with his research, what it would do to help people. He would go into detail about it. I'm sure BJ had no idea what he was telling him. He would sit there mesmerized by what my dad was saying anyway. My dad really took to BJ. I think it was because he was so much different than me. So full of life with big plans and he always listened to my dad. Unlike me.

"John, are you still there? John?"

"Yeah, I'm here. Just give me a minute."

"What's up man? What's going on? Are you in trouble?"

"No, I'm not in any trouble. There's something I've got to tell you."

"So, tell me. Maybe I can help."

"It's Dad. BJ, dad passed away a few days ago."

Those were the only words that would come out. In some ways, BJ was like a brother to me and another son to my dad. I knew how much this was going to hurt him and I could tell by the long pause that he was taking this news hard.

"John, I'm really sorry to hear that. You know I thought the world of your dad. What happened?"

"We aren't sure yet. All we know is that there was an accident in his lab."

"You always thought that might happen. You told me that more than once."

"I know. Just look at the stuff he was messing with. No one else wanted anything to do with it. That's why he built his own lab."

"Yeah. Nobody but the US defense department. Aren't they the ones spending the bucks on this?"

"Yes, they are, and now they've got nothing."

"I don't know what to say. John, you know how much I liked your dad."

"Yeah, I know, and he really liked you too. He thought of you like a second son."

"I don't know if I'd go that far, but he was a brilliant man and a great guy. You know I won't be able to make it to the funeral service. I wish I could. I'd like to be there for you.

"I know you're on call, so you can't leave town."

"Yeah. We could get the call anytime and I have to be here."

"That's okay. I know. I'm sure my dad would understand."

"What can I do for you?"

"Nothing right now. I've got it under control for now. I'll let you know how it goes and what we find out."

"Please do that. I'd like to know. Tell your mom I'm thinking about her and give her a hug, for me. I'll call you soon."

"Okay man, take care. I'll talk to you soon."

I just sat there with the phone in my hand for a long time. There are others I need to call, but they will have to wait. I needed to do something for myself. I took a long walk down the road leading away from the house and the lab. There's nothing out here except desert, cactus and tumbleweeds. It's a dirt road when you get this far from town. Normally, no one comes out this way. It's just the right place to get my feelings sorted out about my dad. We had a very mixed relationship right from the start. Now looking back, I understand why. We were two quite different people, but in many ways the same. If I had known then what I understand now, I think things might have been different. I guess that kind of understanding only comes with age. I don't know if that would have changed who I was. It's too late to think about that now.

Two hours later I was back at the house and finished making the other phone calls. They were much easier than the first two. My mother spent the day driving into town to buy a dress for tomorrow and meet with Fred at the funeral home one more time. I offered to go with her, but this time she wanted to go alone. It was almost dark when she got back, and I could see that she had been crying. My mother was not one to cry around anyone. I asked if there was anything I could do and she said she was fine and would get supper ready in a little while.

We sat there at the table eating, not saying much when I asked her "What will you do now that dad's gone? You aren't thinking of staying out here by yourself, are you?"

"Johnny, I haven't given that any thought yet. I have no idea what to do, and I won't for some time to come."

"You know you can come and live with me and Mary."

"I don't think so. You have your own life to live. You and Mary don't need me hanging around and getting in your way."

"You would never be in our way. Mary would love to have you live with us."

"You say that now. Anyway, you need to get serious about that girl, Mary. You need to marry her and the sooner the better! Don't let her get away."

Just like my mother. She's not afraid to tell you what's on her mind, whether you like it or not!

"You might be right, but you can still come and live with us."

"Like I said before. I have no idea what I want to do right now. We will see what happens down the road."

Next morning was Saturday. We had a little breakfast, although neither one of us was very hungry. We got ready and headed into town for the funeral service. Just like I thought, only a handful of people showed up. Some real friends of my mother and some of the old ladies from our town who I believe just came out of curiosity and were looking for a free meal. Sheriff Pat came in and sat down right behind mother and me. It was good to see a familiar face. It was a short service. It only lasted about forty-five minutes. When the service was over, my mother slowly walked up to the casket, bent over and kissed it. I guess it was her way of saying her final goodbye. The casket was never open. There was a picture of my dad on top of it. I was all right with that. I prefer to remember my dad the way I knew him, not laying in a casket.

Pat shook my hand and said again, "John, if there's anything I can do, just call."

I reminded him I still needed to meet with him at the lab.

"That's right. How about one o'clock on Tuesday?"

"Okay by me."

We all made our way to the fellowship hall in the back of the church. People came over to give us their condolences as they made their way to the food. The Reverend came over and I thanked him for a nice service.

"John, I'm sorry I never got to meet your dad. I am sure he was a fine gentleman. It's been a pleasure getting to know your mother. I see your mother in church each week. She's a wonderful woman."

As he walked away, I turned to my mother and asked, "When did you start going to church?"

"I'll tell you later."

Lunch was over quickly, and people started to file out. We were just getting ready to leave when the Dean of Engineering at Cal Tech, Theodore Benson, walked in. I was a little bit more than surprised to see him. I was thinking you're a little bit too late, bud. Professor Benson had been the dean for as long as I can remember. My mother was as surprised as I was. He walked right over and said, "I am so sorry for your loss Mrs. Northrup."

"Please, just call me Sharon. We've been friends far too long for any of this Mrs. stuff."

"Yes, we have. Sharon and John, on behalf of all the faculty at Cal Tech, we give you our deepest sympathies and are much grieved at the loss of your husband and father. Your husband was a good man and a great professor. I wish we had more like him. He will be greatly missed. The world needs more like him."

As much as that was nice to hear, I was a little skeptical. The last I remember, they all but kicked him off the campus. I'm sure my mother was thinking the same thing. For once, she held her tongue and didn't say anything.

After a few pleasant words of conversation, Dean Benson turned to me and asked if he could have a word with me. We excused ourselves and walked outside. He turned to me and said, "I have another reason for being here."

I knew it. There's no way he would come all this way to be at the funeral just for my dad. This should be interesting!

"John, I was headed out to see your father this week when I got the news of his passing. I received a call from General James Wellington of the defense department last week. You remember him, I'm sure."

"Yes, of course I remember him. He's been helping fund all of dad's research. Or most of it from the start."

"You're right, and he still is, up until this point. He called me because your father asked for another two million dollars to extend his research. He told the general that he was ready to scale up his experiment. Before the general was willing to give him the money, he called me. He wanted me to come out and see just how far your father had gotten. The general wanted to know my opinion and whether he should keep funding your father's experiment.

"Why you?"

"John, you know that the general and I have worked closely together for many years. They funded the research your father did years ago, right up until the time he discovered it wasn't going to work. That cost them a lot of money and they got nothing for it."

"That's not true. Look at the new batteries they got out of that research. Don't say they got nothing out of it!"

"Maybe so, John, but that's not what they were after and you know it. After hearing of your father's death, the general asked me to come out and find out just what he meant when he said he was ready to scale up the experiment. Do you have any idea what your father meant?"

"Not really, I haven't seen or talked to my dad in five or six months. The last time I was out here all I did was help him redesign the cooling system to keep the generators running full time."

"He didn't tell you what he was doing?"

"Well, yes, he did show me, but I really didn't care. He's been chasing this dream for most of his life. I gave up trying to help. It just seemed like we were getting nowhere."

"The general is coming out to meet with me, and he wants you to be there."

"I don't think that's possible. I need to be here with my mother, and I don't know anything about what my dad was doing anyway. "

"I'm sure he still wants to hear what you have to say about your dad's research."

"Like I said, I don't know that much about what he was doing. I know what he was trying to do, but not how."

"Well, you know a lot more about it than any of us do."

"When is he coming?"

"Tuesday, this coming week."

"No way. I'm not going anywhere right now. My mother needs me here. If he wants to see me, tell him to come out here."

"John, do you realize who this is? He is the only five-star general in the army. He only answers to the president. He has been funding your father for years and has every right to come out and take everything that's in that lab and walk away with it."

"So, what. I don't really care. This whole thing has been a dream of my father's, not mine."

"You would let your father's lifetime of work just walk away? Why wouldn't you want to try and finish it."

"Like I said, it was my father's dream, not mine."

"Your father's dream could help millions of people if it works. Just think of how it would change people's lives and help save the environment."

"The last time I looked at what he was doing was about six months ago. I don't think he is any closer now than when he was then."

"The general doesn't share your opinion. He thinks your dad is close, otherwise why would he ask for that money, and why would he say he's ready to scale up? In your father's letter to the general he said he was ready for a trial test and he just needed to take it to the next level to know for sure. Why would he say that if he wasn't close? No one knows what your father was thinking better than you do."

"Maybe, but I have my own life to live and I'm teaching back in New York. I can't just stop and drop all that for some pipe dream my father had."

"Yes, you can. This is way bigger than what you're doing right now. When you finish you can always go back to your teaching."

"You mean if I ever get finished."

"John, I believe your dad was on to something. He wouldn't ask for the funding if he wasn't."

"I can't answer you right now. I have to look after my mother and her needs before anything else."

"I understand that, but will you at least meet with the general?"

"Like I said before, if he wants to see me, I'll be right here."

"I don't know if he'll come out here, but I'll ask."

"Thanks for coming out. I need to get back inside with my mother."

"John, once again, I'm sorry about your dad. I always liked him and everyone respected him. I'll call you and let you know what the general says."

"Okay, fine. Thanks for coming out. My dad would have appreciated it."

When the last person had left the luncheon, we headed home. It was a noticeably quiet ride home and neither one of us said much until we pulled into the driveway. She asked me what the professor wanted. When I told her, she looked right at me and said, "I will not have you spend your life like your father. He spent his whole life trying to do something that couldn't be done. I will not have my son chasing the wind."

I told her I have no intention of doing that. End of conversation!

Sunday afternoon came and we met the reverend at the gravesite to say our final goodbyes to my dad. Just the three of us and the two men that dug the hole. It was sad. My dad deserved better than this. After all he had done and all the people that worked with him, you would think someone else would have shown up.

The reverend read a little scripture, said a prayer and then it was over. How unsettling to realize that this was the end of a lifetime for a man that worked so hard to make the world a better place. He was a good man, an ok father, a good husband, and a brilliant professor. I don't believe anyone will ever realize how hard he worked. It doesn't seem right, but life moves on and in a short time no one will even remember my dad's name, Paul L Northrup.

At that moment I had no idea just how wrong I was about that!

Monday morning came early and by six in the morning I could hear my mother already in the kitchen making breakfast. I guess that ritual was a way to make things normal, at least a little. By the time I got out to the kitchen, the coffee was ready, and she was bringing my breakfast over to the table. I asked how she was doing and as always, she said, "I'll be fine. You don't need to worry about me."

I knew better by the look on her face that she wasn't telling me how she really felt.

"You know I'll be here as long as you need me."

"You need to get back to your teaching. They aren't going to cover for you forever. I'm sure Mary would like you to get home soon."

"Mary knows I need to be here right now, and don't worry about RIT. They have plenty of staff to cover for me."

"But no one at your level. That's why you're there in the first place. I would like you to help me sort through some of your father's things today. There's no sense keeping all his clothes around here. I'm sure I can donate them to the church. Someone will get good use out of them. Your father hasn't worn any of his suits since the time he stopped teaching five years ago."

"Are you sure you want to do this so soon?"

"Why wait? He's gone. There's no reason not to. Let someone else have them."

I could tell by the tone of her voice that she was bitter and a little angry. I thought that was strange, but I think she felt abandoned by my dad's death. All those years chasing after him and now she's alone. It had to be an awful feeling. We spent the day going through dad's things. He had several suits that looked almost new. We drove into town and dropped everything at the church. They were delighted to have all the clothes and thanked us many times. It was getting late by then, so we stopped at the only diner in town to grab a bite to eat.

I wasn't hungry at the time, but it was some of the best home cooking I've had in a long time. Cooking was never my mother's specialty and she knows it. She has many other great talents, but cooking is just not one of them.

Tuesday started out like a lot of days out here. Crystal clear blue sky, calm air, warm sunshine. Who would believe there would be such a heavy dew in the desert? It really was a nice morning. Standing out back looking out over a vast stretch of desert with nothing but sagebrush and cactus and that stupid fence the army put up. I felt at ease for the first time in a week or more. It was a little cool with a gentle breeze blowing and the smell of the desert came gently to me. My thoughts drifted to Mary. It's been several days since the last time I saw her, and I began to feel the need to hold her once again. I wondered. Would she be willing to follow me the same way my mother followed my dad all those years? Would she give up her career the way my mother did, going wherever I needed to be? That would be asking an awful lot of someone.

I kept busy all morning fixing little things around the house while I was waiting for Pat to show up at one o'clock. Finally, one o'clock rolled around and so did Pat, just like he said he would.

"Hi John. How's it going?"

"As good as you could expect."

"How's your mom holding up?"

"You know, she says she's fine, but you know she's hurting on the inside."

"Yeah, I understand. My mother went through the same thing when my dad passed away. It just takes time, and you can't hurry that."

"Yeah, I know."

"Okay. Let's go open this lab and get you inside."

"Thanks for locking this place down. I didn't want anyone walking around in here and taking anything."

"Yeah, about that. I didn't get it locked up until the day you got here. Don't worry. No one comes out this way unless they're lost. You're five miles off the main road and there's nothing out here except this place."

"Just the same, I want to keep it locked."

"No problem. I'll leave you the keys before I go. The lights should still be working. We got them working during our investigation."

"So, what did you find?"

"Really not much. It looked like an accident. We didn't find anything that would tell us otherwise."

"What did the coroner's report say?"

"Glad you asked. I just got it today. Here it is. You can read it for yourself. It doesn't say much."

"Yeah, I can see that. Says here that there was a faint smell of burnt hair and clothing, but no sign of trauma. No sign of bruising of any kind. It appears he died of asphyxiation and no sign of a heart attack or an aneurysm. How is that possible?"

"You got me John, but remember when I told you that I had to break a window?"

"Yeah, I remember you said that."

"Well, when I did all the glass went inside with a rush of air."

"So, you think that there was some kind of a vacuum inside the building."

"That would explain why I couldn't get the door open. After I broke the window, the door opened right up."

"That doesn't make any sense. How can you create a vacuum inside the building? He wasn't working with anything that could do that."

"You got me. I'm just the sheriff. I don't have the slightest idea of what happened out here."

"Where did you say you found him?"

"Back here. I'll show you. He was sitting at that desk with his head down with all these papers around him. He still had a pen in his hand like he was in the middle of writing something. Oh, hang on a minute. I left something in the truck. I'll be right back."

Pat returned carrying the device. "Here it is. I think it's a recording device. We didn't see it when we took him to the coroner. He gave it to me the other day."

"You said his head was right here on the desk with a bunch of papers."

"Yeah, that's right."

"So, where are all the papers? There's nothing here. The desk is clean."

"I don't understand, John. The papers were all over the desk."

"Well, they're not here now. What happened to them? Did any of your guys take them by chance during the investigation?"

"No way. I made sure that they didn't move or take anything."

"Did they come back for any reason? "

"Not that I know of."

"Well, you better call and check. Those papers might hold the answer we're looking for."

"I'll check, but they had no reason to come back."

"Okay. Let's check around a little more."

"John, just what are we looking for? What was your dad doing out here and what is all this equipment?"

"You're going to laugh, but bottom line he was trying to build a better battery."

"All this to build a better battery?"

"No, that's not all. The battery I'm talking about could power a city. The real trick is to charge the battery. He thought that he could find a way to charge a high-powered battery by using less power than it took to charge it, so if it works, we will have more power than you started with.

"Is that possible?"

"He thought so."

"Where did they come up with that idea?"

"This started years ago when I was too young to understand what he was trying to do. My dad was ahead of his time. He saw the need for a renewable power source that didn't pollute the environment and would give us all the electricity we would need. I guess he was ahead of his time."

"So, that's what this is all about."

"Well, yes and no. The first thing that he spent years on was lightning and that didn't work out, but it led to this."

"Lightning? How was he going to use that?"

"It's a long story and it didn't work. I'll tell you about it another time. For now, let's keep looking."

"Glad to help, but just what am I looking for?"

"What would you be looking for if you thought this was a crime scene?"

"Well, that's pretty obvious. I'd be looking for clues to try and figure out what happened."

"That's just what we're looking for. We need to find something that will tell us what happened here. Don't forget to call your guys about those papers. That might just be the clue we're looking for."

"Don't worry. I won't forget."

"Pat, you did say everything was singed and it smelled like something was burnt."

"That's right. The whole place smelled that way, even your mom noticed it. John, I know this might sound strange to you, but wouldn't you think in a building this size you would find a lot of cobwebs? Look around. Do you see any?"

"No, I don't, and you're right, that is kind of strange. My dad wasn't the neatest guy in the world and he certainly wouldn't have bothered to clean out cobwebs."

"If that's true, what do you think happened inside this place?"

"No idea, but it certainly is strange for a building this size."

"While you're going through your dad's desk and the paperwork in there, I'm going to take a walk towards the back of the building and see if there's anything back there."

"Okay, just don't get lost back there."

While going through the papers in his desk and all the papers in his filing cabinet, I began to realize I could be here for a month looking for a clue. The problem I'm having is that everything I'm finding is old information. My dad was incredibly good about keeping records on his work, so he knew what he had already done. He didn't want to repeat the same mistakes he made the first time. I can't find anything recent that would tell me what he was doing, and it just doesn't make any sense since he always kept daily notes of his work. Maybe I'm looking in the wrong place. I wonder if my mother knows anything.

"Hey John, come back here for a minute. I think I might have found something."

"What do you have?"

"Maybe nothing, but didn't you say your dad was working with high voltage electrical equipment?"

"Yes, very high!"

"This electrical panel smells the same way the alternator on my truck did when it burnt up."

"You're right it does smell burnt, so let's take this panel off the outside and see what the inside looks like. This is the main panel for the building. It may give us a clue."

"Man. That doesn't look right!"

"It's not! This thing is completely fried."

"Do you think that's what caused the fire?"

"Pat, I don't see any signs of a real fire, other than what might have happened to the inside of this panel. The rest of the building doesn't show any sign of a fire inside. I know you said everything was singed and had a burnt smell, but if there was a fire, things would have burned up a lot more than what I see."

"Maybe so, but the inside of this panel certainly was burned out."

"What happened inside this panel could have happened in milliseconds because of all the voltage going through here. This is a complete meltdown. I'm surprised the box is in one piece."

"So, what's that telling us?"

"I'm not sure, Pat, but I know one thing. It was catastrophic whatever it was."

"John, I just got a call. I got to go."

"No problem. Just remember to call me and let me know if your men took any of those papers off my dad's desk.

"I won't forget. I'll call you later tonight. One more thing before I go, John. Those big things out front that you called generators. They smell the same way this panel box does."

"Thanks, I'll check it out when I get back up front."

After Pat left, I spent the rest of the afternoon in the lab reading old notes trying to see where my dad had left off. It didn't make any sense. Where are his notes from the last couple of weeks?

My mother came out at about six. "Are you going to come in and eat, or are you going to start being like your father and stay out here all night?"

"No, I'm on my way in right now."

I got washed up and sat down at the table. Over dinner, my mother started to ask if I found anything that might explain what happened.

"No, not yet, but what I found was that Dad stopped writing down his notes the last couple of weeks."

"That's not possible, your father was emphatic about his notes. He made copies every night."

"Copies? Where are the copies?"

"Come with me. I'll show you."

She took me to a door going down into the basement. I didn't know this place had a basement. In the basement was a fireproof room the army had built with a combination lock on the door. She opened the door and inside was a room full of dozens and dozens of filing cabinets.

"Here is every note your father ever took. The only notes that might be missing are the ones from the night he died."

"I had no idea he had all these notes. Which ones are the last ones?"

"Only your father would know that. He was just a little paranoid about someone stealing his work. I can't tell you where to start, but all his notes are here."

There must have been a hundred drawers to go through. It would take months to find what I was looking for.

CHAPTER 17

I was up and in the lab the next morning by eight. By noon, I still had no clue as to what had happened. After lunch, I headed to the lab once again and Sheriff Pat pulled in just as I stepped outside.

"Hi John. Sorry I didn't call you last night, but I found out nobody took any papers from the lab. In fact, they told me there was nothing on the desk when they got here to do the investigation."

"You're sure the papers were there when you found my father?"

"Absolutely. I remember that night very well. Your mom was so upset. I wish I could forget that part."

"So, what you're telling me is someone came all the way out here and stole the last notes my father wrote."

"I know that's hard to believe, but I don't have any other explanation for the missing papers."

"Who would take them? No one even knows he was out here, let alone what he was doing. It makes no sense at all."

"I agree, but that's all I know. Do you still want some help looking around?"

"Sure. I could use the company and I could use the help. Thanks. I'm going to try and get this control panel up and running. See if you can find anything that might have caught fire and then went out."

"Will do."

I had been working on the panel for over an hour when I heard Pat calling. "What's up?"

"I think you should come and look at this." I walked across the lab to find Pat standing by the collector.

"What is this thing, John?"

"It's the collector for that battery that could power a city that I told you about."

"What does it do?"

"Well, the idea is that the generators send huge amounts of voltage to it. The collector is supposed to collect it, then convert it to watts of electricity that can be used or sent into the grid for everyone to use. Why do you ask?"

"Well, put your ear up against this thing and see if you can hear it humming."

"I can, but that's not possible!"

"Well, come back here and look at this. Every light on the back of this thing is lit up, and this gauge says it's fully charged."

"Oh my God! He did it!"

"Did what?"

"He charged the collector completely."

"Is that a good thing?"

"Pat, this is great! It's beyond great. It's incredible!"

"So, what does that tell us about your father's death?"

"Nothing really, but it was his dream to make this happen. Stay right here. I'll be right back."

I ran to the house as fast as I could looking for my mother. "Mom, where are you?"

"I'm out back."

"You need to come to the lab. I've got something you've got to see."

"Right now?"

"Yes, right now."

I tried rushing her into the lab. "John, slow down. I'm not as fast as you are. Take it easy. I'll get there."

"Mother, come back here and look at this."

"Oh, hi Pat. How are you?"

"I'm fine, Mrs. Northrup, but I think John is losing it."

"Mother put your ear against this.

"Why?"

"Just do it, please."

"Okay, it sounds like it's humming."

"It is."

"So, what does that mean?"

"Come back here. Do you see all the lights are on?"

"Yes."

"Now, look at the power gauge. It says it's fully charged."

"John, does this mean what I think it means?"

"Yes, absolutely! He did it! He made it work somehow. He did it."

Pat looked at me like I was crazy, and mom started to cry.

"Your father worked his whole life to get here, and he didn't live to see it."

"Maybe not Mom, but he had to know it was working."

"I hope you're right John. It cost him his life."

"I'm sure he did. I just wish I knew what happened to his last notes. Then maybe I could figure out what happened."

My mother went back into the house. She said she needed to lie down for a little while.

Pat asked me "So, what do we do with all this power?"

"I don't know right now. I don't think we have any way to put it into the grid."

"I need to call Mary and tell her the good news."

"Who's Mary?"

"She's my fiancé."

"I didn't know. Congratulations."

"Thanks. Oh, I can't wait to tell her."

"Okay then, John. I'm headed back to town. If you need to reach me, you know how."

"Thanks Pat. I never would have walked back here. There wasn't any reason for me to go back here."

"Glad I could help. See you later."

I called Mary as soon as I got in the house. I must have sounded like a nutcase. I was so excited I couldn't talk fast enough. We talked for about an hour and then I let her go. I tried to call BJ. I wanted him to know, but he didn't answer. I was so wound up that night I could hardly sleep. Next day I called Dean Benson and told him the good news. He was happy for my dad, but then cautioned me about telling anyone else. He wanted to speak with General Wellington. I thought that was a little strange, but I guess the army did own it at this point. I got a call from the general that same night. He told me to lock down the lab, to not let anyone in and not to tell anyone about this. He said they would be out in two days.

I spent the next day reading all of my father's old notes, well at least some of them. There was no order to these notes. I'm sure I could figure his filing system out if I had a month or two.

Two days later the general pulled in, followed by a small army.

"Hello John. We need to talk."

"Okay, but what's with all the soldiers and why do some of them have guns?"

"That's what we need to talk about. John, this is Lieutenant Colonel David Stone. He's in charge of all of our intelligence gathering, and this is Lieutenant Scott Adams. He's in charge of all operations concerned with this project. Gentlemen, this is John Northrup, Paul Northrup's son."

"Hello gentlemen. Nice to meet you. I think."

Just then my mother came charging out of the house. "General, what the hell is going on out here, and what are all these soldiers doing here?"

"Good morning, Mrs. Northrup."

"Good morning yourself, General. Would you please tell me what's going on?"

"I was just about to tell John about all this."

"Well, you can tell us both now."

"I'm afraid I can't do that right now. I will tell John. Then he can share what he decides is necessary with you."

"Now, wait just a minute. This is my property and that's my husband's equipment."

"I'm afraid that's not true, at least not for now. The US Army has taken control of this property under orders from the president. This is a matter of national security. I'm afraid you and John will have to leave here by the end of the day."

"You can't do this. This is my home."

"I'm afraid I can and you will have to leave. When this is over, you are welcome to come back."

"Mother, let me talk with them and then I'll tell you what's going on."

"Fine. I'll be in the house, but I don't like this one damn little bit!"

"John, let's go to the lab and you can show me what you told me about the other day."

We headed for the lab and were followed by an entourage of army personnel; the general, both lieutenants, two army engineers and two armed guards. I was just a little intimidated. Once inside the lab, I gave them a tour of all of the equipment and ended up in front of the collector.

"General, put your ear against the collector. Do you hear that humming sound?"

"Yes, what does that mean?"

"Come back here and look at the panel. Do you see that gauge?"

"Yes, it says 100% capacity. Okay, so what does all this mean?"

"It means that Professor Paul Northrup, my father, finally accomplished what he's been chasing all these years. That collector proves that it can be done! There's enough electricity in that collector, or if you like you can call it a big battery, to run a large city for a month."

"Well, he finally did it! He told me in his last letter how close he was. I didn't know whether to believe him, so that's why I asked Dean Benson to come out and see what he thought. When I heard your father had passed away, I was upset and disappointed. I thought at the time that he never had accomplished his goal. Now that I see it, I'm happy for him. He did get it done after all. It's truly incredible!"

"General, did my dad ever share his notes with you?"

"Absolutely. Every one of his notes were copied and sent to me. It was part of the deal for the funding. If he ever made this work, it would become the property of the United States Army. His name would be associated with it and he would get all the credit, but it would belong to the army."

"What were you going to do with it?"

"You're not going to like what I have to tell you, John. What I'm about to tell you is top secret, so you can never tell anyone. About eight or nine months ago, we asked your father to do some experimenting for us. What he did worked! Our engineers took it one step further. I'll let them explain."

"Hello John. Nice to meet you. Your dad was a brilliant man and I really admired his work."

"Thanks, but what did he do for you?"

"We asked him to see just how far the electric beam could go and still be in a straight line and under control. What he gave us was incredible with enough power coming from an even larger generator than the one he was working with. He felt he could control the beam for almost a thousand miles."

"Why in the world would you want to do that? You would never want to put a collector more than a hundred feet away, just like my dad did. General, I don't understand why you would need to do that?"

"John, think about it this way. You know that a lightning bolt travels at 270,000 mph. That's millions of feet per second. We don't have anything in our arsenal of weapons that can even remotely come close to that."

"Are you telling me you're going to use this as a weapon!"

"No. That was never our intent. It will only be used as a defensive weapon."

"Yeah, right! No one has ever used a defensive device as a weapon. I can't believe you would do this. My dad's life work was intended to help people, and make their lives better, not to kill people."

"John, don't be so naive. Think about this. Our enemies can launch a missile at us from over 8,000 miles away. It will hit somewhere in the US in about 20 minutes or less. If we can't stop it, it could mean the end of this country as you and I know it. With this new device, we can destroy that missile within minutes no matter where it is. No one else has anything close to this and they may never have it. Well, I should say almost no one."

"What do you mean almost no one?"

"That's the other thing I need to tell you. Have you ever heard of a man named Conrad Mueller?"

"No. Should I know him?"

"Probably not, but he's been in the news several times."

"I don't really watch the news. I really don't trust what I hear."

"I can understand that. I don't trust most of it myself. So, Conrad Mueller is one of the wealthiest men in Germany. He's a fifth-generation German wannabe soldier. His great-great-grandfather fought in the Franco-German Wars in 1870. His whole family has fought in one way or another. His father was in World War II and was severely wounded when Germany tried to take Stalingrad. Conrad himself was drafted into Hitler's Youth Army at the very end when they were drafting the youth to fight. Conrad was only twelve at the time. He was captured by the Russian army and taken back to Russia where he spent four years in a concentration camp. He blames the U.S. for not making Russia release him sooner. We're not sure who he hates more, the U.S. or Russia. He spent the next eight years or so working and studying. Most of his study was about the German way of life from Hitler's point of view. He found his father in a hospital shortly after he got back. His father passed away but before he did, he made Conrad promise to bring Germany back to its glory days and get revenge on Russia and the U.S. for what they did to Germany. Believe me, he's trying."

"Okay, but what's all that got to do with me? And how did you get so much information on this guy anyway?"

"Let me tell you a little more about this Conrad fellow first. About eight years ago he tried to buy his way into the German government. He did get in, but after a year or so they made him leave. His ideas were way out of line with where the German government was going at the time. They wanted nothing to do with him. At least most of them. Some of those governing Germany liked what they heard and became silent supporters of his. Two years later, he tried to do the same thing in Russia, but barely got out of there with his life."

"Why doesn't the German police take care of this guy?"

"Like I told you, he's very wealthy and he has connections throughout Germany and beyond. When it comes to catching this guy, he and his associates seem to know what's coming before it happens. Every time they tried to catch this guy, he just disappeared. They haven't even seen him in the last two years."

"You still haven't told me why I should care or how this concerns me."

"Yes, you're right. We believe he's been after your father's work for some time now."

"Really! What could he possibly want with it?"

"He wants it for the same reason we do."

"General if he wants it, you know he wants it for a weapon, not for defense."

"We're well aware of that, and that's just what we're afraid of."

"How would he even know what my father was working on?"

"John, your father has published his work for years in almost every science magazine there is. Dozens of people around the world have followed your father's work, so it's no secret."

"Okay, but how could he possibly get his hands on any of this?"

"John, did you ever wonder why the postman came all the way out here every day?"

"No, why?"

"He doesn't go anywhere else out here. People this far out of town go to the post office once a week to get their mail. We pay him to come out here every day to pick up a copy of your father's notes. Your mother knew about the arrangement. She got suspicious about the mailman a long time ago. So, we told her about him. She's kept it to herself ever since."

"My mother is pretty sharp. I'm sure she knew what was going on."

"Yes, she is. We had her checked out."

"What! You had my mother checked out."

"Yes, just like we checked you and Mary out."

"You've gotta be kidding me!"

"No, not at all. We do background checks on the whole family when it comes to something like this. Anyway, around six months ago we started to notice the mailman making a stop at his house every day after his pickup here. We figured something was up when it started to take him an extra twenty minutes to get from there to his drop on our end. We checked out his house one day when he was out. We found a copy machine there and not just any copy machine, but one that was encrypted. At first, we couldn't trace where the information was going."

"Why didn't you stop him?"

131

"We needed to find out where he was sending your father's notes first. We told your father to keep sending his notes, but to leave out any new details."

"Wouldn't the people on the other end figure that out?"

"Not necessarily since your father went back and forth on his research all the time. This was nothing new for him."

"You're right about that. He did go two steps forward and one step back quite a bit. So how did you get the real notes?"

"Once we knew we could trust your mother, she would bring them to school once a week. We just picked them up from her."

"You mean my mother is in on this?"

"Yes. She was glad to help."

"She never said a word to me."

"We asked her not to. The less people that know about what's going on out here the better."

"Okay, so now that my dad's work is over. What's going to happen to the mailman?"

"Nothing right now. We are still hoping to get more use out of him. But when this is over, he will be going on a very, very long vacation."

"Did you ever find out where the notes were going?"

"Yes, we did. They were going to an underground office in England. Then by carrier to a little village on the Rhine River. Then on up the river to Frankfurt."

"Who ended up with them?"

"That we haven't figured out yet. We're sure they are ending up with the people working for Conrad Mueller."

"I don't get it. Why don't you just arrest this guy?"

"Like I said before. We can't find him or his associates. They have all gone underground and seemingly just disappeared. We're sure they have people on the inside of the police department that are sympathetic to their cause. Every time we get close, they move. They just disappear."

"What about the German government and their army? Why can't they take care of this?"

"From what we can tell the German army doesn't think he's a threat. They know about him, but for now they could care less. Besides that, some of them are sympathizers, or they've been paid off. At this point, we are not working with their army. Only a few special ops personnel that we can trust. The army doesn't even know we're there. The German army is nothing like ours. After World War II, what was left of the army was completely disbanded according to the unconditional surrender terms set forth by England, Russia and the U.S. Eventually, after many years, they could have their own police force and then a small army. Their army today is still small as compared to that of many other countries."

"So, how did you find out so much about this guy?"

"Two ways. The German police that we trust have been helping us with some intelligence, but most of our information has been coming from our own people. For the last several months, we've been using our people to run this guy down."

"Let me guess. You've been sending in recon teams to find this guy."

"How would you know that?"

"Lucky guess. I have a friend that does that kind of thing for the Army."

"Well John, as a matter of fact, we know just who your friend is. Brad Johnson."

"How do you know he's my friend?"

"Wouldn't you think he would show up in your background check?"

"He never said a word about this to me."

"The only one Brad can talk to about what he does is his commanding officer or me. As far as the rest of the world is concerned, Brad and his squad don't exist."

"Yes, I know. He at least told me that much."

"He shouldn't have even told you that! It's classified information."

"So, is Brad involved in this recon work?"

"I'm afraid he is. Brad is one of the best we have. He's the only one that ever got close to Conrad."

"You mean he actually met Conrad Mueller?"

"Yes. We wanted to get someone on the inside and Brad was the man."

"What happened?"

"Brad was getting close. Then for some reason, they pulled up and just vanished once again."

"So, now what?"

"I'm not sure right now. Brad is still in Germany and he's trying to find them."

"Is Brad and his squad in danger?"

"They are always in danger. It's what they do. I wouldn't worry about them. Like I said Brad's one of our best. They also have a second squad of elite army rangers supporting them if they need help. Now, let's get back to what your dad was doing here."

"Like I said before, my dad made it work. The collector is fully charged and ready to go."

"What do you mean ready to go?"

"General, you can use this power for anything that runs on electricity or just send it into the grid."

"I don't think that's a good idea."

"Why not?"

"How do we explain where it came from?"

"Who cares where it came from? It's here to be used."

"John, when that much power gets put into the grid every power company on the west coast is going to want to know where it came from. From what you're telling me, there's a lot of free electricity in this thing and the power companies that run the grid aren't going to like people getting free electricity. They're going to want to know how it was produced and who did it."

"I never thought about it that way."

"Don't worry about that right now. Can you show me and these engineers how your father did this?"

"I don't think I can."

"Why not?"

"Come with me and I'll show you. Do you see this panel? This is where all the power to run the generators comes in. It's completely fried. The whole inside is melted down."

"Can't it be rebuilt?"

"Yes, General, but that's just a small part of the problem. Without his notes, I have no idea how to set this up. I could be guessing for months to find the right settings and even then, I might not get it right. Besides that, it's obvious something bad happened inside this lab and it killed my dad. He knew what he was doing and it killed him. I'm not too anxious to do the same thing."

"John, these two engineers have all your father's notes from over a year back. They're right up to speed as to where your father was. That is up until a week ago."

"General, that's fine, but in the last week or two my dad found the key to this whole thing. I think those missing notes hold the key to this project and without them we're kind of at a dead end."

"What do you mean missing notes?"

"When the sheriff and the hazmat team finally got to my dad, the sheriff told me they found him at his desk with his head down surrounded with all kinds of papers full of notes. I told the sheriff to lock the place down and leave everything alone. He didn't think to lock it up for almost three days. He said he didn't think anyone would come out here. A few days later when we opened the lab, there were no papers on the desk. We asked everyone that was out here if they knew where the papers went, and no one knew anything about those papers."

"Sergeant, I want you to take a couple of men with you. Go talk to the sheriff and get every name of anyone who was anywhere near this place. We'll talk to them ourselves and find out just what they know."

"General, the sheriff's a competent guy. I am sure he discerned the real situation in his interrogations."

"Maybe so, but we have better ways of asking."

"What's that supposed to mean?"

"Never mind about that. We have felt for some time now that someone might be watching this lab."

"If you thought someone was watching the lab, why didn't you post a guard?"

"In a way we did. Not out here, but we had several people in town keeping an eye on the comings and goings of most everyone in this little town."

"What were they looking for?"

"Anyone that didn't fit in. This is a small town and the kind of people we were looking for certainly wouldn't fit in here. Your mother knew we were out here. If she saw anything or anybody that she didn't know, she had a number to reach us and we would be right here."

"Why didn't someone tell me?"

"At the time, you weren't here and you didn't need to know."

"My mother and father were in danger, and you didn't think I should know?"

"John, we had a handle on it."

"I'm not so sure about that. If someone was watching this place, then it might explain why the papers are missing."

"It might, but I sure hope not. It would mean they have your father's last notes and we don't. That would be bad for all of us. John, how easy do you think it would be for Mueller's people to duplicate your father's results?"

136

"General, my dad has been working at this for years. I don't even know how this all works and I've read all his notes. And I've been helping him with this off and on for some time now. Why do you even suspect that they are working on this?"

"Two reasons. First, Brad has seen some of the equipment, and secondly, we've confirmed shipments coming out of Saudi Arabia. Generators that are larger than the one your father has been working on have been shipped to Germany."

"Saudi Arabia! How do they fit into this?"

"The Saudi's will build anything and sell it to anyone who wants it, as long as they have the deep pockets to pay for it. Conrad Mueller has very deep pockets and many rich supporters. By the way, this accident you keep mentioning, what do you think caused it?"

"General, I still haven't come up with any kind of answer."

"Okay, John, tell you what. I don't think we can do much more here right now. If you're willing, I would like you to work with these two engineers. Tell them everything that you know about what happened out here and maybe the three of you can figure out what went wrong."

"I would be glad to. Maybe they will see something I missed."

"Good, I'm going into town and start to set up my office. We will run everything through my office. Understand, gentleman?"

"Yes sir, we will report anything we find."

"Lieutenant Adams, all communication will come through you."

"Yes, sir."

"John, one more thing. Dean Benson is coming out to see you."

"Why is he coming out here?"

"He said he has information for you. Something about what your dad did back in the lab at Cal Tech."

I spent the rest of the day in the lab with the two army engineers. I was quite surprised how up to speed they were. They even told me a little about what my dad was trying that I knew nothing about. I went over the whole story with them from the time my mother heard the loud boom to not being able to open the door, calling the sheriff, breaking the window, the air rushing in, and then when they got inside that they couldn't breathe, the hazmat team (which is just the local fire department guys with masks) finding my dad at his desk, already dead. His death was caused by suffocation. No sign of a struggle. The fact that there was a smell like something had caught fire, but no real fire. Only the sign of things being singed. They asked me a hundred questions about what happened and I had answers for most of them. These guys were good, much better than I first thought they would be. They came up with little things that I had missed. I guess two or three heads are better than one. About six o'clock, Lieutenant Adams came into the lab to get me.

"Mr. Northrup, I have to take you to town. You're having dinner with the general."

"I'm sorry. I'm not going to leave my mother out here alone tonight."

"Your mother is already in town sir. She will be joining you at dinner with the general."

"When did all this happen?"

"We've been moving your things to town all day. We have you set up in a vacant house right in town. I think you will like it for now."

"You guys don't mess around do you!"

"No sir. We get things done as fast as we can."

I left the two engineers in the lab. I figured they'd be there most of the night. The lieutenant gave me a ride to town and dropped me off at the only restaurant in town. As I walked in past the guard at the door, he pointed me to where my mother and the general were sharing a glass of wine. There wasn't another person in the place. That seemed awfully strange to me. Everybody in town eats here. I wondered what was going on. As I got to the table, the general poured me a glass of wine.

"Here John, have a seat. I hope you like wine."

"As a matter of fact, I do."

I took one sip and knew right then that this bottle of wine didn't come out of this restaurant's wine cellar, if they even had one. Mary had taught me something about fine wine and this was a good one.

"Nice wine, General!"

"Thank you. It's out of my own collection."

"So, how did you get this whole place to yourself?"

"The restaurant owner was very gracious. People in town will be eating here free for quite a while after we leave."

"Good evening, John."

"Good evening mother. I think there's a few things you haven't been telling me."

"Go easy on your mother, John. She was under orders from me."

"I find it hard to believe General. She doesn't take orders from anyone."

The general laughed. "You're right about that John. Let's say it was a request. Anyway, she helped us out quite a bit."

"Johnny, I didn't tell you because I was asked not to and you weren't here anyway. Why make you worry."

"If I had known, I would have come out."

"I didn't want you to come out. You and Mary are making a real life for the two of you back in New York and that's where you need to be."

"John, your mother has been a great help over the last year or so. She has followed up on everything your father was doing. She gave us up-to-date reports on just where he was and what we could expect next."

"Okay mother, just how were you doing that?"

"Do you think your father was the only one in this family with a brain?"

"No, I didn't think that. I know how smart you are. I just thought you didn't want anything to do with dad's work."

"Well, that was true for the most part, but ever since the General asked for my help, I've been keeping up with what your father's been doing. I was the one who told him his cooling system was too small. Sometimes he would miss the simple things trying to solve the big problems."

"So, you're the one who figured that out?"

"I only knew it had to be fixed, but I had no idea how to do it."

"Mother, I didn't realize you were so good at keeping secrets."

"Johnny, you have no idea how much I know."

"I guess not. You're just full of surprises. So General, what's next?"

"John, I want you to stay here for the next couple of weeks, so you can help my people find out what went wrong. Then try to make this thing work the way it's supposed to."

"General, I can't stay that long, I have classes to teach back in New York."

"Not anymore. I've taken care of that for you. I can have you as long as I need you."

"Okay, that's fine for you, but my fiancé is back in New York."

"We would be happy to bring her out if she wants to come."

"I don't think that will work. She is very devoted to her students. I don't think she will leave them. I'll ask her, but I doubt it. General, what happens if we can't get this thing running again?"

"That might be the best thing that could happen for all of us! If we can't get it working, then maybe no one else can either.

Maybe the secret died with your father. The world might be better off if this never works."

"I thought you wanted it for a weapon?"

"I never said that. We truly only want it for defense. I have no reason to lie to you. As a young soldier, I fought in the Korean war. I commanded troops in Vietnam. I have seen how many ways we can kill each other. The last thing we need is another weapon to kill each other even faster."

"Maybe so General, but if you needed to, you would use it as a weapon, wouldn't you?"

My mother said, "Johnny, that's not a fair question to ask the general."

"Okay then General, were you ever going to share this with the public?"

"Honestly, probably not. Which power company would you like us to give it to? Whoever gets this device will have a monopoly on electricity within months. They will drop the price so low that every other power company in the country will go out of business or sell out to them. Soon they would control all the electricity in the U.S. just to start with. After a few years, they would be able to do the same thing throughout the world. Now wouldn't that just be great for everyone. Can you see where I'm going with this? The world would be forced to buy from one company. Not good!"

"I guess I never thought about it that way. Mother, what do you think of all this?"

"John, I think you're a little naive when it comes to the world around you and world politics. Do you remember years ago when a man said he built a carburetor that could make a car run up to a hundred miles on a single gallon of gas?"

"Yes, I remember something about that, but I think it was just talk."

"No, it wasn't just talk, he really did it. The government bought it and buried it. Can you imagine what would have happened to our economy? Think about how low the price of gas would have gone. The same would happen with this if all the electricity we use was almost free. I hate to think what chaos that would bring. It literally could ruin the world economy."

"Okay then, General. Why do we even want to try to get this thing going again?"

"Because someone out there has your father's notes. We don't want to be the only ones who don't have this device. It's called deterrence by strength."

"Yeah, just what we need, another arms race."

"Call it what you want John, but it keeps our world from destroying itself."

"Oh right, just like the atomic bomb!"

"John, it's been working for a long time now."

"It works all right, right up until some nutcase like Conrad Mueller gets his hands on it, then what?"

"That's exactly why we need your help because we can't let that happen."

"Excuse me for a minute. I need to make a call."

"Johnny, do you need to make a call right now?"

"Yes mother, it's something the general said. I have to call Mary."

"Hello."

"Hi Hun, it's me."

"John, what's wrong? It's one o'clock in the morning."

"I know, sorry to wake you, but I need you to do something for me."

"What do you need?"

"Go to my desk, look in the bottom drawer on the right-hand side and tell me if my dad's notes are there."

"Okay, just a minute."

"John, there's nothing there. The drawer is empty."

"I was afraid of that."

"Why, what does that mean?"

142

"You remember when we got back from the Adirondacks, and I said something was wrong and it just didn't feel right in our apartment."

"Yes, I do. Do you think someone stole your father's notes?"

"I'm sure of it now."

"John, you're scaring me. Should I get out of here or call the police?"

"No, you're not in any danger now. They got what they were looking for a long time ago. You can go back to sleep now. I'll call you tomorrow."

"Go back to sleep? I'm supposed to go back to sleep after what you just told me? Someone was in our apartment and stole your father's notes. I may never sleep here again."

"Mary, it's fine. No one is coming back there."

"Maybe it's fine for you. You're two thousand miles away. I'm here by myself."

"Okay, call one of your friends and have them come over and stay with you. I'll call you tomorrow and fill you in a little more. I gotta go. I have people waiting."

"You better call!"

"I will. Love you Hun. Bye for now."

"General, I'm afraid I know how some of my dad's notes got out there. When my mother called me and asked me to come out and help with a cooling problem, I took the notes my father had at the time home with me. I designed a solution and sent it out to my dad. I put all the notes and my design in the desk drawer. Mary and I went on vacation for a couple of weeks. When we came back, I felt like something was wrong in the apartment. It was, and now I know what it was. All the notes are gone. Someone got in there while we were gone and took all the notes.

"Did your designs for the cooling system work?"

"No General, not really. I had to come back out here later and see what I had missed."

"Could anyone else figure out what was wrong?"

"It will take them some time, but I'm sure they will figure out the problem. I did."

"Yes, John, that's true, but they don't have your knowledge or know what you know about the system. That gives us some time to catch up with these guys. How long do you think it will take them?"

"I don't have any way of knowing that General, but three or four months at least. It all depends on how smart these people are."

Over dinner I found out just how involved my mother was. I was surprised to learn just how much she knew about dad's work. She had been reading all my father's notes for the last year and was very up to date on just how far he had gotten. She could be a big help in trying to find out what went wrong. I will have to make sure she fills in the army engineers when we get back to the lab. The information she has could be invaluable in helping us get the generators up and running again. I think she knows more about what's going on with the equipment than I do.

The army had found us a nice place in town to stay. This house was better than the house my mother was living in. They had brought the whole contents of mom's house out here and set it up close to what it was back home. There was one new additional item - a brand new refrigerator. My mother was pleasantly surprised. The old one had been dying for some time. Next morning, we met the general at the same restaurant and once again it was empty just like the night before. Just us three and the guard at the door. I couldn't imagine what people in town were thinking. They probably thought this was another area 51. I'm sure they would be surprised if they knew what was going on right in their backyard. We were having a nice breakfast and the general was telling us stories about his past adventures he had over the years with the army. I'm not sure that I would call them adventures. They were a little on the scary side. Right in the middle of one of his stories, the guard at the door came over to the table.

"General, I have a call for you."

"Who is it from?"

"Charlie Brown sir."

The general left the table in quite a hurry without saying goodbye to either one of us. A short time later the guard returned and told us that the general would be tied up the rest of the day.

We finished our breakfast and the guard took us out to the lab. As we walked into the lab, we found both engineers already there and hard at work, just like I left them the night before. I bet they had been there most of the night and were right back at it first thing this morning.

"Good morning, gentleman. How's it going?"

"Good morning, sir. Good morning, ma'am. We found some things I'm sure you're going to want to see."

"General, you have a priority one call, and it's on a secure line, sir."

"This is General Wellington. Tell me what's going on."

"General, it's Charlie Brown reporting."

"Brad, you can talk freely. This is a secure line."

"Thank you, General. We had a bad night last night. We got caught out in the open last night and it ended up to be quite a firefight, sir."

"Were there any casualties, Brad?"

"Yes sir. We have two men down. Their injuries are not too severe, but I will be sending them back to the states as soon as I can get them on a plane."

"I understand, Brad. We will make sure they get the proper care."

"Thank you General. They're both good men. They mean a lot to me."

"What else can I do for you Brad? Is there anything you need?"

"General, I'm down two good men. I need to have them replaced as soon as possible."

"I understand. Who do you have in mind?"

"Let me think about that and I'll send you a couple names."

"Let me know as soon as you decide. I'll have them on a plane immediately."

"Thank you, sir."

"Brad, tell me what went wrong. What happened last night?"

"Yes sir. You know we've been trying to find this Conrad Mueller ever since he went underground. We finally got a good lead from one of our informants. We have been following up on that for the last three days. We intercepted a shipment of equipment and followed it to an abandoned warehouse. We kept an eye on the warehouse all day trying to track their activity. We saw little movement around the warehouse. We decided to go in last night and have a closer look. I only took half of my squad and one German special operator with me.

We set our recon time for midnight. We were all in position by 12:30. We spent the next hour getting close to the place. I was sure no one knew we were there. We got alongside the building and we're just about to try the door when all hell broke loose. We started taking fire from both corners of the building. I ordered everyone back. Before we got to cover, one of my guys went down with a shot to the leg. Two of us were able to drag him out of the line of fire. We returned fire and tried to make our way back the way we had come in.

They had our retreat covered. We were boxed in. They must have had snipers on the roof. We were catching fire from all directions. That's when another one of my guys caught it in the shoulder. I knew we weren't getting out of there on our own. I called in the rest of my squad. I had them on standby. They were there in just a few minutes. When they got there, they came in weapons hot and really kicked ass. They caught some heavy fire on the way in, but they cleared a path for us to get out of there. My guess is that we were up against twenty-five or thirty well-armed men. We did well to get out of there with only two casualties."

"It sounds like you were lucky to get out of there at all."

"My men are incredibly good at what they do. They know how to take care of themselves in a firefight. General, I believe they knew we were coming. They knew right where to hit us and just at the right time."

"It certainly sounds like it. How do you think they found out?"

"General, I really have no idea. Up until now I didn't think these guys even knew we were here. I'm afraid they know now."

"Don't worry about them knowing you're there. We knew that sooner or later they would be on to us. They're well connected. I'm not surprised they found out. How do you think they found out about last night?"

"I'm not sure right now. I haven't had time to think about that yet. I hate to say it, but it almost must be someone that's working with us. The only ones that knew what we were up to last night was my squad and a handful of German special operators."

"That sure points the finger in that direction."

"Yes, it does General. I find it awfully hard to believe. I've been working very closely with these guys. They all seem like straight shooters. I think they want this guy as bad as we do.
General, I will be sending my men back to base. I want to stay close by. I'll just play the dumb tourist game and see what I can turn up."

"Okay Brad, but be careful. We didn't know until now just how dangerous this group was."

"They are dangerous. They're well-armed and they know how to fight. They are as good as any I've been up against."

"That's not good for you!"

"No, it's not General. But I know how to take care of myself and my men."

"I know you do, but I still want a report from you every day, no matter what you find. Is that understood?"

"Yes sir. Understood."

Chapter 18

"So, lieutenant, just how late were you guys here last night?"

"Only until around midnight."

"Only? That's a long day."

"Maybe for some. This is our job and we're used to it."

"So, did you find something to show us? You don't mind if my mother comes along, do you?"

"Absolutely. She may want to see this just as much as you. Let's start over here by the window. This is the window the sheriff broke in, correct?"

"Yes, that's the one. Why?"

"We checked outside, and the sheriff was right. Every piece of glass came inside. We didn't find even the smallest piece outside."

"Okay, so what does that mean?"

"Well, come back and look at this. All the glass flew back here. The biggest piece of glass we found was this far back from the window. It's seventy-eight feet inside the building. Judging by the size of this piece of glass and where it ended up, it had to be traveling over sixty-five miles an hour. It didn't get this far in the building just because the sheriff broke the window."

"So, what does that prove?"

"It proves that there was indeed a vacuum inside this building when he broke the window."

"I still don't see what that has to do with anything."

"Johnny, let them talk. I think they have more to tell us."

"We do ma'am. Mind you, this is just a theory and we're still working out some of the details. If we believe there was a vacuum inside, then we need to figure out how it happened. A vacuum like we're talking about can only happen in one of two ways. Someone or something would have to suck all the air out of this building. That's highly unlikely."

I said, "The only other thing would be a fire of some kind."

"You're right John. But not a small fire, a quite large fire and a very intense one."

"Lieutenant, how would that be possible without burning this place down?"

"Good question. We know your father was using high-energy voltage which produces huge amounts of heat. Let's suppose that it got out of control and caused a flashback. That flashback could cause the kind of fire that would suck all the air out of this building. It would also explain how things got singed, but didn't burn up. In a flashback with that intensity, it would use up all the air and then an instant later put out the fire. There would be no more oxygen to burn and there would be no more air to breathe. That could be the reason your dad died of suffocation."

"That's one wild theory you came up with, Lieutenant."

"Yes, it is, but we still have more to show you. Come with us. We spent some time going around the building and collecting animals."

"What kind of animals would you expect to find in this building?"

"Look in this basket John and tell me what you see."

"I see what looks like four mice and a raccoon."

"You're right. Do you see any reason for them to be dead?"

"No, not really."

"That's because they all suffocated. Now look at this jar full of bugs and a few spiders."

"Let me guess. They all suffocated as well."

"Yes, as a matter of fact they did. There's no evidence to show otherwise. We have one more thing to show you. Please come back here with me. Do you see all those air ducts up there?"

"Yes, what about them?"

"Take a close look. They're all caved in from some kind of vacuum, just like when you suck on a straw too hard."

I had to admit these guys were thorough, and very good at what they did.

My mother looked at the Lieutenant and said "It seems like you've proven your theory. However, I'm not convinced about your fire."

"Well Mrs. Northrop, let's go back to where the generators are. The panel John showed us is in the back. It's the one my guys are repairing right now. This panel was completely melted down. It had no cooling system. These generators had the best cooling system I've ever seen."

"You can thank my son for that."

"Yes, I know. When this thing is over, I have a cooling problem for him to look at."

"John, look inside this cooling jacket you built. Tell me what you see."

"It's pretty much wasted like everything else in here."

"You're right, and what does all this tell you?"

"Whatever happened in here...well, the heat had to be incredible!"

"Yes indeed. That's the same conclusion we've come to. We estimate that the heat had to be almost 20,000 degrees for maybe one or two seconds. Long enough to singe everything in the building and burn up every single bit of oxygen in here.

"That's absolutely insane! That's twice as hot as the surface of the sun!"

"We feel the same way. But there's no other explanation for what happened here."

"If what you're saying is true, then it would mean that the air itself caught fire."

"That's what we're saying."

"Is that even possible?"

"We called and talked to some scientists we know. They said in theory it is possible, but no one has ever proven it."

"If this had happened outside the building what would have happened then?"

"Mrs. Northrup, I have no idea and I never want to find out. With your permission we would like to exhume your husband's body. We want to examine his lungs to see if they are burnt like we suspect."

"You won't need to do that. The coroner told me they were severely burnt."

"So, even the air in his lungs caught fire."

"That's what we believe."

"What happened here is insanely scary. I don't think we have any way of trying to make this work again safely."

"We need to let the general know right away."

"Maybe not."

"John, what are you thinking?"

"If we had dad's last notes, they might hold the answers to all of this."

"Johnny, I know we don't have his written notes, but do you still have the recorder your father used? You know, the one the sheriff brought you from the coroner's office."

"Yes, I tried to listen to it, but it was damaged. There's nothing on it to hear."

"Sir, if you would let us have it, we might be able to get something off of it."

"Help yourself. It's right over there in the garbage can. I threw it away when I couldn't make it work."

"Great! Give us a day or two, and we'll see if we can come up with anything."

"You can tell the general what we've come up with today. We will make a full report and have it in his hands in the morning."

"Thanks for all your help, Lieutenant. I don't think trying to start this thing will be a priority anymore."

"I don't believe so, sir. In fact, I'm going to stop my men from any further repair work."

"I would say that's a good idea, Lieutenant. Have a good day."

"Yes, sir. You too."

Our plans for the day were pretty much over at that point. We had only spent two hours with the engineers, but it was a crazy two hours. There was nothing left to do at the lab, so we headed back to the house in the village. Once we got home, I went to the fridge and grabbed a beer. Those army guys had stocked the fridge well! I went out on the porch and just sat there staring at the street. This was a small town, and most of the people that lived here were retired and had spent most of their lives here. I watched many of the older folks out on the street. I'm sure they were sharing the local gossip. If only they knew what had happened just outside of town. They would have enough to talk about for years to come. I wondered just how close my father came to burning this whole town to the ground. Thank God it stayed in the lab.

A few minutes later my mother came out and to my surprise she had a beer in her hand. I said "Thanks, but I already have a beer."

She gave me an odd look and said, "It's for me, not you."

She's just full of surprises these days.

"Johnny, do you think your father knew what was happening in the lab that day?"

"At first, I thought he did, but now I don't think so. It happened so fast. He couldn't possibly have seen it coming. I think he died instantly."

"I hope for his sake you're right. I would never want him to suffer in a fire like that." Mom started to cry. I just reached over and held her hand. There were no words I could say that would take away her pain. Only time would do that.

Chapter 19

"General, you have a call coming in from Charlie Brown."

"Hello Brad, what's up?"

"General, I told you I was going to stay here in town."

"Yes. What have you heard?"

"Word on the street is that people know about the fire fight last night."

"How could they know about that so fast? It just happened last night."

"I don't know right now. It happened way outside of town. No way they heard the gun fight. They seem to know all about it. The only way they could know is if someone told them, or worse yet, one of them was involved in it. They are also saying the U.S. is involved in it."

"How is that possible?"

"I don't know, General. We don't have anything on us that might tie us to the U.S. Even our guns are foreign made. My only thought is that someone is feeding them all this info."

"I believe you're right. Someone is feeding them bad intel. If people on the street are on this guy's side, we'll never catch him."

"We'll catch him, General. These guys always make a mistake sooner or later. I'll be there to nail them when they do."

"I like the way you think, Brad. By the way I've sent the two men you asked for. They should be there in the morning."

"Thank you, sir. I'll bring them right up to speed as soon as they arrive."

"Brad, I'll look forward to your next report."

"I will let you know as soon as I have something."

Chapter 20

I called Mary right after dinner and filled her in.

"John, I feel just terrible for your mom. She must be in shock over all this."

"It has definitely taken a toll on her. I think she is just as upset as to what could have happened as she is about my father dying. I believe she will be ok in time. I have a lot to tell you about my mother. It seems she has been more involved with my dad's work than I thought."

"Why, what did she do?"

"It's a long story. I'll tell you when I get home."

"John, what are you going to do now that you're not going to start the experiment up again?

"I will have to talk to the general. I don't see any reason for me to stay here."

"I would certainly like to have you home with me. You've been gone a long time."

"I know. It feels like forever. I really miss you. How's school going?"

"Great. I took the kids on a field trip and they had a ball. I even think they learned something. I just love them all. I feel like I'm their second mother."

"Well, don't get too close. They will all be moving on next year."

"I know and it will just break my heart when I have to let them go."

"I'm sure it will. Sorry, but I need to go. I want to spend a little time with mom before she heads off to bed."

"Tell her I love her and give her a hug for me."

"I will. Love you. Bye for now."

"Bye, love you too!"

Next morning, I had breakfast with my mother, then I headed out for a run. I was about a mile out of town when an army Humvee came charging up behind me. It was one of the general's aides.

"Sorry sir, but the general wants to see you right away."

I was getting used to this "sir" thing. Kind of made me feel like I was somebody. I jumped into the Humvee. We headed back to town.

"Can we stop so I can take a shower?"

"Afraid not sir. The general said now."

"Okay then. This must be pretty important?"

"I don't know sir. I was just told to bring you to the general."

"Suppose I didn't want to come?"

"Sir, I would have brought you back one way or another."

By the tone of his voice, I could tell he wasn't kidding. I decided I wouldn't put him to the test.

I walked into the general's office still sweating and dusty from a ride in a wide-open Humvee. The back roads around here are all dirt roads. I really needed a shower.

The general was on the phone and he wasn't happy. I couldn't tell much, but someone on the other end of the line was getting a good ass chewing. I'm glad it wasn't me. The general slammed the phone down and wrote some notes in his day planner. He looked up at me and said "What the hell have you been doing? You're a mess."

"Sorry, General. I was out jogging on a back road when your guy grabbed me and hauled me back here to see you."

"He was just following the orders I gave him, John."

"Yes, he did follow your orders!"

"Well, sit down John. Do you need a glass of water or something?"

"Not right now, thanks. Why did you want to see me anyway?"

"I have the report from Lieutenant Adams. This report is not good on so many levels."

"You're telling me."

"I'm very disturbed by what I'm reading here. Do you buy into all this?"

"I didn't want to at first. Lieutenant Adams kept showing me things he had found. After a while, I had to agree with him. The lieutenant knows what he's talking about. There's no other logical explanation as to what happened."

"Your mother was there. What does she think?"

"She thinks the lieutenant could be right. It would answer a lot of questions."

"It would certainly seem so. If he's right, then there is no way we can start this machine up again."

"No, General we can't. Without knowing what went wrong, we are setting ourselves up to make the same mistake my father made. We might just kill ourselves the same way my dad did."

"Yes, I suppose that's true. What bothers me more is what this report implies. If I read it right, the fire that took place inside that lab only stopped because it ran out of air."

"We don't know that for sure."

"Well, the lieutenant is damn sure. This fire could just keep going with no limit."

"I don't know if I believe that! It's only a theory."

"His report makes it sound like a pretty damn good one. I have no idea what to do with this report right now."

"What would you normally do with it, General?"

"I don't really know. I never had a report like this before. This is like someone telling you a volcano is going to erupt. We just don't know where or when. If I send this up the line, people will be jumping all over me with questions that I don't have answers to."

"You're right about that. What happens if you don't send it up the line?"

"Good question. Maybe nothing if nothing happens. If something does happen, then I can kiss my career goodbye."

"General. I certainly don't have your experience in these matters. I don't believe there's anything to worry about. Like I said it's all a theory and no one has any proof this could really happen."

"I hope you're right. This report has me pretty spooked, and I don't get spooked very easily."

"General, do you see any reason I can't leave now? I don't see how I could be of any further use to you."

"I don't see any need for you to stay any longer. You've been a big help John, and I know where to find you if I need you."

"Thank you. General, I will be leaving in a day or two. What about my mom?"

"As soon as we clean out the lab, we will move her back to her house."

"Good. She will be glad to get home. If I don't see you General, it's been fun!"

"Thanks again for your help John. I wish things could have turned out better for all of us."

"Me too General."

Just as I was leaving, Lieutenant Adams came rushing through the door. He was sweating, out of breath and pale as a ghost. I hadn't known the lieutenant long, but I wouldn't have thought he was the kind of man that you could rattle very easily. Whatever he had seen or heard certainly had him wound up.

"General, you need to hear this. You too, John."

"Excuse me Lieutenant, but aren't you forgetting something?"

"Sir?"

"Did you forget how to salute, Lieutenant?"

"Sorry sir." The lieutenant snapped to attention and saluted.

"Now slow down, Lieutenant and tell me what's so bloody important."

"Yes sir. Yesterday at the lab John gave us the recording device his father used. John had thrown it away thinking it was ruined. We were able to retrieve the entire recording."

"What's on it, Lieutenant?"

"Here it is. Listen for yourself."

It was my father's voice on the recorder.

"This experiment is #317 on static charge device P-A-N-3. As of late, the collector is working as designed, however static beam integrity has become unstable as I increase the voltage. I'm concerned about this as I have only reached 82% output. My latest calculations have indicated complete loss of beam integrity at 96%. The beam should hold at 92%. This is the purpose of today's experiment. I have fair beam integrity at 88%. Now increasing to 90%. Some loss of beam integrity, but holding steady. I'm now increasing to 92%. At this point, beam integrity is becoming increasingly unstable. I am losing control of direction and stability. I need to shut the system down. I have initiated the shutdown, but it's not responding. I have now engaged the emergency shutdown system, but that has failed as well and I have lost all control of the system. John, if my calculations are right the system cannot be controlled beyond 88%. The beam is forming into a large ball shape. Please don't let anyone go any further with this experiment I fear that a--"

"I fear what, lieutenant?"

"Sir, that's all that's on the recording. It ends right there."

"John, what do you think he was trying to tell us?"

"I have no idea. From what the lieutenant showed me yesterday, I now believe his theory to be correct. What happened in that lab could happen again and on an even larger scale. If someone builds a system larger than my father's and it gets out of control, I'm not sure just how bad it will get, but it will kill every living thing for miles around."

"Lieutenant, do you feel the same way? Is this really possible?"

"Yes sir, I do. I believe it will be worse than what John is saying."

The three of us just stood there looking at each other. We had no idea what to say or what to do next. After what seemed like forever the general turned to me. "This whole thing was your father's idea. What do you think we should do now?"

"Why are you looking at me? You guys are the ones that handle this sort of thing!"

"John, this is all new to us. We never had to deal with anything like this. Certainly not on a scale like this."

"Lieutenant, you haven't said anything. What do you think?"

"Sir. Can I speak freely with John here?"

"Yes, yes. Say what's on your mind, Lieutenant!"

"Sir, I think the first thing you need to do is call Charlie Brown. He needs to know just how dangerous this situation is. Mueller has no way of knowing what will happen if he succeeds in getting a system online. We believe his system is larger and more powerful. General, he could cause massive damage to Germany without ever knowing it. You need to call the president and tell him. He needs to call the German chancellor and get his support. The two of them need to work together to take this Mueller out."

"Yes, I agree. I will call the president, but first I need to call Brad."

"Call Brad? Is Brad Johnson "Charlie Brown"?"

"Yes John, he is. Your friend Brad Johnson is Charlie Brown. Now that you know that, you need to keep that to yourself."

"I will. What is Brad's role in all of this?"

"Brad and his squad are the front line for us on this matter. He's been chasing this guy for months. He got close last week, but ended up in quite the firefight."

"Is he okay?"

"Yes. He's fine. A couple of his men got hit, but they're back in the states. They're recovering well. Now, if the two of you will excuse me. I have calls to make."

"Yes sir."

As we walked outside, my head was spinning.

"Sorry for not believing everything you told me yesterday, Lieutenant."

"Don't worry about it. I didn't want to believe it myself. It's still hard to believe. Unfortunately, your father's recording proves our theory."

"Just how bad do you think this could get?"

"I have no idea, John. If it happens? It could be the worst thing the world has ever seen!"

The lieutenant gave me a ride back to the house where my mother and I were staying. I got out of the Humvee without saying a word. My mind was numb from thinking about what could happen. I couldn't make sense of it. How could it be that something that was supposed to help mankind had turned into something that could be so destructive? Had we really found a way to set the very air we breathe on fire? I prayed to God that we were wrong! I didn't go into the house just then. I needed to go for a walk. Why do people always think the worst when we get bad news? I'm no different. I couldn't get the image of what could happen out of my mind. I walked around town for over an hour, still sweaty and dirty from my jog. I passed many of the townspeople on the street. I didn't say a word to any of them. I just kept on walking. I walked the length of the town and back. But I still wasn't at ease about the things I now knew.

It was time to face my mother. I went to the house and found her busy in the kitchen. Without turning around, she said "Hi Johnny. If you're hungry, I could fix you something to eat." When I didn't answer, she turned around to look my way. "John dear, you're so pale. Are you okay? You look terrible!"

Chapter 21

"This is General Wellington. Put me through to the president! I don't care if he's in a meeting! Put me through to him right now."

"Mr. President, I have something very disturbing to discuss with you."

"General, can't this wait? I'm in the middle of an important meeting."

"No, Mr. President. I'm afraid it can't wait."

"General, I have most of the Joint Chiefs of Staff sitting right here. Should they be hearing this?"

"Let me tell you first then you can decide who you want to tell."

"Very well. Let me clear the room."

"Okay General, go ahead."

"Mr. President, you're aware that we've been, or I should say, we have been undercover in Germany chasing Conrad Mueller for some time now."

"Yes, I'm aware. He's the man we suspect was stealing information on some new electrical device?"

"Yes, he's the one, sir."

"General, what do you mean we had been undercover?"

"I'm afraid the operation got exposed last week. I'm sure the German government knows about it by now."

"How do they know it's us?"

"They don't, but they will when you tell them."

"What do you mean when I tell them?"

"Mr. President, over the last few days we found some very disturbing information. This electrical device has a very destructive and powerful side to it."

"General, I was told that this device was just to make more electricity available to us."

"Yes, that's true. However, no one, not even the man that designed it, knew this could get out of control. There was no way to know the kind of damage this thing could cause."

"Doesn't he know how to stop it?"

"Sir, I'm sorry to tell you, but he died in his own lab when the device exploded on him."

"Sorry to hear that. Just how bad is this thing?"

"Mr. President, it has the potential to kill untold millions."

"General, how can you be so sure this thing has that kind of power?"

"My top engineers, as well as John Northrup, have verified the facts. They believe if we don't stop this Conrad Mueller, we could be looking at a catastrophic event like we've never seen."

"Who's this John Northrup?"

"He is Paul Northrup's son."

"Does he know how to stop this thing?"

"The only way to keep this from happening is to stop Mueller. That's why you need to call the German chancellor and tell him what he's facing."

"Call the Chancellor? Do you have any idea how he will react when he finds out we've been operating on German soil?"

"No sir, I don't, but you have to tell him. He has to know what could happen and what he's up against."

"General, I don't like what you're telling me. I certainly don't understand it like you do. I want you here when I make this call. Get yourself on a plane as soon as possible. I want you here in my office tomorrow. Understood?"

"Yes sir. I'll be there."

"I'm fine, mother."

"You don't look fine. Come over here and sit down. I'll get you a glass of water. I thought you went out for a jog. You've been gone for hours."

"I did go for a jog. I was about a mile out of town when one of the general's aides picked me up."

"Oh yes. They came here looking for you. I told them where they might find you. Is that why you look the way you do?"

"Kind of. I was with the general for quite a while. We were discussing not starting up the generator again."

"Well, thank heavens for that. I hope they never run that again."

"I told him I would be heading home soon. We both felt there was no reason for me to stay any longer. Just as I was leaving Lieutenant Adams came running in the office. He had retrieved the last recording that dad made."

"Oh, my goodness! What did it say?"

"Nothing good, I'm afraid. He said he was losing control of the static beam. He couldn't shut it down. He said it was turning into a fireball. Then he said my name and told me not to let anyone use the machine. It can't be controlled. His last words were "I fear that a " and then the tape ended."

"Johnny, what does all that mean?"

"Mother, you know as well as I do what we found in the lab. With that information and this recording, it proves just what we thought. We can never let this machine be run again. In fact, all of dad's notes and research must be destroyed."

"I understand what you're saying, John. What a shame that a lifetime of your father's work will be for nothing."

"Yes, but there's no other option. It all needs to be destroyed. There's one more thing. Do you remember a few days ago I mentioned the guy named Conrad Mueller?"

"I think so. Why?"

"The General and I are sure he or someone that works for him stole those missing notes. If that's right, they may be able to finish building a static charge machine and get it running."

"Johnny, that would be unimaginable. It would be absolutely terrible!"

"I know."

"What are they going to do about this guy? They must find a way to stop him."

"The general was calling the president after I left. They will figure out something. I'm sure they'll find a way to stop this guy."

"I pray you're right. Your father never meant for this to happen."

"I'm sure he didn't. Now that it has, we have to deal with it."

"Why don't you go get cleaned up and I'll fix you something to eat."

"Thanks, but I don't think I can eat anything right now. I do need a shower though."

"If you change your mind, just let me know."

"Sergeant! Get in here."

"Yes sir."

"I need you to go and get John Northrup."

"Yes sir."

"Tell him to pack a bag and bring him back here right away. Tell him he needs to go to Washington with me for a few days. He will be meeting with the president, so tell him to dress accordingly."

"Yes sir."

"Call and have my plane ready. I need to be in Washington tomorrow morning."

I had barely gotten into the shower when I heard a loud banging on the door. I thought I heard someone say I was needed in Washington. I turned off the water, so I could hear better. I yelled back "What did you say?"

"Sir. The general sent me to get you. You will be going to Washington with the general to meet with the president."

"I thought I was hearing things! When I didn't respond, the sergeant stepped into the bathroom."

"Sorry sir. You need to get moving. The general's plane leaves in two hours and you have to be on it."

"What!!"

"The general told me to tell you that you will be meeting with the president, so bring appropriate clothing.

"The general just told me I could go home."

"Sorry, sir. There's been a change in plans and you're needed in Washington."

"Why? Who needs me in Washington?"

"I don't know sir. I was just told to get you back to the general. Asap."

"Brad, General Wellington here."

"Yes sir. General, what's up?"

"I'm afraid I have some bad news for you."

"Whatever it is, we'll handle it sir."

"I'm not so sure about this one Brad. We've just found out that the machine Mueller is trying to build could blow up in his face."

"Well, that would help us, wouldn't it?"

"No, not at all. That's the last thing we want to have happen."

"Why is that, General? What's so bad about this guy blowing himself up?"

"Because if that happens, he's going to take millions of innocent people with him. From what we found out and what we believe, the energy and heat from this thing can literally set the air on fire. We believe it has the potential to kill every living thing for hundreds of miles around."

"Is that really possible?"

"Yes! From what we now know, we believe that's just what happened in the professor's lab."

"Yes, but didn't it stop there?"

"Only because it was contained in the building. If it gets out, we don't know where it will stop or even if it will."

"You're telling me Mueller's machine could make this happen?"

"Yes, that's exactly what I'm saying."

"General, right now I don't know where this guy is. What's worse is, I believe he may be building more than one of these."

"What makes you think that?"

"Things I'm hearing on the street. Yesterday I was in a little town called Lorch. I overheard people saying they have been locked out of places they've been going to for years."

"What kind of places?"

"I'm not sure. I think they were talking about castles. Are they big enough to build these machines?"

"I guess. It depends how big the castles are. How can we verify how many machines he might be building?"

"Glad you asked. Send someone to Saudi Arabia. Have them nose around and find out just how many of these generators they've shipped. Then we'll know how many are being built and how many places we need to look for them."

"Good idea, Brad. I have just the man for the job."

"I thought you would."

"I'll call you when I know more."

"Johnny, what's going on?

"I don't have any idea, mother. All I know right now is that I'm going to Washington with the general. I don't know why he needs me there. The sergeant said it would only be for a day or two."

"Call me when you get there and let me know what's going on. Johnny, when you meet with the president, remember who you're talking to!"

"I will. Don't worry. I won't be rude."

"Make sure you dress appropriately."

"Yes mother! Do me a favor and call Mary and tell her I will try to call her tonight."

The sergeant was pacing around the Humvee waiting for me. I jumped in and he took off down the road. I heard him taking a call, but I couldn't quite understand what was being said. Next thing I knew, the sergeant was taking the next right and hit the gas again.

"Where are we going? I thought we had to pick up the general."

"Sorry sir. Change of plans. I need to get you to the plane right away. The general is already on his way there."

The only airport around here was almost an hour away. It's a small airport and I can't understand how anything that the general would be flying in could take off or land there. We didn't say much on the ride to the airport. I would ask a question and all the sergeants could say was "Sorry sir. I don't know." I was beginning to think he had a gag order not to tell me anything. We arrived at the airport in just over forty-five minutes, so needless to say, we weren't going the speed limit.

As we pulled around the one and only hangar, I was surprised to see a gleaming white Learjet 75 Liberty sitting there. This is one beautiful plane. It has a pilot, copilot and one steward. The plane seats six and it's plenty fast. I had no idea the army had such an airplane. We drove right up to the plane steps and boarded. The inside was just as plush as you might think. One of the seats had been removed to make room for a desk. The general was on board sitting at the desk and already on the phone. He waved me to a seat and motioned to the pilot to take off. Two minutes later, we were headed down the runway. I looked out the window and watched the little airport rush by. Just when I thought we would run out of runway, the plane leaped into the air and sent me back in my seat. What a rush! I've been on lots of planes, but nothing like this. This thing is a rocket with wings. I didn't want to go to Washington, but the ride there was going to be fun.

The general was arguing with someone on the other end of the phone. I couldn't tell from the conversation who was winning, but I was glad it wasn't me. Apparently, the General got what he wanted and hung up.

"Sorry about this John, but I was asked to meet with the president tomorrow about your father's device. I want you there to help me explain just what this is and just how bad this could be. I'm sorry you're not going home right now. When this is over, I'll drop you anywhere you like."

"Glad to help, General, but couldn't one of your own engineers go with you?"

"No, I reassigned them, and they're already gone. You're the best one for this anyway. I'm sure you can convince the president that he needs to call the German chancellor and tell him to help us. The chancellor needs to get involved and help us. If he doesn't listen, Germany could be in terrible trouble."

"Does the president know all about this?"

"No. He knows very little."

"How is that possible? Doesn't he know what is going on in his own army?"

"John, people have this idea that the president knows everything about everything. The truth is he only knows a little bit about a lot of things. He can't possibly keep track of everything going on in the world. He depends on his advisers for keeping him up to speed. The only thing he knew before yesterday was that we might get some cheap electricity out of your father's device. Our job tomorrow is filling him in, so he can make a good decision going forward. John, there is something you should know about the president."

"What's that?"

"He has quite the temper. You wouldn't know it from his public persona, but in his office, that's a different story. Believe me, he doesn't like being caught off guard. This whole thing came out of nowhere, and he's not happy about it."

"Okay, that's good to know, I think."

This was no commercial plane we were flying in and this was not a commercial flight. Three hours later, we were landing in Washington. There were two cars waiting for us. As we got off the plane the general said, "See you in the morning" and then jumped into the first car.

I hadn't even said goodbye, when a tall, very fit, well-dressed sergeant grabbed my arm and said "I'm Sergeant Tom Pearson and I'll be taking care of you while you're with us in Washington, sir. Let me take your suitcase."

"Thank you, Sergeant. I'm John Northrup."

"Yes sir, I know. I've been filled in about you and why you're here. I have orders to take you to a hotel in DC and get you settled in."

I jumped into the back of a jet-black Lincoln Continental and off we went. Twenty minutes later we pulled up in front of a fine hotel. The doorman opened the door before I could. He had my bag in hand and we followed the sergeant inside. I knew from the minute I walked in the door I couldn't afford this place. The sergeant went to the desk and was right back with the key to my room.

"Sir, this is the key to your room. If you don't like it, just call the desk and they will find you another room. They have a fine dining room here with a great menu. I would suggest you give it a try. Have a nice dinner, sir. I will pick you up at six a.m. tomorrow morning. Please be in the lobby. You will meet with the general then with the president."

"Six a.m. Isn't that a little early?"

"The general likes to get an early start. One other thing sir. Remember you will be meeting with the president, so please dress accordingly."

"Thank you, Sergeant, my mother already told me that."

"Yes sir. See you in the morning, sir."

My room was bigger than the apartment Mary and I shared. The bellhop put my one suitcase in the bedroom and stood there waiting for a tip, something I wasn't used to. When I opened my wallet, I found I only had two $5 bills. I handed him half the money I had. I hope I can charge dinner. I'm sure it won't be cheap in this place. I called Mary and filled her in on what I knew. She said my mother had called and told her I was headed to Washington with the general. We were on the phone for over an hour. After talking with Mary, I called my mother and filled her in. I took a shower and headed down for dinner.

It was the best dinner I had in a long time. When I asked for the check, they told me it was all taken care of. I was glad to hear that. I couldn't imagine what the bottle of wine cost. I got back to my room and hit the sack. I had an early call in the morning. I laid there in bed thinking about Mary. I was really missing her! I wish she was with me. We could have some fun in this place.

"Hello General. I take it this line is secure."

"Yes Brad. I'm in Washington. Anything new to report?"

"Yes sir, in a way, that is."

"What do you mean in a way?"

"Sir. So far, I've checked out two castles along the Rhine River. Apparently, one of them was open to the public. Now it's closed and locked up. There's no doubt that at some point recently, there was some heavy equipment working around there. No one I've talked to seems to know anything about it. There's a big sign that says repair work is underway. Keep Out. I've been watching the place, but nothing is being done. That seems awfully suspicious to me."

"I agree that does sound very suspicious. Keep an eye on it to see if anything happens."

"The other castle was wide open with people coming and going all the time. I was in the castle myself. I didn't find anything that looks like what we're looking for."

"Okay, Brad. Keep looking around, but be careful."

"I'm always careful, General. What's going on in Washington?"

"I'm meeting with the president in the morning. I need to fill him in on this whole mess. I have a friend of yours with me to help convince the president how bad this really is."

"Who might that be?"

"A young man named John Northrup."

"John is with you? Can I speak with him?"

"He's not here in the room with me. We have him in a hotel downtown."

"I'll bet he's just loving this!"

"Not really. He was on his way home when I grabbed him and brought him to Washington. If all goes well, I can send him home in a couple of days. By the way Brad, Bill Mansfield is on his way to Saudi Arabia. I hope to hear from him in a day or two."

"You picked the right man for the job, General."

"If anyone can find out what's going on there, he can. One more thing, Brad. You need to get your men out of Germany for now."

"Way ahead of you, General. I pulled them back to Austria three days ago. I didn't want them in Germany unless I was with them."

"Good move, Brad. I'll talk to you soon and let you know what's happening on our end."

"Very good, General. Say hi to John for me."

Chapter 22

"Herr Mueller, this is Von Hellman reporting, sir."

"Yes, what do you have to report?"

"The last time we spoke I reported we had lost four men in the attack on our experimental facility. Since that time two more of my men have died from their wounds."

"Sorry to hear that, but they were good men and they died for their motherland. How are the rest?"

"Doing well. They will be ready to fight again soon. Herr Mueller, you asked me to find out who it was that attacked us and how many of them were killed in the fight. I was not there at the time as you know. Colonel Kraus reported at least eight of the attackers fell during the fight. However, they must have carried the bodies back with them. We found no bodies and there was no way to tell who the attack came from."

"That's not what I was hoping to hear. I want to know who is after us."

"I understand sir. We will do better next time."

"I trust you will or I'll find someone who can. Now tell me about the evacuation of the facility. How is it coming?"

"Yes, sir. We are right on schedule. It will be complete in one week from today."

"That's good news, Major Hellman. We no longer need that building so, once all the equipment is out of there, blow up the building. I want no trace of what we are doing there left behind."

"Yes, Herr Mueller. I will personally see to it."

"The installation of all three generator stations is going as planned. They should be ready to go online in just a few weeks. Once that happens Germany will once again be the superpower it was destined to be!"

"Herr Mueller, only you could have made this happen! Your name will go down as Germany's greatest leader."

"Yes, it may indeed. More importantly the German people will remember this time for generations to come. Report to me when the building is destroyed!"

"Yes, sir, Herr Mueller."

"Von Hellman! I was not expecting you."

"Colonel Kraus, is there some reason I should clear my plans with you?"

"No, sir. I'm just surprised to see you here."

"Colonel Kraus, I gave your report to Herr Mueller and he was not pleased. I'm not sure he believed any of it. I'm here to make sure you don't screw up the evacuation of this equipment and get us both shot."

"Sir, everything is going well, and all of the heavy equipment will be out by the end of the week. We are in the process of pulling all the controls out and all records of our experiments are filed and ready for shipment."

"Very good, Kraus. One more thing, Mueller wants the building destroyed after everything is out."

"Why would he want that? We may need it again sometime in the future."

"He said we will have no further use for it. When all three of our stations come online and the world sees the power we control, there will be no need for further experimenting. Once they see the destructive power we have, the world will be on its knees. Germany will rule and no one will dare oppose us."

"Von Hellman, our scientists feel there could be a problem with the generators."

"What problem?"

"They suspect they may not be able to control the power as we first thought."

"Do they have any proof of this?"

"No, not at this time. Only a feeling from what they saw in the experiments."

"Until they have some real proof of this, I don't want to hear any more about it."

"Yes, sir."

"Now show me around the building. I want to see for myself how well you are doing."

I had left a wakeup call for 4:30. When it came, I felt like I had just closed my eyes. I ordered breakfast and jumped into the shower. I was out of the shower when my breakfast showed up and I gave the bellhop my last five bucks and finished getting dressed. I hope my mother would appreciate how I'm dressed. I finished breakfast and headed down to the lobby. I wanted to be early. I wanted to show the sergeant I was no slouch and could keep up with these army guys. I walked into the lobby to find the sergeant was already there. He didn't see me come in since he was too busy making time with a gorgeous blond behind the front desk. As I walked up behind the sergeant, I gave the receptionist the quiet sign. She caught right on as I made my way up behind the sergeant. I started making faces as he was trying to get a date. The young lady did well for a minute or two, but then lost it and started laughing at the faces I was making. The sergeant turned around and jumped to attention.

"Sorry, sir. I didn't see you come in."

"That's all right, sergeant. I can see why you didn't notice me coming in." As we headed out the door, I apologized to the sergeant. "Sorry for sneaking up on you, I just couldn't resist."

"No problem, sir. I wasn't getting anywhere anyway."

"Well, I wouldn't give up on her if I were you.'

"Oh, don't worry, I don't intend to give up on her. I just need a new approach."

"Good luck sergeant, but she might be out of your league. Can you tell me what I'm getting myself into today?"

"Well sir, you already know the general. He's a little easier going than the president from what I've been told. I would be ready for an earful if you know what I mean."

"Yes, I know what you mean. The general kind of warned me yesterday. He said the president has a short fuse."

"Sir, I have friends who have been assigned to guard detail for the president. They told me more than once that the president could put some drill sergeants to shame. I don't know if that helps."

"Oh, that helps a lot. I can't wait to meet our president."

We pulled up in front of where the general was staying. It looked like an old apartment building that was in bad need of a good face lift. The sergeant walked me right into the general's office.

"Good morning, General."

"Good morning, John. Grab a cup of coffee and a seat. Like I told you yesterday, we will be briefing the president on your father's device and what we know about what's wrong with it. The president will not want a lot of fancy scientific talk. Just tell him in plain language what it is, how it works, and what we think will happen. Got it?"

"Yes, sir. It may not be quite that simple, general."

"Why not?"

"General, this is the outcome of a lifetime of my father's work, and you want me to explain a lifetime of work in twenty-five words or less."

"John, I understand how you feel about your father's work. Trust me, the president only wants to know what kind of damage this could cause and enough information to get the German chancellor on our side."

"I'll do my best to keep to the point."

"Good boy. That's all I intend for you to do. Now when we get into see the president, stand up straight and keep quiet until I introduce you. Don't sit down unless you see me sit. Make sure you sit on my right side. Make sure the president has been seated first. Don't interrupt the president unless you like having your ass chewed."

I felt like I was walking into an interrogation. "Anything else I should know?"

"I will try to clue you in as we go along."

"What if I have a comment or want to ask a question?"

"Just tap me on the shoulder and I'll let you know when you can talk. All right, we need to get going. Our meeting is at eight. Did you get anything to eat before you got over here? We could always grab something on the way."

"No, thank you, sir. I ate breakfast already."

Now that I think about it, that may not have been a good idea. My stomach was already turning and we weren't even at the White House yet."

Chapter 23

I've been sitting here watching this castle for two days now. Of all the things the army has taught me to do, sitting around on my ass was not one of them. The general told me to watch this castle, but it's clear to me nothing is happening. It will be dark in an hour or so and I'm tired of sitting here watching. I need to find out what's going on in there. I made up my mind to go in tonight and see for myself what is in there. It's just after midnight and I've spent the last two hours trying to find a way to get inside this castle. I must give credit to whoever built it. A lot of work went into this place and they sure didn't want any unwelcome guests showing up here. While I was sitting on my hands for the last couple of days, I did spend some time reading up on this old castle. What little I read was that it was built between 1850 and 1880. I believe this castle is called Neuschwanstein Castle. I could be wrong. There's so many of them, it's hard to tell one from the other.

I need to get inside, but this is not going to be easy. There is a steel door right here at ground level that was certainly not part of the original castle. The castle sits right on the Rhine River overlooking miles of river in both directions. The east side is facing the river and there is a sheer drop off down to the water. No way anyone is getting in from that direction. The south side is guarded by a twenty-foot-high rock wall that is in incredibly good shape for its age. I could get over that wall easily enough, but I'm just not sure what or who might be waiting for me on the other side. The west side is built right up against a rocky hillside. That would seem an easy way in, but if there is someone standing guard, I'd be a sitting duck! Forget about getting in that way. Looks like that leaves me with the north side or nothing. I had to take the long way around to get to the north side. This bloody castle is huge. I had no idea it would take me half the night to get around it. I finally made my way to the north side. I can see several windows high up on this side of the castle. As climbers go, I'm pretty good, but climbing up this thing was not in my plans.

I only got about ten feet off the ground when I realized just how smooth this wall was. It's got me just a little bit nervous. At the rate I'm climbing, it'll be daylight before I get to those windows. If I had known I was going to be doing this, I would have brought my climbing gear. I'm only halfway up and my arms are already aching. I cut two of my fingers on the sharp edges of the rocks in this wall. I can feel the blood between my fingers. I'm at a point where I just can't find another hand hold and I can see it's beginning to get light out. Sunrise isn't that far away. The only possible handhold I see is three feet to the right and two feet above me. If I weren't so tired and my arms weren't already aching, I know I could make that jump.

I can't go back down. By the time I got down, it would be full daylight. My only choice is to make the jump. I kept telling myself you can make it, you can make it. One long deep breath and I jump. My fingers just get the edge, but there's nothing for my feet to grab on to. I can feel my fingers bleeding more and just as my arms are about to give out, I feel a toehold. I push up with one foot and then find another crack to stick my other foot in. I can rest here long enough to catch my breath and say a little prayer. I still have a way to go to get to those windows, but the stones up here are not as smooth and they're not so perfectly put together. I guess the builders never felt anyone could climb this high.

The rest of the way up was easy compared to the first half. I made it to one of the windows and then found it boarded up. Just what I f--- needed. I rested for a couple of minutes then pulled out my knife. I started digging at the wood and much to my surprise it started coming apart easily. The wood was old and dry. In short order, I had a whole big enough for me to crawl through. It was pitch-black inside and I could feel the boards under my feet cracking and giving away. I put my back against the wall and started inching my way around the room. I hadn't gone far when something hit me right in the face. It scared the crap out of me. I realized it was just a bat. What else would you expect to find at the top of a castle? A few minutes later, I felt what I thought was a door. It couldn't have been more than five feet tall and only two feet wide. I guess the people that lived here must have been small.

It took quite an effort, but I managed to push the door open. It made a lot more noise than I wanted it to. I knew the sun was coming up, but it was still dark as hell inside this hallway. I was making my way along when my head collided with what was a very solid wooden beam. Just how bloody short were these people? I ducked under the beam and kept going. The dust and the smell inside this place were enough to choke a person. I took several more steps and then the floor ended. I put my foot out, but there was nothing there. Great! Now what? I took my belt off and let it drop over the edge. About four or five feet down it hit something that sounded solid but there was no way to tell. I sat down on the edge and hung my feet over the side. I took a deep breath and dropped.

Thankfully, it was solid, and it turned out to be the top of a staircase. I felt my way down one step at a time. It was a tight spiraling staircase, and it was only a little wider than my shoulders. About forty steps later, I came to another door. Of course, it wouldn't open. I put a shoulder to it three times and broke through. I came into a small empty room. I scared the hell out of about 100 pigeons. I was covered from head to toe with dust, cobwebs, and a few spiders. This spy stuff isn't all it's cracked up to be. It certainly isn't like a James Bond movie with all those gorgeous women hanging around.

The sun was streaking through two small windows that lit the room up well. It was good to be able to see again. I was trying to wipe the dirt out of my eyes and I could taste all that dust in my mouth. I felt like I could spit mud. I would have given anything for a glass of water right then. The floor in this room was solid, other than being covered with all this pigeon crap.

There was one small door on the other side of the room, leading to who knows where. Down, I hope. Surprisingly, this door opened easily, leading of course to another narrow twisting staircase. Each step creaked and creaked from old age. I just hope no one was close enough to hear me coming. At the bottom of the stairs was another door. I was only able to push it open about three inches. I could see through the opening that there was a chain holding it closed. It was the first sign that other people had been in this castle. I got my hand through the opening and was able to unhook the chain. This room was well lit from four large windows that looked out over the river. I took time to catch the view from one of the windows. It was a spectacular view from up here. I could see for miles. It was a long way down to the river from up here. A fall from here would kill a man. I checked out the rest of the room. I noticed the sign on the door I had come through. No One Allowed Beyond This Point. So obviously people were allowed in here at some point, so why is it locked up now? I would soon find out.

Chapter 24

Our ride to the White House was uneventful. The general made two calls during the ride. I just stared out the window watching Washington go by. When we pulled up to the guard house, the soldier on duty took a short look at the general, jumped to attention and saluted. "Good morning, sir". The driver drove us right to the front door. I followed the general inside trying to keep pace with him without running. He seemed to be in an awful hurry to get this meeting started. We stepped into a room with a large table that could seat at least forty people. We were the only two in there.

"Sit down here, John. I want to go over this one more time."

After ten minutes of being drilled about how to act and what to say, we were ready. At least I thought I was!

"Okay John, let's go."

I followed the general through the door expecting to see the president. I stopped about three feet inside the room, just far enough not to get hit in the back side by the door closing behind me. I was looking at a room full of high-ranking military officers from every branch of the service. I started to sweat and felt my knees start to shake. The general got my attention and waved me over to where he was standing. He introduced me to at least ten people. There were generals, admirals, vice-admirals and the commander of the Marine Corps. All these men were members of the Joint Chiefs of Staff and of course the secretary of defense was there as well. It's a good thing the general introduced me because my mouth was so dry, I couldn't talk. The general started talking to a couple of these officers and just left me standing there. Thankfully, some middle-aged woman saw my distress. She came over and grabbed my arm. "Come with me, Mr. Northrup."

How in the world did she know my name?

"I'm Mrs. Wingate, secretary to the president. Here, have a glass of water and relax."

"I don't think I'll be relaxing anytime soon."

"John, just remember, these men all put their pants on the same way you do."

"Yes, that might be so, but their pants are a lot more powerful than my pants. How do you know my name?"

"Like I said, I'm the secretary to the president. I know more about what he's doing and who he's meeting with than he does. Trust me, the president doesn't blow his nose without checking with me first."

I had to laugh at that one. "Where is he, and who are all these officers?"

"The president is on the phone. He'll be in soon. The men in this room are all the top leaders of our military."

"Why are they all here? I thought this meeting was with the president, the general and myself."

"From what I understand John, you have some very troubling information for us. The president relies on his Joint Chiefs of Staff to help make decisions on matters like this."

"Glad to hear that, I wouldn't want to make a decision like this on my own. Besides the president, who is the top guy here?"

"Your General Wellington."

"Really! You mean I've been working with the top man in the U.S. military?"

"Yes, you have."

"Well, that explains why everyone jumps when he talks."

"They better, or they'll find themselves stationed in Alaska. You should get back over to the general and don't worry, these guys can't hurt you."

"So, if I mess up, I won't be sent to Alaska?"

"Not unless they draft you first."

"Well, that makes me feel much better."

This old castle would be fun to explore if I weren't afraid of getting shot. As I made my way across the room to the other door, I could see lots of footprints on the dusty floor. No way to tell how old they were. It did however prove that this place had been busy up until recently. The door opened easily and it led to another narrow spiral staircase. I was around halfway down when I heard a voice. I couldn't make out what they were saying, but I could tell they were speaking in German. I speak exceptionally good German. I was just too far away to make out what they were saying. I kept going down one step at a time, stopping to listen for any clue that might tell me what was going on. Two steps from the bottom, I could see into the largest room yet. A quick look around and I could tell this room was being used.

Over by the windows was an old table and chairs. On the floor around the table were many old coffee cups and an assortment of other trash. There had to be dozens of cigarette butts lying with the rest of the garbage left behind. Whoever was using this castle could care less about taking care of it. One of those cigarettes left burning would bring this place to the ground in no time at all. I waited for them to finish their cigarettes and coffee. They finally left the room. I took a slow quiet walk around the room just to get my bearings. I made my way over to the only other door in the room. I stood at the top of the staircase listening for voices or anything that might tell me what was going on. I couldn't hear anything and decided it was safe to start down. This stairway was in good shape. It must have been rebuilt not too long ago.

The next floor down was again bigger than the last one. This room was a little darker than the last two. It only had one small window facing the north. At this time of the year, there was little sunlight coming in. This room was much different than the others. There was a good variety of antique furniture in the room and some old tapestries. It looked to be set up the way it may have been hundreds of years ago. Looking around I found another door leading to another spiral staircase. Didn't they know how to build a straight staircase? These things are hard to get up and down!

This had to be the ground floor. This room was massive and there was a long hallway leading away from me that was completely dark. I'm not going down that hallway! Exploring the room, I found what was a new ramp going down to who-knows-where. I kept working my way around and soon came to the large steel door I had seen from the outside. It was bolted shut and locked. Just as I was turning around, I heard voices coming and luckily, I found a dark corner behind a large stone column. I watched these two men come up the ramp and continue up the staircase. Okay, something's going on down that ramp. Only one way to find out. I started down the ramp, staying close to the wall. The ramp took a sharp right and continued down to the next level. Soon I could hear voices and see lights. The ramp passed through another floor and kept going down. I got off the ramp and started exploring the floor I was on. I could see by the faint light coming up the ramp there was nothing going on at this level. I kept making my way along until I saw the light coming through what appeared to be an overlook to the floor below me. I peered over the ledge and there it was - just what I've been looking for.

I could see what looked to me like two large generators and a third machine at ninety degrees from the generators. There had to be twenty-five or thirty men working on all this equipment. There were wires and hoses running all over the floor leading to the equipment. I wanted a better view, so I kept feeling my way along the wall. I found another overlook and realized all that equipment was mounted to three large flatbed trucks. So, that's how they're doing it! Every time we get close, they just start the trucks and move. I can see at least four men who appeared to be standing guard with automatic weapons. The rest all had on white shop coats and were busy adding to or taking things off the equipment. I was watching for several minutes when I noticed everyone backing away from the machines.

There was a very loud roar and then the generators started to turn. They kept turning faster and faster. I could feel the floor start to vibrate. With all the noise and vibration, dust started falling from the ceiling. Just as I thought the stones would start falling on me and the walls might come apart, they shut the equipment down. Once the noise from the generators subsided, I heard a large cheer from the floor below me. I looked over the edge to see them all slapping each other on the back. It must have been the first time they had run the generators. As I was watching all this, I heard someone yelling in my direction. "What are you doing up there?" I made eye contact with the guy yelling at me. I thought to myself okay stupid you better think fast. You've been made! So, in my best German, I yelled back, "taking pictures." Wrong answer! His response to my answer was "Idiot, no pictures!" He and his partner headed for the ramp. This was not going to turn out good. I needed to get out of there and fast!

Chapter 25

A few minutes later, that gentle lady spoke out with a surprisingly loud voice. "Gentleman, the President." Everyone in the room came to attention as the President came into the room. I just stood there transfixed by the fact that I was in a room with the most powerful men in the world. And now the president of the United States had just walked into the room. I was just a little bit intimidated by where I was. The president walked in like he owned the place. Oh, that's right he does. He told everyone to be at ease and headed for a chair at the head of a large table. Everyone knew where to sit. I suppose it was by rank. I had no idea who outranked who. There was so much silver and gold hanging on these guys, how could you tell? The general all but yanked me off my feet as we headed to where the president was sitting.

"Sit right here, behind me. I will introduce you when it's time."

The general was seated on the right side of the president and the secretary of defense was on the president's left. There were two Marine guards fully armed just ten feet behind the president. I hadn't seen them come in, but there they were big as life. I really wished I were someplace else! The president asked half a dozen questions and got straight no bullshit answers. These guys knew what was expected of them and you could tell they took their responsibilities seriously, and no questions asked. The president wrote down some notes and then turned to General Wellington.

"General, please tell us what the hell is going on in Germany."

"Yes sir, Mr. President. As you know, we've been watching a man by the name of Conrad Mueller. We have felt for some time now that he is not only a threat to Germany, but also to the rest of the world. He is a powerful man with a great deal of wealth. He has many allies around the world and, as best we can tell, thousands of sympathizers within Germany. We know he has his people in several police departments throughout Germany and some high-ranking individuals within Germany's army. He hates both the US and Russia and he has sworn to bring Germany back to the days of Hitler and ultimately to be the only superpower in the world. Mr. President, this guy is a nutcase, but a highly intelligent one and as dangerous as they come."

"Why has he become a priority for us now?"

"Mr. President, we didn't see him as much of a threat until about six months ago. His people are incredibly good at covering their tracks. We found them following the research of Professor Paul Northrup. At first, we didn't know why. We have been supporting Professor Northrup's research for over twenty years in conjunction with Cal Tech in California. His invention for creating clean energy was way ahead of anything anyone else has. Over five years ago, we put him in his own lab. He kept getting closer to something we believe could benefit the defense of this country.

"Wait a minute, General. I thought he was just trying to create new forms of clean energy?"

"Yes, Mr. President. He was. We asked him to try something a little different."

"What was that?"

"Let me explain a little more. Professor Northrup was able to direct a beam of electricity to a large collector. We asked him to see just how far he could control that beam. In time he told us it could theoretically be controlled for a thousand miles.

"That's incredible! So how does it work?"

"Mr. President, that is beyond me. That's why I brought his son, John Northrup here to explain how all this came to be."

"That's fine, but why didn't you bring his father?"

"I will let John explain that as well. Mr. President, this is John Northrup."

Right up to that point I was so busy listening to the General I forgot I was going to have to talk. I stood up and shook the president's hand.

"Hello, Mr. President, I'm John Northrup. It's a privilege to meet you."

I was shaking so bad I could barely get the words out. The president laughed and said "John. Take a deep breath and relax. Just tell us what you know."

"Yes sir, Mr. President. Mr. President, the general is right. This is an immensely powerful device. If it gets used the wrong way and gets out of control, it will be catastrophic. It has the potential to kill millions of people. This Conrad Mueller guy has no idea what he has. We need to stop him at all costs."

"Hold on there, John. I understand there is an urgency to this. The general has already convinced us of that. You and the general are the only ones in the room that understand this machine, how it works and how it came to be so dangerous. So again, slow down and tell us from the beginning just how we got here."

"Yes sir, let me start over. This all started before I was even born."

Chapter 26

Apparently, those two guards didn't think I was much of a threat. Just a worker trying to take pictures that he wasn't supposed to. I ran back to the ramp since it was my only way out. I looked down the ramp and I didn't see them coming up yet. I headed up the ramp to the next floor. This was the ground floor as best I could tell. I hadn't found any way in from the outside, so it made sense I wasn't going to find a way out from the inside. I ran to the door leading upstairs. I opened the door to find myself staring at a huge closet. What the hell? Where's the door to the staircase? I turned around and saw three other doors. Which one? I didn't have time to check them all. My best guess. It had to be the smallest one. Of course, it was on the other side of the room. I headed for it, but it took me right past the ramp. I figured the guards found out I wasn't where they had seen me.

As I passed by the ramp, I could see the top of their heads. They were moving a little faster now. I made it to the door and got into the staircase just as they were reaching the top of the ramp. I made it up to the next floor before I heard them yell. They weren't sure if I had gone up there or not. I knew they were expecting me to answer them. Not likely! I had a few minutes before they figured out that I'm not down where they are. I could block this door. That would slow them down, but it will also tell them I don't want to be found. This room is full of old furniture, but nothing I can use as a weapon. I need to keep moving. My only choice is to go up. I was only five steps up the staircase when a very deep voice said, "Back up!"

I had completely forgotten about the two men that had gone past me earlier. One of them was staring me right in the face. "Back up!" he said again. He was speaking German, but I understood what he was saying. I had no choice but to back down and step aside. When he got down to eye level, I was glad I let him pass. He had to be six four and weigh 300 pounds. He took a long look at me and said "Who are you?"

I told him I was a new truck driver.

"What's your name?"

I gave him a bogus name as quick as I could think of one.

"Where's your badge?"

I could see he had one. I told him I just got here and that they were making one up for me.

"Why are you up here?"

"They told me I could smoke up here."

"Okay, but go up to the next floor. No smoking down here."

I said thanks and kept heading up the stairs. I knew there was one more guy I would have to deal with. I'm not too worried about him. It's the guy going down that has me worried. When he runs into the guards, I don't think my story will hold up awfully long. I was right!

I made it up to the next floor. As I stepped into the room, I found the second guy. He was staring out the window smoking a cigarette. Without turning around, he said "Did you forget something?"

When I didn't answer he turned around and dropped his cigarette. "Who are you?"

I could tell from his tone of voice that he was not as friendly as the last guy. He started across the room towards me. I felt my best move was to meet him halfway. He stopped not two feet from me.

I started my story all over again, but he wasn't buying it. He reached for a radio and pushed the button to talk. I couldn't let him talk to anyone! I had to take this guy out. Just as my first punch was about to land, he reacted and turned away. My first punch didn't have much effect on him. He came right back at me with a good punch of his own. He caught me in the rib cage. I took a small step back and then charged right at him. We both went flying across the room and into the table. It was an old table and came apart as we landed on it. I heard the air go out of him as we hit the table. A piece of the table broke off and caught me right in the shoulder, sending me rolling across the floor. We both got to our feet at the same time. He picked up a piece of the table and threw it at me. I ducked to the side as the piece of the table hit the wall behind me. Just as I turned to face him, a chair came flying in my direction. Okay, this guy is starting to make me angry. I took a quick step to the right letting the chair go by. I leaped forward and in three quick steps I was on him, driving him into the wall. We hit hard, but he pushed me right back and took a swing at my head. I ducked his punch and came back with an uppercut right to his chin. That slowed him down enough to land another punch right square in his face. He went down hard and I hit him one more time just to make sure he stayed down. I was sure he wasn't getting up this time. I rolled the man over and could see he was bleeding from his nose and his mouth. He was semi-conscious, but there was no fight left in him. I needed something to tie him up with. There was nothing around, so I pulled his belt off, rolled him over and tied his hands behind him. I had barely finished tying him up when I heard voices coming up the stairs. They didn't sound friendly! Time to leave! But where to?

I started heading for the staircase leading to the next floor. Just as I got to the staircase, it hit me. This is a staircase to nowhere. There's no place up there to go. Even if I make it to the top, I'll never be able to climb down fast enough to keep from being shot. I could hear them getting closer as they came up the staircase. Then it hit me, that narrow winding staircase. I ran over to the man I just tied up. I dragged him over to the door. Just as the guards were getting near the top, I picked the guy up and pushed him down the staircase. I saw the first guard point his gun in my direction. He got off a couple poorly aimed shots just as the half-conscious body hit him and sent him falling backwards down the stairs. There was no way two people could get by each other on that staircase, so for once I was glad the staircase was so narrow. It bought me a little more time.

Going up was out of the question. There was no going down against the guards. I ran to the window and looked out at the river. It was a hell of a long way down. I wasn't sure I could even jump out far enough to not hit the rocks at the bottom. Time was running out and I could hear footsteps again coming up the staircase. I climbed up on the edge of the window and leaned out. My heart was pounding and I could feel the adrenaline pulsing through my body. I heard gunshots just as I jumped out. I pushed out as hard as my legs would let me. I felt myself falling face down. I knew from all my training jumps in ranger school that this was not the way to fall. If I hit the water face first, it would kill me for sure. I raised my hands up and out in front of me. I felt myself start to straighten up. Halfway down, I was almost straight up and down the way I wanted to be. It felt like I was doing over a hundred miles an hour when I hit the water. I hit leaning back a little too far. The water ripped my shirt and jacket right up over my head. It felt like my arms were yanked right out of their sockets. I was barely conscious from the impact. I tried to move my arms, but they weren't cooperating and try as I might they were barely moving. I could feel the current pulling me down stream. I need air. My lungs are burning, but which way is up? I'm starting to black out. This is not the way I want to die.

Chapter 27

"Mr. President, it all started after my mother took my father to a Save The Earth rally. He became obsessed with finding a way to produce clean energy. My father's goal was to bring us to a point where we could stop using fossil fuel. His first attempt was trying to harness the energy in lightning. After years of work on that with the help of scientists at Cal Tech, he found that even though you could harness that energy, it would never be able to produce enough electricity to really help. Realistically, it wouldn't even cover the cost of building the stations. However, two especially important discoveries came out of all that work. One was the battery that the army now uses in all their equipment. One of those batteries, which is the size of a car battery, can power a car for up to six months. One four times that size could run a tank for a month without being recharged."

"Excuse me, John. General, why haven't I heard about this?"

"Mr. President, I will explain that later."

"I will look forward to that conversation! John, please continue."

"Yes sir. The other discovery to come out of the first attempt was a large collector."

"What is a collector, if I may ask?"

"Mr. President, believe it or not, harnessing lightning was not all that difficult. The real challenge is controlling that lightning. Collecting it and retaining it in something that can absorb it in a millisecond was a much bigger problem. Until you solve that problem, there's no reason to try to collect any lightning. My father was able to do just that. He built a device that not only could absorb all that voltage, but also turn it into usable wattage. My father just called it a collector."

"John, your father is a genius. What he's done is remarkable!"

"Yes sir, he was a genius."

"What do you mean he was?"

"Mr. President, my father died in that lab the general told you about."

"Sorry to hear that, John. I would have liked to meet him. Where is all the equipment he developed?"

"Sir, the army owns it. Everything my father ever did the army now owns."

"General, it sounds like you and I have a lot more to talk about."

"Yes, sir, Mr. President."

"John, please continue."

"Yes, sir. After my father resigned himself to the fact that lightning was not going to fill the need, he came up with another crazy idea. He believed he could make his own electricity and store it in a collector. Lightning is nothing more than static electricity. Simply put it occurs when positive and negative particles build up in clouds until a charge is released in the form of lightning. It can be cloud to ground or ground to cloud lightning. But reproducing this in a lab under a controlled environment is another matter. Theoretically, you can make your own electricity. He was able to use one generator to produce a positive charge and another generator to produce a negative charge. When the charge is released, you get a lightning bolt."

"Excuse me again John, but that doesn't seem possible, and how could you control it? Is that what killed your father?"

"No sir, that's not what killed him. I will get to that. Controlling it also was not that hard. After working with my father off and on for almost three years, I kind of walked away from it. We didn't really see eye-to-eye on where this was going. We hadn't really gotten anywhere in the time I spent with him. Several months later, he convinced me to look at one more idea. It worked! On a small scale in the lab at Cal Tech, he produced more power out of two small generators than what went into them. After that, it was just a matter of doing it on a larger scale."

"Sorry for asking again John, but how did you control the lightning bolt?"

"That sir was the genius of my father! At this point in the development, Cal Tech wanted my father to leave. General Wellington pretty much took over control of my father's work and built him his own lab."

"Why in the world did Cal Tech ask him to leave?"

"Mr. President, that's a story for another day."

"Very well, please continue."

"We tried dozens of ways to control the beam, but nothing worked. Then, out of nowhere my father came up with the idea of using high pressure air. The first few attempts didn't work. We discovered that by introducing tiny little aluminum flakes into the air stream, the beam just followed along and pretty much in a straight line."

"Excuse me again, John. How straight and how far?"

"Funny you should ask. That's just what the army asked us. The answer is very straight, but how far? We're not sure. We never really got to test that. We believe it could be as far as a thousand miles or more."

"Wait a minute. You're telling me you can control a bolt of electricity for a thousand miles?"

"In theory, yes. That may sound like a long way, but consider the fact that lightning travels at the rate of 320 million feet per minute. That's a little over six thousand miles in one second. So, you see, you only have to direct the beam in a straight line for a millisecond to hit something a thousand miles away."

"Oh my God! Is all this true, John?"

"I'm afraid so, sir."

"There was a long pause in the room. I think everyone stopped breathing. Finally, the president asked "Could this be used as a weapon?"

"Yes sir, it could."

"General, you said Germany has one of these things."

"No sir, not Germany. A man named Conrad Mueller has it."

"Excuse me Mr. President."

"What is it, John?"

"I don't care who has it! No one can ever be allowed to use it! It could kill millions of innocent people! It killed my father!"

"Gentleman. I need a few minutes. General Wellington, please come to my office."

"Yes sir."

"The rest of you, meet back here in twenty minutes. Gentlemen, everything you heard here today stays here, understand!" There was a lot of head nodding.

"John, you come with me and the general."

After hitting the water, I was quite sure I was dead. I could hear angels talking, but they're speaking in German. Is that possible? German-speaking angels. I tried opening my eyes, but all I could see was darkness. I thought heaven was all about light. Maybe I went the other way. It feels like I have a heavy blanket on me. I tried to push it off, but the minute I tried to move my arms, severe pain shot through both shoulders. Someone pushed it right back down on me. Feeling that much pain, I knew I was still alive! I could hear a conversation, but it didn't make sense to me. "No, no, not today. Just feed for our horses." Little did I know, the two ladies handling this horse-drawn wagon were answering two armed men who were asking if they had seen anyone along the river today. They wanted to see what was in the wagon, but these two ladies put up such a fuss, they just let them go.

As I found out later, these ladies had been down to the river getting water for the horses. When I came floating by, they pulled me out of the water, put me in the wagon and wrapped a big horse blanket around me. The two men left and we continued down the road. Not too much later we pulled into an old barn. Once they closed the doors and locked them, they uncovered me.

"Who are you and how did you fall into the river?" Both ladies were standing in the wagon with me. One had a shovel in her hand and the other one a pitchfork. I knew I better come up with a good answer.

"My name is Herman Schmitt. I was fishing up the river near some rocks and I fell in and hit my head. Thank you for pulling me out."

"Where do you live, Mr. Schmitt?"

"I live in a little town in Austria. I'm here on holiday to fish."

"Are you here alone?"

"Yes."

"Where are your clothes and your shoes?"

"They must have come off in the river. There's a fast current in that river."

For a long minute, I didn't know if I was going to get hit with a shovel or stabbed with a pitchfork, or both. Finally, they smiled and said, "Come to the house and we will find you some clothes and give you something to eat."

Just as I went to get up, a pain shot through both shoulders and my leg. I looked at my leg and saw a long cut running down the outside of my right leg. It wasn't that deep, but it hurt like hell. I guess I didn't miss all the rocks when I jumped. The two ladies helped me out of the wagon and into the house. They closed the door, locked it and covered up the windows. I asked them why they did that.

The older woman said, "Men have been nosing around since yesterday and asking everyone about a man they're looking for. Are you that man?"

How do I answer them now? "No, I'm not. I told you I was just fishing."

"Okay, we believe you."

"Why do they want this man anyway?"

She said, "He stole something from the castle up the river. We know they're lying. There hasn't been anything of value in that castle for over fifty years. They aren't the police either. We don't know who they are. Something very strange is going on in that castle."

"What do you mean?"

"It's all locked up and no one knows why. That castle has been wide open since I was a little girl. Now, for some reason, it's locked up. It's not the only one either."

"What do you mean, it's not the only one?"

"My friend sent me a letter telling me about another castle that was locked up, but now it's open again. No one knows what went on there."

"Where is the other castle?"

"Way up the river from here. Why do you ask so many questions?"

"No reason. I was simply curious."

The ladies took incredibly good care of me that night. They bandaged my leg and got me a good set of clothes. They fed me more than I could eat. I knew I had to get out of there. I have information the general needs to hear. I'll rest here tonight, but then I've got to get moving. I intended to be up and gone before the ladies woke up. When I woke up, I could hear both ladies in the kitchen making breakfast. As I rolled over to get up, the pain and stiffness made me lay right back down again. Okay, tough guy, you may need one more day of rest here. One of the ladies came in and helped me out of bed and into the kitchen. I asked if they had a phone I could use and they just laughed. "No phone here. You will have to go into town to use a phone."

"Herr Hellman. You have a call coming in."

"Who is it?"

"I don't know. He wouldn't say and he would only speak to you."

"Very well. I will take the call in the office. Keep your men moving! I want this building cleared out by tomorrow night."

"Yes sir."

"Von Hellman here. Who is this?"

"Lieutenant Albert Kraus. I'm overseeing the installation at location one."

"Yes, I know who you are and what you're doing! Is there a problem?"

"I'm not sure. There could be."

"Tell me what is happening!"

"Yes sir. Two of our guards saw someone taking pictures of our work. They chased him to the top of our building where he got into a fight with one of our workers. The worker said he beat him up pretty bad, but when the guards got up to that floor, he was still able to jump out the window."

"Did they get his camera away from him?"

"No one saw any camera. We don't think he really had one."

"Have you caught him yet?"

"No sir. We believe he died when he hit the river. I don't believe anybody could survive that fall."

"I don't care what you believe, Kraus! I want him found."

"Yes sir. I understand. We have been looking for him up and down the river. We found a jacket we believe he was wearing and one of his shoes. We found both items down river from our location."

"Then it makes sense to keep looking down the river."

"Yes sir. We will find him."

"Were you able to identify the jacket? Was it a police officer's jacket or an army jacket?"

"No way to tell sir. There are no markings on it whatsoever."

"How did he get in the building in the first place?"

"It doesn't seem possible, but we believe he climbed the north wall and got in through a small window at the top of the building."

That's highly unlikely. I've been to your location many times and there's no way anyone climbed in from the north side. Keep looking. He must have found another way in. I want this man found. If he's not dead when you find him, bring him to me. I will find out what he knows and then I'll kill him myself. Kraus, double your guard!"

"Yes sir, Von Hellman!"

We stepped out of the conference room right into the Oval Office.

"General, I can't begin to tell you how disturbed I am by what I've just heard."

"I understand Mr. President. I haven't slept well for some time now."

"John, didn't your father realize how dangerous this thing could be?"

"Sir, my father never thought or planned on this becoming a weapon. His soul intent was to make clean energy. That's all. The army were the ones that wanted to make it into a weapon."

"That's not true. We only wanted it for defensive purposes."

"You keep saying that general, but you know perfectly well when the time comes, you would use it as a weapon!"

"Alright you two. That's enough. Arguing about it now won't help us at all. We need to find a way to stop this guy."

"John, tell me what happens when this thing blows up."

"Mr. President, it doesn't blow up like a bomb. We don't know for sure because no one was there to see it at the time, only my father and it killed him. In the lab, my father could send the electrical beam to the collector and it would store the energy with no problem. I saw this happen long before the accident. The problem occurs when you put too much power into the beam and then it becomes unstable and less directed. We believe when that happens, the beam becomes a huge fireball for lack of a better description."

"So, what happens to this fireball?"

"Sir, this is no ordinary fireball. It feeds on itself, burning up the very oxygen around it and then we think it just keeps going from there. This fireball burned the very air inside my father's lungs. That's what killed him."

"I'm so sorry, John. It sounds like an awful way to die."

"Thank you, sir. We believe it was quick. I don't believe he suffered very long."

"So, how do we put this fireball out?"

"I don't believe we can. Like I said, this is not like anything you've ever seen. The temperature of this fireball is over 53,000 degrees Fahrenheit. That's four times the surface of the sun. Even if it were possible to get close enough to spray water on it, it would evaporate long before it ever hit the surface of the fireball."

"You're telling me there's no way to stop it?"

"Yes, sir. That's what we've been trying to tell you. The only way to stop it is to not let it happen in the first place."

"General, I understand how dangerous this is now. I'm not sure how to tell the German chancellor about this."

"Sir, I wouldn't worry about how. It's more important when you tell him. Time is not on our side!"

"Yes, I will call him right after the meeting ends. Let's get back in there. I want the Joint Chiefs of Staff to hear just what you told me. Maybe they will have some good ideas."

"Sorry, Mr. President, but I don't think they will have a clue as to what to do."

"That may be so, but at this point I'm just grabbing at straws."

We went back into the conference room.

"Gentleman, please have a seat. John, please tell them just what you told me.

After about fifteen minutes of repeating what I had told the President, I asked if there were any questions. There were a lot of pale faces at the table, then one of the officers asked "If this fireball gets started, where will it stop?"

"The only thing we know is that if there is oxygen to burn, it may just keep going."

"How fast will it move?"

"Faster than anything you've ever seen." There were no more questions and I saw some tears on some very distraught faces.

"Gentleman, we're done here for now. Keep what you have heard here today to yourselves for the time being. I will get back to you when I have more information to share with you."

"General, let's go make that call."

"Yes sir. John, come with us."

Just as we stepped back into the Oval Office, the president's secretary came in from another door. "General Wellington, you have a call waiting for you and he said it was very urgent."

"Who is it?"

"He said his name is Mansfield. He said you would want this information."

"Yes, I need to speak with him. Please put him through here in the office."

"Hello Bill. What did you find out?"

"It's not good, General. They shipped six generators. That's enough to make three of these devices."

"We thought one was bad enough. Now you're telling me this maniac can make three of these things?"

"Yes, sir. I'm afraid so."

"Okay, Bill. Get back here as soon as you can."

"Will do, General. I also have a copy of the wiring diagram. I thought it might be helpful in some way. I will see you soon, General."

From the look on the General's face, I knew it wasn't good news.

After breakfast, the ladies helped me to a big chair in front of a window with a nice view of the landscape around the house. They went out to the barn to feed and water their horses and other animals. Not long after, I could hear arguing coming from the barn. I managed to get up to have a look. Two armed men were standing outside the barn asking questions. They wanted to search the barn. The older sister, as I found out later, had a pitchfork in her hand and was pointing it at one of the men. He took a step back, pulled out his pistol and aimed it right at her head. The younger sister stepped in front of him and said they could search the barn. As the two men went into the barn, the sisters began arguing. They got louder and louder and got a little out of control. I knew the two men would want to search the house next. I started looking for a place to hide. This was a small house. There was one large room that served as a kitchen and living room, two bedrooms and a large closet that was their pantry. No bathroom, that was outside by the barn. No back door and no way out. In my shape, there's no way I can take on two armed men. The two men came out of the barn and to my surprise just started watching the sisters fight and argue. They laughed a little and then headed down the road. When the sisters came back in, I asked them what the men wanted.

"Same as the last three times they talked to us. They're looking for a man that stole something from the castle."

The older sister looked at me for a long time, then said "They're looking for you, aren't they?"

I could have tried to stay with my story, but the stunned look on my face gave me away. Now, the younger sister stepped right in front of me and asked, "What did you steal?"

Just out of pure reflex, I said "Nothing!" That was stupid. Now they know it's me. Even if I wanted to stick with my story, it was too late. The only question now is how much I tell them. I walked over to the table and sat down. The sisters sat down across from me and their stares were cutting right through me.

"My name is not Herman Schmidt, it's Neil Clement." I couldn't tell them my real name. "I'm here on special assignment to track down a man named Conrad Mueller."

At the sound of his name, they both sat back in their chairs. I asked them "Does that name mean something to you?"

"Yes, he's an unbelievably bad man. We think he's the one that closed the castle."

"Why do you think that?"

"Because everyone knows he's trying to hurt our country. Every time we go into town, we hear what he is saying. That Germany is weak and must take control of its own destiny. He wants to get us into another war. We like our country just the way it is. He's an unbelievably bad man, but some people like him and what he's saying. We have heard that he bribes people to get what he wants, even the police. No one wants to stand up to him and they're all afraid of him. We have heard that some people that had challenged him have just disappeared."

"That's the reason I'm here, he needs to be stopped. Is there anything else you can tell me about him?"

"Yes, he has many men working for him, and they all carry guns. How are you going to stop him?"

"I hope with the help of your government. I believe your government will be willing to help, once they find out what he is up to."

"They should help you. They don't like him either. He tried to get into our government and they made him leave. What government are you working for?"

"I can't say right now, but when this is over, I will come back and I'll tell you everything. Right now, I need to get to a phone."

"We will take you into town in the morning. You need to rest today. It's a long ride into town. It takes all day to go there and get back before dark."

I was in no position to argue and I did need the rest. I hope my men never find out I was rescued by two old ladies.

"This is Von Hellman calling. I wish to speak to Herr Mueller."

"Yes, I will get him for you."

"Good day to you General Hellman. What can I do for you?"

"I wanted to tell you about a spy that was discovered at location one."

"I put Kraus in charge of that site. Why are you there?"

"I am not there. I'm still at the old warehouse making sure it's cleaned out and destroyed. Kraus called me to tell me about the spy."

"Kraus is a good man. Was he able to catch the spy?"

"No, he escaped by jumping out a window near the top of the building and fell into the river."

"Did they find the body?"

"No, they have been looking for two days now."

"I would think a fall from that high would kill any man."

"Yes, sir, but I told Kraus to keep looking just in case."

"Very well. Have them keep looking for one more day. Then don't waste any more time on the spy. I'm sure he's dead anyway."

"Yes, Herr Mueller."

"How is the cleanup coming?"

"Not as fast as I would like. If we go ahead with the destruction of the building tomorrow night, there may still be some small amount of equipment in it."

"It will not matter what is left. Just stay with the plan and blow it up tomorrow night."

"Yes, sir."

"Did Kraus say how the installation is coming at site one?"

"No sir, he did not mention it."

"You will be at that site the day after tomorrow, won't you?"

"Yes, that is my plan."

"Very well then. After you have checked it out, give me a call. I want to know if Kraus is on schedule."

"Yes, Herr Mueller."

"I will call you in two days."

"Miss Wingate, please get the German chancellor on the line for me."

"Yes, sir, right away."

The president retorted to the general. "General, this is not going to be an easy phone call to make. The last time we talked I'm afraid I was a little rough on the chancellor. He can be a little stubborn when he wants to be."

"Yes, sir, Mr. President. I understand, but regardless of how upset or stubborn he might be, he needs to know what could happen."

"General, is your man still in Germany?"

"Yes sir. The last time I spoke with him he was nosing around a castle trying to find out what was going on inside."

"When was the last time you spoke to him?"

"Two days ago. He should be calling in anytime now."

"When he does, I want to know what he found."

"Yes sir."

"Miss Wingate, have you reached the German chancellor yet?"

"No sir, they are trying to reach him. Apparently, he is on a holiday."

"A holiday? What holiday?"

"A vacation, sir. They call it a holiday when they go on vacation."

"Well, they must have a way to reach him. Make sure you tell them this is a case of international importance."

"I will, sir."

"Wouldn't you know it! I need to talk to him about the most important thing he will ever face and he's off fishing or something."

"Yes sir, timing is everything."

"John, I have to ask you one more time. Is this thing as bad as you say?"

"Yes, sir, Mr. President. I wouldn't lie to you. It's really that bad."

"Okay, thank you for being honest. I just had to hear it one more time."

"General, how many men do you have in Germany?"

"Only one man, Brad Johnson. The rest of his squad is in Austria waiting for orders."

"Who's the number two man in the squad?"

"His name is Blowing Wind."

The president started to laugh just a little and then asked, "Is that his real name?"

"Yes, sir. He's 100% Cherokee Indian, and one tough son of a bitch! They call him Chief."

"With a name like Blowing Wind, he better be one tough son of a bitch. Is he any good?"

"He's the only man Lieutenant Johnson would trust with his squad."

"Okay then, that's good enough for me. I may want to send them back to that warehouse if I need to prove this to the chancellor."

"Yes sir."

"Excuse me, Mr. President," Miss Wingate interrupted.

"Yes, what is it, Miss Wingate?"

"They told me that the Chancellor will call you back at his convenience."

"What the hell is that supposed to mean?"

"I'm not sure sir, but I will let you know when he calls."

"Fine. Let me know the minute he calls."

"Yes, sir."

"General, I told you he was upset with me after the last time we spoke. That stubborn arrogant son of a bitch. It's a good thing there's not a bloody war going on right now! He'd miss the whole thing! At his convenience, who the hell does he think he is? I'll give him convenience. Just wait until the next time he wants something from me. He can just sit on his ass and wait until it's convenient for me. He's doing this just to make me angry!"

"Yes, sir, but if he knew why we were calling, I'm sure he would have taken the call.

"I'm not so sure. We told him it was an international emergency and he still didn't take the call. He doesn't even know what's going on in his own damn country! Let's hope he calls back in a few minutes."

We spent the next two and a half hours waiting for his call. The president got madder by the minute. I would never have thought the president of our country knew so many swear words. Everything people had told me about his temper was true and then some! The general tried to calm him down, but only managed to get caught up in the president's tirade himself. I just sat in the corner and kept my head down. Finally, the call came in.

"Sir, I have the chancellor on the phone."

"Thank you. Please put him through." The president took a long deep breath and with a remarkably calm voice said, "Hello Mr. Chancellor. Thank you for calling me back."

"Good day to you Mr. President. Sorry I couldn't take your call earlier. I was tied up with something important."

"Yes, sir. I'm sure you were. Mr. Chancellor, I have some very disturbing information for you."

"Yes, what is it?"

"You may want your military leaders to hear this as well."

"I will decide if they need to hear it. What is your concern Mr. President?"

"Mr. Chancellor, do you know a man named Conrad Mueller?"

"Yes. I know Conrad. Why do you ask?"

"We have been tracking him for some time now. We believe he is a great threat to Germany and even to the rest of the world."

"I assure you Mr. President, if he were a threat to Germany, I would know about it. I know all about this man, about the things he has said and the things he has tried to do. He has no real power to do anything to Germany or anyone else. He just likes to hear himself talk. Trust me, he's no threat."

"I'm sorry Mr. Chancellor, but you're wrong! He's building a weapon that could very well destroy Germany and other countries as well."

"What kind of weapon could he have that we don't know about?"

"It's a machine that was never meant to be a weapon. He's turning it into one. He has it in Germany right now. In fact, we think he has the ability to build three of them."

"Mr. President, how is it you know so much about Mueller and what he's doing here in Germany?"

"Mr. Chancellor, please let me explain. We started watching Mueller and his men here in the states almost a year ago. They were stealing information on this machine and sending it overseas to England and then on to some place in Germany. We followed them for months and tracked them back to Germany. We wanted to get more information on them before we called you."

"Mr. President. Are you telling me that you have men working undercover in my country and I'm just now hearing about it?"

"Yes, that's correct, but only to collect information."

"I shouldn't be surprised! You think because you are the United States of America you have the right to do whatever you want to whomever you please. We are a sovereign country and you have no right to be in our country without our permission. I'm ordering you to remove your people immediately. If he has a weapon and this is truly a threat, we will handle it. Goodbye Mr. President."

"Damn it! He hung up on me! Mrs. Wingate, try to get him back on the line."

"Yes, sir, right away."

"General, do you know any of their military leaders?"

"Not very well, sir. We have a missile base there, but we kind of leave them alone and they do the same to us. My best connection would be through Lieutenant Johnson. He's helped train some of their special forces' units."

"Well, call your lieutenant and see if there's someone he can talk to. Tell him to share all this information with whomever he talks to. Maybe they can convince the Chancellor to work with us on this mess."

"Sir, I can't call the lieutenant right now. He is out of touch right now. I have to wait for him to call in."

"Okay, I'll give you until this time tomorrow. If he doesn't call, I want that Indian guy, Blowing Wind, to take that squad back into Germany and find him."

"Sir, with what the chancellor just said, is that a good idea?"

"I don't give a damn what he said. He doesn't know what he's up against and he won't listen. He's a damn fool! Twenty-four hours, and then I want those men back in Germany. Got it!"

"Yes, sir!"

Next morning, I woke up hearing the ladies in the kitchen once again. The thought of another fine country breakfast with these ladies was okay with me. I was able to get myself out of bed and into the kitchen. I was still sore, but moving much better. After breakfast, the ladies started to boil water and put it in a large tub. I needed to get going and now they're going to take a bath? I got up to go outside, but they started yelling at me. "This is for you. You need a bath. You smell like the river." I tried to protest, but after a few minutes I knew it was a losing battle. These ladies were something else. They insisted on helping me get out of my clothes and into the tub. I was a little embarrassed, but they didn't bat an eye.

That hot water sure did feel good. They took the clothes they had given me and gave me another set of fresh ones. I don't know why they had all these men's clothes, but they fit me well. About an hour later, we were in the wagon and headed for town. I hadn't been in a horse-drawn wagon since I was a little boy on my grandfather's farm. I forgot how slow the ride was. We hadn't been on the road for more than ten minutes when we passed another house. A young lady came running out asking if we were headed to town. Twenty minutes later they finally stopped talking.

The young lady handed them a list with some money, so they could pick up the items and bring them back from town.

This happened twice more. Two other times, people stopped us just to talk and catch up on all the local gossip. This trip into town and back surely would not take all day if it weren't for all the stopping and visiting. Every time someone asked who I was, I became a second cousin from a little town in Austria. We finally got into town. They took me to an older building that served as a post office where there was a phone I could use. Inside the building were a half a dozen older townspeople that were just standing around talking. The ladies asked if I could possibly use the phone. The man behind the counter took a hard look at me and then put the phone on the counter top. He asked me who I was calling and stood there waiting for an answer. I did my best to be polite and told him it was personal. He just looked at me and said three dollars. I didn't have a penny on me, but before I could say anything, one of the ladies reached into her pocket and paid the three dollars for me. Thank you. I owe you.

As I was dialing, I realized everyone was watching me. This was not going to be a private conversation. The first person I reached was an international operator and when the little group of people realized that I was calling the U.S., they all took a little step closer. I gave the operator the number and told her I needed to speak with General Wellington. She put me through, but he didn't answer. That was not like him at all. I had forgotten about the time difference between Germany and the US, but that has never made a difference in the past. He always answered by the second ring. I asked her to try again, but there still was no answer. Now what? I had to get through to him. I told the operator I was one of the general's top men and this was an emergency. I had information the general had to have. I will stay by this phone until you reach him and put him through to me. She assured me she would keep trying until she got through. I put the phone down and when I turned around there were a lot of wide-eyed stares coming from everyone in the room, including the ladies that had helped me. I was going to have a lot more explaining to do to my two lady hosts.

I waited in that little building for the next three hours. By then, the ladies had caught up on all the latest gossip and had purchased all the items they needed as well as things for the neighbors. The ladies were ready to leave and I really didn't have a choice. I had to go with them. If the general hadn't called by now, he probably wasn't going to. On the way back, I kept trying to think of who else I could contact. I couldn't reach my squad. The only way to reach them was with a radio and I had left it in the car I had rented. I could try to get back to where I left it, but it would be too far to walk with my bad leg. The ladies were ready to go. It was getting dark by the time we got back. I helped them unhitch the wagon and put the horses in the barn. Then I had an idea. I asked the ladies if I could take one of the horses and go find my car. They really didn't want to let me, but I think after hearing me on the phone today they realized how badly I needed to talk to the general.

They didn't have a saddle for the horse, so I threw a couple of blankets on him and off I went. The ladies told me to stay on this road and it would take me back to the castle. I had left the car around three miles this side of the castle. Hours later, I still hadn't found my car and still hadn't seen the castle. I was stiff and sore from riding this horse, so I decided to get off and walk for a while. Big mistake! Ten minutes later my leg was throbbing and I was walking slower with each step. I had forgotten I was standing in the wagon when I got on this horse. No way I was going to get on him by jumping up on his back. This was a Morgan plow horse and they are huge. I tried to find something to stand on, but out in the country and dark as it was, I couldn't find anything.

I tried twice to jump on his back, but with nothing to hold onto and with the blankets slipping off, it was impossible. I gave up getting on the horse and walking was out of the question. I had all but given up when that crazy horse laid down. Great! Now he's quitting. I slowly began to wonder...did he lay down for me? I had seen this once in a movie where the horse laid down, the injured girl got on his back and the horse stood up. Only one way to find out. I slowly put my good leg over the horse and took hold of the reins. I pulled back a little and said "Okay boy. Let's go." I don't know if he was reading my mind, but he stood up and off we went. It was hard to tell in the dark, but roughly two hours later I felt I was where I had left the car.

Big surprise! No car. I didn't think I would be that lucky. I started back down the road. Every bone in my body hurt, but I had to get back. I started falling asleep. Try as I might, I couldn't keep my eyes open. I leaned against the horse's neck and tried to rest and when I woke up, I realized the horse had stopped walking. I tried to get him moving again, but he wouldn't budge. I looked around and realized I was back. That horse had brought me all the way back without any help from me. We were standing between the house and the barn. I could see a faint sign of daylight and the lights were on in the kitchen. The ladies must be up making breakfast. I slid down off the horse and fell right to the ground. My legs were numb from being on the horse for the last ten hours. The horse turned and went and stood in front of the barn door. I will never call them a dumb animal again. I half walked, half crawled to the house. I knocked on the door and yelled to tell them who I was.

"John, I am afraid you're going to have to hang around for a few more days."

"General. You told me one day was all you needed me for."

"Yes, but we haven't convinced the chancellor to help us. I may still need you here to do that when he calls back."

"Why do I need to stay when you can have one of your own people talk to him? They know just as much as I do."

"I told you before, John. They have been reassigned. Besides, what could be more important than helping to stop this guy? What you don't understand is that in the army we have a thing called strategic planning. That means you always work on more than one plan at a time. In this case we have an A, B, and C plan. The engineers that worked with you are now working on Plan B.

"So, what's Plan B?"

"I'm sure you've heard the term fight fire with fire."

"Yes, I've heard the term."

"Well, that's the plan. We're going to fight fire with fire if we have to."

"General, am I to understand that you're building your own static charging machine to fight them with?"

"In a way, yes."

"That's lunacy, you can't do that! What if you build one of these things and it does just what my father's did?"

"We think we can control it, thanks to you."

"Thanks to me, what did I do?"

"Your cooling system. We have expanded on it."

"General, the cooling system is not the problem. Controlling the beam is the problem! Once you lose beam integrity, you've lost control and you get a giant fireball."

"My people don't think that will happen. We have a small group of scientists working out the problems. They feel confident they can solve the beam integrity issue."

"I can't believe that after seeing what you've seen you would allow this to go ahead. What happens if they can't?"

"Then we go to plan C."

"I can't wait to hear about plan C!"

"If we find this guy Mueller and the chancellor won't help us bring him down, I'm afraid our only option left is to bomb this guy out of existence."

"Oh, that's a great plan! Start another war with Germany. That would go over really big!"

"I understand it's not the best option, but it's better than having this maniac with a weapon he can use against us and anyone else he chooses."

"General, I'm leaving. I told Mary I would be home by now."

"No, you can't leave just yet. Go back to the hotel and call Mary. Have her come here and stay with you until this is over. We will pay for all her expenses while she's here."

"That's very good of you, General. I'm not sure she will come, but I'll call her and ask."

The same sergeant that picked me up this morning was waiting to take me back to the hotel. First thing I did was call Mary. "Hello Hun, it's me."

"John, where are you? Are you on your way home?"

"No, I'm stuck here in Washington with the general. He won't let me leave. He says he still needs me here."

"How much longer will you be?"

"I don't know right now, but I want you to come to Washington and stay with me. The army will pick up all the costs. How long do you think you can get away?

"I may only be able to stay for two or three days."

"That would be great. How soon do you think you can get here?"

"I will call the school and set up a substitute for the rest of the week. If I leave in the morning, I'll be able to be there by the middle of the afternoon."

"Great, I will be waiting for you. Do you still have the address I gave you?"

"Yes, I have it right here."

"I can't wait to see you. I have so much to tell you."

I had just put the phone back when it started to ring. Who would be calling me?"

"Hello, this is John."

"Hello John. This is Sheriff Pat O'Flynn."

"How in the world did you get this number?"

"General Wellington gave me his number before he left. I called him and one of his aides gave me the number to the hotel."

"It's great to hear from you. How are things back in that little town of yours?"

"Very good. As a matter of fact, it's actually quite quiet. After you and all the army people left the town quieted right down."

"Have you had a chance to check on my mother? How's she doing?"

"That's why I called. She's okay, but she was terribly upset when I stopped out to visit her."

"Why, what's the problem?"

"The army did a great job cleaning up after themselves. They cleaned everything out of the lab and took that huge fence down that was around your property. You would never know they were even there. They moved your mom back to her house and I think that's the problem. I'm sure the army had good intentions when they fixed up the house."

"Yes, I knew they were going to do that. It was part of the arrangement I made with the general. I gave them a list of things I wanted them to fix around the house."

"Well, they did more than fix a few things, I'm afraid. They put a brand-new roof on the place and installed a new kitchen and bathroom. They painted both bedrooms, pulled down the old porch roof and built an enclosed patio. They put a brand-new white picket fence around the yard and made it look like something out of a magazine."

"My mother must have been thrilled!"

"Just the opposite. She's upset about it. She told me that the house was the only thing she and your father had together and now that's gone. I think you better give her a call John. She needs to hear from you. I'm sure she's feeling very lonely out there all by herself."

"I'll call her right away and thanks for checking on her Pat. I owe you a cold beer next time I'm out there."

"No problem. I like visiting with your mom. She's a great lady."

As soon as I hung up, I called, but there was no answer. I called and called, but she didn't answer. I kept calling and the last time I called it was 11:00 out there, but 2:00 o'clock in the morning here in Washington. She never did answer.

The ladies helped me into the house. I didn't realize how cold I was until I got inside. After three cups of coffee, I started to warm up. I had a great breakfast while answering all the ladies' questions. When I told them about the horse laying down for me, they just started laughing and said "We know. We trained him to do that. How do you think we get on him?"

I was tired and sore. I spent the rest of the day in bed. When I woke up, it was the middle of the night. This was my best chance to leave without telling the ladies why. I got up as quiet as I could, got dressed and started out the door. As I was passing through the kitchen, I noticed a half loaf of bread, two large pieces of dried beef and two apples sitting on the table. There was a bag and an old coat hanging on the chair. Was it possible they put all these things here for me? I wasn't going to wake them up to ask. I put all the food in the bag and put on the old coat.

Once outside I started down the road headed for town. I hadn't gone far when my leg reminded me it wasn't healed all the way yet. I started thinking about that horse again. I wonder if they would mind if I borrowed him. I went back to the barn and got him out. I headed back down the road again, only this time I was riding.

I felt terribly guilty, but if they knew why I was taking their horse I'm sure they'd understand. If I can stop this disaster from happening, I'll buy them a new horse. If I don't stop it, then they won't need a horse!

I got into town just as it was getting light. There was no one around at all, so I sat in front of the post office waiting. The same guy I had the pleasure of meeting the day before came walking down the street. He stopped and looked at me and then at the horse.

"They let you take their horse?"

"Yes, they did."

"They must like you an awful lot. They never let anyone use their horses."

"I told him I needed to make a call."

"I know! Why else would you be sitting here?" Once inside he put the phone on the counter and said, "Three dollars."

Oh crap. I forgot about that. I didn't know what to say. I just stuck my hands in my pocket to show him I had no money. I felt something like paper and loose change. As it turned out I had about twelve dollars and sixty cents on me. Those ladies knew full well I was leaving. I swore right then and there I would make it back here if I ever got the chance. I made the call and told the operator to tell whoever answered the phone that Charlie Brown was calling. I waited a good five minutes before I finally got the general.

"Brad, is that you?"

"Yes sir, General it's me."

"Where the hell have you been?"

"It's a long story, General. I'll tell you another time. I found them General. I know right where they are. Well, I knew where they were three days ago."

"What do you mean?"

"They were in a castle near here. I was there and saw the whole operation. In fact, I saw them fire it up for the first time, I believe. They may still be there or maybe not. I don't know for sure."

"Why do you say that?"

"You remember I told you every time I got close to them, they would just disappear."

"Yes, I remember. I read your reports."

"Well, I know why. All the equipment was mounted on flat-bed trucks. If they think they've been found, they just up and move."

"Maybe so Brad, or maybe they are staying mobile, so we can't find them. How soon can you get back to your squad?"

"It may take me a couple of days right now. I'm traveling by slow horseback."

"What do you mean slow horseback?"

"It's all part of that long story. I'll give you the location of the castle and the town I'm in. Send one of my guys to get me. They're all in Austria."

"No Brad, they're not. They're on their way back to the warehouse you found a week ago."

"Why would you send them back there?"

"I didn't. The president did. He ordered me to send them."

"Why would he do that?"

"That's a long story at my end."

"Who's running my squad?"

"The Chief, Blowing Wind."

"Okay, that's good. Get a message to him. Tell him to follow plan Alpha. He will know what it means. It was part of a plan we had to go back in if we needed to."

"Don't worry I'll get the message to him. What can I do to help you get back to your men?"

"I need money, and then I can get myself back."

"That's easy, whatever you need. Give me a wire number where you are and I'll send it."

"There's no such thing in this town. When I get where there is a bank, I'll call you."

"Make it soon. I need you back with your squad."

"Yes sir. I'll call you again soon."

I handed the phone back to the nervous looking old man and headed out the door. I had to laugh to myself a little. What must he be thinking right now? I got back on the horse and headed south out of town.

I had only gone about three miles when I heard a small pickup truck coming up behind me. I flagged down the driver and asked for a ride. She gave me a puzzled look and said, "What about the horse?"

I wasn't sure, but I told her he would find his way home. I turned the horse around and gave him a slap on the rump. He headed back down the road in the right direction. I hoped he would find his way home. The young lady in the truck must have asked me a hundred questions before we got to the next town. I asked her to drop me off at the bank there. When I got out of the truck, I handed her five bucks and thanked her for the ride. She was so happy that she jumped out of the truck and gave me a kiss. I'm really starting to like these German women.

I called the general's office and they wired me a thousand dollars. I rented a car and was on my way back to my squad.

According to the general, my squad was on its way back to the warehouse. I knew right where they would be staging for the raid tonight. Germany is a good size country, about three times the size of New York. From where I was, I could get back to my squad before the raid. I was in no shape to lead it, but I could oversee their plan and give the chief my two cents. I have a lot of confidence in him, but they are all my men and letting them go into harm's way without me just felt wrong.

I made good time and got where my squad should have been. After being there for an hour and no squad, I called the general. "Is the raid still on for tonight? Is it still a go?" It was. Okay then, where are my guys, I wondered. While I was waiting around, I did a little recon on the warehouse and there was not much going on. It's getting late and still no sign of my team.

Finally, around eleven forty-five, I see my men making their way in my direction. The first man I caught up with was Blowing Wind.

"Where have you been, Chief?"

"We got stopped at the border by the police. They didn't buy our story about being tourists and turned us back. We had to find a back way in and that put us hours behind."

"No problem. I have been here for hours and I've been watching the warehouse. I've seen three good size trucks leave the whole time I've been here. Other than that, it's been quiet. Little activity outside of the building."

"What about the guys we ran into last time?"

"I haven't seen anyone that looked like a guard."

"That's really too bad. They gave us a warm welcome last time. I was hoping for some payback!"

"I know how you feel, Chief. I would like that myself. I'll tell you what, if they are there, they're damn good at hiding. I made my way right down to the street we got hit on and no one was there."

"So, now that you're here, what's the plan?"

"You tell me. This is your op."

"My plan was to go in the back door where the truck deliveries come and go. We brought a lot more heat with us this time, so we're ready to kick their ass. If we need to, we can bring the whole building down around them. I was told by the general to take this place down no matter what I had to do. He wants undeniable proof to give the chancellor about what's going on."

"I can understand why the general wants proof. Before we go blowing up the building, I have a suggestion for you."

"What's that?"

"Why not send two men to the other side of the building. Give them an hour, and if they don't see any reason to not go in, then we go."

"Good with me boss. I know just who to send. I'll get them going right now. I brought your gear if you're going with us."

"You don't need me for this and I'm not up to it right now."

"Why, what happened?"

"It's a long story, I might tell you someday when we're both old and gray!"

Chapter 28

I had been waiting for Mary ever since I got up today. It's three thirty and she should have been here by now. I've been sitting in this lobby for hours. I'm beginning to think she changed her mind. She is so devoted to her school kids that it wouldn't surprise me if she decided to stay home. Just after five, I gave up. She's not coming after all. I hit the button for the elevator and waited for the doors to open. Just as the door started to open, I heard Mary calling me. She was a sight for sore eyes. She came running in my direction and when she got to me, she jumped into my arms almost knocking both of us to the floor. She kissed me so hard that I thought my teeth would break. When she finally pulled back, there were tears in her eyes.

"John, I've missed you so much. There were nights I cried myself to sleep missing you. I know it's only been a few weeks, but it felt like months."

I don't want to sound like a cold person, but although I've missed Mary tremendously, I never cry myself to sleep. I love Mary more than I knew I could love anyone. I must admit, as smart as I am about a lot of things, what goes on inside a woman's head is beyond me, to say nothing about how deep a woman's love can be for her man. I guess that's what makes a woman like my mother stay with a man like my father for a lifetime. I'm not sure I will ever fully understand women, but the love Mary has for me is something I will cherish all my life.

"I miss you too, Hun. It's been lonely here without you. I was afraid you changed your mind and were not coming."

"Are you crazy! Why wouldn't I come! A chance to be with you and come to Washington with all expenses paid. Why in the world would you think I wasn't coming?"

"I guess I thought you would have been here sooner."

"I kind of got lost and the traffic around this place is crazy!"

"Where did you leave your car?"

"The valet took it."

"What about your luggage?"

"I told him to leave it at the desk. Do I have to check in?"

"Yes, I guess so. Let's go get your luggage and get you checked in. Wait till you see the room we're staying in. It's bigger than our apartment."

"I can't wait to see it. We have a lot of catching up to do and I'm not talking about conversation."

"You must be reading my mind."

"John, your mind is not that hard to read! After we catch up, I want to see more of the hotel. This place is huge."

"Maybe tomorrow. I have plans for you tonight!"

"So, you think you can keep me busy all night, do you?"

"Well, I'm certainly going to try! I've been thinking about you an awful lot."

We spent the night making up for lost time away from each other. Somewhere during the night, we fell asleep. When we got up it was mid-morning, so we headed downstairs to the coffee shop for a little breakfast.

Mary asked me why the general still needed me here in Washington. Before I could answer, she started telling me about her kids. She said they were the smartest kids in the school. There wasn't a single child in her class that wasn't doing well. She told me about the school, the neighbors, and about what's going on in the apartment buildings. She told me about what's happening in town and half a dozen other things. You never had to worry about what to talk about with Mary. She could carry a conversation all by herself. It was one of the many things I loved about her. I could

227

listen to her for hours. She finally stopped long enough to take a breath and asked again "Why are you still in Washington?"

This time I got a chance to answer.

"I'm not sure how much I can or should tell you."

"Why? Is it a big secret?"

"Yes and no. If it's a secret right now, it won't be for long."

"Why? Tell me what's going on and how you are involved. "

"I'll tell you, but you have to promise to keep it to yourself for now."

"I can keep a secret better than most people I know."

"This is no ordinary secret. Even the president's Joint Chiefs of Staff were told not to tell anyone. Do you remember what I told you about my father's death?"

"How could I forget that? It was a terrible way to die!"

"Yes, it was. When his machine burned up it killed him, but the fire never got out of the building. By some miracle it stopped inside. We believe it ran out of oxygen to burn, but if it had gotten out, we think it would have just kept on going."

"What do you mean 'kept on going'?"

"This thing we're calling a fireball is so hot it burns the very air we breathe. If it keeps going, it will use up all the air there is. It would kill every living thing that breathes air."

"John, what you're saying, is it really possible?"

"We think so."

"Well, it's a good thing they took your father's machine. We don't have to worry about that ever happening again."

"That would be true if my father were the only one that had one. Remember I told you someone stole the prints out of my desk?"

"Yes, I'll never forget that either! I still have a hard time sleeping there alone."

"Well, we believe the people that stole the prints are building three of these machines."

228

"Can't someone stop them? What's the general doing about it?"

"Well, that's why I'm here. The general and the president want me to help them convince the German chancellor that the German army and the police need to hunt this guy down and stop him."

"Why you?"

"Because I'm the only one who really knows just how this thing works and how destructive it could be."

"I thought the general had his own people that knew about this thing."

"He does, but they're not available right now."

"Why not?"

"You really don't want to know the answer to that."

"So, how long will you be here?"

"No way to tell right now. We told the German chancellor about all this, but he didn't believe us. He said that Conrad Mueller was no big threat. He hung up on the president. He said if it were a problem, he would deal with it himself. The problem is he doesn't really know what he's dealing with."

"Can't the president call him back and tell him?"

"Right now, he's not taking the president's calls. It seems they don't get along that well. After the president told him we had people in his country without his permission, the chancellor got upset with him. That's why he's not taking his calls right now."

"Why doesn't the president call someone the chancellor does like, tell them and have them call the chancellor."

"Mary, that's a great idea, you should be working for the President. I have to make a call to the general right now and tell him what you said."

"BJ, my guys are, sorry, I mean 'our' guys said that it's all clear on the other side. Nothing happening and there's no one in sight."

"This is so odd. A week ago, we got shot to hell and now there's no one around here. They couldn't have moved all that equipment out of here this fast."

"Maybe they just left it in there."

"No way, Chief, they need that stuff. Okay, follow your plan, have those two guys meet me and the other half of the squad in front of the building. I'll go with them just to oversee what's happening. You take your team around to the back. Have your guys set the charges by the delivery doors and wait for my call. When I say "go", blow the doors, and hit them hard. When you draw fire from the back, we'll hit the front."

"Okay, boss. Give us twenty minutes to set the charges then we'll be ready to go."

I took half the squad with me and we made our way around to the front of the building. Still nothing. This just isn't right. The other two men we had sent to the end of the building caught up with us out front.

"Good to see you, boss. Where have you been hiding? Out chasing those German girls around?"

"Not exactly! Did you guys see anything at the end of the building?"

"Nothing, it's all dark on that end and we didn't see anyone moving around."

"That's really strange."

"It is awfully quiet around this place."

"Okay, listen up. Before we hit these guys, I want you two to go down to the front of the building and try to get a look in those windows. Then get back here and tell me if you see anything."

"Got it, boss. On our way. Back in five."

"BJ, this is the chief. We're ready back here and the charges are all set. We saw a small truck leave just as we got back here."

"Could you see who was in it?"

"No way to tell, too dark, but they sure were in a hurry."

"Okay, hang loose for a couple of minutes. I've got two guys down in front."

"We're ready whenever you make the call."

"Hey boss, there's nothing going on inside from what we could see."

"Okay, get back here."

"So, you guys didn't see anyone in the building?"

"No sir, just some equipment and a few flashing red lights."

"Okay, then we go."

"Hey Chief, this is BJ. Blow the doors and send your guys in."

Ten seconds later, we heard the doors being blown. The Chief and his guys were on their way in. My head was still trying to make sense of this. Flashing red lights?

"How many of those lights did you guys see?"

"I'm not sure. Maybe a dozen."

"Abort, abort! Do you hear me Chief? Abort, abort! Back off all you guys. Get back. I say again, abort, abort!"

"Back off guys, move back, get away from the building. It's gonna blow!"

There was a huge explosion. It sounded like a clap of thunder and everyone went flying to the ground. One of my guys grabbed me and yanked me to my feet and pulled me out of there. The dust and debris were flying everywhere. Some of the guys got hit by pieces of wood and glass coming from the front wall of the building. It came flying at us like a tidal wave.

My half of the squad got away with only some minor cuts and a few bruises. My concern was for the chief and his half of our squad. I didn't know if they heard my order to abort or not. I kept calling as we made our way around to the back of what was left of the building. There was so much dust hanging in the damp night air that it was hard to breathe and even harder to see.

No response from my guys. As we came around the corner of what was left of the warehouse, I could see what looked like someone moving. We got to our team and found most of them were on the ground. Two of my guys were helping others to their feet. I found the Chief. He was on his knees helping dress a bad wound on one of our guys. The only thing he said when I got there was "Son of a b****. They got us again!"

I said "Don't worry about it. When we catch up with these guys there's going to be hell to pay."

"How are all the guys doing?"

"Not bad considering. We were on our way in when we heard you called to abort. We maybe got forty or fifty feet away when the whole damn building came down around us. I can't believe it, but we're all here and nobody got seriously hurt. Although we might not be hearing well for a couple of days. We're still looking for a fight."

"I don't think there's anyone here to fight Chief!"

"So, what now?"

"Have a couple of your guys grab some pictures of whatever they can see and then let's get the hell out of here. I'm sure all this noise will wake up the neighbors and a few police."

"Boss, how the hell did you know they were going to blow the building?"

"I didn't, at least not soon enough! I sent two guys down to the front to see if they could see anything going on inside. When they came back, they told me that there was nothing going on inside, just a bunch of flashing red lights. When I added it all up, it just made sense. After our run in with them here last week, they must have decided it was time to move. They probably ran out of time to move all the equipment out, so they just blew up the building. I should have figured it out sooner."

"Well, I'm glad you did. Another minute and we'd all be dead."

"I hear sirens, Chief, so let's get out of here before the police get here and start asking questions. I need to call the general and let him know what happened here. He's not going to be happy."

Chapter 29

"I'm sorry sir, but Herr Mueller is sleeping. Can't this wait till morning?"

"I'm not stupid. I know he's sleeping! If this could wait till morning I wouldn't be calling. Now, go wake him up!"

"Yes, Herr Hellman."

"Is there a problem, Hellman? I'm sure you didn't wake me up in the middle of the night to tell me about the weather."

"No, Herr Mueller, there's something I think you should know."

"What's so important that it couldn't wait till morning."

"As you know, I had your orders to blow up the warehouse tonight."

"Yes, I know."

"I made sure that happened just as you ordered. We left the building just after midnight and drove to a position where we could observe the explosion. My driver was watching through binoculars when he noticed a minor explosion on the back of the warehouse. At first, we thought the explosives had not gone off as they should have. He then noticed around a dozen armed men running into the building. Just as they were getting to the building, our charges went off. The building was completely destroyed."

"Then what you're telling me is these men, whoever they were, were killed when the building exploded. How is that a problem?"

"Herr Mueller, I believe these were the same men that tried to take the building a week ago."

"You just told me they ran into the building as it exploded."

"Yes, but I couldn't go back and verify if they all died in the explosion. The police arrived in no time and I had no way to find out who these men were. They could have been part of Germany's own army. They certainly were not the police."

"Hellman, you're worrying for nothing. I'm sure the warehouse was all they knew about and now it's a pile of rubble."

"Yes, sir but suppose these were American special forces. They don't give up very easily and if we did kill some of them, they will never stop until they find us."

"Hellman, I have friends in the German government and if there were American forces operating in Germany, I would know about it. But just to be sure, I will check with my sources and let you know. What makes you think these men were Americans anyway?"

"If you remember, we had a network setup in the United States to get plans and information on Professor Northrup's machine. It was working well right up to the end. I believe they caught on to us and traced the network to England."

"Why do you say that?"

"Because the information we were getting in the end was of no use to us. It was information we already had. One of our spies was able to get into the professor's lab at the very end and retrieve the last notes the professor wrote. Those notes were very new to us and they contained information we never had."

"So, you're telling me there were no more notes to get."

"That's correct. Something happened to the professor. We believe he was killed or died right in his lab. Something happened inside the lab, but we just don't know what it was."

"So, the professor died or was killed, and you couldn't find out why?"

"No, we don't know. We just know that he died and then the army took all the equipment. I'm almost certain they know it was us and that we have plans for the professor's machine."

"It doesn't matter what they know at this point. Whatever they know or don't know, I could care less. I have several military leaders here including Germany's top military leader General Meyer who want to see these machines and just what they're capable of. Once they see how powerful these machines are, they will join us. Germany will once again take its rightful place as a superpower in the world. No one will dare to challenge us. We are awfully close now, Von Hellman, so just stay with the plan. I want you at site one by tomorrow. I will be waiting for your progress report. Now, stop worrying and let me get back to sleep."

"Yes sir."

"Please put me through to General Wellington. I need to speak to him immediately."

"I'm sorry, the general is in a meeting and can't be disturbed."

"Then please give him a message for me. Tell him that John Northrup called and I have a plan on how the president can reach the German chancellor."

"I will see that he gets the message."

"Thank you."

"It sounds like he won't take your call" Mary interjected.

"He's in a meeting and it must be pretty important for him not to take my call. He always takes my call. Mary, I know you want to see Washington, but I need to stay here in the hotel and wait for the general to call back."

"I know. I'm going to explore this hotel and see what I can find."

"Good, you go and do that and I'll wait for you in our room."

Two and a half hours later, Mary came back to the room. "John, you should have gone with me. This place is incredible. It has two restaurants, a beautiful pool and a hot tub. In the basement is one of the best little shopping boutiques I've ever seen. You can shop for clothes, jewelry and their shoes are something else."

"So, what did you buy?"

"Oh, let's see, two dresses, a coat, a fur coat by the way, all new jewelry and three pairs of shoes. A girl can't have too many shoes and it's all being sent to the room!"

"What! I don't think the general is going to cover your shopping spree."

"Don't worry silly. I didn't buy anything. I would have to work for a month just to buy a pair of shoes in this place."

"You had me going there for a minute."

"You're just too easy, Hun. Did the general call back yet?"

"No. I don't get it. How could he have been in a meeting this long?"

"Why don't you try calling him again?"

"I suppose I could. I've never had to call him more than once in the past."

"Just call him and then we can get out of here and go see some of this city. There's so much I want to see here. I want to get going."

"Okay. Just give me a minute and then we can go."

John dialed again. "Please put me through to General Wellington."

"I'm sorry, the general is not here. He left over an hour ago."

"Did he get my message?"

"Yes, I handed it to him as he was leaving."

"Okay, thank you.

Mary asked, "Is he still in his meeting?"

"No, he left an hour ago. He has my message and he still hasn't called."

"What are you going to do now?"

"Well, obviously he's not going to call, so let's get out of here and go see some of this town."

237

"Great, what do you want to see first?"

"Let's go to the Smithsonian Institute. I hear they have some really neat stuff there."

"John, you have quite the talent for understating things."

"Put me through to the general and tell him it's Charlie Brown."

"Yes sir, right away."

"Hello Brad, it's awful early here in the states. What's going on?"

"Sorry to wake your General, but you should know that last night's mission didn't go very well."

"Were you able to secure the warehouse?"

"No sir, the warehouse is a pile of rubble right now."

"Are you telling me you had to blow it up?"

"No sir, we didn't blow it up, they did."

"What do you mean they did?"

"We're getting ready to go in. The place was awfully quiet, and I started to suspect something was wrong. I had the chief split the squad into two groups. One was to go in the back and one in the front. They set charges on the back delivery doors. Before I gave the go ahead to go in, I had two men go down and do some recon in the front of the building. When they got back to me, they said the only thing they could see were some machines and flashing red lights inside. I gave the chief the go ahead to blow the doors and go in. Just as his charges went off it hit me. Mueller's men had set charges to blow the building. I called off the mission just seconds before the building blew up."

"Did any of your guys get hurt?"

"A couple got hit by flying debris, but nothing serious. Just some cuts and bruises. Some of them are a little hard of hearing right now, but they'll be good in a couple of days."

"Sounds like you made a good call there, Brad."

"Yes sir, but I should have seen it sooner. I almost got half my squad killed."

"Well, you didn't, so don't worry about it. Did you get a chance to see if they left anything behind?"

"No sir, we needed to get out of there. The police were on their way just a few minutes after the building came down. Sir, there had to be equipment still in that building. There's no way they got it all out."

"Maybe Brad, but I needed pictures, so I can convince the chancellor of what he is up against."

"Yes sir, I know, but it's a big pile of junk right now."

"Where are you right now?"

"We're still in our location in Germany. My guys got stopped at the border yesterday on their way back in from Austria. I didn't want to have to deal with that if you needed us back in here for some reason."

"Good thinking, so just lay low until we figure out our next move."

"General, I know where they have one of their machines setup. It's in a castle called Reichstein near the town of Trechtingshausen. This castle is huge and it looks to be as solid as it was when it was first built. I know the layout and I'm sure we can take it if need be."

"Yes, Brad, I'm sure you could, but right now we need the German army on our side, including the chancellor and he's not on our side right now."

"Why not?"

"Because he's a stubborn s.o.b! When we told him your squad was operating in Germany, he blew a gasket and hung up on the president before we could convince him about what was happening."

"General, if we take out the guys at the castle then our problems are over."

"Not really, Brad. I didn't tell you the last time we spoke, but we think they are building three of these things."

"What makes you think that?"

"Remember, we sent Mansfield to Saudi Arabia."

"That's right. What did he find?"

"He got confirmation that they shipped six generators to Germany and that would mean they could build three of these machines."

"That's bad news, sir. I only know where one of them is. I have no clue where the other two could be. I'm not even sure that one will still be there when we get back to the castle."

"One thing at a time, Brad. Do you know anyone in the German army that you could talk to? Maybe they could call the chancellor for us?"

"Yes sir. I know just who I could call. General Meyer, he's their top man. I've worked with him many times."

"Good. Call him as soon as you can and then call me back."

"Yes sir. I'll call you soon."

"Okay Chief, get the men ready to move out. We're taking a little trip tonight."

"Where to, boss?"

"We're going to visit a couple of old ladies."

"What? Couldn't we go visit a couple young ladies?"

"Never mind, just get the men ready. I need to make a call."

"Good afternoon. I would like to speak to General Hadwin Meyer, please."

"Who should I say is calling?"

"Please tell him it's Lieutenant Brad Johnson, US Army."

"Please hold. I will see if he's available."

"Hello Brad. It's been a long time. Good to hear from you."

"Yes, General it has been a while."

"So, what can I do for you?"

"General, it's more what I need to tell you."

"I think I know what you're going to say Brad, but please go ahead."

"General, we think, I mean, we know that Germany is in danger. Conrad Mueller is leading a large group of men not only to overthrow Germany, but the whole world if he gets his way. He has a weapon that he can't control and he's planning on using it against your army and then plans to use it against the US and anyone else that tries to stop him. If he does use it and it gets out of control, it could end Germany as a country and many other countries around Germany."

"Really, that's quite a story you've got there, Brad. I heard a little bit about this from our chancellor. He told me your President called to warn him about Conrad. The chancellor and I discussed at length what the president told him about Conrad. We know all about Conrad from years ago. He made a run at our government with all these crazy ideas to make Germany into a world power. He was thrown out because of his crazy talk and since then we have heard little about him and what we have heard has not been good. If he is up to something, we will find out what it is and take care of it. So, Brad, relax and let us take care of our own country's problems. I have a question for you, Brad. Are you the one that's been operating in our country without our knowledge or our permission?"

"General, whether I am or not is not the issue here. Sir, you need to listen to me. Back in the states, we had a professor who was trying to make cheap electricity. He almost pulled it off when it blew up on him and killed him."

"Sorry to hear that. We could all use cheap electricity."

"Yes sir, but that accident proved how dangerous this machine could be."

"Wasn't the machine destroyed when it blew up?"

"I believe it was, but the problem is that Mueller had been tracking the professor's work for quite some time. We believe he is building three of these things right now."

"Brad, even if he was building them, how can a machine that makes cheap electricity be a threat to anyone?"

"Good question. Unfortunately, in an experiment we conducted we found that this machine could produce an electrical beam that could destroy almost anything as far as a thousand miles away in an instant."

"So, the real purpose of this machine was a weapon! I should have known."

"No sir, that was never the professor's intent."

"How do you know that?"

"I have been a friend of the professor and his son from my days in college. I know the professor only ever wanted to help mankind. He never would have built this machine if he knew it was going to be turned into a weapon."

"Okay Brad suppose I believe all this. How do you know Mueller is building these machines?"

"Because we found his network that was stealing information from the professor, sending it on to England and then finally to Germany. We also had someone track down information in Saudi Arabia to verify that they built six of these generators and then shipped them into Germany. That would give Mueller just what he needs to build three machines."

"Brad, I still have a hard time believing Mueller would do this and then turn the weapon on his own country."

"General, trust me. He's crazy with the idea of getting revenge for what happened to Germany in the war and what the Russians did to him after he was captured."

"Yes, I've heard some of the speeches he made while he was part of our government."

"General, if you're willing to meet with me I can prove it."

"Where would you want to meet?"

"Did you hear about a warehouse that exploded the other night?"

"Yes, I heard about it."

"That's the location where I can prove to you all that I've been saying. Mueller's men are the ones that blew it up. If that's not enough, I can take you to a castle where they've already in the process of building one of these machines."

"Okay, Brad. I will meet you at this warehouse tomorrow at noon. I hope for all of us that you are wrong."

"I'm afraid I'm not sir. I will see you tomorrow at noon."

"So, you are here in Germany, aren't you?"

"I will see you tomorrow, General and thank you for taking my call."

"Chief, tell the men to stand down. I need to meet General Meyer at the warehouse tomorrow. I may need the guys to help pick up the trash and go through the rubble and prove that this Conrad is up to no good."

"How are we going to know what to look for? Don't we need someone to tell us what to look for?"

"Yes, we do, and I know just who to get. I need to call General Wellington right now."

"Hello Brad. I hope you have some good news for a change."

"I do, General. I was able to talk to General Hadwin Meyer in Germany's army. I worked with him and his men a few years back. He's going to meet me at the warehouse tomorrow at noon. I need John Northrup there. He will know what to look for to show the general. That's the only way we're going to convince him of what's been happening."

"Not a problem. I will have him on a plane right away. Where do you want him?"

"Send him to Frankfurt. It's the closest airport. I will pick him up there."

"What else do you need?"

"Nothing right now. Just get John over here."

"He's on his way."

"Thanks, General. Talk to you soon."

Mary and I spent the rest of the day at the Smithsonian Institute and with no call from the general, we were on our own. We finally had a day to ourselves. Washington is a great place to visit, but the Smithsonian is at the top of my list. What a place and with over twenty museums and galleries to see, there's something for everyone. Mary and I couldn't decide what to see first. I wanted to see the Air and Space Museum. She wanted to see the Natural History Museum, but I won. I promised we would see the American History Museum the next day. We were in the museum the whole day until we couldn't walk anymore. I promised I would spend all the next day in the American History Museum with her. She wanted to collect information to take back to her class to find out about a possible class trip.

The next morning, we ordered breakfast in our room. We were not in any hurry. We had all day. We called for a cab and headed outside to wait. It was going to be another beautiful day in Washington, sunny and warm. Just as a cab was pulling up, I saw two military police headed my way. They were certainly in a hurry and looked like they meant business.

"Excuse me, sir. Are you John Northrup?"

"Yes. Why do you want to know?"

"We need you to come with us sir. We have orders to bring you to General Wellington's office immediately."

"If this is so urgent, then why hasn't the General called me?"

"I don't know sir, but we need to get you there now."

"What about Mary? Can she come with me?"

"No sir, just you."

As I turned to Mary, I could see the disappointment on her face.

"Mary, you go ahead to the museum. I'll catch up with you later. I don't know what's going on, but hopefully it won't take too long."

I kissed Mary goodbye and followed the MPs to their Humvee. These guys are all business, not like the sergeant I first had when I got to Washington. There was no conversation on the way to the general. Every question I asked got the same answer.

"We don't know, sir. Our orders are to get you to the general ASAP." When I stepped into the general's office, he was on the phone and as usual he was yelling at someone. His last words to whoever was on the line were "I don't give a damn, make it happen."

"General, you sure have a way with people." He didn't laugh.

"John, I have some bad news for you. I know I told you to have Mary come here to Washington."

"Yes, sir you did, and thank you. We're having a good time seeing the sights."

"Well, I hate to tell you this, but you're needed in Germany."

"What! Here we go again! You told me I had to come to Washington, so I did. You said I was only needed for a couple of days. You told me to bring Mary here to spend time together and now you want to send me to Germany? What the hell is going on and whose bright idea was this?"

"John, I know what I said, but things have changed and I need you in Germany."

"Sorry General, but not this time. I'm not going. I'm done with this. You don't understand what this has done to me and my life and how upsetting it's been for Mary."

"John, I want you to help us willingly, but let me remind you. I would draft you for the next three years if need be."

"You can't do that!"

"Yes, actually I can. In an international emergency, I can do most anything I want."

"Oh, I see. Well, what do you need?"

"I need you to go to Germany to identify equipment that was in a warehouse, so that we can prove what we've been saying about Conrad Mueller."

"Who will I be trying to convince?"

"A German general named Hadwin Meyer."

"How will I find this General Meyer?"

"Your buddy Brad Johnson will meet you at the airport in Frankfurt and take you to the site where you will be meeting with the general."

"So, this is Brad's idea?"

"Yes, in a way, but I'm the one asking you to go. So, if you want to get mad at someone, you're looking at him."

"No sir, I don't think that would be good for my future. Brad is going to owe me big time for this one. Can I at least take Mary with me?"

"I'm afraid not. You shouldn't be there for more than a day or two."

"Where have I heard that before!"

"John, there's no reason for you to be there any longer than it takes to convince this general that we know what we're talking about. Then Brad will send you back here to Washington."

"I hope you're right, General. My whole life has been a mess since this all started. I need to get back to the hotel and pack."

"Sorry John, but there's no time for that. Your plane leaves in half an hour. These MPs will take you to your plane."

"What about Mary?"

"I will have someone meet her at the hotel and explain what's going on. What does she know right now?"

"I did tell her a few things, probably more than I should have."

"No matter at this point. You'll be back in a couple of days and then you're out of it. You and Mary can go back to your teaching and forget this ever happened."

"Not likely General. I don't think I will be forgetting about this anytime soon, but it will be nice to get back to a normal life again."

"Okay John, go with these guys, and good luck. If anything comes up that you need to talk to me about, Brad knows how to reach me."

"BJ. I can't wait to see him!"

Two minutes later, I was on my way to the airport with no way to call Mary, so I scribbled a little note and asked the MPs to drop it at the hotel. We pulled up to a gate at the airport. Not the one I had in mind. This was Andrews Air Force field. We drove right up to a huge army transport plane. There were two armed soldiers waiting for me by the back of the plane. They walked me inside just as the tailgate door started to lift. They showed me to a bench seat near the front and asked me to strap in. As I looked around, I could see that it was only the three of us on this plane, other than a few boxes. I asked them, "Couldn't you find something bigger?"

One of the soldiers said, "Sorry sir, Air Force One was not available." He said it so fast and with such a straight face I wasn't sure if he was kidding or not. After twenty minutes in the air, I was told I could get up and move around. There was a head up front if I needed it and lots of food and drinks. They suggested I get some rest. It was a six-and-a-half-hour flight to Frankfurt. I tried to sleep, but kept thinking about Mary. What was she going through at the hotel by herself? I hope those MPs gave my note to her. She doesn't deserve to go through all this. I will have to make a call as soon as I can get to a phone.

Chapter 30

"Tell Herr Mueller that General Hadwin Meyer is calling. I need to speak with him now!"

"Yes sir."

"General Meyer, it's good to hear from you. What can I do for you?"

"Conrad, we have a problem. I just got off the phone with Lieutenant Brad Johnson of the US Army. He's here in Germany and is asking me to meet with him tomorrow at noon by the warehouse that you've been using."

"So, it is the Americans after all. We haven't been sure up until now. They have been trying to derail our little plan."

"Yes, Conrad. I'm afraid so. He's determined to show me proof about what you were planning and his theory about you taking over Germany."

"General, I assure you there's nothing to worry about. My men destroyed that warehouse. There's nothing left there to convince anyone of anything. We made sure of that. Whatever he tells you, I'm confident you'll be able to brush it off as hearsay."

"Maybe, but Brad Johnson is one tenacious soldier. He won't give up when he believes something to be true."

"Go ahead and meet with him tomorrow and listen to what he has to say. After that you can order him and his men out of the country. Tell him if there is a problem, you will handle it. Is that clear General?"

"Yes, but I'm not sure that will be the end of it. You don't know this soldier like I do. He's trained several of my lead men and they all had nothing but high praise for him."

"Meyer, if he becomes a problem, I'm sure you can eliminate him and his men."

"That would be the last thing I would want to do. Now that the chancellor knows something is going on, he's been talking to their president about this. How would I ever explain killing US soldiers who are trying to help us?"

"Meyer, accidents happen all the time. Besides, you won't have to kill all his men, just their leader. That will back them off long enough for us to bring our first weapon online. After that it will be too late for the chancellor, the US or anyone else to do anything about it."

"Conrad, just how far along are you from making this happen?"

"Only a few days. They have already turned one set of generators on without any problem, so we should be ready to test-fire soon."

"I hope you're right, Conrad. Once you fire it, there's no turning back. You'll have the whole world against us once that happens. Why don't you wait until all three weapons are ready?"

"There's no reason to wait. Our first target will be the US missile base here in Germany. We will destroy it in mere seconds. I will then send a warning to any country that may want to help the US. If they dare to help, we will give them a taste of just what this weapon can do. Make sure none of your soldiers are on the base at that time. My scientist told me no one will survive. They are extremely impressed with the destructive power of this weapon."

"Mueller, I've gone along with your plan, but only to bring Germany back to a world power as she should be. There was never any talk about going any further than that. It sounds like you're planning to threaten the world with this new weapon."

"General, you misunderstand what I'm saying. I would only ever use it against our enemies if they ever tried to hurt Germany. Once we have established ourselves as a superpower then it will only be for defense."

"Very well then. That is what I agreed to from the start. I would not support you if you went beyond what we started."

"I give you my word General, we will go no farther. Let me know how your meeting goes with this Brad Johnson. I think I would like to know more about him."

"I will call you tomorrow, once the meeting is over. Good day Conrad."

"Okay Chief, here's the plan. I need to pick up John in Frankfurt tonight, then get back here to the warehouse before noon tomorrow."

"You're going to be on the road all night. Don't you want one of the guys to go with you and help with the driving?"

"That's not a bad idea. Grab one of the guys and tell him to leave all his gear here. He won't need it where we're going."

"We can bring his gear with us and meet you at the warehouse."

"No, I changed my mind about that. General Meyer doesn't know how many of us are here and want to keep it that way for now. I don't know if it was something he said or maybe the tone of his voice. I just have a feeling he's not being honest with me about what he knows about Mueller. He thinks the whole thing is a big story and we should just let it go. That's not the General Meyer I knew years ago. Back then any threat to Germany would have his full attention, but his reaction to this was lukewarm at best."

"Do you think he is involved with Mueller?"

"No, I doubt that. He's too loyal to Germany to have fallen in with this nut case."

"Stranger things have happened, boss!"

"I know. I'll be able to get a better feel about him when we meet tomorrow. I want to see how he reacts to what we show him. That will tell me a lot about where his head is at. Okay Chief. I need to get on the road, so tell who was ever going with me to meet me out front in ten minutes. I want one of our guys to watch the warehouse while I am gone. I want a full report when I get back. You and the rest of the guys stay out of trouble."

"Us, get in trouble?"

"Yeah you! I'll be back sometime tomorrow morning. I will see you before I meet with Meyer."

I was rudely awakened by a rough Landing in Frankfurt. It would have been nice if my two guards, or should I say armed escorts, would have warned me. I will never understand why soldiers carry loaded weapons around when there is no threat of anything happening. They always seem to be ready for a gun fight. I got my feet under me as soon as the plane stopped moving. I headed for the back of the plane, but my escorts yelled at me to have a seat. "You're not getting off until Lieutenant Johnson arrives."

"When will that be, I ask?"

"We'll know when he gets here, sir."

These guys don't waste too many words telling you what they know. I spent the next hour or so pacing back and forth in the plane thinking about what I was going to say to BJ when I saw him. I went from screaming at him, to just giving him a hug and everything in between. Finally, I heard a radio crack. The voice was BJ's. I would have known that voice anywhere. From the day he ran me over in the hall, I could always hear his voice above everyone else in the room. His voice was loud, strong, and commanding. I have no doubt that when he gave an order, people jumped.

He ordered my escort to open and deliver the package. So now, I'm a package? What was that all about? This time we went out a side door with one guard in front and one behind, very military like.

BJ was at the bottom of the stairs wearing all black. Not what I expected. Where was his uniform or at least his fatigues? It was good to see my friend again. I had a hundred questions racing through my head, but all I could say was, "It's good to see you, BJ." I gave him a hug, smiled at him then took a step back and punched him square in the chest. I might as well have punched the plane for all the effect it had. I hurt my hand.

BJ just laughed and said, "You punch like a professor, but I guess I had that coming."

"Yes, you did and a lot more than that! Why did you tell the general I had to come over here? I could have told you what to look for on the generators. I didn't need to come over here just for that."

"John, there are no more generators to look at. Only what's left after they blew up the building. We're going to be looking at pieces at best."

"Who blew up the building?"

"Mueller's men. They took most of the equipment out beforehand. I'm hoping they left enough behind to prove that what we've been telling the chancellor is the truth."

"Are you telling me we're going to meet with the German chancellor?"

"No, we are meeting with General Meyer, a man I have known and worked with in the past."

"Yeah, that's what I was told. Another General. Just what I need. Someone else to give me orders."

"You won't be taking any orders from him, just me. We need to get on the road. We have a long ride ahead of us."

"BJ, before I do anything, I need to call Mary. The general pulled me away and never gave me a chance to tell Mary what was going on. So, if you want my help at least let me make a call."

"Sorry, John. I didn't know that. I'll get you to a phone, but we really need to get going after that. So, make it quick."

We found a phone in the airport at Frankfurt and I called Mary. "Hi Hun, it's me."

"John, are you really in Germany? The two soldiers that took you away this morning came back to the hotel. They gave me your note and told me you were on your way to Germany."

"They told you the truth. I'm in Frankfurt right now, but I won't be here for long. Guess who I'm with?"

"I have no idea. Who are you with?"

"BJ. He's the one who asked for me to come over here."

"So, we have him to thank for this?"

"Yes, he's the one!"

"How long will you be over there?"

"Just a day or two at the most."

"Do you want me to stay in Washington or should I go home?"

"Stay in Washington if you can. See if they can cover for you at the school."

"Okay, I'll stay here for now. I'll certainly be glad when this is over. I'm so tired of worrying about you and what you're going through."

"I'm fine. I'll be back in a couple of days and this will all be behind us. Besides I'm with BJ. What could go wrong?"

Mary was annoyed. "Oh right! What could go wrong? I'm tired of this whole thing, I would like things to be normal again."

"You and I both! Please call my mother and tell her what's going on."

"I'll call her right away."

"I gotta go. BJ is staring a hole right through me."

"Tell him I said hi and that he better send you back here in a day or so. Tell him he better keep you safe or he'll have me to answer to."

"Don't worry. I feel very safe with BJ around. Bye for now."

"OK John. Let's go. Like I said we got a long ride ahead of us."

We headed out of the airport with BJ leading me to a very sleek jet-black BMW with very dark tinted windows. He told me to get in the back and he jumped into the shotgun seat. "Okay, so who's driving or does this thing drive itself?" I could see there was already someone behind the wheel. I didn't even get my seat belt on and we were rolling down the road.

"John, this is one of the guys from my squad. He offered to come along and help us with the driving. Just call him Bob for now, no reason for you to know who he really is. The less you know about us the better."

Suddenly, I felt like I was in a spy movie. For the first time since this whole thing started, I felt like I may be in danger.

"BJ, I have a question for you. I heard you call me the package on the plane. What's that all about?"

"Glad you asked. While you are here, your name is Richard Stevenson. Do you think you can remember that?"

"Okay. Now I'm really getting a little spooked. Why do I have to be someone else?"

"I don't want anyone over here to know that the son of the man that is responsible for this weapon is here in Germany. That wouldn't be good for your health Mr. Stevenson."

"Why, what did I do?"

"Nothing, but this could go one of two ways. If Mueller knows you're here and wants your help building his weapon, he may send his men after you and we may not be able to stop him. He has a small army working for him and he is very well connected in Germany. The other way this could go is, imagine he gets this thing to work and he does what we think he will. Now the whole world will want someone to blame. Your father's dead, so that puts you next in line to blame. Would you want people to know where you were?"

"BJ what you're telling me is a little scary, in fact it's scaring the crap out of me. You knew all this, and you brought me over here anyway?"

"Relax John, I mean Richard. The only ones that know you're here are the general and my squad. That's why the new name while you're here."

"Does this general I'm meeting know who I am?"

"No, and I'm going to keep it that way. When you meet him later today, you are Richard Stevenson, a research scientist who's been working for several years with the army and with Professor Northrup until he died. That's your story, so don't say or do anything that may cause him to think differently."

"This kind of thing might be okay for you and your guys BJ, but I didn't sign up for this and I'm not sure I can pull it off."

"Don't worry Richard, I've got you covered. Have I ever let you down?"

"No, but you never put me in a spot like this before either."

"I wish to speak to General Meyer and tell him it's Herr Mueller."

"Yes, Conrad. What is it now?"

"You are meeting with this US soldier at noon tomorrow, is that correct?"

"Yes, you know I am."

"I would very much like to be there."

"That's not a good idea. Why would you want them to know what you look like?"

"General, I'm certain they already know what I look like. With all the intelligence the US has and for all the time they have been tracking me, don't you think they know what I look like?"

"Maybe, but why go face-to-face with them?"

"Meyer, have you ever heard the saying keep your friends close and your enemies even closer?"

"Yes, of course I've heard that."

"Well, that's just what I'm doing. I want to meet this Lieutenant Johnson you told me about and find out just who he is and how he thinks. You can tell a lot just by meeting someone if you pay attention."

"Conrad, I can tell you all you need to know about him. He's intelligent and he's well-trained in warfare and counter-espionage. He speaks five languages, German being one of them. He's a top man in the US Army ranger division. He's the man they sent me years ago when I asked for help training my own elite force. Why on earth would you want this guy to know who you are?"

"Let me worry about that. I will be going with you at noon tomorrow. Is that clear?"

"If that's what you want. I'll send someone to pick you up."

"That won't be necessary. I will meet you there around 11:00. I want a little time to look around before they arrive."

BJ wasn't kidding. Even in this high-powered car and being on the autobahn, it was a long ride. BJ and I spent a lot of time reminiscing about our days in college, him as a student and me as a professor. We talked about Mary and my mom and my dad. BJ still has a real soft spot for my mom. He asked a lot of questions about how she was handling my dad's death and how she was doing without him. When I told him about her helping deliver correspondence for the army he just laughed and said "I wouldn't expect anything less from your mom. She's quite the lady."

I had never been to Germany, so I had little idea of what this country looked like. As the sun came up on a clear blue-sky day, I was surprised at what I saw. We could have been almost anywhere on the east side of the United States. The green hills and open pasture land reminded me of the hills in Pennsylvania. This is a beautiful country with many small farms and scenic mountains and gorgeous rivers. I was really enjoying the ride and the scenery. If things were different, I would be happy to be here.

We finally pulled up behind an old building on the outskirts of a small village. There was no one around and little chance that someone could see us anyway. Before we could even get out of the car, two of BJ's squad were beside the car, fully armed and checking the countryside. Once inside, I could tell this was where his guys have been hanging out for some time now. The inside was showing its age. Most of the walls have lost any color they may have had and cobwebs hung everywhere. Dust covered everything inside except for the old furniture that someone had left behind. Apparently, the guys had wiped it down, so they could use it. Other than that, there was little trace of them ever being there, however the smell might give them away. I don't think they are able to shower very often in this place. It really made me appreciate the hotel I had been staying at in Washington.

BJ went right to the radio and talked to someone who apparently was watching the warehouse. It didn't sound like they had much to say. A minute later BJ came over to me followed by one of the biggest men I've ever seen. If BJ had been standing behind him, I wouldn't have been able to see him standing there. This guy was that big. "John, this is Blowing Wind, but we call him Chief. If for some reason I'm not around, the Chief is in charge. Whatever you need, he'll take care of it." If someone had introduced me to a guy named Blowing Wind, I would have laughed my ass off, but looking at the chief, I didn't even dare crack a smile. From out of nowhere, one of his guys handed me a pile of clothes and a pair of old boots. BJ wants you to change into these before you leave. Surprisingly, everything fit well. One of the other guys handed me a sandwich and a bottle of water. It was the first thing I'd eaten since I had breakfast with Mary. I barely finished that sandwich when BJ yelled "Time to go."

We got back on the road and headed for the warehouse and now I really started to worry. I had to remember my name was Richard Stevenson and everything else BJ told me. BJ must have seen me getting worked up.

"Just relax, John. You'll be fine. Remember today you're not John Northrup, you're not a professor, you're a scientist working for the army. You're here to help identify this machine and stop Mueller from using it."

"Yeah, easy for you to say."

"Don't worry. I got your back. If Meyer starts asking too many questions, I'll just push you aside and take over. The less you say the better."

"I'm good with that!"

"Your main objective is to find whatever you can to make our case. I'll take care of the rest."

About half an hour later, we pulled down an old road that took us to what was at one time a parking lot. We stopped in front of what was left of an old warehouse. As we pulled in, I saw two army trucks used for transporting soldiers, one US style Humvee, a car that obviously was military and a private car that didn't look army issued at all. There must have been fifty German soldiers going through the debris that once was a warehouse. We stopped a little way back. BJ got on his radio to talk to one of his guys that had been watching the place. Apparently, all these army people had shown up around an hour ago and started digging through the rubble.

We got out of the car and started slowly making our way to the building. They sure did a good job when they blew this place up. I could see debris had been thrown 60 or 70 yards in every direction. I was having doubts that we would find anything of use in proving our story. Before we got too far from the car, armed soldiers stopped us and asked for ID. BJ might have had an ID on him, but I had nothing. Just as they looked at me, a very decorated general yelled something in German and the two soldiers stepped aside and let us go. This man coming our way had to be General Meyer, the one Brad had told me about.

"Hello, Brad."

"Hello, General. I'm glad you agreed to meet me. I didn't expect to see so many others here though."

"Well, Brad, if we are going to find anything in this mess, I thought we could use all the help we could get."

Out of the corner of my eye, I saw a well-dressed gentleman get out of the backseat of a nice BMW. It looked very much like the one we had come in, only he had a driver who opened the door for him. He looked to be in his late 50's or early 60's and around six one or two and very fit. He walked like a man with purpose and held himself like someone not to be trifled with. BJ and General Meyer were still exchanging pleasantries when this gentleman stepped up beside the general. Everything changed in an instant. Brad became as rigid as an oak tree and you could see every muscle in his body tense up like a cat ready to pounce on its prey.

The two men stood there three feet apart staring at each other so deeply you could feel the tension between them. No one said anything for what felt like an hour. Finally, the general started to introduce this man to BJ. Before he could get the words out, BJ cut him off.

"No need, General. I know who he is. Conrad Mueller."

The gentleman responded "Why yes, you're right. That is my name. How is it that you would know me?"

"I know who you are and I also know what you've been up to."

"Well, you have me at a loss. I don't believe we've met before."

"Don't play me for a fool Conrad. You know very well who I am."

"Well, yes, I do, but only because General Meyer told me you would be here today.

"General, why is Mueller here?"

"Brad, let's try to be civil about this. Herr Mueller is here as my guest. He heard that he was being accused of building this weapon and wants to clear his name of this. I felt it was only fair that he be allowed to meet his accusers."

"General. I will not allow this man to interfere with my investigation!"

"He's not here to interfere and that's not your call. You're here as my guest as well and this is my investigation not yours. Do we have an understanding?"

"Yes sir, we do."

BJ never once took his eyes off Mueller. He just kept staring eye to eye and neither one of them even blinked. The general finally asked "Who is this you brought with you, Brad?"

Without taking his eyes off Mueller, he introduced me as Richard Stephenson, research scientist for the army. The general finally broke the staring contest and asked me a question. "So, Mister Stevenson, how long have you been with the army and just what do you do for them?"

Oh crap, I wasn't ready for this. Before I could think of anything to say, BJ jumped in.

"Richard only works for us when we need him. He's highly trained in electrical engineering and mechanical design. He knows just what we're looking for to help prove what we've been saying all along."

Mueller interrupted "I was told this weapon that I'm supposedly building is highly advanced. How would your scientists know what to look for?"

BJ jumped in again. "He was on a special assignment where he actually worked with the man who built this machine back in the states."

"So, you were building this weapon in the US and now you're accusing us of building it? It sounds like you want to blame Germany for your mistake, for letting this weapon fall into somebody else's hands."

I couldn't help myself and before I even realized it, I was almost yelling at Mueller. "He never intended for this to be a weapon. My father, I mean my fellow scientists, only built this machine to make cheap electricity."

Mueller said, "Didn't you just say this was a weapon you were looking for Lieutenant Johnson."

"I misspoke. Richard is right. It was never meant to be used as a weapon. It was only meant to help mankind. Only evil men would turn a good thing into something to destroy others."

This Mueller was good. In no time at all, he had turned the whole attention of this weapon on us and away from him and Germany. Thankfully, General Meyer spoke up.

"Gentleman, let's stop all this accusing each other and do what we came here for. Brad, I have my men pulling out anything that looks like a part of a machine. You and your scientist are free to look at whatever you like. If you find something you want to show me, we will be here as long as you like."

"Thank you, General. We will get to work.

As we walked to the building, BJ said softly to me "I should kill that son of a b**** right now and end this."

"How do you know that will end it? Don't we need to find proof of the machine first?"

"Yes, but I still want to kill him."

Four hours later and we hadn't found anything that could prove that someone is building this machine. BJ and I were getting a little frustrated and most of the soldiers were just sitting around and talking.

We got through just about every piece of junk we could find and still nothing. There was one piece of a wall that we couldn't move. BJ wanted to find a way to lift it.

"I said "After all we've been looking at, what makes you think there's anything under that?"

"I don't care if there isn't anything under it, but we won't know until we move it."

BJ started gathering some of the soldiers, grabbed some chains and jacks and then went to work lifting a large piece of wall. Once they had it about four feet off the floor and secure, BJ and I crawled underneath and started digging. There was a fair pile of debris underneath that piece of wall, but after quite a while we hadn't found anything that would help our case. BJ was pulling at a large bundle of cables and called me over to help him pull whatever was connected to the cables out from under a pile of debris. What we pulled out most people would call junk, but when we got it out into the open, it was just what we needed. A large piece of a cooling coil with all the cables still connected.

"This is it, BJ. This is the proof that they had one of the generators here."

"How do you know?"

"Because it's my design!"

"Okay, but you can't say that when we show the general."

"Don't worry, I won't."

"Ok then, let's show it to them."

BJ yelled for the general. "Would you please come over here? We have something to show you."

"So, what have you got there?"

"General, I will let Richard explain what this is."

"General, this is a large part of a cooling coil for a generator that you would need to build the weapon we've been talking about."

Unfortunately, Mueller had come over with the general and said "That could be off any piece of machinery. It doesn't prove anything."

I said "No, Herr Mueller, this was designed specifically for a static charge generator."

"How would you know that?"

"Because I was working with the professor when he designed it."

"Well, it looks pretty common to me."

"It's not, just look at the way the coils weave in and out of each other. That allows for maximum airflow to increase cooling. No one has ever seen a coil like this!"

Mueller pulled the general aside to talk to him away from us.

"BJ, I think we have the general convinced that we found proof."

"Yeah, I agree. It's hard to deny what's laying right in front of you. The big problem now is proving that Mueller is behind all this."

The general and Mueller came back over followed by some sergeant they brought with them. The general asked the sergeant if he had ever seen anything like this coil before.

The sergeant replied "Yes, Sir. We have coils like that in our tanks. There's nothing special about what he's found."

I almost jumped out of my shoes and yelled "He's lying! They don't have these coils in their tanks. It's impossible! This coil is my design. I mean, I helped design it with the professor. It's not just the coil. Look at the wiring. There's nothing like this anywhere in the world."

General Meyer looked at BJ and said "Lieutenant Johnson, you need to calm your scientist down. I think we all know what we're looking at here.

BJ said, "Yes sir, General. Richard, why don't you take a walk while I talk to the general."

I said "BJ, that coil is proof and there's no doubt they had a machine here!"

"Yes, that may be true. You and I believe it, but they don't. Go for a walk and I'll catch up with you."

Now I was the one getting pissed off. We found proof and BJ was giving up. That piece of s*** Conrad. Why did he have to be here? I couldn't believe it. Why would BJ give up so fast? When I looked back, BJ was shaking hands with the general, then he gave a disgusted look at Conrad and walked away.

I met him at the car. "Why would you just give up like that?"

"Just get in the car, I'll tell you on the way back."

BJ pulled the car out and hammered the gas pedal. I have never seen him so mad.

"So, why are we giving up and why are we running away?"

"We're not! We were not going to get anywhere back there. Nothing we said was going to convince them."

"Why? What makes you say that?"

"Because now I know the general is in on it. He's working with Mueller on this whole thing."

"What!"

"John, just shut up and let me think."

The rest of the ride back was noticeably quiet, neither one of us said a thing. Once back at our little hideout, I got out of the car and headed inside. BJ took a hard fast walk down the street. The Chief looked at me and asked. "Where's the boss?"

"He's walking down the road and I think he's in a hurry to get somewhere."

"No, he's not going anywhere. He's just walking off a little steam."

"Should I go with him?"

"Hell no! Not unless you want your ass kicked. He'll be back when he cools off."

"General Meyer, make sure that piece of coil disappears and make sure no one can ever find it again."

"Conrad, I don't see how that coil would be a concern now. We won't be hearing from Lieutenant Johnson anytime soon. I gave him twenty-four hours to get him and his men out of Germany."

265

"Do you really think we've seen the last of that man? Don't be naive, General. He's not going anywhere. He's a man on a mission, and as long as he's alive, he's a problem."

"So, what would you like me to do about him?"

"For now, find out where he's hiding with the rest of his men and then make sure he gets out of Germany. If he's still here after tomorrow, kill him."

"Don't worry Conrad, I'll put my best people on it. In fact, I will use the very men he trained."

"Are you sure they will be willing to kill him?"

"These men are loyal to me. They will do whatever I tell them."

"Very well then. Get it done. One more thing, General. I want you to find out what you can about that scientist. I don't believe he is who he says he is. He said it was his design and he also said, 'my father is'. Why would he say that? I want to know who he really is. He may be of some use to us."

"I'll see what I can find out."

"Sir, you have a call from Conrad Mueller."

"Put him through."

"Herr Mueller, what can I do for you?"

"Hellman, we may have a problem. I just left General Meyer. We were at the warehouse that you destroyed and we found a coil that was not destroyed."

"Conrad, we tried to get as much of the equipment out as we could before we blew up the building. We ran out of time and had to leave some things behind. Who has the coil now?"

"The coil is not the problem. Meyer has it and he will take care of it. The real problem is Lieutenant Johnson. He is part of a highly trained US Army team. He told Meyer about site number one, the castle at Reichstein."

"How would he know about that?"

266

"There can only be one explanation. He must have been the man they chased out of the castle. They never did find a body. Somehow, he survived that fall."

"Yes. He must have and now he knows where we have our first weapon."

"Hellman, are you on site?"

"Yes, Herr Mueller."

"I have been here ever since we blew up the warehouse."

"How is the weapon coming along?"

"Very well. We have both generators up to 60% and our overheating problem seems to be under control."

"When will you be ready to test it?"

"First, we need to get to 90% before we test it. They are telling me five days before we can fire it. Even after we get to 90%, we still need to move it into position before we can fire it at the US missile base. That is at least two days to move it and set it up."

"Hellman, that is not acceptable. You need to push the men. I want that cut in half. You have three days to be ready. No excuses!"

"Herr Mueller, we will do the best we can, but three days may not be possible."

"If you're not out of the castle in the next three days, you may have to deal with Lieutenant Johnson. I don't believe for a minute that he is leaving Germany. I told Meyer to take care of him if he doesn't leave."

"Conrad, I have over seventy-five men guarding the castle. He will never get inside here."

"I'm not worried about him taking the castle. If he catches you out in the open before you're ready to use the weapon, you may be on the losing side of that fight."

"How many men does he have?"

"I have no idea. He may only have a handful or he may have a full squad of thirty or more. Whatever he has, you need to be ready for him."

"We will be Conrad. I won't let you down."

"I know I can count on you, Hellman. Long live Germany!"

"Yes, sir. Long live Germany!"

When BJ came through the door, he didn't look like he had worked off very much steam to me. He looked at me and then at the chief. "Chief, we need to talk. Our whole plan to have General Meyer help us has gone to s***. We will get no help from him or his army. I should have known when I couldn't reach my German contacts. They just disappeared right after they helped us raid the warehouse. They may not even be alive anymore. I think our only option may be to try and take the castle."

"Didn't you say this castle was built as a fort? We don't have any heavy weapons with us. It may be a big job trying to take an old castle with what we have here. If it's the same guys we ran into at the warehouse, it could turn into one hell of a firefight."

"I know, Chief, but we won't be going in alone. I have another squad of rangers at the missile base right now. Their leader is Casey Jones. I'm sure you remember him from our days in training. I had General Wellington send them over as backup."

"That's good to hear. I trust Casey and he has a good squad of men under him, but I think we may have a problem moving that many guys into place without being seen."

"No problem, Chief. We move our guys first and then I'll have Casey and his guys come in behind us. It will take a couple of days to get us all there and be ready to hit the castle, but with a little luck we can pull it off."

"I'm with you, boss. But going into that castle, you know we'll probably lose a couple of guys."

"It can't be helped, Chief. If they get that weapon online, we'll lose a lot more than a couple of guys. Right now, we must stay low. I always want two guys on watch. I'm afraid my friend General Meyer is going to send someone to pay us a visit."

"Why would he do that?"

"Because he gave me twenty-four hours to get us out of Germany. When he finds out we didn't leave, I'm sure he'll send someone to take care of us. It's just what I would do. So, get two guys out there and tell them to keep their eyes open. These guys won't be regular army. I'm sure he'll send the best he has. They may even be the guys we trained."

"I'm on it, boss. I'll post guys every four hours."

"Good! I'm going to call Casey and make sure he has his men ready to move."

"BJ, can I talk to you for a minute?"

"Yeah, what is it, John?"

"I overheard you talking with the chief. You said you were going to try and take down a castle."

"Not try, John, we will take down this castle and anyone who's in it if we have to."

"Why don't you wait for them to come out? Wouldn't it be easier to fight them out in the open? Wouldn't you have an advantage that way?"

"Yes, but I'm not going to wait for them to come out of that castle and start shooting at us with that weapon they've been building. That would be suicide. Why would you even suggest such a stupid idea?"

"BJ, listen to me. If they want to use that weapon, it must be out in the open. They will have to move it and it won't be in one piece, so they will be unable to fire it. Most likely it will be in pieces on a truck."

"You're right about that! I saw it sitting on flatbed trucks in the castle."

"That's what I'm trying to tell you. It can't be used when it's being moved. They need to move it to a high location before it can be aimed at anything."

"Why is that?"

"Because that electronic beam, that bolt of lightning, can only be used in a straight line. It can't shoot around corners or over anything. The beam must have a straight line of sight with no obstacles in the way. Otherwise, it's useless. One other thing you should think about."

"What's that?"

"You don't have to take these guys down as you put it. All you have to do is destroy one of the generators. If they only have one good generator, the other one is useless. They have to have both working to fire this as a weapon."

"John, you're so right! I knew there was a good reason to have you around. I would have never thought about all that without you."

"You're welcome. So, now can I get on a plane and get out of here?"

"I'm afraid not, John. You just proved to me how valuable you can be. I need you to stick around and see this through to the end."

"BJ, that's not what I agreed to. One or two days, that was the deal. It's been two days and I did what I was asked to do. Now, I need to go home."

"Sorry, John, no way. I can't let you leave. You know too much about this weapon. What you just told me probably saved the lives of half my men. Knowing they have to come out and all we really have to do is destroy one of the generators changes my whole game plan."

"Great. Glad I could help, but you still won't let me go home."

"Like I said when this is all over, then I'll send you home."

"So, what do I do now?"

"We're all going to just sit tight for a couple of days. I need to give my other squad time to gear up. I'll call Wellington tomorrow and fill him in on the plan. Once we get his okay, then we move."

The next day, BJ left our little hideout to do a little recon and call the general. "General Wellington, this is Lieutenant Johnson reporting."

"Hello, Brad!"

"General. I was counting on General Meyer to be on our side and help us out, but he is working with Mueller and won't be of any help whatsoever. In fact, I'm beginning to think of him as the enemy. We found proof and he and Mueller threw it right back in our face."

"I had a feeling something like that had happened. I got a call from the president. He was on the phone with the chancellor. The chancellor told him that there is no threat to Germany or anyone else from Conrad Mueller. He was very insistent that you and your men leave Germany and stop accusing Mueller."

"Is that what you want us to do?"

"Hell no, Brad! We can't stop at any cost. If this is truly as serious a threat as we think it is, there's no way we can stop."

"Okay then, General. Here is my plan for now. By tomorrow, Casey's squad will be ready to back us up. I already have them on the move. They should be on location at the same time we get there. Thanks to John we don't have to try and take down the castle. We're going to wait for them to come out. Once they're out in the open, we will target one of the generators and take it out. With only one good generator the weapon is useless. I'm sure with all the noise we'll be making to take out one of the generators, there won't be any way Meyer or anyone else can deny what's been going on."

"Sounds like a good plan. How are you going to get all your men in place without being caught?"

"I have a plan to move my squad a few men at a time during the day. The second squad will be on the move from the time they start until they meet us on location. They know enough to use back roads and stay out of sight."

"All right then, Brad. You have my approval to go. This might be the only chance to stop this guy. You have to make this happen."

"Yes, sir, I know. Is the president good with this?"

"Not a chance. He thinks I've told you to pull your guys out. Brad, if it doesn't work, we're both out of a job."

"General, if this doesn't work that will be the least of our problems."

"Yes, I suppose you're right about that. When will you be moving your men?"

"Tomorrow night. We're going to stay put for one more night before we move to our next position. That will put us close to the castle."

"Okay, Brad. Good luck. Keep me informed as best you can."

It was a long day sitting around this old building. I was starting to look and smell just like everyone else in this place. No one could go out during the day. Two of the men kept watch from the second-floor windows on three-hour shifts. I spent some time up there myself, but there was little to see. Mostly farmland and a few people walking around. I didn't see a single car or truck go down the road, only a horse drawn wagon. From the excitement and adrenaline rush of yesterday to the boredom of today. Talk about a change of pace. Shortly after what they called dinner (dinner was a poor choice of words for what we were eating), BJ finally got back. Without a word to anyone, BJ, the Chief and one other guy huddled over in a corner for over an hour. They were going over all the details of their plan to make certain they agreed that their plan was good. Taking down the men in that castle wouldn't be easy! I tried to eavesdrop without being obvious. One of his guys pulled me away and said "The boss will tell us what's going on and what the plan is when he's ready to. Best to leave him alone for now."

When they finally broke up, BJ called everyone together. For the next hour BJ laid out the plan. He had drawn a very good picture of a castle with a view from all four sides. I was impressed with the detail of the drawing and his plan. We were all told just what the plan was and how we would make our attack. He drilled each man in the squad until he was satisfied that they knew their role in the plan. When he was finally done, I asked "What do I do?"

"Good question. Stay out of the way."

"Oh sure, now that you don't need me."

"That's not it at all. You need to stay back out of the way until I need you. I will need you to verify that the generator is really destroyed. When it's safe to move you up, I'll have one of my guys come and get you. Until then stay back and out of sight."

"When is all this going to happen?"

"We will stay here tonight. Tomorrow, we will move closer to the castle. I know of a place we can hole up until the next day. That will give Casey and his squad time to get into position. Then we just sit and wait for them to come out and we'll do our thing."

"Good. I'm glad I only have to spend one more night in this place."

"John, you have no idea. This place is great compared to some of the hell holes I've spent time in. It makes this place feel like a 4-star hotel!"

BJ gave the order for everyone to get some rest since we would be walking a long way tomorrow.

I had been asleep for several hours. When I woke up, I heard people moving around. I started to get up, but then this huge hand pushed me back down. The only one I know that had a hand that big was the chief. Sure enough, the chief was staring right at me. He whispered "Stay put!"

He didn't have to tell me twice. I could see well enough in the dark that each man had a gun in his hand. This couldn't be good! I heard a radio click twice and then twice again. BJ was holding the radio. I think he answered back because every few seconds there were more clicks.

This went on for about thirty seconds. BJ started pointing and giving head nods. Everyone seemed to know just what he meant. They all began moving at the same time like a well-oiled machine. They all moved to different spots in the building and for all that movement, they hadn't made a sound. BJ pushed open a side window and disappeared into the dark. The chief gave me one more push just to make sure I wasn't going anywhere. Then he disappeared out the front door as silent as a cat stalking a mouse. How can a man that big move like that? I had no idea what was happening, but I knew it wasn't anything we had planned on. Whatever it was, my heart was pounding so hard I was sure they could all hear it.

Once outside, BJ started making his way to the man on watch. He was well hidden in a small batch of bushes. BJ asked him "What's up?"

"There's movement about a hundred fifty yards up the hill. I saw at least two figures moving down through the trees. I'm sure they're not alone. They never send just two."

"You're right. Those two are only the beginning. Okay, get back to the building, but stay outside. I want some firepower outside with me. I'm going to work my way around back to where you last saw them. I want to get the jump on them before they get down here."

BJ was in his element. This is what he lived for, what he is trained to do. He made his way to a shallow ditch running away from our building. He stayed low in the ditch for a short distance until he was sure they couldn't see him and then he crossed through a weedy field moving uphill until he was even with the spot where the intruders had been seen. Now the hard part was getting close enough to strike without being seen. Slowly hand-over-hand, he crawled in their direction. The dark and breezy night was in his favor and he was down wind of their position. Just where he wanted to be. With the help of the rustling of the leaves, his approach was undetectable. As quiet as he was, there was no way anyone would hear him coming, crawling through the grass as silent as a snake.

Just ahead of him now was a small group of trees and that's where they had to be. He just needed to get closer. Inch by inch, less than fifty feet. There they were, right where the guard said they would be. Thirty feet away, he froze.

One of the dark figures turned in his direction. BJ laid still as a rock and controlled his breathing. He was downwind and flat to the ground. There was no way he could be seen. Still the dark figure kept looking right at him. Finally, he turned back to watch the building. Closer now, less than twenty feet. He could hear them talking and they were speaking German. So, Meyer did send someone out to take care of us. Not tonight. Not if BJ had anything to say about it. They kept talking softly, confident that they were safe and sure that no one knew they were here. Wrong!

They had no idea they're being stalked. Now BJ was only ten feet away and right behind them. He made a quick check around to make sure there were only the two of them. He springs to his feet and he's on them in an instant. He strikes hard with the confidence of a lion after its prey. He takes out the first man with the butt of his gun, a blow that sends him crashing to the ground. He wasn't getting up anytime soon. A lightning quick turn to the second man with the same idea. The man had just enough time to deflect the blow and grab BJ's gun. Now they were both on their feet. The German was every bit as tall as BJ and more than ready for a fight.

The two men both had a death grip on the gun. The German pushed back against his attacker and then pulled back hard, sending BJ flying over his shoulder. They both hit the ground sending the gun flying out of reach. BJ was on his feet in an instant, as was his adversary.

Both men lunged at each other, sending them to the ground once again. BJ got in a good punch to his attacker's head just as a knee landed in his chest. They rolled downhill fighting each other until they hit a tree. The impact broke their grip on each other. BJ was first to his feet and this time he had the advantage. He caught his opponent by the neck and put a solid choke hold on him. The man fought hard to get free, trying to break the death grip BJ had on him, but as his air ran out, he began to give in.

Just as he was about to pass out, he mumbled something in German. BJ recognizes the voice. He loosens his hold just a little and lets the man down to the ground.

BJ's mind was racing. Who is this guy? The voice was familiar, but who?

Holy crap, it's Reinhardt! Lieutenant Reinhardt from the German Special Forces Unit. BJ reached into his pocket for a small flashlight and shined it on the man's face. It was Reinhardt. He was still choking and gasping for air. BJ knew he couldn't kill him now that he knew who he was, but what to do with him? He dragged him back up the hill to where the other man was lying still unconscious. Tying both men to a tree, he headed back down the hill to their hideout. Williams was still standing outside guarding the building. He yelled "That better be you, boss, or you're a dead man."

"Don't shoot, it's me. Go grab a couple of guys and meet me up the hill by those trees. I left two men tied up by those trees. We need to bring them down. I know who they are."

Things were still kind of tense inside. Once BJ got back, someone turned on some lights. He had two men with him I had never seen before. BJ's first question was "Where's the chief?"

Just as one of the guys started to answer, the door flew open. An unidentified man came tumbling through the door, followed by the chief. He was carrying another guy on his shoulder.

Whoever he was, he was bleeding bad. The chief dropped him on the floor and told our medic to take care of him. BJ looked at the chief and said, "Guess who I ran into?"

The chief answered "Wolfgang Reinhardt."

"That's right, how did you know?"

"Because they're still making the same stupid mistakes they were making when we tried to train them years back. These two were yacking up a storm when I jumped them. They never heard me coming until I landed on them."

"That's pretty much the same thing with Wolfgang and his buddy over there."

"Boss, you said they would send someone to look for us, but I didn't think it would be the guys we trained."

"Chief, I was pretty confident that would be just who Meyer would send. Who better to find us than the men we trained."

"Well, it seems like the training didn't work out too well. If these clowns are the best they've got, then we don't have much to worry about."

That's when the man they called Wolfgang spoke up. "Lieutenant Johnson, you have this all wrong. It's true, General Meyer did send us to find you and if need be, eliminate you. We didn't come here to kill anyone. For some time now, Meyer has been acting strange and saying things that make no sense. When he told me to take my unit, track you down and kill you no questions asked, I knew something was seriously wrong. I have no idea what's going on right now, but I know it can't be good. Meyer was way out of line with an order like that."

BJ walked over and untied Wolfgang. He asked him "If you're not here to try to eliminate us, why were you hiding on the hill and where are the rest of your men?"

"I sent two of them to watch Meyer and find out what he's up to. I have the rest of them staying out of sight for now."

"All right, but that doesn't explain why you were watching us."

"I remember you and the Chief very well. From what I learned about you when you were training us, I knew there had to be a good reason for you to be operating in Germany, especially without permission. I'm really surprised you didn't contact me for support. My men and I didn't think for a minute you were here to hurt Germany and I still don't."

"Well, you're right. We're not here to hurt Germany, just the opposite. We are trying to save Germany."

"Save us from what?"

"Yourselves."

"What do you mean?"

"There's a guy named Conrad Mueller. He wants to take over Germany and then the world if he gets his way."

"I know this Conrad. He has Meyer jumping through hoops helping him. Although I don't know what they're up to. I take it you have some idea what they're trying to do?"

"Yes! The short story is that Conrad stole plans from the US to build a static charge machine. His goal is to turn it into a weapon that is incredibly powerful. Nothing like you've ever seen before."

BJ turned to me. "John, tell Wolfgang about your machine."

I said "He's telling you the truth. The machine was built in the US, but it was never intended to be a weapon. Conrad Mueller is trying to build three of these machines. One would really be all he'd ever need."

Wolfgang said, "You're telling me if he only had one of these weapons, he could take over Germany!"

"Yes, and much more."

"Just what the hell is this thing?"

"The machine was meant to make electricity by firing a super charge lightning bolt into a receiver. If you fire the beam at anything else, it could easily destroy whatever you point it at."

"I find this all very hard to believe!"

"Well, believe it. It killed my father!"

Wolfgang looked at BJ. "Is what he's saying as bad as it sounds?"

"No, it's worse. You haven't heard the really bad part yet! Go ahead John tell him the really bad part."

"There's more?"

"Oh yes, there's more. John, tell him!"

"BJ's right. There's another problem. If they try to fire the machine at full strength, it will most likely backfire on them and cause a fire so hot it will burn the very air we breathe. The fireball it will create is many times hotter than the sun. Once it starts, there's no putting it out. If that happens Germany will cease to exist. Every man, woman, child, and animal that breathes air will die. This fire ball, if it gets started, will most likely take out a large part of Europe with it. Truth is, we don't know where it will stop, or if it even will stop."

No one said anything for a few minutes. I think we all were hit by the significance of what I just said.

Wolfgang asked "So, what you're telling me is that no one in Germany or anywhere else would survive?"

"No one and nothing that breathes air. Every human being, every animal that breathes air will die. It will burn everything to the ground."

"Who in his right mind would ever build such a weapon?"

"It was never supposed to be used as a weapon. It was meant to help people."

Wolfgang sat there in stunned silence. Then he looked at me. "John, you said it killed your father. You're the son of the man who built this thing. Meyer wanted us to bring you back to him. He didn't believe your story about being a scientist. He said you knew too much."

BJ interrupted. "Never mind that now. John is safe with us. So, Wolfgang, now that you know why we're here and what we're doing, what are you going to do to help us?"

"Lieutenant Johnson, my men and I will do whatever it takes to help you stop Conrad or anyone else we need to stop. We must stop this from happening. What do you want us to do?"

"Do you think you can get any help from the army?"

"Not with Meyer in charge."

"Okay then, how many men do you have?"

"Including me, I have twenty-six men, minus the two you just put down."

"Yeah, sorry about that, but you were spying on us. I have my squad and a second squad. They will be here the day after tomorrow. That should be more than we need to take down the castle if we need to."

"Take down a castle, what are you talking about?"

"I'll explain later, Wolfgang. For now, call your men, and make sure they're okay. We all need to get some rest. We've got a long hike ahead of us tomorrow."

By five the next morning, we were on the move. Wolfgang left to get his men together and meet us at the rendezvous point the next day. We had too many men to stay together, so BJ broke us up into smaller groups. Each group would find their own way to our next location. BJ gave instructions to each leader and all he would tell us was that we were going to meet a couple of nice old ladies. I was sure it was a code term for something, but I had no idea what it was.

I would find out later what it really meant.

BJ had us moving at a hard pace. I was in good shape, but I was starting to hear my feet talking to me. Finally, we stopped in a little patch of woods just off the road. Lunch was dry with only a little water to pass around. I asked BJ how close we were. I was sorry I had asked.

"Just a little over halfway."

We were back on the move going at the same pace or even a little faster. About the time I was ready to quit, BJ pulled us all off the road.

BJ told us "We're going to hold up here until it gets dark. We're just outside of a little town and I don't want to have to go around it. We'll go through after dark, then we're only about ten miles from our next stop. I hit the ground and was asleep in two minutes.

Someone kicked my feet to wake me up. I felt like I had just fallen asleep. It was dark and time to move. Only ten miles more. Only. My body ached all over and I was falling behind. I just couldn't keep the pace.

We passed through this little town, maybe a dozen small buildings without a single light on. It was more like a ghost town. I wondered if anyone really lived there. About a mile or so out of town, the road started up a hill. It wasn't much of a hill, but it was more than I could handle. I completely stopped. My feet just refused to move anymore. When I looked up the road, I could see the chief coming in my direction. I knew he was going to kick my ass all the way up this hill.

The fear of what the chief might do to me didn't help. I couldn't make my feet move. I closed my eyes and waited for whatever was coming.

Next thing I knew, I was being thrown into the air like a rag doll. I came down on the chief's shoulder looking down and being carried backward up the hill. I felt utterly embarrassed, like when your dad throws you over his shoulder because you did something wrong.

I was too tired to protest, so I let him carry me. If he hadn't come back for me, I'd still be standing there in the same spot.

Sometime later, the chief dropped me on the ground. BJ had told his men to wait there. Apparently, he had run off to check on something. He was back in about a half an hour. He had gone ahead to check out our stop for the night.

I was able to walk the little distance left. We passed a little farmhouse and headed right into an old barn. There were two large horses, a few sheep and about a dozen chickens in the barn. There was still plenty of room for us once they pushed the wagon outside. I found a nice pile of straw in the corner and was just about to fall asleep when two old ladies walked into the barn carrying a lantern and two big baskets of food.

The smell of real food made me want to cry. We must have eaten everything they had in the house. They came out four times. More food and water. Every one of us gave them a kiss and a hug thanking them for helping us and feeding us. They seemed happy to do it. I was just heading back to my corner in the barn when I saw BJ, the chief and two of his guys head out for who knows where. I wasn't sure if these guys were real men or just machines dressed up like men. How could you go anywhere after the day we just put in? Every bone in my body hurt, and all I wanted was to sleep.

Next morning the chief kicked me to wake me up and said, "You better get your ass up or you're going to go hungry."

The two ladies were back with hot coffee, fresh bread, boiled eggs and sausage. They must have been up all-night cooking. Where did BJ find these two angels? It wasn't until much later when I found out the whole story about who found who. I guess the code word for old ladies wasn't a code word after all. Thank God they were real.

All the joy of a good breakfast went away in an instant when BJ called everyone together and started to lay out the plans for later that day.

"All right, gentlemen, bring it in. We've got a lot to talk about, a lot to go over and not a lot of time to plan this out. We are fifteen miles from the castle where they have one of the machines. I've had a long talk with our lady friends and they gave me an earful. It seems for the last week or, so men and machines have been going by the house. The ladies took a wagon ride up there the other day and saw trucks parked all around one side of the castle. They also saw a lot of men standing guard on every level of the castle. That's not good for us. I believe with the addition of Casey's squad and Wolfgang's men, we could take the castle if need be. I don't think we'll have to do that thanks to John. I have a feeling that Conrad wants to use this weapon as soon as he can. He knows that we're looking for him and his machine now more than ever. He has General Meyer working with him and Meyer is doing his best to convince Germany's chancellor that everything is fine and dandy. Meyer is also keeping a lid on this from the local police. So, it's up to all of us to expose Mueller and Meyer and destroy this weapon before he gets a chance to use it."

BJ continued and everyone was focused on him. "John has explained to me that they have to bring the weapon outside and take it to a high point before they can use it. So, that's when we are going to hit them. My plan is to have our second squad guard the road to the south. Wolfgang and his men will guard the road to the north. We will be right in front of the only door where they would come out of the castle with the trucks carrying the weapon."

"Excuse me boss, but wouldn't that make us sitting ducks with a weapon like this?"

"No! Sorry, I left out one little detail. John also told me they have no way of using their weapon until it is set up in place and has a straight line of sight to their target. They can't use it when it's on a truck and on the move."

"Yeah, boss, that's one little detail you left out!"

"So Chief, are you telling me you're afraid of a little lightning bolt?"

"No boss. Not a little one, but a great big ass one! Yes, just a little."

"Well, we won't be fighting the weapon, just the men trying to use it. Okay, back to our plan. From what the ladies told me, I think we're up against around a hundred men. With us, the second squad and Wolfgang's men, that's pretty much one-on-one and I'll take those odds any day. They can't throw everything at us all at once anyway. When they come out, they will form up into a convoy. I believe the first one or two trucks will be heavily armed escort trucks. The equipment itself will come out next, followed by more armed escort trucks. I want to let the first armored escort trucks and the first equipment truck go by. Then, we hit the next truck out with everything we have. Once we take out that truck, everything behind it is stuck in the castle. Hopefully the first armored escort truck and the first equipment truck will make a run for wherever they were headed. If that happens, they will be all yours, Wolfgang. You and your men will need to run them down and stop them. That only leaves about half of their men at the castle with both our squads in place. We should have no problem handling what's left and getting inside the castle. Any questions?"

The chief was the only one to speak up. "So, how is it you're so sure they will have all this equipment on more than one truck? If it's all on one truck and we let the first one go by, we could miss our only chance to end this."

"Good question, Chief. I was in the castle and saw the two generators. Each one was mounted to its own truck. The high-pressure blower was on another truck and all the control panels to run it were on a separate truck. The whole thing is mobile, but it takes four flatbed trucks to move it. All we need to do is take out one of the generators and then the weapon becomes useless."

"Just how did you get in and out of that castle without being seen?"

"Sorry, Chief, that's my little secret. No more questions? Good I want every man to double check your gear. We may only have one shot at this and I don't want to make any mistakes. One more thing. My call sign tonight will be 'old quarterback'. Casey's squad's call sign will be 'wide receiver' and Wolfgang's outfit is call sign 'tailback.' No one is to answer to anything else. Get some rest.

We move out as soon as it gets dark. I want to be in place long before daybreak."

The rest of the day was quiet. BJ took two guys with him and disappeared until just before dark. The chief made his rounds every so often checking and rechecking each man and his gear. No one got any rest, least of all me. So many thoughts kept running through my head and the biggest one was how the hell did I get here? I was perfectly happy teaching back at RIT and living my life with Mary. What was Mary going through? I hadn't talked to her in three days or maybe four. Whatever it was, it was too long. I can't believe how much I miss her.

The ladies brought us more food late in the afternoon. Not too many of us had an appetite except the chief. He ate like it was his first meal in a week. The anticipation of what was coming didn't change his appetite.

When the ladies were done handing out food and talking with the men, they headed back into the house. The Chief went back to the house with them. I was standing at the barn door when I saw the chief come out of the house laughing and shaking his head. I hadn't seen him even smile before that, let alone laugh. When he got close, I asked him what was so funny. All he said was "You'll never find out from me." I wondered why he wouldn't let me in on what was so funny. I could have used a little laugh right about then.

Chapter 31

"Herr Hellman, this is Mueller."

"Yes, Herr Mueller, I was just getting ready to call you. I have good news. The men have been working non-stop and have reached 85% on the generators. We have a slight heating problem, but with a little more work I'm sure we can control it."

"Hellman, tell me how far the beam will reach at 85%?"

"They tell me that at 85%, we will easily reach the missile base from the mountain site we have picked out."

"Have you fired it yet?"

"No, Herr Mueller. Test firing was never part of the plan. We had agreed to reach 90% and then move it to the site on the mountain."

"I'm giving you new orders now. I want you to test fire it as soon as possible and tell me what happens."

"Conrad, we cannot possibly fire it from inside the castle. It could kill all of us."

"Hellman, I know you can't fire it inside the castle. Open the outer door that we installed and aim it out the door. I want the weapon test fired before we expose it to anyone. The worst thing that could happen for us would be to move it out into the open and then not be able to use it. Everything we planned would be lost at that point."

"But Mueller if we test fire it, won't that be just as bad?"

"No, just aim it up into the air. It will be a harmless bolt of electricity. People will have no idea where it came from even if they do see it. How soon will you be ready to test it?"

"If we start moving it into position today, we should be ready to test fire tomorrow afternoon sometime."

"Good! If all goes well, I want you to prepare the weapon to be moved the next day. That will have us ready to hit the US missile base in two days. Hellman, I'm counting on you to make this happen. Don't let me down."

"You have my word, Conrad."

"Very good then. Long live Germany! Hellman, once you are confident things are under control there, I want you to turn this over to Kraus and move to site two. They are behind schedule. I need you to get them caught up."

"Yes Sir."

"Kraus, this is Hellman. Get up to my office right now." Kraus was in Hellman's office in less than two minutes. "Kraus, reporting as ordered sir. What can I do for you?"

"Sit down Kraus. I just got off the phone with Mueller. I think he's losing it! He wants us to test fire the weapon before we move it into position to hit the missile base."

"Sir, that will take two days at least. We would have to move it somewhere outside the castle. Set it up, fire it, then break it down and move it again. We haven't reached 90% yet."

"Kraus, listen to me. That doesn't matter anymore. He's happy with 85% and you don't have to move it. You can fire it from inside the castle."

"Inside the castle! That's not possible. It will kill us all."

"Not if you aim it out the door we installed."

"That may be possible, but I doubt it will clear the hill outside."

"What happens if it doesn't clear the hill?"

"I have no idea. It's possible that it could start a fire just like any lightning bolt. Only this one is many times more powerful than you get in a storm. I've heard our own scientists talk about the power this thing has. They're talking like they're afraid to even fire it at anything. They're just not sure what will happen when it's fired."

"Well, they better be sure because they are going to fire it tomorrow. Tell them to get ready."

"Yes, sir, Herr Hellman."

"Kraus, I'm leaving this in your hands. I've been ordered to site two. They're falling behind schedule and I need to get them back on track. Long Live Germany!"

"Yes Herr Hellman. Long Live Germany!"

Mary asked the operator "Could you please try again? I must speak to General Wellington."

"I will try one more time, but he hasn't been picking up."

"Did you tell him it was Mary Williams calling?"

"I left your name with him yesterday. He knows you've been trying to reach him. Wait, I have him on the line. I will put him through right now."

"Hello Mary. General Wellington here. How are you?"

"How am I! How do you think I am! I'm going crazy sitting in this hotel! I haven't heard from John since he called me from Germany and told me he'd be home in a couple of days. General, be honest with me. Is John all right? Is he in any danger?"

"Mary, I'm sure John is fine. I spoke with BJ just the other day and he said John was fine, but he needed him to stay there for a few more days. That's all I can say right now. I hope this is all over in a couple of days. I will make sure John gets home safely."

"That's just what you said last time, General. You said you sent John to Frankfurt, right?"

"Yes, that's where we sent him."

"Is he still there?"

"I can't answer that, Mary."

"Just tell me yes or no. Is he still in Germany?"

"I can't tell you, Mary. You must understand. What he and BJ are doing is of national importance. I can't talk about it with you or anyone else."

"Can you at least tell me if his life is in danger?"

"Mary, he's in the best hands he could be in right now. BJ won't let anything happen to him, trust me."

"General, if you can't or won't tell me anything more than that, then I'm going to Frankfurt myself and find John."

"No, Mary you're not! That's an order!"

"Sorry, General, but I'm not in your army and I don't take orders from you. I'll do what I want and you can't stop me."

"Mary, I can stop you and I will if you don't listen to me. John would not want you to be over there. Trust me it's not safe for you to be there right now."

"You just told me that John was safe and now you're telling me it's not safe for me. Which is it, General?"

"Mary, you know I can't give you details on what's going on over there. You'll just have to trust me and stay here until John gets back."

"That's awfully hard to do considering everything you told me lately has been a lie."

"I haven't lied to you, Mary. Everything I told you was the truth at the time. It all changed after John got over there. I expect to hear from BJ in the next day or so. When I do, I will ask about John and give you a call."

"Do I have your word General?"

"Yes, Mary. Absolutely. I will call as soon as I know something."

"Okay then, I will stay here in Washington for now."

"Very good, Mary. I will call you soon."

The first thing BJ did when he got back was to call us all together once more. "Listen up men. We were just up by the castle and it's just like the ladies told us. We saw over twenty guards stationed all around the castle and at different levels inside the castle. The plan is still the same. We all get into position and then wait for them to come out. Once they start to move, you all know

289

what to do. If anything changes, I'll make the call. Stay on your radios and listen for my orders to strike. All right. It's dark enough and time to go. We've got all night to get there, so take your time. Once we get there, get settled in and stay put. This could be a long wait."

We headed out in groups of threes and fours. BJ didn't want us all walking in one big group just in case someone spotted us. I was with BJ and two other men in the lead group. We walked along at a good pace and this time I was able to keep up. About two hours later, we took a short break.

BJ passed the word that we were only a mile out and it was time to get off the road. We started up a hill and into the woods. The going was easy at first, just a little brush and small trees. Gradually the hill got steeper and the underbrush got thicker. I was only fifteen or twenty feet behind BJ, but in the dark and fighting through the brush and trees, I lost sight of him many times. Good thing the guys behind me kept me moving in the right direction. After what seemed like another two hours, we came to a little clearing. BJ was down on one knee looking at something down the hill. He handed me his night vision binoculars and said, "Take a look."

There it was just as plain as day. The castle we've been talking about was much bigger than I had imagined. This was the first castle I had ever seen, except in a book or on TV. It was impressive to say the least. It had to be a hundred feet tall and three hundred feet across. I could make out the different levels of the castle. I could only guess how much there was below the ground. Sitting there in the dark, it was an intimidating building. The thought of trying to shoot our way in was inconceivable to me. My mind drifted back to medieval times when knights would storm a castle like this. What a battle that must have been!

BJ began to place his men up and down the hill just where he wanted them. I asked him "Where do you want me?"

He handed me a small radio and said "Do you see those three big trees up the hill? I want you up there, behind those trees. Stay put until I call you. Once we have things under control, I'll call you down and then you can make sure we've destroyed at least one of the generators."

"BJ, I know you're looking out for me, but from up there I won't be able to see anything."

"That's the idea, John. If you can't see anything, then no one can see you to shoot at you."

"Good point. I'm on my way."

Getting up the hill was a job. There were times I had to grab small trees to pull myself up. When I finally got up to the three trees, I found a nice place between them and sat down for a rest.

The next thing I knew the sun was coming up. It looked like a scene out of a story book. I was high up on a hill looking down on an ancient castle surrounded by lush green vegetation and trees with a beautiful blue river running behind it all. The sun was glistening off the river and lit up the side of the old castle as it rose into the sky. I found myself wishing Mary were here to see this. Then reality set in. I was so glad Mary was back in the states where she was out of danger. The thought of what was going to happen here today had me more than a little scared. I started looking around for BJ and his men. I knew right where they were, but I couldn't see any of them. I also knew that the second squad and Wolfgang's man were down there somewhere. I couldn't see a single man anywhere. I guess that's a good thing. If I could see them, then they wouldn't be very good at their job.

As the sun came up and it got lighter, I could make out small figures on and around the castle. From where I was, that was all I could see. The morning passed without any activity around the castle. I got a little bored, so I took a little hike up to the very top of the hill. It wasn't that far, maybe a hundred feet or less. What a spectacular view. I could see for miles. Germany was indeed a beautiful country. Too bad this jerk Conrad was trying to ruin it.

After a few minutes, I made my way back down to my hiding place. Just as I got there, I saw a huge door opening at the bottom of a ramp leading to what I believe was the basement of the castle. That must be where they built the weapon. Great! Now, I'm calling it a weapon. They must be getting ready to bring it out. As much as I was afraid of the fight that would soon take place, I was also a little curious to watch it all happen.

Unbeknownst to us, inside the castle Kraus was carrying out the orders he had been given by Hellman. All the men who had been working on the weapon protested the order.

"Kraus, we are not prepared to fire it at this time. We certainly do not want to fire it from inside the castle. We have no way of knowing what will happen. To fire from a confined space could be extremely dangerous for all of us. The air pressure alone could kill someone if they cross in front of it. We don't believe the beam will clear the hill outside. Even if it does, it will bring unwanted attention to what we've been doing here."

"Your concerns are of no matter. We have our orders from Conrad himself. We are to test fire the weapon by tomorrow afternoon. If all goes well, we will then move the weapon tomorrow night and be ready to hit the missile base the next day. I don't care if you must work all night to make this happen. I think you better get started. You will fire it by tomorrow afternoon. Do you understand?"

"Yes sir, we understand!"

By mid-afternoon the next day, they told Kraus they were ready. The weapon was moved into place. It had been aimed out the door and up over the hill, just as Conrad had ordered. If this worked, Conrad would be in control of Germany within three days. The world would never be the same.

The large steel door was opened. Kraus gave the order to start up the generators and prepare to fire. As the generators came up to speed, they turned on the high-pressure fan. It roared like a jet engine and sent pieces of hundred-year-old dust, dirt and everything that wasn't nailed down flying out the door in front of the castle.

The scientist gave Kraus the signal that they were ready. He signaled to fire. Just as they were about to throw the lever, one of the generators lost power and started to slow down. A critical fuse had just blown. It would only take a few minutes to fix it.

As I sat there trying to imagine what this battle would look like, I heard a large noise coming from the castle. I looked down the hill at the castle only to see it disappear in a cloud of dust. What just happened?

I couldn't believe that trucks coming out of the castle could possibly make that much noise and a cloud of dust that big. Within a minute, the air blast hit me. There was only one reason for that amount of air pressure to be coming out of the castle. They were trying to fire the weapon and it was aimed right at me. I knew I might only have seconds to get out of the way. I leaped to my feet and made a beeline for the top of the hill. I did a headfirst over the top and went tumbling down the other side. I kept going down until I was well below the hilltop.

I had left my radio, backpack and jacket right by the trees and right now I really could care less. Then I realized I had no way to tell BJ I had moved. I was well down the hill and safe if they did fire the weapon.

I started to make my way across the side of the hill to a spot where I would be safe to go back to the top. I had almost reached the top when I heard a tremendous roar and what sounded like a blast from a ton of dynamite. I saw pieces of trees and tree limbs flying. The ground shook under my feet and the flash was blinding. They had done it. They had fired the weapon and it worked. God, have mercy.

The world will never be the same. I wanted to cry, scream, curse at my father and pray for help. Then I got mad, madder than I ever thought I could be. I had to get to BJ. He had to stop them no matter what the cost.

I had to get back down the hill to where I last saw him. I realized that BJ had seen the lightning bolt hit the very trees he had sent me to hide behind. The trees had exploded instantly into a million pieces and there was a hole in the ground you could have buried a car in. There was no way anyone who was within a hundred feet of that blast could have survived.

BJ had left his place of concealment and headed up the hill to look for me, knowing full well I was probably dead. When he got to where I was supposed to be all he found was part of a burned backpack. He never told me, but he just stood there looking in the hole and crying.

I made my way back down the hill to where I thought BJ would be. The cloud of dust around the castle is beginning to settle. I had to find someone quick or I would be seen running around. I was making my way around when I was yanked off my feet. The Chief pulled me down. "Why are you running around like a lost dog?"

"I have to find BJ!"

"He went up on the hill looking for you. I'll call him and tell him you're down here."

The Chief radioed BJ and told him I was with him. I heard BJ tell the chief "Hang on to him. I'm going to kill him when I get down there."

I didn't know if he was serious or not. When BJ got back down to us, I could see the relief on his face. He came up to me and gave me a hug around the neck and then a love tap alongside my head.

"How did you know you had to move?"

"Easy. When I saw and felt the air blast coming out of the castle, I knew they were trying to fire the weapon. Why they didn't fire it right away, I don't know. I knew they were trying because I was with my father once when he fired it in his lab. You must bring the generators up to speed then turn on the high-pressure fan. Once that's running for a minute, you can fire the weapon at whatever you want. I don't think they were firing at me. I think they just wanted to shoot it up into the sky. They just misjudged the angle."

"Well, it's a good thing you moved when you did!"

"You're telling me!"

BJ checked in with everyone to make sure no one was hurt. They were just a little surprised by how powerful the blast was. Outside the castle, things looked a little chaotic. Men were running everywhere, and no one seemed to know what to do or where to go. The last thing they were thinking about was us. I told BJ that I was pretty sure they wouldn't be firing it again. He decided to move some of his men closer. I was told to go back up the hill and stay out of the line of fire just in case they did fire it again.

Nothing else happened that afternoon that we could see. It was starting to get dark and I had left my backpack and jacket at the site of the blasts. I wasn't going to go looking for them. There was nothing left of them anyway. It was getting cold and I was hungry. I made my way back down to BJ. "What the hell are you doing back down here?"

"I'm getting cold and I haven't had anything to eat all day."

"Poor boy. Welcome to my world! Take my jacket. There's food in my backpack. Take what you want and then get your ass back up the hill where you belong."

"Yes, Sir, but before I go, I want to give you an idea."

"I can't wait to hear this."

"What if I go down there with a white flag and talk to them. I'm sure they have no way of knowing what will happen if they reach 90 or 95% on the generators. If I could convince them of what they may cause, they might just surrender the weapon without a fight."

"Are you out of your mind? They just fired it and successfully I might add and now you think they're just going to give it up because you said it will explode on them!"

"BJ, as bad as that was, I'm sure they were only at 80 or 85%. I told you what happened in the lab when my dad went past that. It's worth a try and if it works no one gets killed and we stop all this."

"I don't know John. It's a crazy idea, but it might just work or they might shoot you on sight."

"Not if I'm carrying a white flag."

"John, there's no guarantee they're going to honor a white flag. Men like these don't live by the same moral code you and I do. Even if they don't shoot you on sight, they may not let you go once you're in there."

"BJ, I really want to give this a try. I believe it'll work."

"Stay here. I'm going to talk this over with the Chief. I want to see what he thinks and we need a backup plan if this goes south on us."

Twenty minutes later BJ was back. "The Chief thinks you're nuts, but he agrees it might just work. You are the son of the man who invented it, so just maybe you can convince them how bad this is. We'll give it a try and see what happens."

"What do you mean we?"

"I'm going with you. You can convince them to give up the weapon and I can tell them what will happen if they don't."

"That's fine with me. I'll be glad to have some company."

We waited until after dawn which came way too soon. I didn't get any rest all night. I kept going over what I would say to these guys once I got in front of them. It was just about the middle of the morning when BJ tapped me on the shoulder. "Are you ready for this?"

"No, but let's go."

We started down the hill. When we got to the road, BJ pulled out a white flag and started waving it. It didn't take long for them to see us. They came running at us and pointing their guns right at our heads. We just stood there with our arms up. The first man started to ask us questions. "Who are you, and what are you doing here?" BJ was very direct. He told them who he was and then explained who I was. He told them we needed to see whoever was in charge and said the information we had could cost everyone here their lives if we don't get a chance to talk to someone. That got their attention and they started leading us down the ramp into the castle.

The afternoon before, just after they had fired the weapon, things had gone terribly wrong just as their scientist had predicted. They should have never fired it inside. Two men were dead. They thought they were safe where they were, however, they got pulled into the air blast and were killed instantly when the weapon was fired. Two others were burned and those without ear protection couldn't hear anything. One man got killed when he was caught by the air blast and blew out the door.

Even with all that had happened, Kraus told Hellman that it was a successful firing and he ordered the men to get the weapon ready to move. They had spent the night taking the equipment apart and getting ready to move it to the mountain site. They were about half done when they brought us to see Kraus.

"Herr Kraus. These two were out in front of the castle waving a white flag and asking to talk to you."

"Who are you?" said Kraus "and what makes you think your white flag will keep you alive?"

"My name is Lieutenant Brad Johnson of the US army rangers, Division 504 Special Forces. This is John Northrup. He's a scientist and he's the co-inventor of this weapon you have. He has something to tell you that is going to save your life and the lives of all the men you have here in this castle."

"Again, why should I listen to anything you have to say?"

"I have over a hundred men outside waiting to take you down. This is your only chance to end this without bloodshed. If you want proof, send one of your men outside. Tell him to look up the hill."

Kraus sent a man out front. BJ called the Chief and told him to have half the men stand up and wave. Two minutes later the man came running back in. "It's true. He has men all up and down the hill." Kraus still didn't want to listen. BJ must have one big set of brass balls! He got right in Kraus's face and said "Listen you stupid F---ing German! We are trying to save your worthless hide!"

That did the trick.

"Okay, then talk."

"John, you're up and make it good."

"I want to talk to your scientist. The men who actually built this machine."

Kraus asked "Why do you need to talk to them?"

"They are the only ones who will understand what I'm saying."

Kraus called for three men to come forward. He said "These are the men who built this weapon. Tell them your story."

I said, "First of all, this was never meant to be a weapon!" For the next twenty minutes I told them the whole story, right through to where my father had died in his lab and what we think will happen if it backfires outside. Two of the men just stood there and turned as pale as a person could get. The third man grabbed my arm and pleaded with me to be sure I was telling him the truth. He said they felt there was a danger of something like that happening. They felt it all along because their calculations just didn't work out. When I was done talking, BJ turned to Kraus.

"We'll be leaving now and give you time to think about what we've told you. Don't take too long. My men are itching for a fight. I want your answer before dark. You know where to find me when you want to talk."

We turned and walked right out the door. Kraus was speechless. He just stared and watched us leave.

As we were leaving, I heard his scientist pleading to Kraus to give up the weapon and leave.

I was shaking like a leaf and I asked BJ "What do we do now?"

"Just keep walking and hope they don't shoot us."

We got off the road and started up the hill. We found the chief and filled him in on what happened. He asked "So what do you think they'll do? Do you think they bought it?"

"We'll know soon enough. I gave them until dark to let us know."

"Herr Hellman. We have a serious problem. We are surrounded by US Special Forces. A Lieutenant Johnson and a young scientist came in under a white flag. They told us all about the weapon and what could happen if we use it. My people agree with what they were told. They no longer want to go along with the plan. They want to turn the weapon over and leave."

"Kraus listen to me. Whatever they told you is a lie. Of course, they want you to give up. They don't have the ability to stop you. If they did, they would have done it by now. They're just trying to scare you into surrendering, so don't listen to anything they say. Lock them in the castle and leave them there."

"I'm sorry, sir. I can't do that. They left after talking to us."

"You let them leave?"

"Yes sir, they came in under a white flag and I had to let them leave."

"You're an idiot, Kraus! You had their leader and the man I've been looking for. You just let them walk away. I should shoot you myself! Get the weapon ready to move. Tell your guards to be prepared to fight if they must. I want that weapon on site by tomorrow night and ready to fire the next day. Do you understand me?"

"Yes sir. I will do my best."

"Kraus, keep your mouth shut about this. If Mueller finds out, he will shoot both of us."

Kraus got his people together and gave the order to finish preparing the weapon to be moved. Two of his scientists begged him not to do it. They pleaded with him not to ever fire it again. Kraus wouldn't listen. Hellman had convinced him that it was all a lie. He believed the Americans couldn't stop him and he was going to follow his orders even if it killed them all. He threatened to shoot anyone that didn't follow his orders.

We waited outside for them to come out and surrender. It was starting to get dark and no one had appeared. In fact, most of the guards had disappeared inside the castle. BJ turned to me. "John, this is not looking good. They have pulled all their men inside to get ready to make a run for it."

"How do you know that?"

"It's what I would do if I were in their place. If they were going to give up, they would have done it by now."

Just as he said that two men came running out of the castle. They headed right for us waving their hands and yelling for help. The only two guards left outside started shooting at them. BJ gave the order to take out the two guards. There was a hail of gunfire and the two guards were dead.

Unfortunately, the two men running from the castle didn't make it. They were both lying in the road not moving. I felt so bad for them. They had tried to get away because of what I had told them. It was my fault they were dead.

As I was looking at them, I told BJ I thought one of them moved. BJ grabbed two of his guys and headed down to see if one of them was still alive. I watched him from where I was but couldn't tell anything. They grabbed both men and brought them up to where I was. One of them was dead and the other one was still alive, but in bad shape. The medic went to work on him and tried to stop the bleeding. BJ looked at me and said, "I think these are the guys you talked to."

"Yes, both of them." BJ started asking the man questions, but the man couldn't answer all that well. He did manage to tell us they weren't giving up. Someone named Hellman had given the order to go ahead with the move and he said everything that you told us was a lie. This man said he believed us and asked us to save Germany. BJ asked him where the other two sites were. All the men could mutter was "Nearby, nearby." Shortly after he said that, he was gone. The medics said he lost too much blood. I didn't realize it, but I had tears running down my face.

BJ grabbed my shoulder and said "John, this is not your fault. They knew what they were doing. They made their choice a long time ago when they got involved. They could have walked away then, but they didn't. You need to move on and let this go. I want you back up the hill and out of the way. This is going to get really ugly, really fast."

BJ was right! Once it had become completely dark, a large truck came charging out of the castle with no lights on. BJ came on the radio and told everyone to hold their fire until he instructed otherwise. The truck came to a sliding stop sideways in the road. The men inside jumped out and started firing blindly up the hill. They just kept firing at who knows what since they had no idea where any of us were. After two or three minutes of this, they stopped. They realized no one was shooting back at them. They started laughing. You could hear them mocking us. Where are all the brave US soldiers now? The cowards have all run home to their mommies. They continued calling out insults and started lighting up cigarettes and slapping each other on the back. Soon, a second truck came out. It stopped by the first one for a minute. They talked for a moment or two and then the truck started off down the road. The first flatbed truck carrying one of the generators came out of the castle and started down the road. BJ called

Wolfgang and told him to get ready. Within minutes, a second flatbed carrying the second generator came out of the castle.

Just as it got to the road, BJ gave the order to light it up. They hit that flatbed with four grenade launchers and stopped it dead in its tracks. The guys opened on the truck that was sitting sideways in the road.

All the men that had been laughing at us just minutes before, now lay dead beside the truck. They never got a shot off in their own defense.

BJ's plan had worked perfectly. That flatbed truck was stopped right where nothing could get by it. Now all we had to do was destroy the generator.

Easier said than done!

Gunfire started coming from several places in and around the castle. We returned fire as best we could, but they had high ground and trying to get at the generator wasn't possible at this point. BJ ordered Casey's squad to draw fire away from us. They were there in seconds and opened with everything they had. They launched more grenades at the castle and the gunfire they laid down was incredible. It did just what BJ wanted. He moved down the hill with several of his men using the truck in the road for cover. Just as they were about to go for the flatbed, a dozen more men came running out of the castle to try and get the truck moving again.

They fired right at BJ and his squad, pinning them down behind the truck. Several of them kept firing as others climbed into the cab and pulled the dead driver out. The gunfire just kept coming.

All those muzzle flashes looked like fireworks on the 4th of July, only there were real bullets behind each one. I couldn't see how anyone could survive through all that.

Suddenly, there was a huge flash and an explosion down the road. Apparently, Tailback (Wolfgang) had taken on the first two trucks that had left the castle headed north. I hoped they were successful.

BJ called for his men still on the hill to direct their fire at the flatbed. They unleashed a firestorm of bullets at the truck. I could see at least four men go down and the rest went running back into the castle.

BJ and his men made a beeline for the flatbed. They tossed a grenade in the cab just to make sure it wasn't going anywhere. Next came the generator. Kraus and his men had apparently built a steel box around it and the bullets were just bouncing off it. BJ and his men set a charge on the truck next to the box and made a run back to the ditch on our side of the road. Seconds later, the charge went off with a huge blast. The flatbed was blown in half, but the steel box still looked like it was in one piece.

The gunfire stopped all at once. The stillness after all that had just happened was unnerving.

BJ came on the radio. "This is 'old quarterback'. Wide receiver, hold your position. Wait for my orders and report in."

"This is 'wide receiver'. We have taken out the first two trucks. Their men are dead or we have them tied up. The generator is still in one piece and we have no way to blow it up. It's in a metal box. I have one man dead and two wounded. The rest are good to go."

"Good work. Sorry about your man. Hold your position. We have the second flatbed truck disabled and the same with the generator. It's still in a box. We're waiting to see what their next move is."

Five minutes passed, then ten, then twenty, and a half hour later and still nothing from the castle. BJ came on the radio "Wide receiver, report in."

"All's quiet here. Nothing moving anywhere."

"Tailback, report in."

"Same here. All quiet here."

"Listen up everyone. I don't like this. They can't leave and they know they can't fight their way out. Something's up and I just don't know what it is right now. Stay sharp. I have a bad feeling about this."

It stayed quiet for a long time. I started to relax and lay down with my head against an old log. I couldn't believe it, but I was starting to drift off. Just then, I thought I heard a branch snap behind me. A minute later, I heard another branch snap. So, something or someone was coming down the hill behind me. Whatever it was, it was heavy. I could hear it getting closer and closer. Not wanting to scare it, thinking it had to be an animal, I slowly reached for my night vision goggles and very slowly rolled over to look up the hill. What I saw made me freeze! What I first thought was a bear, moments later turned out to be a man. A man carrying a gun.

Then I saw a second man, then another and another. We are being attacked from behind. Little did we know, Hellman had sent reinforcements. These men, whoever they were, had come at us from over the hill. The first man was now less than thirty feet from me and coming right at the log that I was laying against.

I moved very slowly, inching closer to the log. I tried to become part of it. My heart was pounding so hard, it hurt. Now he's passing right by me on the other side of the log. I suddenly noticed I had stopped breathing. I took a long slow breath and waited for him to pass by.

I lifted my head up to see over the log. I could count at least eight to ten men making their way down the hill to where BJ and his men were. If I talk on the radio to warn BJ, they'll hear me and kill me for sure. If I don't, they will ambush BJ and his guys and most likely kill most of them. I couldn't let that happen.

I waited till they were down the hill a little way. I said a quick prayer and pressed the button on the radio "BJ, they're behind you, they're behind you!"

The man closest to me turned and fired. He must have fired at least ten rounds at me. I felt a burning sensation go up the inside of my leg and there was an instant pain in my chest. Then I felt a bullet hit me right in the forehead.

I could feel the blood coming through my pants and running down my face. I was starting to black out. My last thought was about Mary.

BJ had heard John's call and the subsequent gunfire that followed. Damn, he thought. John put his life on the line to warn me and my men.

BJ yelled into his radio "John, John answer me man, please answer me. Son of a b****! Someone is going to pay for this big time."

"Wide receiver, get your men back to the castle. We're being attacked from behind. Tailback, move your men up the hill and make a sweep in this direction. See if you can intercept these guys."

Just then, gunfire broke out coming from the castle again.

BJ thought. Now, I know what those bastards were up to. They were just stalling, waiting for reinforcements. He shouted "Chief, we're going into this castle right now. Launch everything you have at the ramp door." Seconds later the front of the castle lit up like a roman candle. They raced across the street and down the ramp. The grenades had done just what they were intended to do. There were six or seven men down as they charged in. Three more fell, as they tried to stop BJ's squad.

"Chief, now that we're in here, I want you to take five other guys and clear this castle out floor by floor and don't try to be the first one up those staircases. They're small and you'll barely fit. If you find Kraus, try to take him alive. I'm taking the rest of the men and heading back outside. I want to catch these guys coming off the hill."

Chapter 32

"Hellman, this is Kraus. We've lost the castle."

"What do you mean, you've lost the castle?"

"Both of the trucks carrying the generators have been destroyed. One of them is blocking the ramp."

"Kraus, listen to me. Get the rest of your men and get out of there. And report to site two as soon as you can."

"Hellman, you don't understand. There are no other men. I'm one of the last ones still alive here. The rest of the men are either dead or they've been captured."

"Kraus, you have to find a way out of there. Don't let them capture you and don't let them take you alive. I have sent reinforcements. Try to hook up with them. They should be there by now."

"I will do my best to get out of here. There's an old tunnel under this castle. I think I can get out through that."

"What about the scientists? We need them."

"They're all dead. They tried to run out on us and were killed."

"All right, then get yourself out of there. I will be pulling back the reinforcements soon. I don't want to lose good men over nothing. I will call Mueller and tell him what's going on."

"Mueller, this is Hellman. We have lost site one. I just spoke with Kraus and he told me they were attacked and have lost control of the castle."

"What about the weapon? Is it still on its way to the mountain site?"

"No! Both trucks carrying the generators were destroyed."

"How is that possible? You had over a hundred men guarding the castle. How could they have been overrun?"

"I don't know sir. Kraus told me they were either all dead or they had been captured. Whoever attacked the castle was incredibly good at what they did. Do you think it could possibly be our own Army?"

"No. I know who it is. It's Lieutenant Johnson and his men. I still don't understand how thirty men could defeat a hundred men inside a castle. There's more to this than we know. I'm going to call Meyer and find out what he knows about this. I told him to take care of this Johnson, either kill him or run him out of the country."

"Mueller, I'm sure that Johnson is the same man that went into the castle and tried to talk Kraus into surrendering."

"When did that happen?"

"Just hours before the attack. Johnson and a young scientist who was with him told Kraus and his people that the weapon could backfire and burn them all to death. I told Kraus to ignore them and get the weapon out of there. That's when the attack happened."

"All this was going on and you didn't think I needed to know?"

"I thought Kraus could handle it."

"Well, I guess you thought wrong. I will call Meyer. He needs to get control of whatever happened at that castle."

"How are you coming with the weapon at our second site?"

"In two days, we should be ready to move it if all goes well."

"Hellman, does anyone know where site two is?"

"Not to my knowledge. We've been very good about keeping it a secret."

"Good. Get the weapon ready to fire. You may need it to defend yourself. I will get back to you after I talk to Meyer. I may come up there myself!

"Yes, Herr Mueller! Long live Germany."

"Hello, this is General Meyer."

"Mueller here. Why didn't you take care of that Lieutenant Johnson like I told you?"

"Listen Mueller! I did take care of him. I sent my best team out after him and a full squad of twenty-six men. Their leader Wolfgang reported he had found Johnson and killed him. Why, what happened?"

"Well, Wolfgang lied to you! Last night Johnson showed up at the castle. I now believe that Wolfgang has joined forces with Johnson. That would explain how they could overrun the castle and take out a hundred of my best men and destroy the weapon in the process."

"Mueller, I don't believe for a minute that Wolfgang would do that. He's been a loyal soldier to Germany most of his life."

"Well, believe it, Meyer. He deserted you."

"If that's true, then we're done. We must stop now before anyone else gets killed."

"Meyer, listen to me. We are not done and nothing has changed. We still have two more weapons and several hundred men willing to fight for us and Germany. We're going to stay with the plan and see this through. I need you to take a detachment of soldiers up to that castle and get this under control. When you get there, you're going to arrest Johnson and Wolfgang and then you're going to make them disappear for good. If word of this gets out and gets back to the chancellor, you can make up some story about a training operation that went bad."

"Mueller this is insane! How in the world do you expect me to cover this up when my own men know what's going on?"

"You only have to control the situation for two days, then we will be ready with the next weapon. Once we have that, it won't matter what happened at the castle. We will be in control and it will be too late to stop us."

"Mueller, just where is the second weapon and what makes you think you will be able to use it against anyone?"

"We have it up in the mountains at a deserted mining town about fifty miles from the castle. Do you know the place I'm talking about?"

"Yes, I know right where it is. I've been there before."

"Good, so when you get things under control you can meet me up there. The weapon should be ready by then."

"All right. I'll do my best, but if Johnson and Wolfgang have joined forces, they won't go down easy."

"I don't care what it takes. Just get it done this time!"

It was still dark when BJ got back outside. He sent half of his men down the road where he hoped they would catch Wolfgang coming our way. The rest of his men took cover behind what was left of the truck and the steel box protecting the generator.

"Wide receiver, this is, old quarterback. Where are you?"

"Wide receiver here. We are halfway up the hillside just starting our sweep on your right. No contact yet."

"Good! Keep moving in and let me know when you're at twelve o'clock from the castle."

The squad waited and listened for anyone coming down off the hill. Just when it seemed that nothing was going to happen, the first dark figure stepped into the road. Then another and another and in short order there were twenty or more men moving our way. BJ gave the order to hold fire. Seconds later, the dark figures in the road opened on them. They started firing in their direction, but not really aiming at them. Bullets were flying all around them. They returned fire as best as possible, but the heavy fire coming from the dark figures kept them pinned down well.

"Tailback, this is 'old quarterback'. We're getting the crap beat out of us. Get back here to the castle. Get back here on the double! Wide receiver, bring your guys down the hill. We're pinned down here." Within minutes, Wolfgang and Casey's squads came sweeping in from both sides. They opened fire and drove the attackers off the road and back into the woods. Seven men lay dead in the road. The attackers kept firing from the trees and then just as fast as it started, it was over. All was quiet.

"Everyone hold your position. They may come back at us any second." Ten minutes past and still nothing happened.

"Everyone, report in."

"This is Wolfgang. Nothing moving here. We're all good and no one was hit."

"This is Tailback. All's quiet on my end. No one hit. We're all good." That was hard to believe. The Germans lost seven men and we had no injuries. There must have been a guardian angel looking out for us in that fight.

Then suddenly it hit me. John was laying somewhere up on that hill. He gave his life to warn us about the ambush. How will I ever explain this to Mary? I guess I will just tell her how brave he was, that he gave his life to save me and my men. I'll never forgive myself for not letting him go home when he asked.

"Wide Receiver, take half your men and start up the hill on the right. Tailback, start up on the left and make a swing towards Wide Receiver. Keep a lookout for the guys that just hit us. I think they took off, but stay sharp, just in case. Find John and bring him down.

"We'll find him. Don't worry."

It had been quite a night. BJ headed back into the castle just as the first hint of daylight was appearing in the sky. He hoped today would be better than yesterday. BJ radioed the chief.

"Hey Chief, where are you?"

"I'm up on the third floor. At least, I think it's the third floor. I'm in a room with a lot of old furniture."

"Okay, I know right where you are. I'll be right up."

"Good, because I have a surprise for you."

"What did you find?"

"Just wait and see."

I made my way up to the room where the chief was and when I walked in there was the chief with his hand around Kraus's neck.

"I told you I had a surprise for you."

"Yes, you did."

"Where did you find him?"

"He was running for a little hole in the wall on the ground floor of the castle. One of the guys caught him trying to crawl out through an old tunnel."

Well, this is going to be a better day than yesterday, that's for sure.

"What do you want me to do with him?"

"Leave him right here with me. We're going to have a long talk. Chief, will you go help the guys find John? He's somewhere up on the hill and I want his body brought down."

"Sure boss. We'll find him."

Who the hell was slapping me in the face? "Johnny, Johnny boy wake up."

I opened my eyes to see the Chief and Wolfgang staring down at me. I couldn't believe I was alive. I looked at the chief and spoke. "Be honest with me. How bad is it?"

The Chief and Wolfgang lost it and started laughing!

"What's so funny?"

"Johnny Boy, you must have nine lives. We thought you were dead when we first found you. The medics said you had a pulse, so they went to work on you, but there's really nothing wrong with you."

"What do you mean? I got shot in the leg, I got hit in the chest and I think a bullet hit me right in my forehead."

They just started laughing again. "Johnny boy, you're fine. Your leg got cut from a piece of a rock that splintered from a bullet. Your chest hurts from your radio being hit and blowing it into a hundred pieces and apparently one of those pieces gave you a little cut in your forehead, but it won't even leave a scar. Other than that, you're fine."

"But that can't be right. I felt the blood soaking through my pants!"

Once again, they started laughing! "Johnny, there's no blood, but it looks like you peed your pants."

Right about then, I was wishing I had gotten hit by at least one bullet. How would I ever live this down?

The Chief pulled me to my feet. It was true. I was fine. My chest hurt, and I could feel the bump on my forehead. My pants were still damp, but not from blood. The Chief got on the radio to call BJ. "Hey boss. We found John and we are bringing him down."

I grabbed the radio from the chief. "Don't you dare tell him what happened to me. I will tell him myself."

The Chief just grinned and said, "I hope you can make up a good story because the truth is pretty damn funny!"

"Where is BJ anyway? Why didn't he come looking for me?"

"He's in the castle with Kraus. They're having a little talk."

"Is Kraus still alive?"

"Yes, he is. We caught him running away. I imagine the boss has him singing like a bird by now."

"Kraus, we tried to warn you, but you thick headed Germans don't listen to anyone. Now you're my prisoner and your men are either dead or they will be our guests for a long time."

"Why would I believe you? It was all lies and you were just trying to trick us into giving up for no reason."

"No, Kraus, I'm afraid not. It was the truth and your scientists knew it. They tried to surrender and you killed them. The young man I had with me was the son of the man who invented this machine that your people turned into a weapon. It killed his father by doing just what we warned you about. Now, his son is dead at the hands of the assholes following you. He was my best friend. I should cut your F----- head off, Kraus! All right Kraus. This is only going to go one of two ways. You're going to tell me everything you know about what Mueller is doing and where the other machines are and then I'll turn you over to the German army in one piece. Or, if you don't tell me everything you know, I will turn you over to them in little pieces."

"Lieutenant Johnson, or whatever your real name is, you think you're so tough, but I know you Americans have rules. You can't do anything to me."

"Wrong, Kraus. Those rules only apply during war. This is not a war and there are no rules. I can do whatever the hell I want to you and no one will care. I'm going to start by chopping off your fingers one by one until you start talking. You have one minute starting now until I take your first finger.

"You're all talk and you don't have the nerve to go through with it."

Before Kraus could finish what he was saying, BJ pulled out his knife and Kraus's little finger on his right hand dropped to the floor. Kraus let out a scream and started cursing BJ.

"Now, do you have anything you want to tell me, Kraus?

"I will never tell you anything."

An instant later another finger fell to the floor. Kraus let out another scream and cursed BJ all the more.

"You're down to two fingers and a thumb on that hand. The next one you lose will be the thumb. Start talking, Kraus before I get mad and take the whole hand."

"Alright, alright. Mueller and Hellman have two more machines. One is in the old, abandoned mining town about two hours from here. I don't know if the other one is there or not."

"Who is Hellman?"

"He is Mueller's right-hand man. He does whatever Mueller tells him to do. He is second in command."

"What was their plan for the machine that you had?"

"We were going to move it to a site on a mountain near here."

"What was your target?"

"Your missile base. We were going to destroy it as a message to the US and anyone else that interfered with our plan to take over control of Germany."

"What's the target for the other weapons?"

"I don't know."

"Kraus, you're about to lose that thumb."

Kraus pleaded, "I swear I don't know. You can cut off my whole arm and I still won't be able to tell you what I don't know."

"What were your last orders?"

"I was to bring whatever was left of my men and go to the old mine."

"You know, Kraus, I'm starting to believe you, but if I find out you lied to me, I swear I'll find you and cut your stinking head off!"

That was just about the time the Chief and I walked into the room where BJ was holding Kraus. BJ was so involved in getting information out of Kraus that he never turned around. I was shocked to see blood running down the side of the chair coming from Kraus's hand. I saw what looked like two fingers laying on the floor. I had all I could do to keep from throwing up after seeing that. BJ was just staring at Kraus and he was holding the bloody knife he had used to cut off Kraus's fingers. The chief yelled at BJ "Boss, I have Johnny here."

Without turning away from Kraus, BJ yelled back "Why the F--- would you bring his body in here?"

"I thought you might want to see him."

BJ turned to face the chief and the rage on his face shook me right to the bone. Once he saw me standing there, you could see the rage leaving his face, replaced by unbelief. After the shock of seeing me, he yelled at the chief to get me the hell out of there.

I had seen many different sides of BJ, but the one I saw that day will live with me the rest of my life. How could a man that was so full of life, cared so much about his friends and just having fun, turn into a man so full of hate! It wasn't until years later that I got my answer and began to understand. The chief took me outside and gave me some water. He could see how shook up I was. He said to me "Johnny boy, you're going to just have to forget what you saw in there."

"Forget! Forget! How the hell am I going to forget BJ cutting off someone's fingers! How do you forget something like that?"

"I'm sorry you saw that. Kraus must have refused to talk and the boss did what he had to do to make him talk.

"I don't care if he doesn't talk. BJ had no right to do that to him."

"John, tell me this. What happens if we don't find the other weapons and Mueller starts to use them?"

"Thousands or maybe millions of people die."

"John, do you think the boss cares if Kraus loses a couple of fingers to save a million people? What would you do to save all those lives?"

"I don't know, but I don't think I could ever bring myself to torture someone like that."

"Well, maybe you should be thankful there are men like BJ who will do whatever it takes to save the lives of innocent people from men like Kraus and Mueller."

"I understand what you're saying, Chief. I just wish there were some other way."

"Sometimes there is no other way, Johnny Boy."

A short time later, BJ came out of the castle looking for a medic to take care of Kraus. He talked to the chief and Wolfgang

315

for about ten minutes before he headed over to me. When he got to where I was sitting, I just sat there looking up at him. I couldn't read the look on his face. There was no sense of his being glad to see me or that I was even alive. We just looked at each other for a long time, neither one of us quite knowing what to say. Finally, BJ said "Glad you're alright."

Then he just turned and walked away. That was one of the hardest moments of my life. The innocence of our friendship was gone. I had seen a man I didn't know existed and who lived inside a man I knew as Brad Johnson. I hoped he would stay inside and never come out again. I also knew that when the time came and the need was there, the man that lived inside Brad Johnson would come out and he would do whatever he had to to get the job done.

The chief came over and sat down. He said "Just give the boss time. He did what he had to do, so that we can put an end to this. We now know where Mueller is and where he's keeping the other machines. Without that information, we'd be up the creek without a paddle."

"I know and I understand, but it's just not something I could ever do."

"Johnny Boy, I've been with the boss from day one and we have always been a recon unit. We have seen things that shook us to the core - men, women and children being killed or tortured for no reason. We were never able to help the people we saw suffering and dying. Now we can and a lot of that pent up rage is coming out. So, try to understand, this is not who we are. It's who we must be to get the job done. You'll never understand unless you've seen what we've seen, but you can still be a friend to the boss. So, give him a little room. He's just doing his job."

"I will and I will always be his friend no matter what. I wish I had never come over here. I wish I could go home and forget this ever happened."

"Johnny Boy, we all feel that way. You're going to have to find a way to live with this, just like the rest of us."

Just then Wolfgang came walking over to get the chief. "Hey Chief, BJ wants to see us. He's up on the road by the burned-out truck."

"Okay, tell him I'll be right there. Rest easy, Johnny Boy. This will all be over soon."

"I hope you're right, Chief. All I want is to go home." The chief was wrong. This was far from over!

"Okay Chief and Wolfgang, I need both of you to help me out."

"Whatever you need us to do boss, just say the word."

"That goes for me and my men as well, BJ."

"Thanks for all you both have done and thank your men as well. They have all done a great job to this point, but it's not over yet. This is what I know from talking to Kraus. Mueller and some guy named Hellman have two more weapons. One is in an old mining town not too far from here. Kraus doesn't know where the other one is or what the targets are. He doesn't know if the weapons are ready to be used. We know they can't use them if they are on the move. If we can find them and wait for them to move the weapons, then we can hit them the same way we did here."

"Boss, don't you think they know that this time. They may just be waiting to see what we do before they make their move."

"Yes, Chief, I thought about that, but then it becomes a waiting game, and we win if that happens."

"Excuse me BJ, but how do we win by waiting? If we wait, aren't we giving them more time to finish building the weapon?"

"Yes, that's true Wolfgang, but even if they finish building the weapons, they can't use them until they have a clear line of sight to the targets. Mueller will have to move them to use them and that's when we hit them. Wolfgang, do you know where the old mining town is?"

"Yes, I know right where it is. I've been up there many times. It's uphill all the way from here and we don't have the transportation we need to get there with any speed. The roads were washed out years ago and were never fixed. If we hike it, it will take a full day to get there."

"All right, this is what I need you both to do right now. Get your men together and clean this place up, clear the road, and bury those bodies. I will have Casey post guards overnight. Make sure your men get fed well and get some rest. We head for the mining town at first light."

"Okay boss."

I was just sitting there staring at the ground when BJ came over with two of his men.

"John, I want you to work with these two guys and get inside those two steel boxes that are holding the generators. Find out if they're still in good working order or if they can be salvaged."

"Why would you want to salvage them?"

"John, if Mueller has two of these weapons and tries to use them, wouldn't it be wise to fight him with the same kind of weapon of our own?"

"No! BJ, it wouldn't. Haven't you been listening to what I've been saying ever since I got here! If you use this thing it could blow up in your face and kill all of us and everyone else for miles around."

"I heard you, John, but didn't you say it was safe at a low-level output?

"Yes, I did say that, but it doesn't mean it's safe to use. It could still kill us all if we don't use it the right way and I'm not sure I even know how to do that!"

"Well, John, that's where you come in. You'll just have to make sure we use it safely."

"No way, BJ. I'm not going to do any such thing!"

BJ stepped right up to me, grabbed my shirt, pulled me nose-to-nose and said "This is a national emergency and I need you to do this! Do I make myself clear?"

"Yes sir" was the only response I could come up with.

BJ just walked away and left me with the two soldiers and from the look on his face I was sure he meant every word he said. That other man living inside him had just shown his face again. The two soldiers and I spent the next three hours getting inside the first steel box and checking out the generator. From everything I could tell it was in good shape and ready to be used. The second one was down the road and I prayed that it had been destroyed. I didn't know it at the time, but BJ was off talking to General Wellington.

"Hello General, this is Charlie Brown reporting."

"Brad, it's good to hear your voice. I haven't heard from you in almost three days. What's been going on over there?"

"It's a long story, General, but the bottom line is, we have one of the machines and a guy named Kraus. He was in control of the castle and this machine, but after a little persuasion he gave us the location of the other two machines. Well, one for sure. They are in an old mining town not too far from here."

"Brad, who's controlling the other machines?"

"Some guy named Hellman. He's Mueller's lap dog."

"Is Mueller in this mining town?"

"I don't know. I couldn't get anything more out of Krauss. I don't think he knows where Mueller is."

"Brad, I want those machines taken out, but I want Mueller just as bad!"

"I understand General. I'll do my best to catch him."

319

"So, what's the plan now, Brad? When are you going after the other machines?"

"We plan on leaving here first thing tomorrow morning. We need to regroup today and secure the castle. I have John going through the two generators we captured from Kraus."

"Very good, Brad. I want those generators brought back here to the states. I take it that John's okay. Mary keeps calling everyday asking about him."

"Tell Mary, he's fine. I don't really know why, but he's good."

"What do you mean?"

"Well sir, between you and me, John should have been killed twice by now, but he barely has a scratch on him."

"Why, what happened?"

"General, I only know the details about the first time. Nobody seems to be willing to tell me what happened the second time. When I ask, they just laugh. When I get back, I'll find out and let you know."

"Okay Brad. As long as he's okay. Make sure he's safe. I promised Mary he would be okay with you."

"Yes sir, General."

"Brad, I'm leaving for Germany tonight. I will be at our missile base in the morning. I want to be there when you get Mueller, so call me at the base tomorrow and let me know your location. That way I can send support if you need it. Brad, one more thing. How are all your men? Do you have any casualties?"

"General, it's hard to believe, but we didn't lose a single guy in the battle for the castle. Wolfgang did lose two of his men, but the rest are ok. All my men are in good shape and all of Casey's squad is good and ready to go."

"Brad, who's Wolfgang?"

"General, he is the leader of Germany's special forces group. They were sent out to eliminate me and my guys. I was able to convince them that they are on the wrong side of this. They helped us take down the castle and they are going to help us take down Mueller as well."

"Are they the same men you went over there to train a few years back?"

"Yes sir, the same guys."

"Does their commanding officer know about this?"

"No, I don't believe he knows yet, but he must suspect something by now. His commanding officer is General Meyer. He's the one that sent Wolfgang out to eliminate us. Meyer is working with Mueller and that's why we can't call on the German army to help us. Meyer has control of the local police as well and is spreading lies to the chancellor. He's trying to control the whole situation."

"That sounds impossible."

"I know General, but so far, he's been able to do it. The chancellor has complete trust in him and whatever he says the chancellor believes."

"Brad, that would explain why our president can't convince the chancellor of what's going on."

"Well, General, once we show the chancellor what's really been going on over here, he'll have to believe us."

"Brad, you're sure you can count on Wolfgang to help you out. What he's doing is treason and he could be shot for helping you."

"I trust him, General. He knows what he's doing. He's putting his country first over his own life. He knows what he's doing will help save Germany from Mueller and what he's trying to do. He already lost two men helping us, so I think that says it all!"

"Okay Brad, it's your call. I'll be at the base in the morning. Call me once you're on the move. Let me know if you need any support."

"Will do, General. I will talk to you tomorrow."

"Hello Mary, this is General Wellington."

"Thank goodness you called, General. I'm going crazy sitting here in this hotel. How is John? Is he on his way home yet?"

"Mary, he's fine. I just spoke to Brad and he assured me that John is doing well."

"Oh, thank you General. That's good news, but when will he come home?"

"I'm sorry to tell you, but it will be a few more days until we can get him out of there and get him home."

"General, every time we talk it's a few more days. Do you really think I believe you anymore? You told me the same story over and over. Can I even believe that John is all right? Why can't I talk to him if he's alright?"

"Mary, I've told you before, John is not in any kind of trouble over there. He's just helping Brad with a difficult situation."

"So, why can't he talk to me then? Don't they have phones over there?"

"Mary, once again, he can't talk to you right now because of what he's doing and where he is. It's a matter of national security."

"Yes, General, you told me that a dozen times and I still don't understand."

"Mary, I'm going to Germany tonight. I will look into getting John home as soon as possible, so just hang on for a few more days and this will all be over."

"Yeah, General, same old story - just wait."

"Mary, I'll call you as soon as I have John on a plane. I must go now. Goodbye."

"Hello Miss Northrup. This is Mary calling."

"Hello dear. How are you?"

"Not so good. You know John is over in Germany helping General Wellington do something and I have no idea what it is. The general keeps telling me he's coming home and then he doesn't. It's always a couple more days. I know he's lying to me."

"Mary, listen to me. I don't know for sure what John is doing over there, but I'm sure the General is not lying to you. Things change and his plans need to change with them as well."

"I understand that Sharon, but I want John home just the same."

"I know dear. I want him home as much as you do."

"Sharon, I can't sit here anymore. I decided to go to Germany myself and find out what's going on."

"Mary, I wouldn't do that. Didn't the General tell you it was dangerous over there?"

"Yes, he did, but if John is okay and not in any danger, why wouldn't it be safe for me?"

"I don't know Mary, but I think you should stay here and wait."

"I can't just sit here anymore. I have to go!"

"Okay, Mary. Call me when you get there and promise me, you'll call."

"I will, I promise. Goodbye."

Mary was on a plane and headed for Frankfurt, Germany the next morning.

The two soldiers and I headed down the road to the second generator. When we got there, four of Wolfgang's men were standing guard. Wolfgang's men had done quite a job on the truck when they took it out. The truck, or what was left of it, was in a ditch four or five feet below the road. The steel box was laying on its side with a big dent in one side of it. I had no way of getting inside. The side that had a door was lying face down against the ground. Without a crane, there was no way I was getting inside to check out the generator. The two soldiers told me to stay put and said they would be right back. About an hour later, they were back with a torch and started cutting their way into the box. Great. Now I would have to crawl around inside this box and try to see if these generators were any good. About three hours later, I felt that they were in working order, although it is hard to believe looking at the dent in the side of the box. The generators may have been in good shape, but the truck carrying the controls to run them was destroyed and there was no way to fix that! I had a great feeling of relief come over me. This was one machine that would never be used as a weapon again. As we walked back to the castle, I started to think about how nice it would be when I get home and get to be with Mary again. I miss her so much it hurts. BJ was waiting for us and expecting a good report.

"So, John, what did you find? Can they be used?"

"Sorry, BJ, I'm afraid not. The generators are fine, but the controls to run them were destroyed. There is no way to salvage them and it would take months to build a new control panel, even if you had the parts."

"Okay fine, we'll just have to go without it. John, when this is over, I want you to oversee the shipment of the generators back to the states."

"Why me and why should we ship them back? Why don't you just destroy them right here?"

"I have my orders from General Wellington. He wants them shipped back to the states and that is what you are going to do."

"BJ, you know what the army will do with them once they have them back. This will just start all over again!"

"That's not for me to decide. John, I have my orders and what the army does or doesn't do is not up to me."

"So, you just blindly follow orders even when you know you shouldn't!"

"Yes, John, people much smarter than me make the calls. They're the ones running our country, not you and me!"

"BJ, that's b******* and you know it. They are no smarter than anyone else. They don't realize what can happen with these machines if they get out of control, but you do. Don't let them make the call on this. Do what you know is right. Destroy these machines and end this."

"All right, John, that's enough. This conversation is over. Just do what you're told. I have other things to take care of right now."

As BJ walked away, I realized I wasn't going to change his mind and he was going to follow orders no matter what. It was getting late and I was hungry. I went looking for something to eat and to my surprise I found that some of Wolfgang's men had come up with real food for a change. Beef and potatoes were a real treat from the usual Army K rations I've been eating. I asked them where they got all this food and they just smiled. BJ had given orders for everyone to get a good night's rest and be ready to move out early the next day. It was getting dark, so I went into the castle and found a good place to sleep for the night. I must have laid there for two hours. All I could think about was Mary, my mother, what tomorrow would bring, what the army would do with my father's machines, would Mueller give up without a fight, what would happen if he got his machines working, how many people would he be willing to kill to get control of Germany. There was no way I could get to sleep. I got up to take a walk outside. Maybe I could clear my mind outside.

Once I got outside, I couldn't believe how dark it was. You could hardly see to walk. The night was cool and clear. The stars I could see were just incredible! This far out in the country, there was no light to interfere with the night sky. For just a moment, all my thoughts went away and I felt at peace. I walked less than a hundred feet from the castle when I felt something being pushed into my back. A very deep voice told me to stand still. My first thought was that one of the bad guys had come back. I was sure I was going to die right there.

"Johnny Boy, what the hell are you doing out here? You could get yourself killed by one of the guards. They tend to shoot first and ask questions later."

Thank God, it was the chief! "I'm so glad it's you, Chief. I thought I was going to be killed."

"You might have if you kept walking. No one is supposed to be out here."

"Sorry, Chief, I couldn't sleep. Too much going on in my head. I thought I would go for a walk and maybe I could stop thinking so much. Why are you out here? Are you on guard duty?"

"No, Casey has that job. I'm out here for the same reason you are. I keep thinking about that blast we saw come out of the castle yesterday. I've seen a lot when it comes to weapons, but I've never seen anything like that before."

"That's because there's never been anything like that before, Chief."

"I'll be honest with you, Johnny Boy. I'm a little concerned about facing anyone that has a weapon like that. I'm not afraid of death, just the way I might die."

"Chief, are you really not afraid of dying?"

"Everyone dies, Johnny. No one leaves this world any other way. There's only one way out! I was raised Indian. We believe that a spirit lives inside each one of us. We are blessed by our great Mother Earth to live this life we have. We are part of this world for only a short time. We believe that death is only the beginning of a journey to a far better place."

"I think I'll stay right here as long as I can, Chief, just the same. I guess I don't see death like you do."

"Johnny, haven't you ever felt the presence of a greater power in the universe? The presence of a being that is far, far greater than you or me? That's the Great Father Spirit. He put Mother Earth here and gave us life. He will bring us and all men into that great spirit world to be with him. That's why he put us here in the first place."

"It sounds like you're talking about God."

"You people may call him God, but we see him as our Great Spirit Father."

"I wish I could feel the same way you do about dying and what comes next. I just don't think I could get there."

"Johnny Boy, when this is all over, you and I will have to have a long talk. Right now, we need to get back inside the castle before someone shoots us."

I did finally get to sleep thinking about what the Chief had said. I woke only a few hours later to the sound of men preparing for battle. I walked outside where the first hint of light was showing in the eastern sky. It looked like it would be a beautiful day. It was what the day would bring that had me so anxious. I saw men cleaning rifles, checking pistols, loading backpacks with food, water and ammunition and putting on their war paint. I guess this is what men do when they go to war. But this was not a war as we think of war. These are good men trying to stop one evil man from possibly destroying his own country. No one had declared war, but men would die today fighting for what they believed in. That has been the cause for an untold number of wars in the past, so in that way this was very much a war. I hope and pray these good men will win the day and save us once again from the evil that lives inside some men's hearts.

BJ was gathering up his leaders and giving last minute details of his plan. Wolfgang and his men would lead off, followed by Casey's squad. BJ and his men would bring up the rear making sure no one got up behind us. Once we got to the old mining town, the plan was to split up into three groups and each one of the units would try and find where Mueller was keeping the machines. Once they were found, we would rejoin the other groups and make a unified attack. All of this hinged on the fact that the machines had not been made ready to use as a weapon. If they had, then all bets were off. A new plan would need to be made. We really wouldn't know what we were up against until we got there. BJ sent Wolfgang and his men off down the road, followed by Casey's squad five minutes later. BJ came up to me, pulling Kraus along with him. Kraus's hands were tied behind him. BJ handed me a pistol and showed me how to use it, then said "Kraus is all yours now. If he runs or tries anything, shoot him! I need you to carry this backpack as well and don't lose it."

"Why, what's in it?"

"Never mind what's in it. Just make sure you don't lose it. I will need it later."

The pack must have weighed sixty or seventy pounds. He told me to follow right behind the second squad and in front of his men, so he could keep an eye on me and Kraus. I had just fallen in line behind the second squad when I felt, as much as heard, something coming up the road behind us. I wasn't the only one to hear it. Everyone in the second quad turned around to see what was coming. The noise got louder and louder and you could feel the ground under your feet start to vibrate. We all saw it at the same time. Coming right at us was the biggest tank I'd ever seen. Someone yelled to take cover and men went running in every direction. I just stood there frozen in place thinking we are all going to die right here on the spot. Someone grabbed me and pulled me off the road. I hit the ground so hard, it almost knocked the wind out of me.

When I got my wits about me, I looked down the road and to my disbelief I now saw two tanks side by side filling up the whole road. They just kept coming up the road. I was sure no power on earth could stop these giant beasts of destruction from killing each one of us. They rolled right up to the castle and stopped. I saw what I thought was a Humvee pull around in front of the tanks, followed by at least fifty soldiers and a hundred or more behind the tanks. Everything just stopped. It was like time had frozen us all in place.

After several minutes, an older man wearing a very impressive uniform stepped out of the Humvee. I was not far up the road and it was easy for me to see that it was General Meyer.

General Meyer oversees the entire German army. I remembered him from our meeting at the warehouse. I wondered if he was here to help us or take us all as prisoners. One way or the other, something was about to happen. Two other officers got out of the Humvee and stood one on either side of Meyer and the three of them made quite an impressive front. From behind a castle wall, out stepped BJ. He walked to the middle of the road followed by the chief. They couldn't have been more than fifty feet from Meyer. Then slowly, everyone of BJ's men stepped out in the road backing up their lieutenant.

I was the only one not out on the road supporting BJ. As I went to get up, I realized I had lost track of Kraus. Looking around I found him lying in the ditch right behind me. I pointed my gun at him and told him to get on his feet. I was sure he would want to be part of this. I had just gotten myself and Kraus to our place in the road when I heard hard fast steps coming up behind me. It was Wolfgang and his men. They came right up to where I was and took a position covering the road behind me. Wolfgang kept going until he ended up side by side with BJ and the chief.

The odds were not in our favor. In total, we had ninety-two men. We were facing over a hundred and fifty men and two big ass tanks and this was not looking good for our side. Casey, BJ, Wolfgang, and Chief stood shoulder-to-shoulder looking at Meyer and his men. Every man standing behind our leaders was prepared to fight to the death if need be. No one said a word for a good three or four minutes. They just stared at each other. Finally, Meyer broke the ice and said "Lieutenant Johnson, you and Wolfgang should tell your men to stand down. No one needs to die here today. This can all be over peacefully and you will be free to go back to your base and then home to your beloved America."

BJ said, "I don't think so, General. You know why we're here and we aren't going anywhere until the job is done."

"Lieutenant Johnson, you have no authority here. In fact, you shouldn't even be here. I can have you shot where you stand as a terrorist in my country and you, Wolfgang, you have committed an act of treason against your country. You will go to prison for the rest of your life if you don't lay down your guns and give up."

Wolfgang said, "General, you're not my commanding officer anymore and you no longer deserve to wear the uniform you have on. If anyone has committed treason here, it's you. You fell in with Mueller and his plan to take over Germany and who knows what other countries! Did you really think you could get away with this? Germany is far more than one man. It's a people that believe in fair government, a government run by those people, not by a dictator or any one man. Someone tried that years ago and that didn't turn out so well. Meyer, you're the one who's going to spend the rest of his days in prison. Your men need to know the truth. Meyer is not the man you think he is. He has betrayed Germany and you. He and Mueller are planning to take over Germany and rule as dictators."

Meyer started walking toward BJ. At least thirty guns went up, all pointing at Meyer. He stopped dead in his tracks. He held up his hands and said "I only want to talk, that's all."

BJ yelled "Everyone, just take it easy." I heard BJ call my name. "John, bring Kraus up here right now. I pushed through the men in front of me until I got to where BJ was. I pushed Kraus up next to BJ. I turned to leave, but BJ grabbed me and said, "Stay right here, I may need you."

Meyer stepped right up to us and said "There is no way this is going to work out for you lieutenant. Tell your men to stand down and end this!"

"That's not going to happen, Meyer. Do you know who this is?" as he pulled Kraus up in front.

"Yes, I know who he is. What happened to his hand?"

"Unfortunately, he lost a couple fingers in our little battle yesterday."

"Is that true?" asked Meyer.

Kraus looked at BJ and said "Yes, it's just like he said."

BJ said, "Don't worry about how it happened. Our medics took good care of him. I want you to know that Kraus has been extremely helpful and has given us all kinds of information on you and Mueller. Like where he is and what he's up to. He also told us that you have been involved from the start. He told us how you have lied to your own troops and kept the truth from your government and your chancellor. How you have manipulated the police force and kept them away from things like the warehouse when it was destroyed. All this information is in the hands of our intelligence people back in the states, soon to be shared with your chancellor. Oh yes, we are sending along a whole bunch of pictures to prove what we've said. Sorry, Meyer. Kraus sold you and Mueller out. This is over for you and Mueller. You can't buy your way out of this one."

Meyer just stood there speechless. He had nothing to say. He was a man totally defeated. The look on his face said it all. He knew he was finished.

"Lieutenant Johnson, please tell me one thing. Is this weapon as powerful and dangerous as you have been saying?"

BJ turned and looked at me. "John, go ahead, tell him."

"General, my father had no idea that what he was doing would end up as a weapon. This machine was supposed to help men, not destroy them. It killed my father, and yes, if it gets used the wrong way and gets loose, it has the potential to kill every living thing for miles around. We have no way of knowing how far it will reach."

Meyer was in shock and you could see the fear on his face. There were tears in his eyes. When he spoke again, he was a man in total humiliation. "I've been a fool. I got caught up in Mueller's plan to bring Germany back to a world power. I believed him when he said this would be good for all men, that it would bring lasting peace to all of us. I truly had no idea it could bring such destruction to us or anyone else. If this is all true, then you must let me help you stop Mueller. I know right where he is and what his plan is. Maybe I can talk him into giving up this crazy plan and surrender himself and his men."

BJ just stared at Meyer for a long minute and then said "I don't think so, General! You sold out your men, your country, you lied to your chancellor and now you want me to believe that you would help us take down Mueller. Why in the world would I ever trust you?"

"Because Lieutenant, like you just said, my life is over. When the chancellor finds out what I've done, I will never see the light of day again if they don't just shoot me. Helping you put an end to Mueller will at least give me a little self-respect after what I've done."

Wolfgang pulled BJ aside and talked to him. "Listen, BJ. I have known Meyer for almost twenty years. Up to this point, he has always been a man of his word. I think he really believed Mueller when he told him how good this could have been for Germany. I would trust him. If he says he will help us, I believe he will."

"All right, Wolfgang, but he's your responsibility from now on. If he survives this, he is still going to spend the rest of his life in prison."

"I agree with you, but for now he has two tanks and a hundred and fifty men we absolutely need."

"Okay fine. If we now have his help, let's go see what he's willing to do."

BJ and Wolfgang came back, grabbed Meyer and the chief and then disappeared into the castle. They needed to come up with a new plan.

The rest of us were left standing around looking at each other. After a few minutes, we all started to relax now that we weren't going to start shooting each other. Some of Wolfgang's men went over and started talking to Meyer's men. Apparently, they knew each other and had served together. I grabbed Kraus and found a place in the shade to sit and wait. BJ was drilling Meyer about what he knew. "Alright, Meyer. Start talking. Just exactly where is Mueller and how many men does he have? Are both of the other two machines in the same place and are they ready to use?"

"Lieutenant Johnson, this is what I know. One of the machines is in that mining town for sure. I don't know what building it's in and I wouldn't think Mueller would put two machines in the same place. He always wants a back-up plan in place. He's always been insistent about that and that's why you only found one here in the castle. The last I knew, he had over three hundred men ready to fight with him. They are all very loyal to him and I believe they are good fighters too. Mueller has a man who is his field general. Hellman is his name. I have only met him a couple of times. He carries out all of Mueller's orders. He told me that Hellman was at that old mining town and that he promised Mueller he'd have the machine ready in two days. That was yesterday, so I would think it would be ready to fire tomorrow sometime. Hellman is a man of his word. If he said it would be done, I would count on it."

"Meyer, what is his target now that we messed up his plans to hit our missile base?"

"I don't know, lieutenant. The plan as far as I knew was to destroy the missile base as a warning to the US and anyone else that tried to stop him from taking over Germany. He promised me that that would be all he would do. After that the weapons, or as you call them 'machines', would only be used for defense."

BJ looked at the chief and shook his head in disbelief. "General, I find it hard to believe someone with your background and experience would fall for a line of crap like that."

"Lieutenant, you need to understand the history of our country and all of the killing and loss of life I've seen, the instinct of men to kill each other and to bring war against his fellow man. Then one day someone comes along and says he has found a way to bring a real lasting peace to the world. It's hard to ignore that it might just work. Wouldn't you take a chance at saving millions of lives by stopping all the wars that have gone on since the beginning of time?"

"No, General, I wouldn't! I might not have your years of experience, but as you said, men have been killing each other from the day Cain killed his brother Abel and I don't believe for a second that anyone other than God himself can stop it. What you've done is to let a mad man get his hands on a weapon that could kill millions of people, not save them. So, General Meyer, just how do you plan on helping us stop Mueller?"

"Lieutenant Johnson, I believe Mueller will listen to me. When I tell him everything I now know, he just might believe me and give this all up."

"How are you going to make him listen to you, General?"

"Let me and my man go into that mining town first. The rest of these men follow close behind, but stay out of sight on the outside of town. If I can talk him down, you can come in and arrest him. If he won't give up, then we'll all pull back and join up with you. I will leave the plan of attack to you at that point."

"Okay, General, I will give you your chance to talk him down, but let me tell you how this is going to work. Once we find out what building he's in, you will stand out in the street and when you talk to him, I will be listening to everything you say by radio. I will have two of my best shooters aiming their rifles right at you. If

I hear anything that even sounds like a double cross, you'll be dead before you take your next breath. Do you understand me?"

"Yes, Lieutenant. I understand you fine. After all I've just told you, you still don't trust me."

"Don't take it personally. I don't trust most people anyway. Okay, everyone listen up. This is how it's going to go down. Because the general here showed up and screwed up our whole plan for the day, there's no way we can get into that mining town today. According to what you told me, Wolfgang, it will be after dark by the time we get there now."

"That's right, BJ. There's no way to get there before dark now."

"Well, that may just work out in our favor. I want everyone on the move in the next half hour. General Meyer, you will lead the way with those two tanks of yours. Once we get close, I'll take Wolfgang and six of my men and recon the town tonight. If we get lucky, we will find Mueller and his weapon before he even knows we're there. That's the plan so let's get everyone moving and go stop this nut job!"

General Wellington, a four-star general and head of the Joint Chiefs of Staff for the president of the United States, landed in Germany early the next morning arriving at the army's missile base by 8:30. The first thing he did was send off a coded message to Lieutenant Johnson. Open communication in Germany was not a good idea. The base commander was sure people were always watching and listening to everything that was happening at the base. It wasn't just the Germans that were listening. Germany was full of spies from other countries always trying to find out just what the US was up to. If any one of our enemies found out about what was happening right in their own backyard, there's no telling what they would do to the US or to Germany. The general's message was short and to the point. "Charlie Brown, where are you and what can I do to support you?"

Charlie Brown's answer came back minutes later. "General, we are on the move and we have joined forces with General Meyer of the German army. We now have a force of 240 men and two tanks. I think we have what we need to get the job done. Is it possible to get any air support?"

"Message to Charlie Brown. You know we have no fighter planes in Germany, but we do have two attack helicopters that can make it to your location in about an hour and a half. I will investigate getting air support from Germany's Air Force.

"Thanks, General. I will let you know where and what we need."

General Wellington was not happy about being left out of the action. He was a fighting general and wanted very much to be where the fight was, not sitting on the sidelines being told to wait. However, he did have one of his best men leading this operation and he would trust him to win this fight.

Chapter 33

Mary's plane landed in Frankfort just before three in the afternoon. She got a taxi to a hotel and then headed out to find John. With no real idea as to how to find him, she started asking people out on the street if anything strange had been happening lately. All she got was some funny looks and a few harsh words from some people she spoke with. One old man was kind to her and asked her why she was nosing around. After a short explanation, he told her he had heard about something a little odd from his brother who lived up north from there. Something about an old warehouse falling down, but he had no details. He suggested she go talk to the local police. She found the police station and asked an officer at the desk if he had heard of any military action in Germany lately.

"Sorry Ma'am, but no. Even if I did, I wouldn't be telling you about it. You're obviously a US citizen. What goes on in Germany is none of your business anyway."

Mary just stood there as tears started to roll down her face. The officer started to soften up a little. "Ma'am why are you asking in the first place?"

She started to tell him about John and then realized she couldn't tell him the real reason why John was there. She realized she might be committing treason if she did. So, Mary made up a story as best she could about her and John fighting and how she had to find him and make things right. Now the officer became very suspicious of her.

"Ma'am when you first walked in here you were asking me about military action in our country. Now you're telling me you and your boyfriend had a fight. Just what the hell are you up to, lady?" Suddenly Mary became nervous and afraid. The officer knew she was lying to him. She said sorry for bothering you and made a quick exit out the front door and down the street. The officer came out of the front door yelling for her to stop. She just kept running and after a block or two the officer gave up and went back to the station. Mary walked around for several hours, sometimes crying, and sometimes getting angry. Where was John, was he alive, was the General telling her the truth, was she ever going to see the man she loved so much again? How would she live without him? Mary started to make her way back to the hotel. About two blocks before she got there, she saw the man who had told her about the warehouse falling. He was very polite and asked her if she had any luck finding John.

"No, and I don't know what I'm going to do now. You're the only one who told me anything, even though it was only about an old warehouse falling down."

"Well, miss, I really didn't say that right. The warehouse didn't fall, it was blown up by somebody. My brother said that the police up there told him it was no accident. Someone blew it up deliberately."

Mary's heart skipped a beat. That's the exact kind of thing that John would be involved with. Well, maybe not John so much, but he was with BJ and that sounded just like BJ all day long. She was so excited she kissed the man and ran back to the hotel. Now Mary had something to go on. First thing in the morning she would head to the town that the man on the street had told her about. Tonight, she would call General Wellington and tell him what she had turned up. Wouldn't he be surprised! Mary got back to her room and got right on the phone to the general. A woman answered and asked her who was calling. Mary told her who she was, lied and said she had important information that the general was waiting to hear. After what seemed like a long time that woman came back on the line. "I have the general for you and I will put him through now."

"Mary, this is General Wellington. What is so important that you lied to my secretary."

"General, for your information I'm in Germany and I found out what town John and BJ are in. I found a man on the street and he told me about a warehouse that somebody blew up. I know it has to be where they are."

"Mary, listen to me. Stop talking and listen to me. Do not talk to anyone about what you know. Tell me where you are and I will be over to get you as soon as I can get there. Stay in your room and don't leave until I get there. Do you understand me?"

"Yes, but why?"

"Never mind why, Mary. Just promise me you won't leave your room."

"Okay, fine. I'll stay in my room."

"Mary, I will send someone to get you as soon as I can."

Mary ordered room service and because she spoke exceptionally good German, she found a show she liked on the TV. An hour and a half later, there was a knock on the door. That must be the general. She opened the door to see two large men standing in the hallway. They asked her "Are you Mary?"

"Yes, why?

"We have been sent by the general to pick you up. Please come with us and we will take you to him."

Mary didn't like the tone in this guy's voice. She looked at them and said "The general said he was coming here. Why didn't he come himself?"

The man answered, "He didn't tell us why. He just said to bring you to him."

"I think I will call him first."

"No, don't try to do that."

"Why not?"

"He's in a meeting. That's why he didn't come himself."

Mary had a very uneasy feeling about this. These two guys weren't dressed like any kind of military personnel she had ever seen. However, it wasn't the first time the general had sent people to pick her or John up. She grabbed her purse and a jacket and headed for the elevator with one guy on each side of her. Once in the lobby, she started for the front door.

One of her escorts grabbed her arm and spoke. "We're parked out back." He turned her around and pushed her towards the back door. Every instinct in her body started screaming at her! This is not right. These are not men sent by the general. Mary's mind started to race and her heart was pounding like a freight train! How do I get away from these two men? They are twice my size. She dropped her purse and as one of them stopped to pick it up, she made a run for it. Mary was in good shape and quick. She dodged the first guy and ran for the front door. She got halfway there when a big hand grabbed her foot and sent her headfirst to the floor. She rolled over just as her attacker reached for her. She kicked as hard as she could and got him square in the chest. He wasn't expecting that and it sent him falling backwards onto the floor.

She was on her feet and running for the door and as she ran, she yelled for help, but the only ones in the lobby were two old ladies and the girl behind the desk. She was three feet from the door when one of her attackers knocked her to the floor again. This time she hit hard and it knocked the wind out of her. She caught herself gasping for air, but still tried to get her feet under her. Too late. She felt herself being picked up and carried to the back of the lobby. Fight as she might, it was no use. They had her. They took her out the back of the hotel to a van. They opened the door and threw her inside. She landed hard hitting your head on the floor and then passed out.

The order came down the line. It was time to get on the road and head for this mining town once again. I grabbed Kraus and headed down the road. We had been sitting around for hours while BJ and the rest figured out what they planned on doing. No one told us anything except where to get in line and make sure to keep up. I still had charge of Kraus and the backpack. All that sitting around and I never thought to look in the backpack until I picked it up and started walking.

Apparently, the game plan had changed. Now, General Hadwin was taking the lead with his two tanks and one hundred and fifty of his men. That was fine with me. If someone was going to get shot, it was surely the lead guys. About two hours into our march, the road came to an end. What had once been a road was nothing more than two runs in a field. The walking became hard and slow. I was glad those two tanks were breaking down the brush that had been growing up on what once was a road. We were making slow progress when everyone came to a stop.

We had come to a washout that even the tanks were having a hard time with. When I got to the edge of the wash, it was thirty-five or forty feet deep and had to be a hundred feet across and filled with rocks and boulders the size of small cars. Looking across, I could see that they had tied ropes to the tanks and were using them to climb out the other side. There was no way I was going to make that climb with this backpack. Down into the wash sliding on my ass most of the way, I did get to the bottom. You had to pick your way through the rocks and debris that the water had washed down the mountain. I couldn't imagine the amount of water it would take to wash away this much land and carry some of these boulders this far down the mountain. I'm glad I wasn't here at the time.

Kraus and I made it to the far side. Now for the climb out. Kraus started up the rope, but I stopped him. "You stay here until I get up and then you can climb out." Just as I was about to try to climb out, a piece of rope hit me on the head. Someone shouted at me to tie the rope around me and they would pull me up. Whoever that was up there knew I was probably not going to make the climb on my own. I found out later the chief had given orders to help me out. In fact, two of his guys had been keeping an eye on me and Kraus all day long. I should have known!

Once everyone was out of the wash, we took a twenty-minute break. Word passed down the line that we weren't halfway there yet and there was no way we were going to make it in daylight. It ended up being after midnight before we got to where BJ wanted us. Hours before I had given the backpack to Kraus. I put my gun in his face and said, "You drop this and I drop you." I was starting to act and talk like BJ and that scared me just a little! I just sat down when I was told to move up front with Hadwin. When Kraus and I got to Hadwin, I was kind of glad I was there. Hadwin and a few of his leaders were sitting around and eating real food. We hadn't had much to eat that day, just what we could eat on the move. The chief was there and when he saw me, he just smiled. "You look like you've been run over by one of these tanks."

"Thanks Chief, I feel like it. Where is BJ?"

"BJ, Wolfgang and a half dozen men went into that old mining town. They're going to find out just where Mueller and his men are. They should be back by daylight."

"How far are we from the town?"

"Best we can tell in the dark, about a mile or so."

"Don't you think we should get a little closer in case BJ needs our help?"

"No, I don't think so, Johnny Boy. BJ can take care of himself. He stopped us here for a reason and this is where we stay for now. Get something to eat and then sac out. Tomorrow is going to be a busy day."

Kraus and I got our fill of food. I let Kraus walk to a tree and relieve himself. After he came back, I tied him to a tree for the night and lay down myself. I was asleep in minutes, even while thinking what tomorrow might bring. What seemed like minutes turned out to be several hours, BJ was shaking me and telling me to wake up. "John, get up. I want you to hear this."

About fifteen minutes later, BJ had all the leaders in a group and started telling us what they had seen in town.

"Okay everyone. Listen up. Wolfgang and I were able to get into town easily, almost too easy. There were half a dozen guards around, but they weren't doing a particularly good job watching the town. We got past them with no problem. There isn't much left of that town. Most of the buildings are old wooden structures that are falling down. There are only two buildings in town big enough to hold Mueller, his men, and the weapon. The first one we checked out was empty with no sign of any activity. We moved on to the next one and we hit the jackpot with that one. We saw sixty to seventy men in and around the building, far less men than we were told about. The machines, or what we're calling weapons, are inside and all covered up with canvas. There's no way they will be ready to use anytime soon.

I couldn't help myself from butting in. "Excuse me BJ, but that makes no sense at all. If this Mueller is as smart as we think, and I believe he is from our meeting at the warehouse, it makes no sense that he wouldn't be ready for us. He must know we're coming for him and besides Kraus told us that this guy Hellman promised to have the machines ready in two days. That's today!"

"John, I don't know why they're not ready. I'm glad they're not. Chief, tell them what you found."

"Sure. Just like BJ said the guys were half-asleep. We walked right past them and checked out behind every building. When we got to the building where Mueller and his men were, we found an old Russian helicopter, a Mil-Mi-26, behind the building. That's how they got all that equipment up here. We knew they didn't drive it up here on trucks. We were able to get in the back part of that building and BJ is right. The weapons are all covered up, but they're right inside that building. The building is huge. It must be two and a half stories or three stories high with over twenty rooms leading off the main room where the weapons are.

If they don't give up, it'll be a real battle getting them out of there."

General Hadwin jumped in the conversation. "Not really, Chief. If they don't surrender, then I will bring the building down on top of them with these two tanks and there won't be anyone left to fight when I get done with them."

BJ chuckled and said, "I like the way you think, General."

BJ started laying out the plan. "It's now about 5:30 and it will be light in an hour. General Hadwin, this is now your ball game. We're about thirty minutes from town. I want you and your tanks on the move by 7:30, so that gives me and my men time to get in position around the town to watch and see what happens when you call Mueller out. I want you to roll up to that building by nine. Mueller doesn't know that you have flipped sides. When you start to talk to him, he may not believe you at first. If that happens, have one of your tanks level the building next to them. That should get his attention. Remember what I told you. I will be watching every move you make and listening to every word you say, so one false move and I drop you right where you stand."

"I assure you, Lieutenant, you can trust me. I want this to end as much as you do. I want Mueller behind bars where he belongs."

"Okay then, everyone knows what their job is. We've got about an hour before we move. One more thing. General Meyer take Kraus with you and let Mueller see him. That may help convince him to surrender. Everybody else, get your men ready to move out. I want this over by noon and hopefully we will all be on our way back home by then."

As everyone started to move away, I grabbed BJ. "Listen to me, BJ. I have a bad feeling about this. It doesn't add up."

"Thanks, John but this is what I do. I think you need to leave this one to me."

"No, BJ, you're going to hear me out on this. You dragged me over here and halfway across Germany, almost got me killed twice and now damn it, you're going to listen to me. You and I both know it's not wise to underestimate your enemies. I think that's just what you're doing. Mueller and his men have been two steps ahead of you from the start. He has fooled everyone in Germany including the chancellor and the head of this army. Now, you think he's gotten so careless that you can just walk into this town and he is going to roll over and give up? I think he's setting you up. He's goading you into this. It's just too easy!"

"John, I hear you, but maybe this time we deserve an easy one. I've been waiting a long time to bring this bastard down and today that's just what I'm going to do. You stay here in camp. I'm leaving twenty men behind to watch the camp and you can listen on the radio and hear how this all works out. Now if you'll excuse me, I need to call General Wellington and tell him what's going on today. Now, go find a good place to watch what we do to Mueller!"

"General Wellington, this is Charlie Brown. Am I free to talk?"

"Yes, go ahead Brad."

"General, we are just outside of the mining town I told you about. This is the plan."

Ten minutes later the general had agreed with BJ's plan. He would send in the two helicopters he had at the missile base to back up BJ and his men. Everything was set in motion. General Meyer, his two tanks and a hundred of his men were on the move. I prayed this would all work out as planned, but I had a bad feeling it wasn't going to. After pacing around the camp for a while, I grabbed two soldiers and a set of binoculars and headed up a hill just outside of camp. The view from up there was good. I could see the tanks were just outside of town, right on schedule like BJ wanted. It wouldn't be long now. We will know soon how this all turns out.

It's too bad it had to come to this. This little mining town is set between two beautiful mountains. It's easy to see why it was built here. Plenty of mountains to dig into. I kept watching from the hilltop and right on time I could see the tanks roll up in front of a large building. BJ said to the general "This is really strange, General, not any of Mueller's men have put up any kind of fight or tried to stop you at all. Maybe the sight of those two tanks made them think better about putting up a fight."

I could see General Meyer standing side-by-side with Kraus and two of his officers. He ordered Mueller to come out and talk. "Mueller, this is General Meyer, head of the German Army. We have you and your man surrounded. You need to come out and surrender before anyone gets killed here today."

Two minutes later, the front door of the building opened. Out stepped an older man dressed in a military uniform, but it wasn't Mueller. It was Mueller's right-hand man, General Hellman.

"General Meyer, we know who you are and you know who we are and you know why we're here. So, let's stop pretending we don't know each other. In fact, General, if I remember right you are supposed to be on our side, helping us bring Germany back as a world power where we belong. What happened to you, General?"

"I never wanted to be part of this Hellman. Mueller conned me into thinking this could actually work. I was a fool to listen to his lies!"

"General Meyer, I see that the Americans have poisoned your mind. Herr Mueller will be disappointed that you have deserted us."

"I didn't come here to talk to you, Hellman. Where is Mueller?"

"Herr Mueller is here. He told me to speak for him. He's listening to everything you say. You can be sure of that. I see you have one of our lieutenants with you. Kraus, have you deserted us as well?"

Kraus answered "I didn't desert you, but if I had known before what I know now, I would have never gone along with your plan. The weapon you have that you think you can control, well, you should know you can't! Sooner or later, it will get out of control and kill us all. You and Mueller need to stop this right now and turn these weapons over to General Meyer."

"Kraus, I always knew you were a weak-minded man. You never really had the backbone for this. I told Mueller that from the start and I was right and now you can die with the rest of these cowards."

Meyer yelled "Hellman, listen to me. No one needs to die here today. Go back in there and tell Mueller and the rest of your men to come out with your hands up and I promise you no one will shoot. You have ten minutes to comply or I'll give the order for these tanks to bring this building down on top of you."

Hellman scoffed. "Well, thank you General Meyer and how gracious of you to give us ten minutes to comply. I will take your kind offer back to Herr Mueller and his men. I will let you know what our answer is in precisely ten minutes."

Watching and listening to what was taking place in town, it was obvious things weren't going at all the way we thought they would. I heard BJ talking to General Meyer after Hellman went back inside the building. BJ said "Meyer, what the hell is going on with this Hellman? Has he lost his mind? He and Mueller are trapped in that building with no way out and they can't possibly think they can fight their way out. Their only chance to live is to surrender."

"Lieutenant Johnson, I don't understand it myself. Hellman acts like he and Mueller are in charge, like they're holding all the cards. He was too calm and two bloody sarcastic for a man in his position. I wanted to walk up to him and slap him right in the face."

Just then one of the soldiers who was with me tapped me on the shoulder. "Sir, look behind that building. We have them trapped in and they're all running out the back up into that hill behind the building. That won't do them any good. We'll just hunt them down one at a time, so why would they even bother? They should know they can't get away that easily. There's no place to go up here. It's all mountains."

In an instant, it all came clear to me. It all made sense now. All the pieces just came together! They're not running from us. They're running from Mueller. He's not in that building at all. He's somewhere up in one of these mountains with the real weapons.

"Give me the radio. I need to warn BJ right now. BJ, this is John. You need to listen to me."

"John, get off the radio. Whatever it is, it can wait till later."

"BJ, it's a trap! There are no weapons in that building. It's a decoy. Mueller is setting you up. It's a trap. Get out of there."

"John, what are you talking about? I saw the weapons and the men in that building last night myself."

"BJ, whatever you saw, it was not the weapons. You said they were all under tarps, so you could have been looking at a pile of boxes for all you know. Trust me. It all makes sense now. They let you get in and out of town last night easily, so you would believe you had them trapped. The fact that there were so few men when we were told they had hundreds. Kraus told us that Hellman promised to have the weapons ready yesterday and why didn't Mueller come out to talk? Because he's not there. Believe me. He's with the weapons right now and he's probably aiming them right down on top of you and General Meyer. For God's sake, trust me BJ. Pull everyone back, please. It's a trap!"

"Meyer, have you been listening to what John just told me?"

"Yes, I have. He's right. It all makes sense to me now. That's why Hellman was so damn smug when he was talking to me."

"Okay then. Get your ass out of there now and pull those tanks back fast."

From my perch on the hillside, I started scanning the mountain sides. There it was. About a mile from town and halfway up the mountain side, a large opening to an old, abandoned mine shaft. No sooner had I seen it when a cloud of dust and debris came out of the opening, followed seconds later by one of the brightest lightning flashes I'd ever seen. My warning was too late. The lightning bolt hit the first tank.

Chapter 34

She heard something that sounded like someone calling her name, but she wasn't sure she knew that voice. Her head hurt like hell and she couldn't seem to open her eyes.

"General, I think she's starting to come around, but please go easy on the questions. She has a pretty severe concussion."

"Ok, doc, just a few questions."

"Mary, can you hear me, this is General Wellington. Mary, try to open your eyes. Can you see me?"

"Yes, I see you, but you're all fuzzy and you keep moving."

"That's alright Mary, it will get better, trust me."

"Where am I and why does my head hurt so bad?"

"Mary, do you remember what happened to you last night?"

"I think so. I had dinner in the hotel restaurant. I had a couple of glasses of wine with dinner. Is that why my head hurts so much?"

"Mary, what hotel did you stay in last night?"

"You know the one here in Washington."

"Okay Mary, that's fine. Now I want you to listen to me. The doctor here is going to give you something to help you sleep. You'll feel better when you wake up."

"Okay, but can I have something for my head? It really hurts."

"I know Mary, we're going to help you with that. You just rest for now."

"Doc, how long will she be like this?"

"No way to tell right now, General. I want to keep her under for a couple of days and then we'll try waking her up. Until then, there's nothing more we can do for her."

"Okay doc. Let me know if anything changes."

"Yes sir, I will."

"How are my two marines doing?"

"They'll be fine. One has a broken arm and the other one has some badly bruised ribs. Other than that, they're both fine. They're right down the hall if you want to go see them."

"Yes, I will stop down and see them. I want to get the story right from them. I already have the police's version. Can you believe they actually wanted to arrest them?"

"Why?"

"The police claimed that they didn't have to do what they did to those kidnappers. If it were up to me, I would give them both medals."

"I agree with you, General. They deserve a medal."

"Okay doc. I'm going to see my boys now. Keep an eye on this young lady for me."

"Don't worry, General. She's in good hands."

"Good morning, gentleman. I can see you're both doing well."

"Yes, sir General. We are both doing good. We should be out of here in a day or so."

"Glad to hear that. I want one of you to tell me just what happened last night."

"Well, General, you sent us to pick up that young lady, Mary. As we walked into the hotel lobby, there were two older German ladies who came running up to us and yelling something in German. Neither one of us speaks German very well, but we understood the words 'young lady'. They were pointing to the back door. So, we ran out the back just in time to see one of those assholes throw her into the back of a van. We both took off running across the parking lot to the van. The guy on my side picked up an old board of some kind and took a swing at me. I blocked it with my left arm. I think that's how my arm got broken. Anyway, I landed a hard right fist right square in the guy's face. He went down, but got right back up and came right at me again. We both slammed into the side of the van and hit the ground. I got to my feet first and grabbed him by his long hair. I slammed him into the side of the van three times. The third time he went down in a pile and never moved again. I had no idea that I had broken his neck the last time I drove him into the van. I didn't really mean to kill him, sir. It just happened. I was so hyped up from adrenalin, I really didn't think about what I was doing. I'm still trying to get my head around the fact that I actually killed another person."

"Don't worry about it, son. You did what you had to at the time and no one will fault you for that."

"What about you, soldier? What's your version of what happened?"

"Sir, it's just like he said. We saw them throw the girl in the van and we started running in their direction. My guy came at me swinging both fists. Sir, I almost started laughing. That was a huge mistake on his part. I was a two-time golden glove boxing champion by the time I was eighteen. I joined the corps and put on about thirty pounds and my boxing only got better. I let him take a swing at me and then I just started pounding him in the face. I'm sure the third time I hit him, I broke his nose. He went down in a pile and I was sure he wasn't getting up. That's when I turned to see what was going on with my buddy. I couldn't believe it, but that a****** got up and ran me into the side of the van. I'm sure that's how my ribs got so bruised. I turned around and hit him twice in the face and once in the throat. I'm sure that crushed his larynx. He won't be singing any songs anytime soon. After that, we both jumped into the van to help the young lady. We weren't even sure at that time it was Mary. She was bleeding so much from her head wound, you could hardly see her face. Apparently, someone had called the police. By the time we got the bleeding stopped, the cops were there. They called an ambulance and brought us all to the hospital. That's pretty much it, sir. I hope we didn't cause you too much trouble. We just did what we thought we had to."

"You two did exactly what you should have done. It's what you were trained to do; help and protect people. You should be proud of what you did. You saved that young lady's life. If you hadn't got there as soon as you did, she would be dead. She lost so much blood, if she hadn't gotten to the hospital when she did, the doctor said she would have died in that van for sure."

"How is she, sir?"

"It's too early to know for now. The doc is going to keep her under for a couple of days and then when we wake her up, we'll know more."

"Please, let us know how she makes out, sir."

"I will. You too just rest up for now. I will make sure you get sent back to the states to recover. You both deserve a little vacation for what you did."

"Thank you, sir,"

"Doctor, is there anything I can do for Mary before I leave?"

"Yes sir, General. Mary is in for a long rehab and she's going to need someone to be with her a lot; someone she knows and trusts."

"I know exactly who to call. I will have her here in a couple of days."

"That would be good, General. I won't wake her until she gets here."

"Thanks for all your help, doc. I'll call you in a day or so."

What followed that lightning bolt was a nightmare I will never forget as long as I live. The whole side of the tank began to glow. A door on top of the tank flew open and someone tried to get out. They never made it. The tank exploded in an instant. In a way, it was a blessing. The men including General Hadwin and Kraus who had been standing near the tank had burst into flames from the heat of the lightning bolt. The blast killed them instantly. Others were on fire and running in every direction trying desperately to pull off their clothes. The blast was so powerful that it pushed the other tank sideways at least thirty or forty feet. The explosion leveled two small buildings on the street and blew out every remaining window in town. The fireball must have gone a thousand feet in the air. There was so much smoke, dirt and debris in the air that I could hardly see the town. We watched in utter disbelief at what had just happened. General Hadwin and a hundred of his men were gone. They had all died in seconds with no chance of surviving. I kept looking at the town hoping beyond hope that someone had survived. Several minutes later as the dust was settling down, the shape of the town was coming back into view and we could see bodies everywhere. None of them were moving. Some of the bodies were still burning and I prayed that they were dead. The radio cracked and I heard BJ calling for General Meyer. He must know that he's dead, but he called his name three times. Each time you could hear the sorrow and the pain in his voice. Finally, Wolfgang and the Chief came on the air. They all had the same report. As far as they could tell, everyone that had gone into town was dead. Now we know why Hellman had been so cocky when he was talking to General Meyer. It was a setup. The ten minutes Meyer had given him he had used to get himself and his men in the building out the back.

For the next few minutes as the dust continued to settle, BJ and his leaders tried to come up with a plan to retrieve bodies and see if anyone in the other tank had survived. While they were still talking, they got their answer. The tank began to move and, in my heart, I was glad that someone had lived through that, but in my mind, I was screaming 'don't move'. If they stayed still, Mueller might think they were dead and leave them alone. Just as the tank began to move and head for the building where Hellman had been, the two helicopters General Wellington had sent showed up over town. I heard BJ try to order them to leave the area, but they hovered over town in disbelief at what they were seeing. They desperately wanted to help, but BJ kept telling them to get the hell away from town. BJ knew just what I knew; that Mueller would target the other tank and that's exactly what he did.

Seconds later, another lightning bolt hit the second tank. It had almost reached the building when it exploded. It sent so much metal and other debris into the air that it took out one of the helicopters in another thunderous explosion. The other helicopter was hit, but was able to stay in the air. A minute later it was gone out of sight.

The blast from the second tank destroyed the building Hellman had been using as a decoy. The building must have been set up to explode if anyone went inside. Several large explosions happened right after the tank blew up. By that time, BJ and everyone else had started to pull back. There was no way to tell where Mueller would aim his next lightning bolt. We didn't have to wait long to find out.

For the next twenty minutes or so, Mueller would target another building in town. Soon the whole town was in flames and every building had been destroyed or was burning. Mueller was a madman with the ultimate weapon.

Later, when BJ and everyone that was left got back to the staging area, BJ came right up to me, grabbed me, and asked. "How the hell is Mueller able to keep shooting that thing? You said it would blow up in his face."

"No, BJ, that's not what I said. I said if he tries to use it at 90% or more it would blow up. Obviously, he's only using it around 80%. Did you notice how straight and round the lightning bolts were? That tells me he has learned to control the weapon and he knows enough not to exceed 80%."

"John, you're telling me he did all this at just 80%?"

"Yes, and if he keeps it at 80% there's no telling how long he can keep firing it. There's only one thing that will stop him from firing the weapon."

"Just what the hell would that be, John?"

"Fuel. He needs fuel to keep the generators running. When it runs out, he's done."

"Great, John! The only problem is we have no idea how much fuel he has up there. This could go on for a long time. I'm going to call General Wellington. We need to bomb this a****** off the mountain."

"BJ, I don't think that will work. Mueller picked his spot well. Look where he is. You will never bomb him out of there by dropping bombs on top of that mountain. It must be a thousand or fifteen hundred feet of solid rock from the top of that mountain down to where he is. If you try to go straight at the opening, he'll burn you out of the air before you get within a mile of that opening."

"Okay, John, thanks for nothing. You're so good at telling us what won't work, try thinking of something that will work. You go to work on that, Johnny Boy. I've got to call the general and tell him we got our ass kicked today."

"Hello general, this is Charlie Brown reporting in. I've got some really bad news for you. General Meyer and a hundred or more of his men are all dead, along with both of his tanks being destroyed. General, I've never seen anything like it. This weapon is, I don't even know how to describe it. It hits you in an instant. You don't even see it coming. I saw men burst into flame and some just disintegrate instantly. General, I'm not sure we can stop this guy."

"I know what you're saying, Brad. The men that came back in the helicopter were talking like crazy men. Some of them claimed it was a lightning bolt from God. One man said it was a volcano that erupted. They were all scared as hell. Just what happened out there?"

"Sir, Mueller is held up in an old mine shaft halfway up the mountainside. He must have lifted the equipment up there by helicopter. That's the only way he could have done it."

"Brad, this is going to get worse before it gets better. I just got off the phone with the German Chancellor. He's demanding to know how we are involved, and he wants to know why he can't reach General Meyer."

"General, please tell him that General Meyer died a hero. He gave his life trying to stop Mueller. Tell him we are working with the German army and we are doing everything we can to stop Mueller."

"Brad, I have an idea how to stop Mueller."

"What's that, sir?"

"I'm sitting here at our missile base with over a hundred missiles. If you give me the exact location of that mine, I can send one of these missiles right down that mine shaft and end this."

"That just might work, General. I can do better than give you the location. I can laser mark it for you, so you can't miss it."

"Okay Brad. How long before you're ready to give me a target?"

"Give me forty-five minutes to get into position. You'll get my signal right at the launch desk. As soon as you see it, let that bird fly. Let's kill this guy once and for all!"

The general went right to the commander of the missile base. "I want a BXT 240 ready to launch in ten minutes."

"Sir, not to be disrespectful, but no way in hell! First, I can't launch any missiles unless I have confirmation of an attack. I need permission from the German army, my own commander back in the states and besides a BXT 240 will bring down a mountain. You just don't light one of these things off without a good reason. What in the world would you be shooting it at anyway?"

"A mountain, Commander. Now, get it ready!"

"Sir, I don't think"

The General cut him off. "I'm not asking you to think! I'm giving you an order as the Commander in Chief of the US Army! Now you can carry out this order or spend the rest of your days behind bars."

"Okay, gentleman. You heard the general. Prepare to launch number one."

Twenty minutes later, the signal and location came up on the screen.

"General, we have confirmation of the target," the commander remarked.

"Well, then launch. Get this bird in the air. Commander, how do I know where it will hit?"

"General, do you see that dot on the screen? That's the target. This line is the missile."

"How long before it gets there?"

"From here it's only about three minutes. Just keep watching the screen, so you'll know when it hits. Okay, General, the missile is about a minute out."

"Commander, I'm watching the screen and that line just disappeared. What happened?"

"I'm not sure sir, it looks like something happened to the missile. It seems like it just exploded in mid-flight."

"How is that possible? Did someone shoot it down?"

"No sir. There's no way anyone shot that missile down. It's the fastest and most advanced missile we have, so no way anyone shot it down. We would have seen that anyway. It must have been a malfunction of some kind."

"Well, then get another one ready!"

"Sir?"

"You heard me, get another one ready. I'll call my man on the ground and tell him to mark the target again."

"Brad, this is General Weldon. You must mark the target again. Something happened to the first missile."

"No, General, nothing happened to the missile. Mueller shot it down."

"That's not possible. That missile was still fifty miles out."

"I know, General, but I heard it explode and I saw the lightning bolt that took it out. Now you know what we are up against. General, you better find out where that missile blew up. I'm sure it did some damage wherever it went off."

"Okay, Brad, no more missiles. Brad, I know you have a lot on your mind right now, but I want you to know about Mary."

"Why, what happened to her?"

"She came to Germany looking to find John even though I told her not to. She got kidnapped while we were trying to get to her. Two marines I sent to get her were able to rescue her. Unfortunately, she got hurt and is in an induced coma right now. The doctor doesn't know how well she will come out of it. I have sent for John's mother to come and stay with her. There's nothing we can do for her right now. We just must wait and see when she wakes up. I'll leave it up to you if you want to tell John or not."

"That's bad news, General, but let me think about telling John. I may not. I need his head in the game right now. If he's worried about Mary, he may be too distracted."

"Okay Brad that's your call, let me know what I can do to help you guys out there."

"I will, General."

"You must be Miss Northrup. I'm Doctor Keller. I have been treating Mary ever since they brought her in here three days ago."

"Please, just call me Sharon. How is she doing?"

"Well, as you can see, she is resting quite comfortably. We are pleased with the way her head wound is healing up. However, that is the least of our concerns. She has a severe concussion. The first time we tried to talk to her, she didn't remember where she was. She thought that she was still in Washington. That tells me that her short-term memory is a problem. We didn't go any further with evaluating her at the time. Now that you are here, we will try waking her up and see what she remembers. Forgive me for asking, but just how do you know Mary, if I may ask?"

"I have known Mary for some time now. She and my son met in college. I keep waiting for them to get married."

"So, they were students together?"

"No, not exactly. John was a professor at the school and Mary was a student there."

"Sharon, I don't want you to be alarmed about what Mary may remember or what she doesn't. She may remember you and not others or she may remember everyone. In most of these cases the person's memory will come back slowly. Once they get around familiar places and things, it will help them draw on their past. That's the main reason I wanted someone like you here. She will need to see a face she knows, but even with you here she may be scared."

"May I ask why your son didn't come with you?"

"Didn't the General tell you?"

"No ma'am, he didn't mention it."

"Doctor, I think you better ask the General. I'm not sure how much I can say about John, but if he could be here, he certainly would be. He loves Mary ever so much."

"Okay then, Sharon, are you ready? I'm going to give her a shot and it should wake her up. You can start talking to her anytime now. She'll be able to hear you even if she doesn't seem like she's awake."

"Mary, Mary, dear. It's Sharon, John's mother. Do you know who I am?"

"I'm not sure, who did you say you are?"

I'm Sharon dear, Miss Northrup."

"Oh yes, Miss Northrup, yes, of course I know you, but why did you come to Washington?"

"I came here to be with you, Mary."

"That was nice of you. I'm sorry, but I can't seem to open my eyes. I don't know why."

"That's okay, Mary. I can see you and you look beautiful."

"Oh, thank you. I feel so tired."

The doctor said "Sharon, ask her to tell you the last thing she remembers."

"Mary, what's the last thing you remember, dear."

Mary responded "I think I spent most of yesterday in the Smithsonian Institute, in the art building. It's so wonderful. You should go."

"What else Mary?"

"I went back to the hotel and had some dinner. I think I went to bed after that. Sharon, I'm not sure where I am now. Can you tell me where I am?"

Sharon told her "Mary, you had a fall and hit your head and you're in the hospital. We are taking good care of you."

The doctor looked at Sharon and said, "Ask her if she remembers John."

"Mary, do you remember John, your fiancé?

"I don't have a fiancé. I'm too busy teaching my students to have a boyfriend. Who's John?"

"No one for you to worry about right now, dear. You just rest and let us take care of you."

"Okay Sharon. I think that's a good idea. I'm very tired. I think I'll sleep now."

"You do that, dear. I'll be right here when you wake up."

The doctor said to Sharon. "I can see you're upset right now, but the fact that she knows you is a great sign and in fact, it's more than I hoped for. She knows you, she knows she's a teacher and she remembers she was in Washington at the Smithsonian, so that means that a lot of her memory is still intact. She will get more as time goes by."

"Doctor, why does she know me and not John?"

361

"Sharon, there's no understanding why some parts of a person's memory come back and other parts don't. It may be months before we will know the full extent of her memory."

"Doctor, when will she be able to travel back to the states?"

"I would think in a few days, but she will need a lot of rehabilitation. Just walking will be a challenge for her, so she will need a lot of support."

"Don't worry about that. I will see to it that she gets all the care she needs."

Chapter 35

"Chief, get Wolfgang and John. We need to figure out how to stop this maniac." BJ turned to us and spoke. "All right, guys. We're all that's left after this morning. Mueller hit us big time. John, I'm sorry I didn't listen to you sooner. You warned me, but I was too thick-headed to hear what you were saying."

"BJ, I'm sorry I didn't put the pieces together sooner. If I had, all those guys would be alive right now."

"Don't go there, John. The only one to blame for their deaths is Mueller. We need to find a way to stop him."

"BJ, I've been thinking about this and we do have some things going for us."

"Like what, John?"

"Well, first off, we know right where Mueller is. He can't get out of there without going through us. He can't surprise us anymore and the biggest thing is he can't shoot at us with that weapon."

"Why not?"

"Because he has a limited range to aim that thing, so if his targets aren't right out in front of him, he can't shoot. The mine may be a shelter for him, but it also limits the range he can aim that weapon. We could just sit here and starve him out. It worked for the Roman army when they took over Masada."

"Thanks John, but I'm not going to sit here for days or weeks waiting for Mueller and his men to starve to death or commit suicide."

BJ turned to Wolfgang and said "I think we can take advantage of the fact that he can't shoot that damn thing at us. "Wolfgang, you said you've been up here in the past. How much do you know about the mine shafts up here? Is there another way out?"

"Sorry, BJ, not that I know of. Most of the mine shafts up here have been deserted for years. I came up here as a kid and we are in and out of almost every mine up here. They all ran into a dead end. One way in and one way out."

"BJ smiled and said "Good, then we have him trapped in his own grave."

"Excuse me, BJ, but you're doing it again!"

"Exactly what am I doing, John?"

"You're underestimating Mueller. That crack I made about him starving to death, I didn't really mean it. Do you really think he would let himself get trapped in a mine with no way out? I don't believe for a minute that he would let that happen. He must have another way out. I think you should try to figure out what he's up to and beat him at his own game."

The Chief said "Boss, I think you should listen to Johnny Boy. He makes good sense to me."

"I have to agree with the Chief on this one," said Wolfgang.

"I have to agree with you both. I think John's on to something here."

"Okay, John, what do you think his next move is?"

"Well, Mueller has to get out of there somehow, so I would say we need to figure out how he's going to do that. Wolfgang, you said there was no way out. Is that right?"

"No way that I know of."

"If he had to dig his way out, how long do you think that would take?"

Wolfgang shook his head and said "It could take months or maybe a year. That mountain is two miles thick. The mine he's in only goes back a couple thousand feet."

BJ asked "What are you thinking, John?

"Okay, let's suppose he tries to connect with another mine that already exists. How long would that take?"

Wolfgang said. "It depends on how close the other shaft is and how would we ever figure out what shaft he was trying to dig to?"

"Easy. Send a few men into each shaft near the one he's in. If he's digging in their direction, they should be able to hear them. Wolfgang you're the only one that knows the mountain, so which shaft is he likely to try and connect to."

"I'm not sure, but it would have to be one that is big enough for him to move the equipment through. There's only three that are that big. The rest are way too small."

"Okay then. We send a team into all three and see where he's coming out. Remember, he can't use the weapon while they're being moved."

"You're right, John. All we have to do is deal with his little army."

"BJ, I didn't say I had it all figured out."

BJ turned to Wolfgang. "Wolfgang, draw us a map of where to find these shafts and let's put our teams together and be ready to move by dark."

Wolfgang had the map drawn up in less than an hour and it had surprisingly good detail. Two of the mine shafts were close by and the third one was a long hike away. BJ kept it simple- shaft A, B and C. BJ and a few of his men would take shaft A, Wolfgang and his men would take shaft B and Casey would take his men into shaft C.

All three teams set out just as it was getting dark. We could still see the mining town burning as the sky turned dark. Over a hundred of our men still lay dead in the street, but even after dark we didn't dare try to retrieve them. That would have to wait until this was all over. Every man among us wanted to avenge our fallen brothers. Those of us left at camp sat and listened on the radio for any indication that one of the teams had found the right shaft.

BJ's team was the first to reach their shaft. After approaching the entrance very slowly, they found no one near the outside. Once inside they found that it was pitch-black inside, damp and cold. They advanced slowly, step-by-step, feeling their way along the walls, expecting any minute to run into someone or trip over a booby trap. The only thing that greeted them was the smell of some dead and decaying animal that was ripe in their noses. If someone had been using this mineshaft, you would think they would have gotten rid of whatever was causing that smell.

Wolfgang was closing in on shaft B and they were about a hundred yards out when they heard voices. Wolfgang told his men to stay put while he made his way closer. Wolfgang crept along through the trees and brushes until he was right on top of whoever it was that was talking. They were talking and laughing about what happened in town that day. Wolfgang's rage was building to the breaking point. He wanted to jump out on these two men and kill them with his bare hands. Just as he thought he couldn't hold himself back any longer, a third man came up and ordered the other two back inside the mine. He ordered them to keep digging out the shaft. He told them to make sure they were through by morning. That's all Wolfgang needed to hear. He made his way back to his man and got on the radio. "BJ, we found the right shaft. It's my shaft, shaft B. I overheard men talking about being done by morning. I will meet you back at camp. Call back Casey. No reason to have them keep going."

Two hours later, they were all back at camp. BJ pulled everyone together and laid out the plan of attack. They would split up into three groups and cover the entrance to the mine shaft from three different directions. BJ's man would cover the mine shaft head on, Wolfgang would cover the shaft from the right side and Casey and his men from the left side, but up on the mountain above the mine. That would get him and his men a good view of what was happening below. They could provide good cover fire from up there and tell BJ and Wolfgang just when and where to move. All three groups started to move out now that the plan was set. It was time to end this. BJ turned to me and said "John, where is that backpack I gave you?"

"I have it right here." I handed it over to BJ and asked, "So, what's inside?"

BJ looked at me, smiled and said "John you've been carrying this for days and you never looked inside?"

I said "No. I guess I didn't really care what was inside. Why, should I have looked inside?"

BJ said "If you had you probably wouldn't know what you were looking at anyway. A while back Wolfgang and I decided that these machines or weapons should never be left to anyone or any country ever. Wolfgang gave me a new extremely high explosive that we were going to use to destroy the machines once we had control of them."

"BJ, you made me carry this stuff around on my back all this time! What if it had gone off with everyone around me!"

"Relax, John. The stuff as you call it, can't go off by itself. That's the good thing about it. I have the other component to make it ignite. You need to put the two together, but when you do you better find a deep hole to hide in. I was going to use it on the weapons, but now I'm going to use it on Mueller. All I need to do is get close. This little backpack will do the rest."

I looked at BJ and said "Getting close to Mueller might not be that easy. You know he will have his best fighters around him."

"John, I didn't sign up for this because it was easy. Don't you worry about me. I promise you this ends today!"

BJ, Wolfgang and Casey all headed out with their men. They all knew they were outnumbered two or three to one, but they never hesitated to take on this fight. These men were special. They were men of their word and they had sworn to protect their country from all enemies even if it meant giving their lives to do it. Today, some of them would do just that. Wolfgang and his men were the first to get into position, followed by BJ and his men. Casey had a little harder time getting up the mountain to his position. The side of the mountain was steep and covered with large rocks and trees. A good place to hide behind, but not easy to get to. Once in position, he was in good shape to cover the entrance to the mine shaft. Everyone was in position and waiting for some sign that Mueller and his men were coming out.

Just as the first signs of light were creeping over the mountain, BJ came on the radio. "Heads up, everyone. I see movement in front of the mine. There's about a dozen men and a bulldozer coming right at us. No one starts shooting until I say so."

"BJ, this is Wolfgang. I have at least two dozen men coming out and heading in my direction."

"Wolfgang, hold your fire as long as you can. I want them right in front of us before we open on them. Casey, what do you see from up there?

"Wolfgang is right. There must be twenty or thirty men moving in his direction and more coming out of the mine. We should be able to thin them out well from up here. I have two 30 caliber machine guns aimed right down on top of them."

"Good, Casey, but hold your fire. Let's see just how many more come out before we open on them. For the next ten minutes, it was hard to believe what they were seeing. More men and three trucks came out of the mine. John had really called this one right. Mueller's plan was to just roll away after leveling the town. He had the men and equipment to do just that. The only problem with this plan was he didn't count on BJ.

"BJ, this is Wolfgang. These guys are right in our face and they'll be stepping on us any minute now.

"Casey, this is BJ. Open up on them and draw them away from Wolfgang."

Casey and his men let hell rain down on them. Mueller's men started dropping like leaves on a windy fall day. They were so busy looking ahead they never thought to look up until it was too late. All the men who had been moving in Wolfgang's direction, now began shooting up at Casey's position. That's when Wolfgang and his men opened on them from behind. For Wolfgang and his men, they were easy targets. By the time they turned back around, more than half of them lay dead on the ground. The shooting became more and more intense as Mueller's men found cover and started to return fire. Some of Mueller's men started to retreat into the mine, but this gave BJ and his men an opening to move closer. Up to that point, BJ and his men had held off firing and so Mueller's men didn't even know they were there. Casey and his men kept up the hail of gunfire from above. Every now and then, one of Mueller's men would step out to fire up the hill at Casey's position. They made an easy target for Wolfgang and his men to take them out. The way this was going, this would all be over soon. That's the way Wolfgang saw it, anyway.

Just as BJ was making a move for the front of the mine, dozens of men came charging out of the mine firing their guns in every direction. The gunfire was so heavy and so intense, all BJ and his men could do was take cover. Two of Mueller's men had come out of the mine with a grenade launcher and turned them loose at Casey and his men up on the mountainside. Before they could shoot them down, they had taken out one of the thirty caliber machine guns and killed three of his men. After losing one of the machine guns and three of their comrades, Casey's men came back fighting even harder. Two of Wolfgang's men crawled up to within a hundred feet of the mine. Shooting from a well-protected rock outcropping, they laid down a withering barrage of gunfire. That gave BJ and his men the opening they were looking for to get back into the fight. They had been pinned down by the last rush of men coming out of the mine. BJ's forward attack was slow-moving. Mueller's men were hiding behind that bulldozer and piles of rock that had been taken out of the mine years before. BJ and Wolfgang continued to move closer from the front and the side. Casey was picking off Mueller's men from above when suddenly, his men made a run for it back into the mine. BJ and Wolfgang moved to within a hundred feet of the mine. Casey held this position above the mine and everyone took a deep breath. The question now was who would make the next move?

Nothing happened for the next twenty minutes or so. BJ moved closer to the opening until it got to the point where there was no more cover. One more step and he would be leaving himself wide open to anyone shooting at him out of the mine. Minutes passed and all was quiet then, without warning, a hail of gunfire erupted from the mine. Everyone dove for cover. This went on for the next couple of minutes. Whoever was shooting was doing so blindly. They weren't hitting anyone, but they were keeping everyone at bay. This happened two more times with no one getting hit. This wasn't getting Mueller anywhere. BJ began to wonder what the point was. Why would Mueller waste ammunition, shooting blindly out of the mine? John's voice was ringing in Casey's ear, reminding him that Mueller is smart. He always has a backup plan, but what the hell was it this time? We have him cut off and no way out. Why is he stalling? He must know he's trapped. Just then Casey came on the radio "BJ, I'm sure I saw a movement behind you. I don't know how many, but I know I saw men moving up on you." BJ instantly knew! Hellman! It must be Hellman. He and his men had run out the back of that building yesterday before it blew up. I thought they had just run off into the mountains. That's why Mueller's men were stalling. They were just waiting for Hellman. Just as BJ got his men turned around to face the oncoming threat, Hellman and his men opened on them and at the same time Mueller's men came storming out of the mine once again. They were caught in the crossfire. BJ and his men were in a dangerous spot. Casey poured down fire from above on top of the men coming out of the cave, but there were just too many of them to stop them all. Wolfgang came at Mueller's men from the side. They hit them hard, shooting and charging at them from the trees. Mueller's men were so focused on running straight ahead that they never saw them coming. They were so close to each other it turned into hand-to-hand fighting. The Chief and his men were far better at fighting hand to hand than Mueller's men were. In no time, the Chief and his men, with the help of Casey's men, started picking off those that were trying to run back into the cave. They had stopped the threat to the back of BJ's men. BJ was busy trying to stop the charge from Hellman and his men. BJ and his squad were far outnumbered, but they were well-trained and steady as a rock under fire. They kept picking off their attackers one by one as they ran headlong at their position. There were just too many of them to stop them all from getting through. It soon became a one on one, face to face fight for survival.

BJ grabbed his pistol and was able to shoot two men as they ran at him. He didn't see a third man coming at him from the side. He felt himself go flying to the ground with his attacker on top of him. The man reached for a knife, but BJ was able to kick free and get to his feet just as the man was about to stab him in the back. A shot rang out from nowhere. BJ's attacker lay dead at his feet with a large hole in the side of his head. BJ turned to see the Chief standing there. No time to say thanks. There were other attackers to take down. BJ and the Chief charged head-first into a group of five attackers sending three of them flying backwards. The Chief still had his pistol out and finished off the two that were still standing. BJ finished off one with this knife and the other two just lay there on the ground with their hands over their head. Neither one of them wanted to take on a man the size of the Chief. BJ looked around and realized the fighting had stopped. Every one of Hellman's men were wounded, dead, or had given up. The question now was where was Hellman? BJ began looking around. He soon found Hellman lying face down on the ground. When he turned him over, he saw that he was still breathing.

"Can you hear me Hellman?"

A very weak voice said, "Yes, I hear you."

"Hellman, I'm Lieutenant Johnson. This is all over for you and Mueller. The two of you have accomplished nothing by what you've done, except getting a lot of people killed, and for what!"

Hellman slowly opened his eyes and looked at BJ and said, "No matter what you think or what happens here today, it's not over and this doesn't end today."

BJ said "What do you mean, Hellman? Answer me. What do you mean?" No words ever came out of Hellman again. If something else was to happen in the future, Hellman wouldn't be part of it. He was dead.

The chief grabbed BJ. "Boss, leave him lay. We have our own men to take care of." One of BJ's men was dead and five others had some serious wounds that needed attention. The medics did what they could, but these guys weren't going to fight anymore today. The chief and BJ rounded up the eighteen men that had surrendered and they stripped them down to a t-shirt, their pants and boots and set them off carrying one dead soldier and five seriously wounded soldiers. BJ had two of his men march them back to camp. By now it was mid-afternoon and each side had taken up a position to wait and see what the other one would do. Casey held his spot on the mountainside after sending his lost men back to camp with the others. The chief and BJ had tried to take account of the men Mueller had lost and as best they could tell, he had lost over a hundred and sixty men. The question was how many more did he have. How many more would he be willing to sacrifice before he would give up?

Chapter 36

"Hello, Sharon. I'm glad I caught you here. I see Mary is resting well."

"Hello, General. Yes, she's resting quite well. She worked hard at a rehab session today. The doctor said she could head back to the states any time now."

"Yes, I know. That's why I'm here. The doctor called me to let me know how she was doing."

"General, I have to make arrangements to get her home."

"No, Sharon, you don't. I have already done that. Tomorrow morning, two US Army medics will be here to take you and Mary to an army transport plane. They will be with you all the way home and you will be landing at Andrews Air Force Base in Washington. From there, they will take you and Mary to the Walter Reed Medical Center. Mary can stay there as long as she needs to recover and she will have the best care there is. I have arranged for you to stay at a hotel close by. Don't worry about the cost. That's all being covered by the army. It's the least we can do for you and Mary."

"General, that's wonderful. I don't know how to thank you."

"You don't have to thank me. I have grown quite fond of Mary. She's the kind of girl I would want for a daughter if I ever had one."

"Yes, General, I feel the same way. I hope someday she will be my daughter, but if she doesn't remember John that probably won't happen."

"Sharon, we just need to keep hoping for the best and leave the rest to the Lord."

"I pray every day for her, General."

"So, do I Sharon, so do I."

"General, any word on my son?"

"Well, yes and no. Sharon, I'll share this with you, but don't tell anyone else at this point. I think you already know what's been going on over there."

"I have my suspicions, General."

"Well, Sharon, you probably are right. For several weeks now we've been chasing down a man named Mueller. We've been close a couple of times, but he's been extremely hard to catch."

"General, is he the man that stole my husband's plans to build a static charge machine?"

"Yes, he's the man. We have two special forces units from the US and a special unit from the German army working to bring him down."

"General, is Brad Johnson in charge of one of those units? If he is, then I know right where my son is."

"Sharon, I can't say any more about that. You have to understand this is all top secret."

"You don't have to say anything more, General. I think I can put the pieces together on my own. General, please bring my son home in one piece."

"Sharon, I'll do my best. I'll do everything I can to make that happen."

"Yes, I'm sure you will, General."

"Sharon, I have to go for now. I'll see you and Mary back in Washington. Have a good trip."

"Well, good morning, Mary dear. I'm glad to see you're waking up!"

"Oh, hi Sharon. How long have I been sleeping?"

"Well dear, you've been asleep for a long time."

"Sharon, I remember the doctor telling me he wanted me to rest today, then he gave me a shot to help me sleep. I wasn't really tired at the time."

"Mary, that's not the real reason he wanted you to sleep. After you went to sleep, we took a little trip. You are now back in Washington again. While you were asleep, the general had you flown back to the states and brought you here to the Walter Reed Medical Center. You'll have a new doctor and nurses to take care of you."

"Sharon, are you leaving me here?"

"Absolutely not, dear. I'm going to be here with you every day until you don't need me anymore."

"That's good. I don't want to be here by myself."

After an intense firefight between BJ's men and Mueller's men, things were disturbingly quiet. It had been more than an hour from the last time any shooting had occurred and BJ was getting anxious about what to do next. BJ called Casey up on the mountainside, asking if he had seen any movement. Casey replied that there was nothing moving at all up there. The mine shaft opening was about a hundred feet up the mountain from the valley where BJ and his men were waiting. That mine shaft must have been dug out over fifty years ago. The opening was large enough to drive a tractor trailer right inside. All the area in front of the mine had been cleared away leaving no easy way to approach the opening without being seen. The only cover was the trees that BJ and his men were hiding behind and that bulldozer Mueller's man had left behind during the firefight. The chances of charging into that mine were slim and none. After sitting on their butts for almost two hours with nothing happening, BJ decided to make a run for the mine.

He took three of his men and crept up to the very edge of the tree line. After waiting a few minutes, they made a run for the abandoned bulldozer. An eruption of gunfire came from the mine forcing them back to the protection of the trees. Although BJ and his guys didn't accomplish anything, they knew that Mueller and his men were still in the mine and guarding the opening. BJ began to worry that Mueller might try to find a way to get out of that mine shaft higher up on the mountain. BJ was worried about Mueller using the higher mine shaft, the one he had used to rain down destruction on the town. BJ sent Wolfgang and his men up there to guard the opening or if he could, set charges and blow the opening. Around an hour after Wolfgang had left, there was an explosion up on the mountain. Wolfgang and his men returned to report that no one was ever coming out of that opening again. The charges they had set sealed the mine shaft completely. Now the only way out for Mueller was to attack BJ's position head on and if he did, BJ's men would be ready.

Casey held his position above the mine. Wolfgang was back in the tree line adjacent to the mine and BJ and his men were directly in front. If Mueller thought he was coming out the front of that mine, he would be facing a hail of gunfire. Nothing had happened for some time now. The sun had set softly over a quiet peaceful mountain. The darkness had sent evening shadows dancing across the face of the mountain, making the men nervous and anxious about what they were seeing. Were they just seeing shadows or were Mueller's men creeping out of the mine? It was a very dark night with no moonlight and a cloud filled sky had covered even the starlight. It was hard to even see where you were walking.

BJ warned everyone to stay sharp. The Chief had moved very quietly up to the very front of the tree line. He was the first to see Mueller's men moving in their direction. He warned BJ that Mueller's men were only about fifty yards out. BJ told Wolfgang to launch flares. When the flares lit up the night sky, Mueller's men were caught out in the open with no cover. The flares had caught them off guard and as they stood looking up, BJ and his men opened on them. Mueller's men tried to return fire, but being blinded by the light, all they could do was fire blindly into the darkness. The hail of gunfire from above and the crossfire from the darkness was devastating on Mueller's men. By the time the flares hit the ground, not one of Mueller's men was still standing. They were either dead or dying. BJ had Wolfgang put up two more flares and a couple of the medics tried to go to the aid of those left alive, but gunfire from the mine sent them back into cover.

That was all BJ could take! He got on the radio and called Wolfgang. "Get over here to where the Chief and I are." As soon as Wolfgang got there, BJ started laying out his plan. BJ said, "The Chief, two of my guys and I are going into that mine and blow them all to hell." He called Casey on the radio and ordered him to move his men down with the rest of his men in front of the mine. He told Wolfgang "I want you to wait twenty minutes, then send up two more flares. As soon as the flares light up, you tell everyone to pour as much gunfire into that opening as you can. We will be undercover on the right side of the opening and try not to shoot us. Once the flares go out, stop shooting. I hope by then everyone close to the inside of that mine will be dead or driven back by your gunfire. The Chief and I will make a run into the mine and set the charges in this backpack. If we don't make it, these two guys will get it done. Okay let's go. Like I said, twenty minutes, then open up on them."

Exactly twenty minutes later the flares went up. Wolfgang gave the order and a devastating amount of gunfire poured into the opening of that mine. If anyone had been in the entrance of that mine, they were dead by now. Once the flares hit the ground and went out, BJ made his move. As fast as he and the Chief could, they ran straight into the mine followed by their backup team. Running and carrying a seventy-five-pound backpack full of high explosives was not easy. Once inside, they made their way along the side of the mine feeling the wall as they went. It was pitch black inside and every so often, they tripped over loose rocks and a body or two.

Now fifty feet inside and no resistance; one hundred feet in and things were good so far. BJ turned to the Chief and quietly said "Okay Chief, I'm going to set the timer for three minutes. I need to run this in another fifty feet, then we need to get the hell out of here fast."

The Chief looked at BJ and said, "Okay boss, move fast and be careful." BJ set the charge, stood up, took one step and then a single shot rang out. A lone gunman who had somehow survived the hail of gunfire hit BJ square in the chest and then the gunmen fell dead from his own wounds. BJ dropped to his knees and grabbed his chest. Blood started running out on his fingers and down his arm. He was hit bad and he knew it. The Chief grabbed him and let him gently down to the ground. The Chief said "Boss, how do I stop the charge?"

"You can't," said BJ. "You have to run it deeper into the mine. Then you get yourself and the other two guys out of here. I'm not going to make it. The Chief picked up the backpack and ran like a man possessed deeper into the mine, threw the backpack, and ran back to BJ. Once there, he yelled for the other two to come and help. They picked up BJ and started for the entrance of the mine. Shooting started coming from somewhere deep in the mine. The Chief yelled "Just keep moving. We need to get out of here."

Outside the mine, Casey and Wolfgang had moved right up to the entrance of the mine just in case BJ needed their support. Little did they know what support he would need. Casey and Wolfgang were right there to the surprise of the Chief. As dark as it was, they couldn't see who the Chief was carrying. The Chief yelled for more help to carry him out and find a medic right away. The Chief gave orders for everyone to move back to the tree line. The charge was set to go off any minute.

Mueller's men inside the mine had no idea what was coming. They had slowly started to make their way back to the front of the mine. Walking in the dark, they stepped right over the backpack with no idea of what was in it. No matter, they only had seconds to live.

The Chief, Casey and Wolfgang got everyone back to the tree line. They had just made it when it felt like the very ground they were running on shook beneath their feet. The shock wave sent them all falling to the ground. The whole mountain shook from the force of the explosion. A huge fireball came roaring out of the mineshaft. Rocks and debris started falling from the sky and the explosion caused a landslide of rocks, trees and all kinds of debris came pouring down the side of the mountain right over the entrance to the mine and buried the entrance completely.

The chief fell to the ground and covered BJ with his own body protecting him from the fallout of the explosion. Once on his feet again, he picked up BJ and took him safely out of harm's way. The chief started yelling again for the medics and only then did everyone realize that it was BJ the chief had been carrying.

Chapter 37

Mary had been at the Walter Reed Medical Center for just over two days now. The doctors were pleased with her progress physically, but her memory was not showing much sign of improvement. Sharon was with Mary in her room when the doctor came in. The doctor said, "Good morning, Mary. How are you today?"

Mary looked up and said, "I feel better today. Thank you."

The doctor turned to Sharon and said, "Glad to see you again, Sharon."

Sharon said "Good morning, doctor. I will be here every day until you say Mary can leave."

"That's good. I'm sure Mary is glad you're here."

Mary said "Oh yes. Sharon is my best friend. She helps me every day. She keeps telling me little things about my past, things I can't remember. I think Sharon knows more about me than I do. Doctor, when will I start to remember more."

The doctor looked at Mary and said "Like I told you yesterday, I can't give you a time or date when you will remember your past. All we can do is work each day and see what comes back. Everyone I have worked with in the past gets some of their memories to come back, but it takes time. It may come back tomorrow or next week or a year from now. Something you may see or do will trigger something and you will get another piece of your memory back. I have seen many people get all their memories back. We just don't know how long it takes. We will just keep on helping you get there. While we wait, I want you to keep working on your physical skills."

Mary smiled and said "I will. I'm almost to the point of standing on my own now."

"That's good. Mary, you keep at it. I will stop by this afternoon and see how you are."

As the doctor was leaving, Sharon followed him out of the room into the hallway. Sharon stopped him and asked, "Doctor, Mary is doing well with her physical recovery and you can hear from her speech how much better that is. From what I have read about most cases when these things come back, the person's memory also comes back. That doesn't seem to be the case for Mary."

The doctor looked at Sharon and said "What you've read is true in most cases, but not always. Mary seems to be progressing differently. I don't want you to be alarmed. Mary has only been healing for a short time now, so give her time. I'm sure she will continue to improve."

"Doctor, it's hard to be patient. I want so much for her to get better. One more question. Have you heard from the general?"

"No, I'm afraid not, Sharon. He must be pretty busy not to call. As soon as he does, I will let you know."

"Thank you, Doctor. You know where you can find me when you hear anything."

"Yes, I know right where to find you, Sharon. See you later."

Once word spread that BJ was down, everyone gathered around the medics working to save his life. The chief was on the radio to General Wellington. "General, this is the chief. BJ's down. He's been shot in the chest and needs help right now. You need to send a helicopter. He needs to get to a hospital as soon as possible."

"Chief, I will have one in the air immediately. Has Mueller been put down?"

"Yes, sir. He and his men are buried under tons of rock. It's over."

"General, get that chopper out here now or BJ won't make it."

"It's on the way, Chief."

Sitting in camp waiting to hear how the attack was going was almost worse than being there. We had no way of knowing what was happening other than bits and pieces of what we heard on the radio. Then we heard, saw, and felt a huge explosion. We took one look at each other and then decided without saying a word to go and see if our comrades needed our help. Everyone scrambled for a weapon and started heading for the site of the explosion. Someone threw a rifle at me and I gladly took it. I wasn't even sure I knew how to use it, but I was willing to fight if I needed to. BJ had told me to stay put, but I wasn't going to be left behind; not now. It was hard keeping up with these guys. They were moving double-time trying to get to the fight as soon as they could. We covered the distance in just over half an hour. When we found the rest of our unit, they were all just standing around in a big circle. Some of the men were down on one knee and I could see they were praying. I started looking for BJ, but was not able to find him through the circle of men. I started asking where he was and one of the soldiers standing there turned to me with tears running down his face and said "BJ's down. He's been shot."

From the look on the soldier's face, I believed that BJ was dead. I just stood there in disbelief, not BJ, not Iron Man BJ, not our leader, not my best friend. "How?" I asked.

The soldier shook his head and said, "I don't know, you'll have to ask the chief."

I said, "Where's the chief?" He pointed to an open field. I could see men putting out flares for what reason I had no idea. I ran to the field and found the chief and as he turned to look at me, he said "I can tell from the look on your face you heard about BJ."

I could barely get the words out. "How did he die, Chief?"

382

"Johnny Boy, BJ's not dead, but he's close. If we don't get him to a hospital soon, he will be dead."

Life just came back to me! "He's not dead? Where is he? Can I see him?"

"Slow down there, Johnny. The medics are working on him and there's a chopper arriving here any minute. They are going to take him right to the hospital. Come with me. Maybe he can hear your voice."

When we got to where the medics were working on BJ, they let me kneel next to him. All I could say was "BJ, it's Johnny. Can you hear me?"

My heart was stuck in my throat. He looked so bad. One of the medics said to take his hand. That he might squeeze my hand if he hears me. I picked up his hand, but there was no response. The medic said "Try again, only louder!"

"BJ, can you hear me?" This time he gently squeezed my hand.

The medic said "That's a good sign, don't let go of him and keep talking. It may be just enough to help keep him alive. He needs to keep fighting, so don't stop talking to him." Minutes later, I heard the helicopter coming in. They picked up BJ and took him to the chopper. They loaded BJ, both medics and me into the chopper. I never let go of his hand.

When we lifted off, the doctor who had come with the chopper took over from the medics. He started to cut away BJ's flak jacket to get a better look at the wound. BJ had been hit right in the middle of his chest. Now with the light from the inside of the chopper, I could see the wound and how much blood he had lost. No matter how much plasma they gave him, blood just kept seeping out from the hole in his chest. The doctor radioed ahead to the hospital telling them what they needed to do to be ready. I kept squeezing his hand and talking to him. Once we landed, they said "You need to say goodbye now. We need to take him right into surgery. I held his hand one last time and said goodbye to my best friend, not knowing if he heard me or if I would ever see him alive again. I fell on my knees right there by the helicopter and prayed.

The chief was still back at the mountain next to the old mining town. He had a big job on his hands. He needed to round up everyone, including the prisoners, and hike two days out to where they could be picked up by the German army and taken to the US missile base. There they could rest and then be sent back to the states. The German army would be responsible to dig into the mountain and retrieve Mueller's body and any equipment that was not destroyed in the blast. Everyone, especially the Germans, wanted to make sure that the machine could never be used again. General Wellington called the president and gave him the good news about the weapons being destroyed. The president called the German chancellor and gave him the good news. They became allies after that, but not the best of friends.

I had been left alone there by the helicopter praying by myself. I made my way into the hospital and went looking for anyone who could tell me what was going on with BJ. I was told where I could go and wait. I was sitting by myself waiting and after several hours fell asleep. I hadn't slept in over thirty-six hours and just couldn't stay awake. I was awakened by none other than General Wellington himself. "Hello there, John. How are you doing?"

"Hi General, that depends. How is BJ doing?"

"No word on BJ yet, John. When I was told the extent of his injuries, I flew in two of the army's best trauma doctors from Walter Reed. They have a lot more experience treating these kinds of wounds than the doctors here in Germany. If anyone can pull him through this, they can. They just got here and have gone in with the other doctors. We should know something in a couple of hours."

"Thank you for doing that, General. BJ is worth our best efforts to save him."

"You don't have to tell me, John. BJ is one of the best soldiers I've ever had serving with me."

"General, I need a favor."

"Whatever you need, John. What is it?"

"General, I haven't talked to Mary in almost two weeks and she must be worried sick. I really need to talk to her. Do you know if she is still at the hotel in Washington?"

"John, I need to tell you about Mary. She's not at the hotel."

'I'm not surprised, General. She probably got tired of waiting for me and went home."

"No, John, that's not it. She did get tired of waiting, but she didn't go home. She went to Germany looking for you."

"Why would she do that? Didn't you tell her what was going on?"

"Of course, I did, John. But what I could tell her, anyway. Mary is a very stubborn young lady and I couldn't stop her from coming over here."

"Is she still here General?"

"No, John. She's back in Washington at the Walter Reed Medical Center.

"What is she doing there?"

"John, Mary came over here looking for you and she found out some information she shouldn't have. She called me and started telling me what she knew. I didn't know she was here at the time. Once I realized she was here in Germany, I told her to stop talking and that I would be right there to get her. She had no idea how much danger she had put herself in. I sent two marines right out to get her."

"General. I don't understand. Why would she be in danger?"

"John, we have a lot of enemies in this world. They seek whatever US intelligence they can find. Germany is not the US. People here are always surveilling us and watching everything we do. Someone, we don't know who yet, heard Mary talking and went after her. They got to her just before my two marines did. My two marines were able to rescue Mary. Unfortunately, she got hurt during the rescue."

"Is that why she is in the hospital? I need to talk to her right away."

"John, you're not going to be able to do that. One of her attackers threw her in a van. She hit her head hard when that happened. The Marines saved her life by stopping the bleeding. She has a very severe concussion and I'm sorry to say this, but at this point she doesn't remember who you are. It doesn't mean she won't, but right now she doesn't know who you are. Your mother is with her and Mary knows her, but Mary remembers little about her past."

"General, how can she remember my mother and not me?"

"John, you're asking questions I can't answer. As soon as we get back, I will take you to see her doctor and he can answer all your questions."

I was trying hard to understand what the general had just told me. This woman that I love with all my heart could not remember me. What if she never remembers me? Just as the impact of what the general had said hit me, one of the two surgeons from Walter Reed came out and spoke to the general. "We have done all we can for Lieutenant Johnson here. We have stabilized him as best we can. If he is still stable in the morning, we will fly him back to the states. I know a surgeon who specializes in this kind of trauma. The bullet is so close to his heart, I don't want to do this without her. She is the best there is at this type of surgery."

The general asked "Is he going to make it?"

The surgeon shook his head. "Honestly, General, I can't believe he's even alive."

The general said, "I will make all the arrangements to get you and the Lieutenant back to Walter Reed, so just tell me when he's ready to be moved."

"He needs some recovery time. I will let you know in the morning, General."

The general left to make arrangements and the doctor left to go back to surgery. I was left alone to think about Mary, BJ and how I might lose my best friend and a woman I've loved all in the space of just a few hours. I have never felt so alone in all my life. Was God punishing me? What did I do to deserve all this pain? After hours of sitting there, I fell asleep on the bench. I was awakened this time by a marine telling me we needed to go. I was taken to the airport and onto another military transport plane. BJ was already on board with his doctors and the medics who had saved him out in the field. Also on board were a half a dozen of BJ's men who had been wounded while fighting Mueller. I started thinking about that son-of-a-b**** and I was glad he was dead. If there really is hell, I hope he's in it!

We were off the ground and headed home and five hours later we landed. There was an ambulance waiting to transport BJ right to the hospital. The wounded men and I were taken by an army truck to the hospital and dropped off at the emergency department. Not being wounded, I was left alone once again to find my way around. I finally got directions to where they were operating on BJ. The general showed up around an hour later.

"General, do you know what's going on with BJ?"

"No John, they haven't told me anything yet. We just need to be patient and wait."

"General, is Mary here in this building?"

"No, John. She's in the rehab center across the street. I just came from there. I spoke with her doctor and told him you were here."

"How is Mary doing? Can I go see her?"

"No, the doctor wants you to wait a couple more days. Mary is doing well with her physical recovery and she is remembering more about her past. The doctor wants a couple more days before he will let you see her. He doesn't know what seeing you may do to her. I talked to your mother while I was there. I told her about BJ and the fact that you were here. She said she would be over as soon as she got done helping Mary through her rehab session."

The general and I spent the next two hours talking about the cost of taking down Mueller. It had cost the lives of many good men and one more good man's life was hanging by a thread. I looked up to see my mother coming down the hall. I could see tears running down her face. After giving me a long hug that I needed so badly, she took my hand and sat down. She started telling me about Mary. She told me how good Mary was doing. While we were talking, a woman walked up dressed in surgical clothing and introduced herself to us. She was the surgeon they had been talking about in Germany.

"I just finished working on your soldier, General. He's one of the toughest young men I have ever worked on. I must be honest with you, He must be living on sheer willpower. He is stable at this point, but the next 48 hours will tell us if he's going to make it or not. We're going to keep him sedated for at least that long. If his vital signs are good, then we will wake him up and see if he regains consciousness. Until then, there's nothing else we can do."

The general said "What do you mean if he regains consciousness?"

The surgeon said "General, Lieutenant Johnson is lucky to be alive at all. I took out the bullet and repaired the damage as best I was able, but I can't do anything about the blood he lost. We gave him four transfusions during surgery, but when the body loses that much blood it affects all your organs. Like I said, we won't know anything for at least 48 hours, so until then I suggest you pray for that young man."

The general thanked the surgeon, said goodbye to me and my mother and disappeared down the hall. My mother and I sat there in the hallway. She shed more tears and we talked about how full of life BJ had always been. We laughed about all the trouble he got into and yes, we prayed. I prayed more in the next two days then I had in all my life up to that time. With the permission of Mary's psychologist, I could see Mary if she couldn't see me. Those were the longest two days of my life! Every time I saw Mary, I walked away crying. Would my love ever love me again? Every time I sat next to BJ, I would talk to him and pray that soon he would answer me. Finally, the two days were over. I was in BJ's room by eight that morning. The general came in around ten and the doctor finally showed up around 11:30. When the doctor came into the room, he looked at me and the general and said "His vitals are good and his blood pressure is good, so we're going to try and wake him up. Don't be surprised if he doesn't respond. His body has been through a great deal. He may come to and he may not. His own body and mind will decide when it's time. Are you ready? We both nodded and the doctor started the procedure to wake him up. Twenty minutes later, there was no change. After an hour, the doctor said "It could be days before he's ready to wake up. I must be honest with you in cases like this sometimes the patient never wakes up. All you can do is keep talking to him. Tell him anything you like, no matter what it is. You never know what may trigger a response."

The doctor left and the general and I sat talking for over an hour. He eventually had to leave himself. I was left alone with my best friend and for once, I could say whatever I wanted and BJ couldn't argue with me. I really wished he could. My mother came in later and said Mary's doctor wants her to go through a stress evaluation before they will let me see her. I asked how long that would take. She said, "They will do it tomorrow and let us know." I spent the rest of the day with BJ. Where else would I go? It was a long day and I was exhausted. I left, but the next morning I was back. I had brought a magazine and was reading it to BJ, when I heard someone call me 'Johnny Boy'. Only the chief calls me "Johnny Boy."

"Johnny Boy, how are you doing?" I looked up to see the chief standing in the doorway. I was so happy to see him. I jumped out of my chair and ran to him and gave him the biggest hug I could. I started asking him questions so fast, he couldn't answer them.

"Hold on there, Johnny Boy. One thing at a time. The chief looked past me and then said "How's the boss doing?" I told the chief that BJ was doing well according to his doctor. I told him they tried to wake him yesterday, but he hasn't said anything or even opened his eyes. "I keep telling him to get his lazy ass out of that bed, but so far nothing has changed."

I had been so excited to see the chief, I didn't even see Casey standing there behind him until he said "Hi, John." I gave Casey a big hug and told both to come in and sit down. For the next two hours, they filled me in on what happened after I left in the chopper with BJ.

The German army met them as they were hiking out. The Germans had taken control of the prisoners and went back to what was left of the burned-out mining town. They had gone back to retrieve their comrades' bodies. Wolfgang, Casey, and the Chief had gone to the missile base to write reports and get debriefed. They said goodbye to Wolfgang and were flown back to the states. When they arrived, they were debriefed again and then put on leave until further notice.

We had been talking for hours when my mother walked in. I introduced the Chief and Casey to my mom and told her a little about how we had become good friends. My mother politely pulled me out into the hallway to tell me some good news. I would be allowed to meet Mary the next day at one o'clock. However, I would not be allowed to tell her who I was or anything about our past together. I was excited and sad all at the same time.

I spent the rest of the day and most of the night with the Chief and Casey. Occasionally, one of us would go over and hold BJ's hand and talk to him. I went back to my hotel room to sleep and to get ready to meet Mary the next day, but I was back in BJ's room by nine the next morning. It was easy to see that the Chief and Casey had never left. We talked and laughed a little until noon. I had told them the whole story about what happened to Mary. I had a hard time telling them why she was there at the hospital. The Chief gave me a big hug and said, "Just trust that things will work out." Just as I was leaving, in walked the general. Casey and the Chief both jumped to attention. The general said, "At ease men, I'm here to get John."

I said "General, I'm on my way to see Mary." The General grabbed my shoulder and said "That's why I'm here. I'm going with you. It's my fault she's here and I want to be there for both of you. Mary knows who I am and maybe seeing you and me together will help in some small way. I just want to do whatever I can to help."

I was a little shocked to see this 4-star general so thoughtful and caring so much about me and Mary. I said "Thank you, General. I wasn't expecting you to do this."

The General said "John, I think a lot of you and Mary. I will be forever grateful for all you've done to help in Germany."

"I said "Thanks, General, let's go see Mary."

As we arrived in the hallway outside of the rehab center, my mother and Mary's psychiatrist were waiting for us. The doctor said "John, this is how I want to proceed for Mary's sake. Your mother will go in first and we will let her have a few minutes with Mary. Then you, the general and I will walk in together. We will approach Mary slowly and the general will introduce you as a friend of his. You can say hi and shake her hand, but that's all. If I see any kind of a bad reaction, you must excuse yourself and leave. Do you understand? I know what you're going through, but Mary is my only concern right now."

I replied "I understand, doctor and I will do whatever you say. I want Mary to get better more than anyone."

He said "Ok, then, let's go. Sharon, you go ahead and go in and we'll be in shortly."

After my mother had been with Mary for a few minutes, the doctor tapped me on the shoulder and said "Okay, John, let's go." The three of us walked into the rehab center together. My mother was standing by Mary. She had a nurse on each side of her and she was just coming off a walking device. We were making our way to her and were just about there when Mary looked up and saw the general. A big smile came across her face and she said, "Hi General" and started to wave at him. Right in the middle of her saying hi to the general, she looked right at me.

The smile left her face and was replaced by a dark look of confusion. We were less than twenty feet away when the psychiatrist stopped me in my tracks. He said, "No closer, John." I looked at Mary. Her face was one of total confusion. She started to shake and the nurse grabbed her just as she dropped to her knees. She put her hands on her face and started to cry. Her crying got harder. My mother tried to help consult her, but the psychiatrist told the general to get me out of there. The general grabbed my shoulder and turned me around. Everything in my being wanted me to run to Mary, but the general was pushing me to the door. I could hear Mary crying even louder now. We were just about to the door when I heard Mary scream out my name. I stopped and turned to see Mary reaching out for me with both arms. She kept calling my name. I pushed the general out of my way and ran as fast as I could to Mary. I hit my knees, threw my arms around her and pulled her to me. She hugged me around the neck and we just stayed there on the floor crying in each other's arms. When I looked up the nurses were crying, my mother was crying along with the psychiatrist and even the general had tears running down his face. In fact, the whole room was crying or cheering for us. Everyone started to clap. When Mary caught her breath, she looked at me through her tears and said "Where have you been? I've been waiting for you for so long."

I said "Never mind that. I'm here now and I'm not going anywhere." I helped Mary up and we made our way to a table. The psychiatrist started asking Mary questions. Mary was able to answer all of them. Then he asked her to tell him about me. Mary looked at me and said "He's the love of my life. That's all you need to know, doctor."

The psychiatrist laughed and said, "I can see that!"

My Mary was back! We all laughed, and the doctor stopped asking questions. We all calmed down and started talking about Mary's sudden recovery.

I had only been with Mary a short time when an orderly came in asking for a John Northrup. I said "I'm John Northrup. Who wants to know?"

The orderly said, "A man called the Chief wants you to return to Lieutenant Johnson's room immediately." All my joy started to disappear. I turned to Mary just as she started to ask me what was wrong with BJ. "Why is he here in the hospital?"

"Mary, mom will tell you about that, but right now I have to go! I must see how BJ is doing. I promise I'll be right back." This couldn't be good. The Chief knew I was seeing Mary for the first time. He wouldn't call me away unless it was bad. A hundred things went through my head as I ran out of the rehab center. I ran as fast as I could, down the hall and out the front door across the street to BJ's wing of the hospital. In the lobby, I hit the button for the third floor. I couldn't wait. I headed for the stairs instead of taking the elevator. I found the stairs and was up the stairs two steps at a time and then down the hall to BJ's room. As I approached his room, Casey was sitting outside in the hallway with his head down and his hands folded. I could feel my heart dropping to the floor. As I rushed into the room, I ran headlong into the Chief. If he hadn't caught me, I would have bounced right off him back out the door. The Chief had tears running down his face and as he grabbed me and hugged me, and softly said "I think he's going to be alright. He's asking for you." I pulled away from the Chief and rushed to BJ's bedside. I picked up his hand and said, "I'm here, BJ, I'm right here!" The doctor was there and he said to go ahead and keep talking to him. BJ looked more dead than alive. He was trying to say something, but it was so soft I didn't hear it. I put my ear close to him so I could understand him. I said, "It's John, BJ, can you hear me?" He said "I heard you in the chopper, so you think you're going to kick my ass, do you? Bring your lunch, it will take you all day." I started to laugh and then cry. That was just like him to say something like that.

Casey had come back into the room and when I told them what he said, they all started laughing. The doctor told us all to say goodbye and made us leave the room. He said BJ needs his rest and that's enough for now. Out in the hallway, there were high fives and a lot of happy tears. We were talking and laughing when the Chief asked, "How's Mary?" My joy over BJ had almost made me forget that I left Mary back in rehab. I told them what had happened when Mary saw me. There were more high fives and tears of joy. I said goodbye and promised to be back the next day. I ran down the stairs across the road and back into Mary's arms.

Now, I know there must be a God! He must have heard my prayers because he answered them all. Life was good again and now I prayed that it would stay that way. Pretty naive on my part. We all know better!

Epilogue

Life had begun to return to normal, well, at least our new normal. I spent every day for the next three weeks going to rehab with Mary and visiting BJ. You could see Mary getting better and better every day. I spent many late evenings in her room just watching her fall asleep. One evening, just days before she was released, Mary started getting a little frisky with me. I closed the door and before I knew it, we were making love right there in the hospital. I didn't know it was possible to love someone as much as I love Mary. I thought we were being quiet with our love making, but when I walked out of the room, I think every nurse on the floor had a little grin on her face. Ask me if I cared.

Several days later, Mary got the doctor's blessing to leave. She got a clean bill of health both physically and mentally, however she never did remember her attack and rescue in Germany. In fact, she didn't even remember going there. Her psychiatrist was okay with that and told me not to bring it up anymore. I had been staying in a hotel close to the Walter Reed Medical Center, courtesy of the US Army. I now got to share it with Mary. Over the next two weeks we finally got to visit all the sights in Washington that we had planned on before all this happened. We would spend our day sightseeing and our evenings with BJ.

Three weeks after BJ's amazing recovery, he was on his feet and taking a few short steps. I must mention that the nurse who is helping BJ was one of the most gorgeous nurses I've ever seen. It was just like BJ to have the prettiest nurse in the hospital. I still don't get it. What does he have that the rest of us don't? Mary and I were both getting very anxious to get back home and really get our lives back to normal. She had called her school and was told her class was waiting for her return. My position at RIT was still there if I wanted it. I very much wanted to get back to teaching. BJ

395

would be in recovery for the next three months. We promised him we would be back to visit as often as possible. I told the general that we would be leaving, but before I left, he asked me to write a report on all that had happened in Germany. I said I would, and I was okay with that until I started to write it. I had to write a report on everything I was trying to forget.

Mary and I made our way back to Rochester, New York and picked up our lives pretty much where we had left off. The days turned into weeks and the weeks into months. We got married which made my mother happy. Shortly after that, I was able to tell my mother she would be a grandmother and that brought tears to her eyes once again. I was able to get back and see BJ about once every three weeks. His progress was incredible. I should have known, after all it was BJ. In a little over four months, he was ready to return to duty, at least he thought he was. The army wanted to put him behind a desk. BJ fought with the army over that until they finally agreed to let him try returning to fieldwork. Occasionally, I would run into Casey and the Chief while visiting BJ. During one of those visits the Chief had told me he still wanted me to come visit him on the reservation he grew up on. He said, "I still want to have that talk with you, the one we started that night at the castle."

With permission from my wife, I did go and spend four days with the chief. I can't say it changed my life. However, it did give me a whole new perspective on life and what comes after that life.

One time during a visit to see BJ, I ran into Wolfgang. He had flown in from Germany to visit BJ. He was doing well and had been promoted to lieutenant major. He told me he had spent many weeks in the mine trying to dig out what was left of Mueller and his machines.

Life was going along as it should; things were quiet and in about four months I was going to be a father. I was more than a little nervous about that. Then one night, I got a call from BJ. He told me that General Wellington had retired. I said good for him, he deserves to retire. BJ told me that he heard the general didn't really retire. He was forced out by the president. I was dumbfounded! Why in the world would the president force the head of the joint chiefs of staff to retire?

The answer came two weeks later. The phone rang about seven in the evening. It was my mother. She was serious and said "John, I need you to come out here to see me. I need your help with something."

"What is it?" I asked. She said, "Never mind. Just get on a plane and come out here." I gave up trying to figure out what was going on. If my mother didn't want to tell me, I knew I would never convince her.

Two days later, I landed near Lake Havasu and drove out to my mother's house. My mother met me in the yard as I got out of the car. She gave me a hug and without saying too much she took my hand and led me right to my father's old lab. I walked into the lab with her and there sitting at a table was General Wellington, BJ, the Chief and Casey. A momentary feeling of joy came over me as I saw them all sitting there. However, a closer look at the somber look on their faces turned my feeling of joy into a feeling of dread. A hundred thoughts ran through my head. Why are they all here? Why aren't any of them in uniform? Why meet out here in the middle of nowhere? All my questions were about to be answered.

The first one to speak was BJ. "Hello, John. It's good to see you. I wish this were just a friendly visit, but it's not. You better sit down. The general will fill you in."

The general looked at me and said "John, I have some bad news for you. If I remember right, you had a good look at the weapons, or machines as you call them. When they came out of the castle, they were still in good working order. Is that right?"

I said "That's right, General. I was told you were going to bring them back to the states to have them destroyed."

The general said "Yes, John, you are correct. I did have them brought back to destroy them and I believed that's what was done. I was adamant about their destruction with the president. I found out later that the president had gone behind my back and had the machines hidden away. He put men to work on rebuilding them and getting them to run again."

The general had barely finished speaking when I jumped out of my chair and yelled at the general. "How could you let that happen? You know how dangerous those machines are." BJ grabbed my arm and told me to calm down and sit back down.

BJ said "Why do you think the general was forced to retire? He got into a battle over this with the president and that's why the president made him leave."

I looked at the general and said "Doesn't the president realize how dangerous these machines are? Does he know how much damage they could cause if they get out of control? Why would he do this?"

The general shook his head and said "John, it's an old story. Every government wants to have the biggest gun and that way they think they have the upper hand on their enemies. They call it having the biggest deterrent."

I looked at BJ and said "After all we went through, all the men that died, I just don't believe it. I have nightmares about what happened! Now, you're telling me it's not over."

BJ put his head down for a moment and then looked up at me and said "John, yeah you're right, it's not over and we have more to tell you."

"I said "More, what more could you have to tell me? Isn't this bad enough?"

BJ said, "Yes it's bad, but there's more you need to know."

"What more could I possibly need to know?"

"John, when we blew up that mine, we were sure we killed Mueller and destroyed the other two machines. In fact, the German chancellor put Wolfgang in charge of overseeing that was the case. Wolfgang worked with the team to dig into the mountain to make sure the machines were destroyed and that Mueller was dead. It took them three months to get into that mine. The machine that Mueller used against us was there. They made sure it will never be used again. Unfortunately, they only found one machine. That means that the other one is still out there somewhere. Wolfgang told me they never found Mueller's body, so as far as we know Mueller may still be alive. Worst of all, he may still have one of the weapons."

I just sat there in total disbelief, and no one said anything. The nightmare was starting all over again. I looked at BJ and said, "This will never be over."

BJ stood up and said "Wrong! It will be over and we're going to end it. John, that's why you're here today. Your mother is willing to let us operate out of your father's lab and no one knows we're here. You, me, Chief, Casey, the general and Wolfgang - we'll all be part of the team that will bring this nightmare to an end. Wolfgang has already started putting a team together in Germany. With his help and the general's connections and what we already know, we can stop this. So, John, are you in?" I could see the confidence on BJ's face.

I said "What choice do I have? Of course, I'm in!" BJ slapped me on the back and said "Great! Let's get to work."

ABOUT THE AUTHOR

Born in the early fifties and a lifelong resident of upstate New York, I was raised on a farm with one sister and four brothers. It didn't take long for me to learn the value of hard work. Growing up in the country, there was always time for adventure and spending long summer days exploring the woods, streams, and ponds around home. Those days of exploring lead to a growing imagination for storytelling. After years of telling stories, my adventures have led me to writing my first book.

Made in the USA
Middletown, DE
27 July 2022

70007379R00225